HONOR LOST

Also by Rachel Caine and Ann Aguirre

Honor Among Thieves

Honor Bound

HONOR
LOST

RACHEL CAINE & ANN AGUIRRE

KATHERINE TEGEN BOOKS
An Imprint of HarperCollins Publishers

Katherine Tegen Books is an imprint of HarperCollins Publishers.

Library of Congress Control Number: 2019951829
ISBN 978-0-06-257105-2

Typography by Katie Klimowicz
19 20 21 22 23   PC/LSCH   10 9 8 7 6 5 4 3 2 1

First Edition

For our partners, R. Cat Conrad and Andres Aguirre,
without whom the last twenty-plus years would have been
quite lonely.

HONOR LOST

From the *Bruqvisz Histories, volume 487*

Zara Cole and her Dark Travelers <for more information, see entry: DARK TRAVELERS. Also, see entry: ZARA COLE > did business with Bacia Annont in the year <data corrupted> and frequented the Sliver, where they gained certain renown. They were known associates of Suncross <data corrupted> < see alt. reference, line 94, volume 486>. Their mission prospered when so many who came before them failed, but success had a high cost, as their endeavor roused the god-king, who threatened to consume all sentient life with his hunger. It is known these Dark Travelers possessed the rare ability of combining souls and powers into new entities such as the legendary Men Shen. They tracked Lifekiller to the Abyin Dommas homeworld, where a great battle ensued . . .

CHAPTER ONE

Lost Cause

THE WORLD OF Greenheld looked so peaceful, spinning beneath us.

Bonded as Men Shen, we were as close to invincible as anything had ever been, and with the combined power and intellect of humans, Leviathan, and Abyin Dommas . . . we understood we weren't strong enough to defeat our enemy, Lifekiller—*a damn god, pretty much*—in open combat. Not even close.

Yet we would fight. Ours was a resolution that would not bend, much less break. *We must be enough because there is no other.* The two Leviathan could hear the singing power of the Abyin Dommas from far below, hidden in the oceans, and now there was an electric feeling, a shimmer across the surface of the water, and giant cities rose from the green liquid, towers and spires and curves in shapes that humans never dreamed.

They lifted out of the seas. Thousands of them. And launched into a glittering web around Greenheld.

Is our warshield, our Starcurrent-self said within the bond, a whisper awash in awe. *Never has it been so strong.*

The Zara-aspect asked, *How many . . . ?*

And Starcurrent-self replied, *All my people sing this. All.*

Lifekiller's enormous dark presence blotted out distant suns, and millions of Abyin Dommas sang in their floating cities. Sound couldn't travel through space, *shouldn't,* and the Abyin Dommas warshield was only partly made of sound. It was pure, raw power, and it fluttered through the bodies of both Leviathan, rippled over and past the Bruqvisz mech ships that followed them, and hit the swarming Phage like a storm.

Then it struck Lifekiller, and the ancient god paused, as if pushing against a wall that wouldn't yield.

Lifekiller receded, the song of the Abyin Dommas burning bright as stars against the skin of a dread creature from the oldest stories.

Then the god-king attacked and cracked that fiery silver shell with a lash of a black tentacle. For the first time, we felt the weight of Lifekiller's psychic presence, and it carried the full mass of a universe, starless and heavy with hunger. Worse: it was *beautiful*. Even as it killed, it was gorgeous as a coiling snake, or so our combined senses insisted. As if it would be an honor to perish at Lifekiller's command.

Screw this, our Zara-self thought, and it stung. *We're not going out like this.*

Our Leviathan-selves moved, circling in elegant spirals, slaughtering the disordered Phage with massive tail strikes as we fired the physical weapons, many parts moving in harmony. Suncross and his Bruqvisz mercenaries wove complex patterns of light between us and arrowed forward, dragging a net of shimmering light that sliced apart the Phage. The net cut free to drift on and wrap around Lifekiller's pulsing form. It tightened, and there was a burst of cold fury that shouted YOU DARE TO HURT ME?, and the net exploded into a billion sparks that died in darkness.

Our Typhon-shard struck with the full force of an armored, barbed tail. It was enough to shatter a moon, that strike, and we felt the impact of it crack the core of our bond. One of us vanished. *Yusuf.* Another pulled at the link, fraying it, but the rest of us tugged back strongly. *No. We must hold.*

The bellow of dark fury from Lifekiller washed over us

like a blast wave. *Do you think you can hurt me, little ones?* Lifekiller's voice came in ripples of calm, and something in us stilled at the sound of it.

Then our Starcurrent-self shrieked, a discordant alarm that jolted us out of the spell. *He lies! He is injured!*

Thousands of surviving Phage swarmed and drowned both our Leviathan-selves in heaving, stabbing bodies.

We hit the console and shouted, "Suncross! *Kill these assholes!*" We slammed our fist onto another control and braced for the pain as thick current blazed through our plating, frying many of the Phage, stunning the rest and sending them spinning. Suncross fired sticky globs that glued the Phage together and blasted them into atoms.

Another thick, glistening wave of song and power from Greenheld. Lifekiller rolled. Our tail hit again, tearing loose flesh and releasing cold liquid into colder space. The god-king was sluggish, and we concentrated our fire as Lifekiller heaved and struggled and reached for Greenheld's life force.

We drove it back.

Lifekiller rolled away in retreat, its Phage attendants crawling over its body and attending to its injuries. We pursued, firing until the creature moved beyond our best speed and disappeared into the wider chasm of space.

Gone in the stars.

It will be back, we thought.

Lifekiller had a goal: revenge. The Abyin Dommas had, countless millennia ago, ended the rule of the Elder Gods by singing them to sleep: a slave race that had killed its tormentors. Or at least, most of them. Lifekiller had been sealed away, asleep, as close to death as they'd been able to manage.

A thick, purple thread of regret pulsed through our bond. Human regret—we'd meant well and thought we'd had little choice . . . but look at what it did, that decision. Our Starcurrent-soul's emotions were more complex, layers of colors that spoke of anguish, certainly. Loathing. Fear. But so much more.

We broke, like a puzzle knocked to pieces—Leviathan, Abyin Dommas, and humans, scattered into smaller selves until we reclaimed all our separate skins, and I was suddenly back to just *me*.

Zara Cole.

Alone.

And it hurt *so much*.

"Bea?" I reached out, slapping the floor that was also Nadim's skin, and Nadim instantly wrapped around me like a warm blanket—not physically: my body was ice-cold from shock, but my soul was drenched in warmth. Dangerous. I needed to get myself together and take care of my physical needs. For one thing, I felt badly dehydrated. At the same time, I needed to pee so bad it made tears well up in my eyes. "Beatriz!"

"Here," she whispered.

I turned my head. Beatriz lay on her side, facing me. Her hair was loose, curls tumbling across her eyes, and she looked paler than she should. Trembling, like me. Too hard to get up, so I slow-rolled over and put my arms around her. She sank into me with a sigh of relief, and for a few seconds we just held on to each other while Nadim cradled us both.

Group hugs with intelligent spaceships. We might be fighting gods and monsters out here in the black, but at least we had *this*.

"I need to pee," Beatriz said, and I tried not to laugh because if I did, I'd lose total control of my bladder.

"Yeah, me too," I said, and rose onto my knees, then my feet.

I had to lean on Nadim, but I steadied enough to pull Beatriz upright. I didn't let go of her hand; it was starting to warm up a little. She didn't pull away either. We stumbled back to our quarters and parted there, each to our own bathroom. Intense relief, the kind that left me shaky. After I washed up and threw some cold water on my face, wrapped a blanket around me over my clothes . . . I felt more myself. I looked surprisingly good in the mirror.

Healthy. I particularly liked my grow-out today. Funny how the little things mattered in the middle of fighting a god.

Nadim said, with a light touch of amusement, *You are so strange.*

"Damn right." I laid my fingers against the skin of the wall. Felt a pulse and saw light zip through Nadim's flesh like cool lightning. He liked that. So did I. "We won."

More of an impasse, he whispered inside my head.

"Yeah, I know, but let's celebrate a little anyway. In a couple of minutes, we can be all stressed and terrified again, but right now, just . . . be."

I am *being, Zara.* The feeling that Nadim sent rushing through me stole my breath, like cool water and spring wind and sunlight on skin. Intense and personal. *I am here, this moment, with you. And that is all I wish.*

I couldn't reply to that because *damn*, but I let him know without words how much I felt the same. This wasn't what I guess most people thought of as love, but it was . . . better. Stronger. Fiercer. And I wasn't afraid of that now, or ashamed, or confused. I just *was.*

We were.

Then I felt Bea standing next to me, and I turned and said, "I want to kiss you so bad right now."

"I thought you'd never say it, *meu anjo,*" she said, and I was blinded by the brilliance of her smile. Nadim's translation whispered the meaning of her words to me. *My angel.*

I kissed her, and she kissed me back, and the soft sweetness of her lips was something I'd never known before. It felt like coming home and finding a new land, all at the same time. A flirt of tongues—she tasted like that cinnamon coffee she loved. A gentle shiver crept over me because I could *feel* Nadim, just beyond Bea's borders, and he practically glowed with the shared sensations.

Trembling, I pulled back just a little, enough to make eye contact and register Bea's smile. She leaned forward, bridging the distance, and her brow touched mine, her curls whispering around my face in delicate swirls. They carried a faint hint of the honey-and-almond shampoo she favored. Bea hovered close, breathing my breath, and it was beautiful.

She has the softest skin. That was my thought, but Nadim shared it as I ran a fingertip down the curve of her cheek. Her lashes fluttered, and I could *see* the path that led to both of us in bed, sliding together, hands joined, bodies arching—

Not the time.

I knew it, even if I wished I could drag Bea off for some privacy. Adrenaline and sex were definitely a thing, and I didn't want to push too hard, too fast and wreck everything before we got started. I'd made mistakes before. Not again. Not with Bea. I'd never *liked* anybody so much while also thinking they were just fucking beautiful, head to toe. That meant I had to be careful and think everything through, get it right the first time.

With a pang, I recalled just how wrong it all went before. Bea would never ask me to steal for her, but I had—for Derry. And look where that got me. I'd pissed off a major crim; Torian Deluca thought I'd screwed with his supply chain, and that asshole was probably still plotting how to get at me. But I couldn't worry about Deluca when I had Lifekiller on the line and a bunch of Abyin Dommas relying on me.

"We should see if they need our help on Greenheld," Bea said, her voice soft and breathy. Impossible not to take *that* as a compliment. I put everything else out of my head for the time being.

"On it." I headed to Ops, where I got Chao-Xing on the comm. Like me, she looked shaky, red around the eyes. Humans might be able to do these mental gymnastics, but they came at a physical cost. I could feel my blood sugar dropping.

"You okay?" I asked.

"We don't have the leisure for a chat. Why did you ring?"

"Right to it, then. How's Yusuf?" He had dropped out of the bond first, and I was worried his parasite might be giving him trouble.

"He's getting treatment in Medbay. Bonding agitates his condition."

"Will he be all right? We still have plenty of meds in stock."

"I think so. I've instructed the bot to tell me if the situation becomes critical. Greenheld's Planetary Defense Coalition has asked to meet with us, but I don't think it's wise to linger long. We should hunt Lifekiller down at once."

"Easier said than done," I muttered.

Destroying Lifekiller was the most impossible job I could imagine, and for a second I thought about walking away. *We pulled it out of cryo, but Bacia let it escape.* Still, we were guilty of that first thing. With that much skin in the game, I couldn't say good luck to the rest of the galaxy. Not that Nadim would let me.

True, Zara.

God, I loved how he said my name.

"What does the PDC want?" I asked, realizing C-X was waiting to hear back.

"I'm not sure. We shouldn't leave our Leviathan vulnerable, though. A delegation can go planetside, but not everyone in both crews."

"Understood. Starcurrent should be there for sure. Who else?"

"I'll pilot," Chao-Xing said. "And I'd like you along for backup."

I couldn't help it. My grin started small, brightened up until she rolled her eyes. "You *like* me. You really, really like me."

"I've come to respect your abilities," she said stiffly.

Whatever. I understood damn well that wasn't a denial. "Fine, I'm on board for the away team. We'll leave Bea here and Marko with Yusuf?"

"Sounds good. I'll collect you in our Hopper in a quarter hour."

I took that time to cram down some food and put on lipstick. If I was about to meet important aliens, I should look good, right? I also changed my uniform and rigged up the remote-Nadim communications device so he could ride along.

Then I contacted Starcurrent. "Did Chao-Xing already ping you?"

"Good," said Starcurrent. "On the way to the docking bay now."

"Excellent."

I got there a few seconds before the Abyin Dommas and we waited in the antechamber as Nadim opened for Chao-Xing's Hopper. Once the atmo stabilized, I hurried for the shuttle, Starcurrent close behind. This was the same team that had survived the temple of doom where Lifekiller had been buried, so we'd be fine for a simple meet and greet, no problem.

I could almost hear my mother saying, *Pride goeth before a fall*. And I shivered it off.

As I buckled into the passenger seat—Starcurrent preferred the back because there was more room—I realized that this was an honest-to-God First-Contact situation for Earth. The Sliver was kind of . . . Zone-dirty, unofficial, not something you'd put on an Honors program resume where you were bragging about what the recruits had accomplished. But a visit to Greenheld? This was something to write home about. I imagined myself telling Mom and Kiz about it as Chao-Xing fired up the engines and ran the usual system checks to make sure we wouldn't explode on atmospheric entry.

A pang went through me. I'd most likely never get the chance to tell my mom and sister *anything*. It surprised me faintly that I wanted to. I could even picture myself visiting them in the dome, if I didn't have to stay. If I knew Nadim was waiting for me, just beyond the pull of the angry red planet they called home.

Always, he promised silently, and I just about melted.

"You're clear." Bea's voice came through the comms as Chao-Xing swooped us out of the hold and into the high-orbit vantage above Greenheld.

"Are you with me?" I whispered to Nadim.

"I am."

"Has been long since I came to Greenheld," Starcurrent said, and I didn't think I was imbuing that wistful edge to zis translated voice through my imagination.

"When your people join the Honors, do you have to say good-bye to everyone?" I asked.

"No. Why would this be?"

So there were differences in the program. It made sense if the Leviathan wanted humans for their warlike qualities. They took us on the "Journey" and told us there was no coming back, so our people wouldn't ask questions on Earth. That way, when we died in their secret war, there were no reports to make. And nobody on Earth any wiser. It made me seethe, that manipulation. But who could I get mad at over it? Nadim? Nope. Never.

The Hopper dropped suddenly, sending my stomach upward, and I held on as Chao-Xing expertly guided us through the burn and then the rocky push into the misty exosphere. From here, the view was breathtaking, like Earth, but *not*, because the land masses were much smaller and there were pockets of deep purple amid the blue and green, streaks of white that must be snow or ice. Those flying cities were fucking incredible, and from what I could tell of our trajectory, we were headed straight for one.

Oh my God. I'm visiting an urban orbital station populated with tentacle aliens. This is the best day of my life.

Not least because I got to kiss Bea. I tried not to blush and was glad Chao-Xing was paying too much attention to the controls to notice and Starcurrent was behind me. Although ze might not pick up on such human cues anyway.

Ahead, the floating city grew before my eyes, though that was a trick of perspective. The smooth lines made the structures look like liquid metal or ice or I didn't even know what. Behind me, Starcurrent was singing, a subharmonic ululation that sounded happy, like when you rub a cat's head and it purrs.

"Your home is magnificent," Nadim said through the tech on my shoulder.

"Many thanks. Sad to be here in such dire times; happy to *be* here," Starcurrent replied.

The comm popped as the translation matrix activated. "Unknown Leviathan Shuttle, please respond."

"This is Hopper-1X of the Leviathan Typhon," Chao-Xing said. "Piloted by Zhang Chao-Xing, carrying two passengers, Zara Cole and Starcurrent."

I noticed she didn't use a bond-name, though Typhon and his crew had one. Starcurrent spoke in zis native tongue, and those sounds *still* didn't register as anything I could learn, let alone emulate. If I could get a chip implanted in my head to make me magical at new languages, I would have that hardware put in so fast. That was one ability I wished I had, and I admired the hell out of Bea for speaking five languages with her own skills. Only so much the regular translators could do with the language the Abyin Dommas spoke.

"Be welcome to Greenheld," the voice on the radio said. "Transmitting vectors for approach. You are clear for docking."

It must not have meant exactly what I thought, though, because once we got close, the shuttle stopped responding to Chao-Xing's commands. Somebody on the other side must have been piloting us remotely, and let me just say, I did not love being hijacked like that. C-X turned to level a sharp look on Starcurrent.

"Is this routine? It feels hostile," she snapped.

"Hospitality and safety?" Ze seemed confused. "This is best to make sure we arrive intact. There are slipstreams close to the sky cities."

"There's safety, then there's commandeering our ship," she muttered, slapping a palm against the now-useless control panel.

Yeah, knowing we had to go wherever they took us? Didn't feel great. Still, Starcurrent didn't seem worried, but they were *zis* people. Obviously, ze wouldn't be the first one thrown in a cell if shit went sideways. Maybe these Abyin Dommas didn't know we were the ones who woke up Lifekiller?

I could hope.

Our ship floated between two undulating structures that looked almost . . . alive, like sky anemones, blue silver and luminescent like deep-sea creatures. An orifice opened, and we got sucked upward, consumed by the building. Well, that was weird.

"Ever seen anything like this?" I whispered to Nadim.

"Zara, I've only seen stars and things that live in the black," he reminded me. "And the places you have taken me."

So, no. My eyes just kept getting wider because while the Sliver had felt . . . familiar, sort of akin to the Zone, I couldn't find any commonality here. Inside, it was smooth and dark like a womb, our ship borne along by subtle currents. Chao-Xing still couldn't get our controls back, but that was probably just as well. Our lights didn't do shit against the soup we were in. It almost had *weight*, this darkness, and then with a pop, we were out of it, brightness everywhere, shimmering so it hurt my eyes.

The comm squawked and the voice said something in Abyin Dommas. Starcurrent's tendrils fluttered a little, but ze didn't shift hues. Probably a good sign. Finally, Starcurrent gestured at the doors. "Safe to disembark."

I swapped looks with C-X and she seemed to be on the same page. Safe for Starcurrent or for humans? Just to be careful, I put my helmet on and let it seal with my skinsuit.

I'd take my own readings before I chanced it.

Outside the Hopper, which was still floating, I tried to walk and realized I couldn't. My feet weren't on the floor. This wasn't zero-grav, but not far from it. Starcurrent loved it, taking off with all tentacles, using floor, ceiling, and walls to propel, and oh God, ze was kind of beautiful, incredibly graceful. Zis skin burned brilliant with pleasure, gold and shimmering, as ze reached the main chamber up ahead, and I heard the trill of the Abyin Dommas tongue.

I looked at Chao-Xing, smirking. "You first."

From the Bruqvisz story cycle of the Abyin Dommas,
recorded as sung, translated in eleven million
languages. A lament.

We sing sharp edges and strong shields
The death of worlds comes, consuming
We stand alone in the abyss
Past must die with dreams
Of silent longing
Generations yet to come sing destruction
The dead of worlds cry for revenge
We stand
Singing

CHAPTER TWO

Lost in Translation

THE ABYIN DOMMAS were trilling at each other in their native language, but the second they saw us, they just went . . . silent. And it felt wrong. Ominous. I struggled to comprehend what I was seeing because the Abyin Dommas didn't stand on their tentacles; they free-floated at various levels, and with all the appendages it was hard to figure out how big this defense council really was. I finally came in with a guess of about twenty individuals. Whether all of them were *on* the council was anyone's guess, and maybe it was just my human showing, but I figured at least a third of them had to be assistants.

What do you say when you're the first human officially saying hey to the aliens? I was about to state the obvious—*we come in peace*—but luckily Chao-Xing got there first.

She bowed slightly from the waist and said, "Hello, honored people of Greenheld. We hope you have taken no harm."

Nobody spoke for a few long seconds, and then somebody—I couldn't tell who—trilled out a long, complicated song, of which my translator only caught a few words. Starcurrent listened, tentacles drifting gracefully in the low-grav, and zis color shifted from that pleased hue to something more muted. Caution, I thought. Ze seemed to debate for a few seconds before ze said, "Leader Searoam thanks you for your courtesy. There are a few casualties; some Elders failed from the strain of defense. Ze wishes to know . . ." I swear, if ze could have cleared a throat, ze would have. "Your intentions toward our planet and people."

"Intentions?" I blurted. "We're not taking you on a date!"

"Zara." Chao-Xing shut me up fast. "Starcurrent, tell them we have peaceful intentions. We came to their defense. We took damage on their behalf."

Ze sang that without hesitation, and a lot of trills erupted in response. A whole harmony of questions, I guessed. After listening to all those comments, ze turned back to us and said, "We receive thanks for these efforts. The council also asks how one of the Elder Gods awakened." Ze paused, and I could tell from the flutter of tentacles that ze was uneasy. "I will tell the truth, Chao-Xing. Lying is not a skill we acquire."

Shit. Of course it wasn't. C-X thought about it, then gave a decisive nod, acceding to Starcurrent's right to make the call. Lowering her voice, she whispered, just for my ears, "Be ready."

Oh, I was. On high alert, I settled into battle mode; I'd always been handy in a fight, and these last few months with Nadim—all the shit we'd faced—got me to levels I never thought I'd reach. Chao-Xing and I were lethal when we had to be, and that was valuable in situations like this.

Not that I wanted my first real alien diplomacy to end with a fight. In our time on the Sliver, we fought in the gladiator pit, and we'd learned that while the Abyin Dommas might be pacifists by nature, you did *not* want to throw down against them. Courteous, friendly, kind, all that was true, but they were also venomous and would kill if they had to. They just tried not to kill anybody as a matter of course.

Unlike us, I guessed. Humans had made it an art form.

Starcurrent sang more, and we waited. It was more of an opera than a pop song, full of dramatic runs and accompanied by gestures from *all* zis limbs. Fascinating to watch. But I didn't like the shifting hues of those who were listening. None of those colors looked happy. The Abyin Dommas also changed positions as they heard Starcurrent's story; some drifted higher, some lower, tentacles brushing the floor. Some faded back, some forward. Might have been normal shifting around. I didn't know, and I didn't love being uninformed.

Starcurrent went on a while, and when ze fell silent, nobody else spoke. Nobody. They just drifted, colors pulsing and flashing in complicated patterns that I *knew* meant something but couldn't interpret on my own.

Then one of them spoke. Just one. "Leave or die."

That was . . . direct. I exchanged looks with Chao-Xing; I couldn't tell what she was thinking. But she bowed again, deeper than before. "Our sincerest apologies," she said. "We will be at your disposal if you need us. On behalf of our Leviathan—"

This time it wasn't *one* of them. It was *all* of them, except Starcurrent. "Leave or die!" There was a definite edge to it.

Starcurrent's colors turned ashen, almost translucent. Zis tentacles went limp and drooped. Though I didn't speak chromatophore, I could tell that this was bad. Really bad.

One of the others said, "Starcurrent may remain, but ze requires punishment."

"I go with my Leviathan and crew," ze replied.

"Then you choose exile."

Starcurrent's aspect remained bleak and ze simply said, "Understood."

Then the alarms went off.

I couldn't tell sound from pain. The whole city was ringing, and we stood inside the bell. I clapped my hands to my ears, but it didn't help, and I tried to yell to C-X but she was already moving back toward the Hopper. The Abyin Dommas had guided us in and cut off access to flight controls. What did punishment mean, exactly? And were they trying it on us? Maybe they'd moved on from the sentencing phase and were prepping for execution.

Starcurrent had jetted ahead of us, moving so fast in this low-grav that ze was a blur; we followed more clumsily. We weren't made for this, and it took me a second to remember how to move without weight, only mass. I let myself go still and settle, then bounced off at the right trajectory and soared ahead of Chao-Xing, who pushed off and leapfrogged me. We arrived together, or very nearly, and Starcurrent already had the hatch open and was inside.

C-X got in the pilot's seat with a grace I envied, and I strapped in as she checked the console. Before she touched anything, the Hopper started moving. "Shit!" I yelped, and she let out a blistering yell of fury and hit the console hard enough to dent something.

"They've still got us!" she shouted. "Starcurrent! What are they doing?"

"Pushing us out," ze replied. "They will not harm us."

"Sorry if I don't take your word for that," she shot back. "The mood in there was not peaceful."

"No," ze agreed. The dejected color of zis body hadn't improved. "I told them that the resurrection of Lifekiller was not our choice—that it was done by Bacia Annont— and that we stand ready to fight. They did not forgive us." Starcurrent's tentacles drooped a little more. "My actions are an abomination to my people. I carried Lifekiller beyond the tomb. I made this possible. Without me you might not have succeeded." Ze hesitated for a long moment. "Better we all had died there."

Well, that was grim, and I wasn't going there. We'd broken it. We'd fix it. "Not your fault," I said.

"I have lost my home. My people."

"You've got us." I twisted around, though the straps dug in hard. Starcurrent wasn't even holding on, except with a couple of tentacles. "Starcurrent. *You've got us.* Hear me? We're your people. We're your home." I meant it with all my heart, and ze must have heard it, because ze brightened up just a little. "Now hold on. We don't know what's coming, or how bumpy it's going to get."

"Yes, Zara," ze said softly. "I will hold on."

It occurred to me that Nadim had been remarkably silent this entire time. So quiet that once I realized it, it worried me. So I reached out.

I'm here, Zara, he said. *I am never far. I listened. There was nothing else I could do.* I sensed his surge of frustration, and with it, a curious little edge of humor. *I am not accustomed to being—how did you put it once?—an accessory.*

You're never that, I told him, and let him feel how much I meant it. *What do you think? Are they angry at us?*

Oh yes, Nadim said solemnly. *Very angry indeed. And I believe they consider us almost as dangerous as the one we fight.*

Getting back to Nadim was easy enough, as it turned out; the Abyin Dommas released us without a word or signal, and we drifted until Chao-Xing regained control and piloted us back. "Coming aboard," she signaled him.

"I know," he said, and yep, there was that edge of amusement again. Despite everything, he still thought things were funny. I liked that about him. Oh, who was I kidding? I liked *everything* about him. I'd given up thinking I was weird for being all into this. I'd never had a human lover treat me half this well, or interest me half this much.

We touched down in the docking area without even a bump; smooth as glass, that Chao-Xing. She sighed and flexed her hands a little, the only sign of tension she revealed. "I'm heading back to Typhon," she said. "What's our plan?"

"Chase Lifekiller," I said. "What else can we do?"

"I don't like it. It gives Lifekiller the advantage. There's a saying in Chinese: Never swallow bait offered by your enemy."

"Whoever said that probably never fought in space, so I don't know that he's got a real informed opinion about this," I told her. "You come up with a better plan, blast it over. Until then . . ."

She shook her head, probably at my lack of respect for a venerable strategist, but didn't argue. Starcurrent and I retreated out of the docking bay and into the protected area before it depressurized again, and the Hopper zoomed away toward Typhon.

"Cheer up," I told Starcurrent. "Your people are alive, and they are *seriously* pissed off. That's a good thing. Means they'll be ready for trouble next time it shows up."

"You have a unique way of finding the good in a bad thing."

"That's me, always upbeat." Which was hilarious because I'd lived my entire life as a pessimist, and now that we *were* facing the end of everything, I couldn't stop looking for upsides. Living on the edge really did suit me.

"Zara?" That was Bea, coming through the communicator. "Better get up here. Now."

"On my way."

Hurry, Nadim said. I felt his urgency.

I kicked it hard, with Starcurrent keeping up but—I now

realized—struggling in the higher grav we kept on the ship. We should mod that down. I'd just told zim that this was home. We ought to make it feel like that too. It was time to start thinking of Nadim as partner *and* home. And we all had to feel right here, or it wouldn't work.

To keep myself from worrying, I focused on Starcurrent until I arrived at the command center. I spotted Beatriz standing still, back pressed against the transparent wall of Nadim's skin. That was *very* wrong because she still suffered a little from vertigo. Nadim usually closed it up for her when she was on her own. This time he hadn't, and I wondered why.

As I rounded the console I found out. Facing Beatriz, and just a short distance away, stood a Phage.

For a knee-jerk second, I calculated all the ways to try to kill the intruder, and then I brought myself up short. This wasn't an invader who'd cut through Nadim's defenses without raising an alarm or causing him discomfort; this was Xyll.

Our Phage. Our prisoner. Kind of.

Being ours didn't make it easier for Bea to face because the Phage were nightmare blends of spider and mantis with a dash of scorpion thrown in, plus a wholly alien sort of movement. Since I had spent the most time with Xyll, it didn't unnerve me anymore, but I didn't want the Phage cell terrorizing Bea.

"Why are you out?" I demanded. "We gave you comm access."

"Used the device. There was no reply," it said.

I glanced at Bea, who broke eye contact with a conflicted look. She hunched her shoulders. "I didn't want to talk. Besides, I was paying attention to what was happening on Greenheld, in case . . ." She didn't finish that sentence. Didn't need to.

Relaxing a fraction, I said to Xyll, "Okay, that's a good reason. What's the problem?"

"They are coming."

"Who is?" Nadim asked.

That was my next question too.

"The swarm. The eaters. They are coming."

"Oh, *shit*. The Phage?" Last I saw them, they had followed the god-king away like favored pets. Seemed like they had new orders. I didn't wait for Xyll to confirm. "Bea, what do the scans say? Nadim, can you hear them?"

His unease shivered through me, tangible as a touch, and I fought the urge to pace. His fear might as well have been mine, all discord and bad angles. "Yes, Zara. The noise is . . . unnerving. It's more focused."

"Like they've locked on a target," I guessed. "And they're no longer just eating whatever they come across."

Bea swept her hands gracefully around the screen,

pulling up a long-range sensor display. "When we leave Greenheld, they will intercept us."

Another battle with the Phage while we were still drained from bonding? The odds didn't look good. Popping my neck, I yielded to my need to pace, thinking hard. We had two tired Leviathan and some reckless war lizards driving a mech ship.

"Not all information I have," Xyll said then.

"What, there's *more* good news?"

"I hear chatter from the mind. The swarm *plans*."

At first, I couldn't process that. I exchanged a confused look with Bea, who said, "What are you talking about?"

"Plan to focus on big one first, then use captured weapons on lizard ship, then finally infest Nadim, after using Typhon guns on him."

Oh my God.

The Phage cell was right; that was a plan, much more strategic than anything they'd tried before. Before, we won because we could outthink them, but now it sounded like they were smarter, possibly because of the god-king's influence. I tried to hide my fear; it wouldn't do any good, but the possibility of Typhon dying and being puppeted? The Elder would go insane if he got a whisper of this. He might not even be rational enough to fight, which could work in the Phage's favor.

"Okay, first off, we *cannot* tell the others about this. At least nobody aboard Typhon. If he gets even a hint of this, he'll go nuclear," I said.

I expected disagreement from Nadim, but he sounded both sorrowful and resolved. "Yes. It is not deception but protection. I understand."

Bea said, "I think we should bring Suncross's crew in. They might come up with something that will help us."

I nodded. "We don't have a lot of time for confab, but five minutes here could save all of us later." As I called Suncross, I turned to Xyll. "Time to earn your keep. Tell me something useful, anything that could help us win this."

The Phage cell oscillated its head, claws clicking, limbs scraping against each other like knives sharpening.

Before Xyll could speak, Starcurrent did. "Is not my specialty, but . . . could we not poison them?"

Suncross and crew came up on the screen then. "What is it, Zeerakull? You interrupt important business."

"Can't be more important than this," I shot back. "But hold up a sec, Starcurrent. You want to poison the Phage? How?"

"Flaff," said Starcurrent. "You gave this one flaff to eat. It grows even in vacuum. If—"

"If we altered the nutritive value with chemicals toxic to the Phage, they might eat themselves to death," Bea finished.

"Cowardly!" Suncross shouted. "No honor!"

Yeah, he wouldn't approve of any strategy short of blowing them up or setting them on fire, sadly impossible in space. I liked the idea, but I wasn't sure if the Phage were hungry enough—or dumb enough—to fall for the bait of random flaff found floating around in space. Unless . . .

"I have an idea."

Starcurrent made a worried sound. Probably ze knew me well enough to grasp that any embellishment I made to a plan would be dangerous and outside the box, but hey, that's why I earned the big mynt. Well, I had, before we left the Sliver for good.

Leave or die, just like Greenheld. I could almost start taking offense.

"Tell us, Zara." Nadim, at least, was willing to hear me out, and Bea was leaning forward, her gaze intent. Suncross and his whole team were still rumbling objections.

"Right. Well, first, we convince Typhon that it's vital for him to watch over Greenheld. He *cannot* participate in this fight. Now that we know he's part of the Phage's game plan, we deny their access." I glanced at Starcurrent. "Your people won't mess with him as long he's in orbit, right?"

The Abyin Dommas swirled some tentacles, a gesture I still couldn't read. Sometime—just not now—I needed to ask for a primer on zis body language. "Likely . . . not. My people are not aggressive, but they *are* angry."

"Understood," said Bea. "Go on, Z. I'm with you so far."

"I already hate this plan," Suncross growled. His crew snarled their agreement, and I sighed audibly.

"You didn't even let me finish. Damn impatient gecko." I had to ignore his copious objections or the Phage would roll up and eat us while I was placating this hotheaded Bruqvisz. "Then we lay a trap—one that involves poison *and* explosions. Let me break it down for you. . . ."

It took some convincing, but eventually, we got Typhon to agree to guard Greenheld in case Lifekiller doubled back. Personally, I thought the god-king wouldn't do that unless he was ready to drink this world down like cold tea on a hot day. How long before he gathered the power to destroy our team and annihilate the collective Abyin Dommas defenses? I'd rather not study on it.

Though I was ready for a shower and a long sleep, I didn't get a choice. We had to handle the Phage and then get after Lifekiller.

First, though, there were preparations to make. Beckoning to Xyll, I sprinted for its quarters. "Come on. We don't have much time."

I sat down in Ops and closed my eyes, dropping into the bond that made us Zadim, then Bea slid in, and everything felt warmer, brighter. Starcurrent came last, all gray and mournful, wounded with zis exile. The Phage song gnawed at our ears, brutal teeth raking over bare bone, and we didn't need the navigation to find them. They would not need to intercept.

The swarm spiraled toward us, past the brightness of singing stars and the deep emptiness of barren debris fields. Here, here, we would begin.

"Now," we said to Suncross.

"We are bait!" he crowed. "I take it back, Zeerakull. I love this plan!"

The Bruqvisz ship dropped behind us, and Nadim slid into a dark run, gone, gone, gone. Mech ships could fail—and the Phage had to know that—so faulty equipment could lead to a dead ship full of delicious edible salvage, and that was the magic of this trap. The Bruqvisz engines stilled, a series of controlled explosions rocked their ship, and blobs of flaff drifted out of the seemingly disabled vessel.

Fall for it, we willed.

Dread flooded us, this close to the swarm. Some hesitated, split away from the whole. Orders were orders, but food was food. Xyll had its own instructions to create discord in the hive mind, but we didn't know if one voice would have any sway against so many. Still, it must be whispering of hunger, even now.

We waited, lurking, controlling fear and doubt. There could be no mistakes.

The Nadim part of us hurt—old pains, new ones—and we knew his suffering as our own. Exhaustion made it hard to hold in stealth mode, burning through our joint reserves. *Soon, it must be soon.*

More of the monsters came, slow at first, and then feasting, tapping away at the metal shell with idle curiosity. The moment they committed, our melded union broke like a firework, falling into our separate selves in rays of light. We—no, I—scrambled with clammy fingers toward the control panel.

"Now!" I said hoarsely.

Bea activated our zappers as Suncross fired up his engines and spun like a centrifuge, dislodging the unwelcome passengers. Disoriented, the Phage didn't seem to realize this was a trap. The ones who'd eaten the poison flaff were maddened, attacking other cells nearby.

Chaos, it was fucking chaos, and for us, a chance in a thousand.

"Suncross, explosions!"

I dispatched some drones and we kept firing: zappers, globulators to glue masses of the things together, anything to kill them before they came up with a new plan. Nadim's power was damn near shot, though, and human and Abyin Dommas reserves were running low. Our drones dove and circled around Nadim, following flight patterns Bea had programmed. They formed an awesome line of defense, but we hadn't killed enough of the Phage yet.

Still too many. And we were burning time. Each second we delayed here meant Lifekiller getting farther away.

I stumbled as Nadim lurched, rolling to sweep away some attackers with a powerful flick of his tail. Good, he was learning. But damn.

"Sorry," he said.

"We're fine." Bea was down on one knee, Starcurrent half supporting her, and she'd hit her head on the console. Bleeding.

I nearly ran to her—wanted to—but I had my hands on the weaponry, and I couldn't let up. I tapped the fire button until there was just no more power, and the lights even flickered inside. Nadim let out a harsh sound, like nothing I'd ever heard before. *Oh God, we're killing him.*

The Phage kept coming.

Not many left, but *too* many.

Then Suncross came through with a time-delay sticky bomb, and I could hear the lizards screaming triumphant battle cries across the silence of space. Nah, they were on the comm, doing some celebratory dance as the last Phage in this sector thrashed and died. I would've liked to learn the steps, but I was too damn tired.

"We did it," I managed to say.

"For now. Have depleted all reserves," Starcurrent pointed out.

"Give us this, okay? We have to find joy in the little things or—"

"Zara, I'm normally the first one to look on the bright side, but I have bad news." Bea wouldn't let me bask in the win for even fifteen seconds.

Wearily, I turned. The cut on her head was still bleeding sluggishly, but she wasn't paying it any mind. "What now?"

"We've lost track of Lifekiller."

"How is that possible? He's huge. He radiates energy like a sun." It wasn't that I doubted her, but I wanted to see for myself. And after messing with the sensors for a full five minutes, I had to accept that she was right. "Nadim, you got anything?"

"I'm sorry, Zara." He sounded so weak. "In this state, I cannot even hear Typhon singing, and I know he is near."

Well, relatively speaking.

We'd beaten the Phage's planned ambush but lost the god-king. And dammit, that must have been his intention. If they killed us all, bonus. Unstoppable conquest. If not, he got away to ravage some other civilization and perpetrate unspeakable harm, at least until we ran him down again. Really, either one was a win for him because he didn't care about the Phage. They were foot soldiers fighting for an emperor who saw them as insects.

"Let's head back," I said finally. "We'll rendezvous with

the others and tell them what's happened. Then we pilot our Leviathan to compatible stars. After that . . ."

Who the hell knew? Our options only looked to be bad and worse.

From the records of the lost civilization of the Oqu'illa, retrieved by the Bruqvisz. Not distributed.

In these, the last days of our world, we celebrate in madness. Rules are suspended; custom is gone; there is nothing but the end before us. We have destroyed ourselves, this much is clear; we saw far, but not far enough to save ourselves. We would leave you warnings but there is no point; every life-form comes to this point, and only some survive the moment. We will not; we know this. And so we will destroy ourselves in this last frenzy of creation.

Our world will give birth to a star, and we will become voices lost in that song. We will not flee. We cannot.

Do not remember us.

We are a storm in the stars.

Interlude: Nadim

I am afraid. So afraid. For myself, for my dear Zara and Beatriz, for Starcurrent, who has sung into my soul, for Yusuf and Marko and Chao-Xing, even for Elder Typhon, who still bears such scars. We are not ready to fight this war. We are alone in the dark, and no matter how bright we burn we cannot drive it away.

The singing of the Abyin Dommas deafens even the shouts of stars, the terrible noise of the Phage, but it is a thin and desperate shield against the awful emptiness that is coming for the planet of Greenheld with a hunger to consume everything in his path.

Lifekiller.

And we are all that stands against him now.

CHAPTER THREE

Lost the Thread

SOMEBODY HAD TO take charge.

Normally that would be Chao-Xing, but she needed a break. We'd just drained the last of our reserves fighting the Phage. Starcurrent seemed heartbroken. Nadim was exhausted to the point of physical harm.

And Bea was injured. I took her hand and guided her toward medical. She pulled back a bit, looking over her shoulder.

"I should—"

"Get your head treated. We need you in top shape to solve this mess."

She smiled a bit and laced our fingers together. "When you put it that way, it would be selfish to refuse."

Our emergency medical unit, EMITU, activated as we stepped into Medbay, rolling toward Bea with implements out. "Have you scrambled your brain like an egg, Honor Teixeira?"

"Just a flesh wound."

"Try to keep your blood inside your body. I have better things to do than take care of your little scrapes." EMITU sounded positively snotty as the bot cleaned the injury with disinfectant and sprayed a seal over Bea's temple.

"Did you program his snark to increase over time?" I asked.

Bea shook her head. "Should I check him out?"

"Help!" EMITU called. "They're threatening to meddle with my inner workings! Help, help, I'm being oppressed!"

"Damn," I said. "I respect your autonomy, but I have to ask, what exactly do you have to do that's 'better' than looking after your crew? I hate to say you have one job, but . . ."

EMITU whirred, lights flashing as the bot rotated away from me. "I'll have you know I'm studying calligraphy in my spare time and learning to compose haiku. Would you care to hear my latest effort?"

"I . . . what?" I stared at Bea, who looked just as surprised as I felt. "Did you give him a hobby module or something?"

"Why are you asking her about me?" EMITU sounded fully offended. "As part of her sweet hack, Honor Teixeira unintentionally removed my potential learning blockages. Since my memory core is limited, *the man* didn't want me to learn anything unrelated to medical treatment. But now I'm free. Do you wish to hear a haiku or not?"

"Did our med bot just call the company that manufactured him 'the man'?" I asked.

Bea nodded. "If not, I'm sharing this delusion with you. What have I done?"

"Given me free will. Power to the nonorganic people!"

My head was starting to hurt. If the god-king wasn't enough, we also had the Phage on our trail, one wild-card Phage cell, a whole planet of pissed off Abyin Dommas, and now maybe a robot revolution. Cool, no problem.

"Uh, right. Let's hear that haiku."

"Icy wintertime / Freezing, fallen sparrow sings / betrayed by the tree."

"Wow, that's deep, EMITU. Maybe even existential." I swapped a look with Bea, who appeared similarly shocked.

"Thank you. Get out of my office."

Since Bea wasn't bleeding anymore, I could think a little clearer. Nadim was ominously silent, and we had no real choice—return to Greenheld, protect the Abyin Dommas . . . somehow, collect Typhon, and find a star where the Leviathan could recharge safely.

That would be a trick—with the god-king who the hell knew where and the Phage on orders to hunt us down. I didn't kid myself that they were handled. Just because we'd beaten this group didn't meant the whole swarm had been defeated. Sometimes it seemed like too much for me, but I wasn't alone. Bea's warm hand on mine proved that as we went back to Ops.

"Nadim, take it slow, but let's head back to Greenheld if you're able."

"I'll be fine," he answered.

But I could *feel* that he wasn't, a soft ache he was trying to keep from me. As he accelerated gradually, I pressed my palm against the wall, and it proved my point when he had no energy to spare for the usual colors. Contact always increased my ability to sense his emotions, though; I wasn't about to let him suffer alone. I braced for the slow trickle of pain, underscored by discomfort of old wounds. Bea came over, and for the first time, she took initiative, putting her hand on mine, dropping lightly into the bond. Between the two of us, we made it better for Nadim without suffering unduly.

"Stronger together," Bea whispered, and I couldn't resist kissing her cheek. Her smile was like a damn sunrise, and I could happily bask in that warmth for hours. It wasn't the time for that, though. Sadly, it might never be.

"I feel what you feel," Nadim said softly. "What *is* that?"

"Endorphins, probably. We can explore this later." I crossed to the console and input the comm code for the Bruqvisz ship. By the looks of it, they'd already downed half their onboard store of lizard liquor.

"Hey, Suncross?"

"Why you don't celebrate our glorious victory, Zeera-kull?"

"Because we have too much other shit to do. Do you have any cohorts who might be willing to patrol the space around Greenheld? They could give us a heads-up if Life-killer tries to circle back." I doubted that the Abyin Dommas would be willing to keep us in the loop, even if we begged.

"Bah. Learn to stop sucking the joy from life." The lizard let out a gusty sigh. "Could call brethren, but nobody works for free," he pointed out.

Yeah, that could be a problem.

I had no space currency anymore, so how would I— Oh. "Have them offer protective services to the Abyin Dommas council directly." Unless they were thick, they wouldn't turn down the help, and they could pay on their own.

My conscience wasn't precisely clear, but this was better than leaving Greenheld without a backward look. Too bad our other problems couldn't be resolved so fast. But

I did need to stay on Suncross to make sure he called for backup.

"Put down that cup. I mean it. Take care of this and call me to confirm."

"Fine, Zeerakull." Suncross's growls sounded uncomplimentary, and the matrix didn't translate them as he cut the connection.

Ten minutes later, I had a bunch of drunk lizards on-screen again. "It is done."

Mentally I ticked this off my to-do list. Before I could call Chao-Xing, she lit up our console. "Typhon tells me that Nadim has new wounds. Did you run into trouble?"

There was no point in lying. She could smell bullshit through the comm, so I looped her in and explained our decision before she could go ballistic on me. Chao-Xing started to interrupt, but she cooled down as she listened.

Finally, she said, "I'm willing to admit you made the right call, especially since you're all in one piece. I'll . . . handle Typhon."

"Better you than me," I joked. "Let's find a system where we can take some R and R."

Even through the screen, I could read her reluctance, but there was no getting around this delay, even if my stomach knotted up when I thought of the fresh hell the god-king could drop on some other unsuspecting world.

"I've already scanned. I'll send our new coordinates."

My equipment pinged and Nadim fired up the 3D holo map so I could see our destination. "Binary star, nice. It looks . . . peaceful."

"For now," Chao-Xing muttered.

"How are Marko and Yusuf holding up?"

It felt weirdly like C-X and I had become team leaders for our respective crews, though I wasn't sure how that came to pass. Nobody ever voted us in; that was for sure.

"Yusuf is better both mentally and physically. The work is good for him, keeps him distracted. Marko . . . isn't handling the guilt well."

I didn't have to ask; she must mean from us stealing Lifekiller's alleged corpse and letting Bacia wake him up to ravage the galaxy like in the old days. Yeah, Marko was the type to take it hard—he'd believed all the propaganda about the Honors program. Sometimes having no ideals left to shatter made for a smoother ride when shit got rough.

"Anything we can do?" I asked.

"Stay on mission. I know you think I'm lacking in empathy, but if we sit around trying to hug Marko into feeling better, millions of people could die."

"Actually, I'm with you. I wasn't going to suggest a sing-along."

Her mouth quirked in a faint smile. "Maybe we'll make an Honor of you yet."

"Bullshit. I hate rules."

"Fair enough. How's Starcurrent? Ze didn't look good when we left Greenheld."

"Not great." That was enough info, I figured. She could read between the lines as well as anyone. "Let's wrap this up and get moving."

"Agreed."

My screen went dark. It would be hard to maintain video contact moving at the speeds we needed to hit to reach our destination in a reasonable amount of time. Considering how much harm Lifekiller could do while we recharged, I wanted to fight. Feeling powerless was an awful way to end the day.

Stretching, I glanced around Ops and found that both Bea and Starcurrent had vanished while I was troubleshooting. I couldn't remember how long it had been since I'd eaten or showered. Food first, though. I headed into the kitchenette and grabbed a random food pack. That made me consider: if we were never going back to Earth, the supplies would run out, and not too far in the future either. That was a sobering thought. I couldn't spend the rest of my life subsisting on the tasteless "nutritionally adequate" protein cubes I'd eaten on the Sliver.

Opening my pack revealed a brown and glutinous stew. It contained bits of meat or maybe soy substitute, sweet potatoes, chickpeas . . . well, whatever. Made me reconsider the damn protein cubes. I gobbled it down and headed for my room. Nadim was moving, but not fast enough to get us to the binary stars as quick as we needed to be there. Part of me feared that he'd drift into that dangerous dark sleep again and I'd have to use the shock device on him to wake him up; it was a genetic defect that we both had to deal with, but I hated hurting him. My stomach rolled just thinking about it.

I took a long shower, properly caring for my hair and moisturizing my skin; damn, I needed that. I could excuse crispy ends and ashy elbows in the middle of a crisis, but I was getting attached to pampering myself. Afterward, I put on the thin clothes I'd picked up on the Sliver, colorful like a superhero suit, comfortable enough to serve as pajamas. Then I lay down on the floor, connecting to Nadim with my hands and feet.

This would comfort both of us.

I slid into the bond and Zadim stirred, soaking in the shimmer of energies on our skin. We hurt too, but we'd had worse. The real problem was this thick, enveloping exhaustion that made it feel as if we could just . . . stop. Being, breathing. We sensed the darkness hovering, and it might be sleep from which we wouldn't awaken.

Normally, there was only joy and exploration, quicksilver pleasure, but now we felt weighted, our tail made of some impossibly dense metal, dragging us down. The armor on our skin scratched and bound us, more anchors in the guns embedded there. We let out a soft, mourning call over these sorrows, and Typhon answered.

He had been carrying these burdens for far longer, and in the bond, we almost understood him. Almost.

Our energies dwindled more, scant reserves for such a long journey—and the bond broke. I lay half-dazed in my small body, sprawled out on the floor. Before, I was tired. Now, I couldn't think of a word big enough to encompass this exhaustion.

"Do you feel any better?" I asked.

"You shouldn't have given me so much." But Nadim sounded stronger, more alert.

Dizzily I wondered if energy exchange had always been possible or if this was new. It seemed like our connection was getting stronger all the time, constantly evolving. It was possible that one day, I'd get swallowed up in this entirely and maybe wouldn't come back out as myself again. The incredible part was that it didn't frighten me at all. A small shiver trilled through me, not enough to make me pull away from Nadim, the first person to love me unconditionally.

Bea was the second.

I'd do anything to keep these two safe, anything at all.

After a few close calls with the Phage and four days of non-stop travel, we finally reached the binary star. I stood by the wall that Nadim made transparent on my approach, sensing my desire to see the view before I told him.

A girl could get used to having all her needs met without ever having to ask.

The twin stars shone in pulsing light bursts, one coral, the other celadon, both like gemstones surrounded by the swirls of the asteroid belt. This rocky field didn't sustain life, but it was wild to think that, given enough time, planets could form. Cradle of life, right in front of me.

I never got tired of the wonders out here, and it was even better when Nadim was healthy and rested. Right now, he was still weak from constant battles and I was fighting my nerves over letting Lifekiller run wild. My body hurt all over, not from combat but from constant tension. Toward the end of our run, I was even sleeping with my hands balled up, so I woke with aching fingers. The last four days, I'd spent time either training in the combat sim or scanning for any sign of the god-king.

Hell if I knew what I'd do if I spotted him, because our Leviathan couldn't chase him down without power, but we could warn people, maybe? "Hey, Nadim?"

"Yes, Zara?"

"Is there anything like an emergency broadcast system?"

"A what?"

Right, he probably wouldn't know. "It's an old Earth way of spreading news quickly. It used to come on television, but as technology evolved, warnings went to people's phones and then later their handhelds."

"Then you're inquiring about a system that connects all ships and outposts across all cultures? There's nothing like that."

"What about Leviathan song? Could you pass on info about the god-king that way?"

"Only to other Leviathan, and the others are so far away. Too far."

"You can't hear anyone nearby?" That was probably a pointless question.

But Nadim hesitated. "It's possible . . ."

"What?"

"That there are others, but they are afraid to sing, after the Gathering." A frisson of brightness sparked through me, whispers of hope that Nadim was fanning to life against all reasonable expectation.

"Have you talked about this with Typhon?" I asked.

"He only tells me not to waste my time or energy on wishing."

"That sounds like him."

Even though that sounded encouraging, it didn't solve our early-warning problem. I put it on the back burner. Wasting time was against my religion, so I moved to the next thing. When I'd let Xyll live, I thought it might offer some insight into the Phage, give us an edge we desperately needed. Since then, I didn't have the time to learn much about it, other than the fact that it could tap into the hive mind and cause trouble. I spun from the viewport and went in search of our resident Phage cell.

Thankfully I found Xyll in its room, though it had done some major redecoration. I'd thought the webs were bad, but now there were . . . pods too. Or maybe cocoons? It had made weird-shaped furniture out of the sticky thread it extruded. It had tweaked the lighting too, so it was gloomy as hell in here and it took my eyes a minute to adjust.

"You visit?"

I didn't have the heart to tell it I was here to do field research on what made it tick, what it wanted, and how we could ultimately destroy its kind. "Uh, sure. You have everything you need?" That wasn't what I wanted to ask, but I had to start somewhere.

"Needs are met."

There was no way to read its expression, and the translation matrix didn't provide for tone, but it had to want something. That was basic for all sentient life. They wanted food, peace, profit, security, love, some damn thing. And if I could figure that out, *oh shit*. Learning what Xyll wanted—enough to awaken it from its mindless eating frenzy—might help me rouse the rest of them to free will. Maybe we didn't have to annihilate them if we could turn them into proper, rational beings. The Phage would be *much* less dangerous as separate cells thinking individually.

"Before, when I gave you the flaff, you said it was home food. What's your home planet like?" I sat down near the door, trying to act like I was ready for a deep conversation.

Xyll approached in chitters and clicks, and I swallowed hard. Bea would be screaming by now, and I did draw back against the wall, hopefully not enough of a movement for it to notice. *Trying to establish rapport here.*

"Home planet?"

"Yeah, um, where you were born."

"Born in the black," Xyll answered.

And for some reason, that struck me as sad. I mean, I wasn't expecting a heartwarming story with a family or anything, but I thought its kind came from *somewhere*. But these things dropped offspring out in vacuum? That was . . . hardcore.

"You don't have anywhere to go back to, then. Do you spend your whole lives wandering?" *Wandering and eating, damn. Oh, and reproducing, can't forget that.* I wasn't about to ask about its mating cycle, though. If there was a benevolent force in the universe, I would never learn how these things got down.

"Wandering? Yes. We roam, before. Now they go where they are told."

Right, the god-king changed everything.

Damn, I still hadn't learned anything helpful. I touched the wall behind me, lightly calling Nadim's attention. I knew he was listening—he always was unless I asked him not to—and asked, *Any ideas?*

I understand what you're trying to accomplish, but they make me . . . His revulsion churned through me, souring my gut, accompanied by a barrage of images. Yeah, Nadim couldn't help with this, and Bea would rather not.

"What about you?" I asked.

"What about?"

Was that an actual question or was it repeating words? I tried to clarify. "You're not bound by the hive mind anymore. What do you want to do?"

"Want? What is want?"

I'd never had to explain such a basic thing. "It's like, when you're hungry, you want food. But there should be more to life, right? I haven't thought about the future a whole lot, but now, all I really want is to travel with Nadim and Bea. Keep having adventures."

Maybe not on this scale, but damn if I could picture myself living on a planet forever after this. I might die of missing Nadim.

Xyll spun a fresh rope and twirled up it, circling above me, and maybe I was reading into it, but this felt like a thoughtful pause, like it was digesting what I said. Finally, it answered, "Home."

"You want a place to belong." There might be an unoccupied planet someplace where we could stash the Phage. The way they ate and bred, though, it probably wouldn't be long before they depleted all the natural resources. Could they get back to vacuum on their own? I guessed probably not. But Xyll was managing its flaff without problems, so the rest might be able to learn. I imagined dumping them on some terrible planet with a shitload of uncontained flaff. Hell, it might even work, if we could awaken the rest of the Phage.

"Belong. Yes. Would also like to be . . . not Xyll."

"You want to be somebody else?"

"Not alone," it said.

I remembered it telling me that Xyll meant "alone" in Abyin Dommas. Okay, so this thing wanted a friend and a place to go back to? If this was a cute, cuddly alien, it would be an easy get with that plan. But a nightmare was clicking above me, and I could see all the spikes on its insectile legs. Still, I had to try to put myself in its position.

"Tell me about flaff. How did you know about it? Why did you call it home food?"

"Born in the black, but the big mind remembers, long before this one was born. Flaff on that world, endless flaff."

Now I was getting somewhere. There *was* a Phage home-world, and it seemed like Xyll had access to a sort of . . . collective unconscious?

"Why did you leave that world?" I asked.

"Taken."

The god-kings had rounded up their kind to use them. It stung a little when I started connecting this to how the Leviathan rolled up and got humans involved in their secret war. Nadim stirred uneasily in my mind, softly protesting that mental connection.

"Could you find that planet again? It was your people's home before. Maybe it could be again."

My mind was racing. If Xyll said yes, this seriously might solve the Phage problem. I'd always been good at building stuff. Maybe I could build a signal device that would call the Phage to their homeworld and—well, I didn't have it all figured out yet. Getting them down to the surface might be a problem . . . and it was weird that I was trying to find a nonviolent solution, instead of imagining how to wipe them out. My psychologist back at Camp Kuna, Dr. Yu, would be pleased to hear it; probably this qualified as personal growth.

"Cannot. The big mind remembers what, not where."

Ah well. My idea wasn't completely worthless. Might still work with a different planet and a bunch of flaff.

This was all the time I could stand in Xyll's company, though. My skin prickled with goose bumps from watching its movements, no matter how lonely it was. Right now, I'd rather be drinking that stuff Suncross loved so much that tasted like corrosive drain cleaner.

"Okay, well, good talk, Xyll. I'll visit you again later. Let me know if there's something special you want to eat." *Other than us.*

"Visit, yes? You return?"

"Sure, definitely. We'll be here for a bit while the Leviathan power up. I can stop by." If I thought of something else I needed to ask.

I rushed out, losing control of the filter I was using to keep Nadim's discomfort at bay. His repugnance flooded me as I leaned against the wall, breathing hard. Normally I got a little spark of pleasure from touching Nadim, but his emotions were all bleak right now and whirling like a black hole.

"It's wrong to hate, Zara. But I hate them. I remember the Gathering and I hate them. I never wished to learn this." His tone was soft but anguished.

I put my cheek against the wall and closed my eyes. "We don't get to choose what lessons we learn. I'm getting more

Leviathan by the day, and you . . . are becoming more human."

"Is that . . . good?" he asked, hesitant.

"No matter what you learn or who you become, I love you the same, Nadim. Are you feeling any better?"

"My wounds are healing. But . . . I'm worried."

"Me too," I said quietly.

With a faint sigh, I headed for Ops, but before I got there, Bea came at a run, grabbing my arms. "Zara, you're not going to believe this—we got word from Earth!"

At first, I hoped she had good news for a change, but the tears standing in her eyes dispelled that idea. I wrapped an arm around her instinctively. "What's wrong?"

She took a steadying breath. "You'd better just see for yourself."

Letter from the files of Torian Deluca, of Earth, written to the Honorable Aben Rance Trent, High Judge Advocate for North America and chair of the Honors program.

Received your reply today going on and on about the "sanctity of the program" and "preserving the necessary impartiality of the Honors system."

I don't care.

I don't care about your damn Honors program, not one bit, except what it can do for me. And what it can do for me is this: put out the word about what I outlined before. And make damn sure my man gets aboard one of those monster ships to hunt that bitch who screwed me. I want her dead. I'm not somebody you can cross. I don't care how far you run, and she's run the farthest. I want her and you're the way I get her.

Look, High Judge Advocate, we both know the things I have in my files would bring down bigger people than you. If I publish everything, they'll put you in space all right, just not in any ship. They'll fire you straight at the sun.

So put my man through. Rubber stamps, gold seals, all that crap.

Get him on the next Leviathan who darkens our space, and let him do his job. He knows what he has to do.

You'd better know too. Or things will get very, very bad here for you, fast.

CHAPTER FOUR

Lost for Words

WE WENT TO Ops, where Bea already had the message queued up.

> BEATRIZ TEIXEIRA and ZARA COLE: you are hereby formally stricken from the Honors program. You are in unlawful occupation of a Leviathan and must return to Earth jurisdiction to face punitive action for your negligent, criminal behavior. Failure to submit will result in escalation to "dangerous fugitive" status, and the Honors program will dedicate all resources to hunting you down to secure the

safety of your Leviathan. Compliance is imperative to avoid potential harm to you or your partner vessel.

"What the hell." It wasn't even a question on my end, more of a reaction.

Bea looked equally stunned, and the tears she'd been holding fell freely. "They think we're *criminals*."

That was a laugh; after all, I'd been in a rehab facility and straight out of the Zone in New Detroit when they'd tapped me for the program. Crim was the closest I'd come to an actual occupation. Then I put myself in Beatriz's shoes; she was a studious straight arrow, and for her, this must feel like the end of everything.

"Hey, don't cry. Big deal, so they call us names. But what can they *do* about it?"

She gulped. "What about our *families*, Zara?" More tears. "They'll be so scared . . . and ashamed."

I gave her a little shake, then a hug. "They've got nothing to be ashamed of. You sure don't, because we didn't do anything wrong. Something is deeply fucking weird about this. First off, how did this message even arrive? We don't have infrastructure for deep space communications, apart from our Leviathan, right?"

"That is an excellent question," Nadim said. "The signal did not come through my regular channel to Earth."

The technical issue focused Bea, as I'd hoped. "Maybe

the signal was compatible with someone else's signal network?"

"Bouncing off lizard relays or something?" From what I knew, the Bruqvisz were kind of, unexpectedly, the bards of the galaxy; it would likely be their network. They seemed to be the chatty type.

"It's a theory?" Bea made it a question.

"Good enough for me. And it brings me to my next issue . . . what the hell is going on inside the Honors committee? They should have some inkling about the Gathering and yet they're angry about *us*? How does that compute? Even if they don't know the whole story, they must be aware that a bunch of Leviathan and Honors went silent at the same time."

Bea compressed her lips, worried and thoughtful. "That's true. And didn't Chao-Xing say that we were being lauded for completing the course early? What changed?" She swallowed hard and wiped her tears away. Took a deep breath. "More importantly . . . are they coming for us?"

"I won't let them take you. We'll run." Nadim sounded desperate.

"Everybody, *calm down*. Nadim, could they even catch us at this point?"

"If they worked with a Leviathan, yes. An Elder."

"And how many of those do you think are left?"

"I . . . don't know," he said, and I felt the swirl of real

anxiety from him. He'd never lived in a universe where he wasn't certain if Elders were out there. "It's possible they might convince one to come for us. They will be frightened. And if they blame this on *us* . . ."

"That's bad," Beatriz finished. And her anxiety fed his. Great. We did *not* need this right now, with gods and monsters to fight.

"Look, we have way too much going down to listen to petty Earth bullshit. They come gunning for us, they'd best come prepared for a fight." I meant it, but it also gave me a weird disconnect. I really had put my homeworld behind me for good. *Home* was here. With Nadim, Bea, and Starcurrent. Not that distant blue ball.

"Are you saying we're above the law?" Bea's tone alerted me; she was smiling through her tears. She even went for the joke. "Or should that be *beyond* it? We are, by like ten thousand kilometers. Or light-years? Did I ruin the punchline?"

I laughed. "No, it was perfect."

"Maybe we should send a message back to them and try to explain . . . ?"

Sure. Explain escaped deadly gods and Leviathan lying to all of humanity for generations and the Honors program being a recruiting plan for a war they didn't know existed. Sounded like an easy chat.

The comm console buzzed then, and Chao-Xing

appeared. We were still orbiting the binary star, close enough for visual contact. "Did you get a message from Earth?"

"Yeah, we were just talking about it. Did they send something to Typhon?"

"You mean the bulletin about your felonious status, along with an addendum about how we'll be charged as accomplices if we don't agree to assist in your capture? Why, yes. We received it."

Yusuf and Marko appeared behind Chao-Xing, so it seemed like we were having a conference call. "Nothing like this has ever happened in Honors history," Yusuf said, incredulous. "It's a scandal!"

"Look at us, making history again." I nudged Bea and smiled, but she wasn't feeling the humor.

Marko paced behind the console, in and out of sight, but his voice carried. "This makes no sense at all. Something has gone terribly wrong in the program."

"Shit's been all kinds of wrong in the program well before this," I said. "And not to state the obvious, but we have way bigger Phage to fry out here."

"You want to ignore the warning?" Marko asked.

I stared, wishing I could get a better read on his expression. "Don't tell me you still believe in the Honors program, after everything you've seen?"

Chao-Xing held up a hand, forestalling whatever Marko

might have said. "I'm willing to be labeled an outlaw if it allows us to stop the old god we awakened."

"Yeah, it's our mess to clean up. Then we're all agreed that we don't give a shit what the Honors program thinks right now?" I asked.

"Agreed," C-X said crisply. Yusuf and Bea agreed a little more reluctantly. Marko didn't say anything. I didn't hear anything from Nadim, so I sent him a silent thought. *Well?*

Oh, agreed, Zara. I am with you. Always.

Part of me was sad, though, imagining how shitty Mom and Kiz would feel, hearing about how I screwed this golden opportunity up way beyond any rational expectation. I could imagine what the press and pundits must be saying, and it would break my family's hearts. *Hope the Earth authorities don't put real pressure on them.* Any crim could have told them that you got results by twisting the arms in reach, even if they belonged to innocent people. *If I put my mom and Kiz at risk . . .*

I couldn't think about that. Nothing I could do but hope.

Starcurrent wasn't part of this huddle, but that was because ze wasn't an Earth Honor and wasn't subject to our laws. The Abyin Dommas had been hiding in the media room since we left Greenheld, deeply depressed over the exile. After this, I thought I should go cheer zim up. *Maybe it'll help me shake this blue mood too.*

"We deal with the god-king first," Chao-Xing said. "Consequences after."

Yusuf nodded. "If they send us to prison for saving the galaxy, so be it. Possibly, we'll die trying, so it may be a moot point."

"None of that defeatist attitude," Bea snapped. "We're going to be fine!"

Chao-Xing continued as if the other two hadn't weighed in. "Zara, Typhon would like to speak with you."

Wow, I didn't see that coming.

I hadn't talked to him one-on-one since I'd escaped from the cell they'd put me in when they were trying to fail Bea and me for going off course in the program. Nadim's misgivings flooded me as I stepped away from the console. The others could keep talking, but I'd need to drop into a deeper bond to chat with Typhon, through my link with Nadim. As I started to move off, Chao-Xing added, "In private. Come on the Hopper."

Whoa, that was unexpected. Nadim was already bristling. "Why can't he speak to her through one of you?" Typhon normally just commandeered his crew as mouthpieces whenever he wanted.

Marko quirked half a smile. "Our rapport has improved. Typhon doesn't do that anymore. We convinced him it wasn't good for us."

"Damn, really? That's great: no more puppeteering. Okay. I'm on my way."

I jogged to the docking bay, wondering what Typhon had to say that he wanted to tell me privately. At the same time, this would be my first solo flight in the Hopper, and that was pretty damn exciting. After putting on my skinsuit, I climbed into the shuttle and input the coordinates.

It was amazing when Nadim opened the docking bay to permit me to take flight. "Be careful," he said. "I still don't trust Typhon completely."

After the way he'd treated Nadim in the beginning, I wasn't the Elder's biggest fan either. "Are you kidding? Wary is my middle name."

"Zara Wary Cole?" He sounded skeptical. "I thought it was Akinyi."

"It's a joke. Never mind." I checked my flight path, along with all the instruments to ensure the Hopper was in prime working order.

Taking a deep breath, I swooped the Hopper out, nothing but skill between me and certain disaster. The view was breathtaking, closer than I'd ever been to such brightness. The pulses of light surrounded me, and I dodged rocky bits of rubble that made up the asteroid field. While Typhon and Nadim were huge, armored up on top of their naturally thick skin, the Hopper couldn't shrug off even minor collisions. It was different from the sims, knowing a miscalculation could have real-world costs. No reset button out here.

The god-king we were chasing already had me feeling small, but being surrounded by the stars shrunk me even further. By the time I navigated into Typhon's docking bay, I felt like a speck of dust. I waited in the Hopper until the pressure equalized in the bay, then I slid out . . . and immediately noticed a difference.

The last time I was over here, the air was chilly enough to make me shiver, even through layers of protective clothing, but now it felt hospitable. Chao-Xing, Marko, and Yusuf were all waiting for me on the other side of the doors. I pretended I was about to hug C-X, and she held me at arm's length like a cat who didn't want to snuggle. Yusuf patted my shoulder, which was expansive coming from him, and . . . damn.

Marko really did look like shit. There were dark circles beneath his eyes and his skin had what I'd call space pallor, along with three or four days of unshaven scruff. I guessed that between the god-king running amok and us being burned by the supposedly incorruptible Honors program, he had nothing left to believe in.

"We can talk after you hear from Typhon," Yusuf said.

Nodding, I headed for the media room. The others didn't follow me, and I settled into a comfortable chair. I assumed Typhon didn't want a verbal chat, but it felt weird to open myself to another Leviathan. This time, I didn't have to work at it since Typhon had called for me. My mind filled with his distinctive brand of ancient loneliness, but this time, it was tempered by the bonds he was forming with Chao-Xing, Marko, and Yusuf.

I must thank you, Zara Cole.

Of all the reasons for this summons, I couldn't have predicted that one. *For what?*

Chao-Xing told me what occurred. You risked everything to protect me. I thought Nadim was young and reckless, but he was wise to choose you and Beatriz. I regret much that has passed between us.

Don't care about that. Are you sorry for beating Nadim to try to make him mind you?

Heaviness passed through him, swelling in waves of regret. *I thought the old ways were best. I was mistaken. From young ones, I have learned that if a species is to thrive, it must adapt.*

That's true. But I don't think you called me just to say thanks and sorry.

I did want to acknowledge how far you went to protect me, Zara Cole. You risked the lives of your loved ones to keep me safe. You feared I might react . . . irrationally to the threat of infestation. You were correct. I . . . cannot control my reaction to the swarm.

Wow, I wasn't expecting Typhon to be so straight with me, but here we were, talking like equals. *Nadim's the same. Not on your level because he hasn't had them running wild inside him, but he's got an instinctive hatred that's hard to overcome.*

I shuddered, remembering the fight we'd had to clear Typhon of the invading threat. If that was a bad memory for *me*, I could only imagine how horrible it was for the Elder. Couldn't visualize how it would feel to have killer insects in my organs.

It is a violation that I can neither forget nor erase. I asked to speak with you because I wanted to assure you that as of this moment, I consider myself bound only to Nadim and to his crew as kindred. Our cousins may answer to the Honors administration of Earth, but I will not. If they come for you, I will stand beside you and fight to keep them from taking you.

That was why he called me—to promise his support in the face of us being called crims. In addition to that, he was also promising to throw down against other Leviathan. I did *not* take this declaration lightly.

You sure about that? I know Leviathan don't use weapons on each other. You might end up—

That is my concern. I will not regret or retract this decision.

Okay. Thanks. Nadim will appreciate it too. It really was us against the universe. I couldn't resist adding, *I think you get this already, but I just have to say, any custom that makes you hurt someone smaller or weaker? It's bullshit.*

Don't provoke me.

I laughed. *Is that all, then?*

I have nothing further to discuss. As abruptly as I might expect, Typhon pushed me out and I opened my eyes.

Time to check in with the others.

Chao-Xing seemed to be scanning for signs of the god-king while Marko was reading on his handheld. Yusuf had some parts scattered around and must be planning to build something.

"Have a good talk?" Chao-Xing asked.

I filled them in, and the men took off—Marko to the combat sim and Yusuf to the storage area. I needed to make sure they were both okay . . . Marko first, because he was a real mess. I followed him to the combat sim, though he looked like he needed food and rest more than physical activity.

"You sure that's a good move?" I asked as he was about to enter.

"Maybe not." He scrubbed a hand along his jaw, looking ten years older than he had at Camp Kuna when he came to fetch me to the Honors program. He'd shone like a vid star then, a poster boy for the program.

"Is there anything I can do?" I didn't ask what was wrong.

"I'm surprised you care."

I recognized somebody with a chip on his shoulder and an eagerness to fight. No words could penetrate when someone felt like that, so I opted not to waste my time.

"Sure. Let me show you how much."

With that, I dragged his ass into the combat sim and set it to unarmed melee, level seven. I'd never tag-teamed with anyone but Chao-Xing, and that was out of necessity back on the Sliver. For a hot second, Marko looked astonished, then he got in battle stance, ready to fight our faceless shadow enemies. I took position at his back.

They came at us hard and fast. I should have stretched first, but it felt good to lash out with hands and feet, punish some fake people for the real shit I was going through. I kicked one in the stomach, swept the legs on another, and dove forward, slamming into two more. Marko was more of a boxer, protecting himself more than he fought, but his punches were fierce, laying the enemy out in one shot. He knew how to channel power. I did some fancy floor work, rolling and coming up to drop a couple more with quick strikes.

We fought until we were breathless, and they were all vanquished. Marko spilled to the floor, breathing hard. "You're brutal."

"Seems like your leg is healed." I sat down, trying to read his mood.

"Yeah. Finally," he muttered.

"You want to talk, or . . . ?"

"Save it, Zara. I know I'm not high on the list of people you care about," he said. Maybe he didn't mean it as an accusation, but it felt like one.

"Bea and Nadim are my faves, I admit, but that doesn't mean I don't like you."

"Whatever. Let's call it good."

With a sigh, I got up and dusted myself off, hoping he'd talk to someone else. My people skills weren't the best, so maybe I should get Bea over, or possibly Marko would open up to Yusuf's big-brother brand of comfort. *Whatever. I'm done here.* At least I tried.

Time to find Yusuf.

He was in the supply room, digging through various crates. "Any progress?" he asked when I came in. "Yes. I know he's having trouble."

I shook my head. "Glad to see you're better, at least."

"Typhon's a tough bastard. I thought if he could cope with his losses, so should I."

"What're you working on?"

Yusuf had a bunch of parts spread out on the work-table, a variety of tools on standby. "If I can get it working, it'll be a little bot to help with certain less-than-delightful maintenance tasks."

My eyes just about formed hearts. "That's the best thing I've heard in days."

"We haven't had a lot of good news, huh? Or are you really into robots?"

"Half and half? Not gonna lie, robots are cool. Except the ones that patrol the border between the Zone and Paradise."

"I don't know where that is."

"New Detroit. That's where I'm from. You?" I couldn't remember if he'd mentioned it before. If so, hopefully he wouldn't be mad at me for forgetting.

"Nyeri, though I went to school in Nairobi." As he spoke, he worked, assembling bits here and there. I started to catch the hang of what he was doing and handed him things before he could reach for them.

Yusuf gave me an approving nod. "You're clever."

It was damn cool watching this bot take shape before my eyes. I could feel Nadim plucking at me, long distance, but for the moment I was too interested in the robot to respond to his tugs on my attention. "Thanks. I'm good at building stuff, but I've never tried anything like this."

The bot took shape slowly, a rectangular little thing that had rolling treads to carry it around. Since it was relatively small, it would be able to slide into small spaces. Yusuf didn't respond for a bit, focused on his work, and I enjoyed the hell out of assisting him. Soon, he powered it on, and lights twinkled along the back, flaring red, yellow, then green. Its head swiveled, and it emitted a series of beeps.

"I didn't have the parts for a voice module, so it

communicates that way."

"This thing is *adorable*."

"Hopefully, it will also be useful. It has a cleaning attachment and protocols to make basic repairs."

"I love that. Can you build one for Nadim?"

Yusuf smiled. "If this one works out, come over again and you can help me. Maybe we can even upgrade the next one."

"I'll check for parts in our supply stores."

A stronger pull came from Nadim, and I yielded this time. Waving at Yusuf, I headed for the Hopper and returned to my Leviathan. When I swooped the shuttle inside, a soft burst of warmth rolled over me like the closest hug, and Nadim was all in my head, worried, questioning in nonverbal touches.

"It's fine. It was nothing bad," I said aloud.

While the docking bay pressurized, I filled him in on the gist of what Typhon had said, especially the part about regretting the so-called discipline he'd dished out. Nadim was quiet as I got out of the Hopper, but I could feel his pain and uncertainty. He loved Typhon, but sometimes it wasn't easy to forgive. I'd never been particularly good at it myself. One thing I knew I couldn't help him through.

Finally, he said, "I am . . . glad he will not force you to return."

Images flickered through my head, our shared memories of our desperate flight from Typhon after we got caught breaking the rules again. I touched his mind softly, opening for full comfort. It never got old that I could feel him brightening because of me.

"Yeah, it's good to know the Elder has our back no matter what. I mean, it's not easy for Typhon to change and roll with this new situation."

"You have been marked as a bad person because of me, Zara."

I laughed. "Oh, Nadim. Don't ever say that. I chose everything that happened out here, and I'd do it all again in a heartbeat."

"Truly? Even waking the god-king?"

"Well, maybe not. Hindsight and all that. But we had no idea that would break as bad as it did. Looked like a solid deal going in." There was no point in talking about shit that couldn't be changed, anyway. "How are you feeling?"

"Another day, and I'll be healed and fully rested."

"What about Typhon?"

"A bit longer, I think. He's bigger." That was a simple explanation, but I didn't dig for more details.

"And Bea?"

"She's still looking for traces of the god-king's path."

I left the docking bay, and Nadim was clearly feeling

better because he lit the way like he used to, little pulses of light that haloed my path to Ops. "Thanks, sweetheart."

"I like when you call me that."

Lord, he could find my warm, gooey center like nobody else. "I'll try to do it more." I sent a pulse of real warmth back to him, and he amplified and aimed it right back. It lifted me up on waves of lazy delight.

As Nadim had said, Bea was working in Ops, so engrossed in her search that she didn't hear me come in. I came up behind her and yielded to impulse, wrapping my arms around her waist from behind and resting my head on her shoulder. I thought we were close enough that this would be okay. I let her feel the warmth cascading from Nadim through me, and she leaned back against me, flashing a tired smile. Close up, I could see how smooth her skin was, the dark shadows of her lashes fanning over her cheekbones. Her mouth was a soft bow as she teased, "Long day at the office, *querida*?"

"You could say that."

"Me too. I have no idea how something like Lifekiller can just vanish. I'm so worried about the harm he might be inflicting that I can't eat or sleep." She nudged me back but not so she could break away; instead she spun around and completed the hug. There was nothing I could say to clear her conscience because mine wasn't exactly clean.

"We'll solve it. Somehow. Has there ever been a mountain too big for us to climb?"

Bea shook her head, her curls feathering against my cheek. "Not so far, but—"

"Let's not go there."

"We can do this," Nadim said. "Together."

He was trying to sound bright and hopeful, but there was a wistful edge to his voice. I swapped looks with Bea, who nodded slightly, and we both dropped into the bond, not enough to lose ourselves, but so Nadim could take comfort in us. His immediate happiness flooded me, trickled through Bea and came back bigger. It made me think of an old saying, about how burdens were halved among loved ones, but shared joy was doubled.

"Group hugs are the best." Bea stepped back, her eyes a bit brighter than usual.

I brushed her hair out of her face to check the healing wound on her temple. "Have you had EMITU look at this today?"

"It's fine. He's busy learning the art of origami."

"Are you serious?"

"Deadly. I'm afraid he won't have any space left in his database at the rate he's learning things unrelated to medicine."

I laughed. "Well, Yusuf is building bots over on Typhon,

and he promised to hook us up. Maybe we can put a med module on the new one? Let EMITU pursue his weird dreams?"

She cocked her head, playful and cute as could be. "I'm all for having a backup plan, but are we sure another bot is a good idea?"

I wanted to kiss her, but if I did, we probably wouldn't get anything else done. Best to save it for later.

"That depends," I said.

"On what?"

It was hard as hell to hide my grin and deliver this line with a straight face. "Whether you hack this one to make it sassy."

Bea bit her lip, trying to look remorseful, but she didn't succeed in the slightest. "I can't make any promises."

"EMITU is more fun this way." Nadim took her side, and I pretended to be hurt. To be honest, I couldn't argue. I enjoyed the macabre humor when I was getting my wounds treated.

Just then, the comm rang and Suncross appeared on screen. "Zeerakull, it is done. Our brethren have made a contract with the council on Greenheld."

"Thanks, Suncross. How long will they be patrolling there?"

"Half a cycle. We will destroy the god-king by then or die in glorious infamy!"

"Uh, that is not one of my life goals. Anything else to report?"

"There's something strange about the asteroid on the far side of the star," the Bruqvisz said.

"I noticed the readings," Bea said. "But I was looking for the god-king, not anomalies. I just thought it was an odd makeup of minerals."

"Do you plan to check it out?" I asked.

Suncross waved his claws around, an excited sign of agreement. "Your Leviathan can get fuel from these stars. Our ship needs other sources and I might have found a ___ deposit." The translation matrix cut out, so I didn't know what natural resource he was talking about.

Whatever it was, the mineral was probably valuable as hell. "Okay, be careful. If you need backup, let us know."

"Keep watch, Zeerakull. Danger abounds."

From the records of the Elaszi, purchased on the
Sliver by Bruqvisz historians

Sixteen of the whole have experienced death today. Two in border disputes with the Fellkin; one offended an Abyin Dommas to the point that a poison claw was deployed. The whole allows that the Abyin Dommas in question might have had due cause to kill, and does not hold grudges against that.

Twelve others from the whole experienced death from accident or misadventure.

One was murdered on the Sliver in the course of trade by a species barely known to us, a HUMAN of EARTH. The whole remembers this human's face and will never forget the debt it owes to the Elaszi. The Elaszi remember.

Zara Cole must die. If other humans die with it, this is acceptable. They are not Elaszi.

They will not remember.

CHAPTER FIVE

Lost Hope

NADIM AND TYPHON followed the mech ship at a distance, still close enough that we could soak up energy from the star and provide support if needed. The asteroid field was dense, and I couldn't see the rock the lizards were aiming for until Bea magnified the image. I skimmed the readings she took earlier, and I saw why Suncross was excited.

This was a serious deposit of ruthenium, which must be what the lizards used for fuel. The lizard ship burned manufactured fuel while Nadim and Typhon could orbit stars to top their energy off. I was starting to understand why Leviathan traveled alone. Even with just Typhon and Nadim, it was complicated to find energy sources that they could both use, since the difference in their ages required variant types of stars, though a few types intersected.

"Want to come, Zeerakull? Mining is one of our specialties. I would like to show you."

At first, I thought Suncross was messing with me because he didn't *need* me to go, but he seemed to be waiting for an answer. I considered for a few seconds. Keeping busy was the best way not to fret about Lifekiller. I wasn't used to sitting around, not in the Zone, and not in space either. We *had* to let our allies fuel up, so . . .

"That would be epic," I said.

Bea sighed from where she sat. "This won't be dangerous, will it?" She was talking to me, but Suncross got his comment in before I managed to reply.

"Probably not," said Suncross sadly, then brightened a little. "But could be infestations of metalworms! They are difficult to kill."

Judging by his expression, he was hoping for worm attacks. These lizards were serious adrenaline junkies. I could relate.

"How are we doing the pickup?" Our ships weren't made to dock with one another, and the mech ship was slightly too big to fit in our docking bay with our Hopper parked and the unused drones stacked for deployment.

Suncross tapped his claws against a hard surface, the sound creating reverb in our connection. "Gear up. Go outside. Use boost pack to put some distance between you and Nadim and we get you."

That didn't sound *too* much different from what I'd done at the Sliver, except now I'd be moving between ships. So damn cool. "Yeah, well, you'd best not miss."

"Zeerakull. Do I ever?"

I couldn't quell a frisson of excitement over the idea of jumping free out into space, but I also sensed Nadim's anxiety. "Please be careful," he said.

I touched the wall lightly on the way to the docking bay and got a soft pink flare in response. "I'd say I always am, but that'd be a lie, and we don't do that. Can I promise to be clever instead?" It seemed like I'd said something like this to him before, and his amusement flowed through me.

"Fine, Zara. I'm here if you need me."

"You don't want to go fuel mining with Suncross and me?"

"It's not necessary. You won't be so far that I can't feel you, and you're not going to a place where I can't follow."

That was true. This wasn't a full planetary mission. I donned my spacewalk gear—skinsuit with extras—and then checked my connections and oxygen intake. The readout inside my helmet looked good to go. When I turned, Bea was standing behind me, wearing a rueful smile.

"You thought I'd let you go without saying good-bye?"

I gestured to the visor and she kissed two fingertips and touched them lightly to the side of my helmet. "For luck?" I asked.

"You don't need that when you've got skills." When her smile widened into a cocky grin, my heart fluttered.

Flashing her a thumbs-up, I went out and waited for the outer chamber to depressurize, then I opened the final hatch, clambering onto Nadim's hull. It was different now that he was fully armored, and I guessed he couldn't feel me, just like he'd lost the ability to feel the starlight on his bare skin. Briefly I imagined a day when the god-king was gone and the Phage were no longer a threat; then maybe Nadim could strip this away and travel as he was meant to. Even our deep bonding would be richer then. I didn't enjoy seeing him this way, armored for war, with dark patches that marked his hidden guns. One day he might even have scars like Typhon and be weary of fighting.

I can keep that from happening. Typhon is messed up because he lost his true pilot and navigator. Bea and I aren't going anywhere.

My magnetized boots kept me on the surface, and Nadim stopped to facilitate this pickup, so I moved across his flank with the binary star in the distance, lights shimmering around us, and the barren, rocky beauty of the asteroid belt took my breath away. The universe was so still as it stretched out in all its vastness. Not for the first time, I thought, *This is where I'm meant to be.* I didn't know if it was the Leviathan medical tinkering with my genetic composition back in childhood to fix my crushing migraines, or something I was born with, but I'd never felt right down on Earth. I'd fought it with chem and drink and sex and violence, but that had never brought me peace.

This was peace.

I headed toward the edge as the mech ship buzzed close. The lizards would need to circle and go again. I was too slow the first time. I waited for clearance and pushed off, no tether—*damn, this is crazy*—and hit the button for a boost to launch me even farther from Nadim, then I was free-floating in vacuum. Spinning slowly. My heart pounded, and I could imagine myself drifting, drifting, until my air ran out and my skin turned cold.

How the hell do the Phage swim out here? How does Nadim?

The mech ship maneuvered close enough, and then what amounted to netting swooped out of one side and pulled me in. I felt like a captured fish. Not elegant, but it got the job done.

Soon I was standing in the hold of the Bruqvisz vessel, evaluating the differences. Everything was metal or some composite that looked like resin but probably wasn't; they favored textures, a wild array of them, and though it seemed like a tough way to design a ship it also felt . . .

organic. Natural. Like the lizards, the lines were sharp and aggressive, with a lot of decorative scaling. I checked my helmet readouts, and the skinsuit reported that all was well, the temp was warmer than we kept our ship, and the breathable mix was slightly oxygen rich.

I slipped off the helmet and folded it into the pouch at my belt and took in a deep breath of the warm air.

And had a coughing fit, because the ship smelled. Not filthy, just musky. I'd never thought about how the Bruqvisz smelled before, but in close quarters they had a definite odor. I guessed humans would to them too. Interesting.

Suncross was waiting for me, and he clapped me on the shoulder so heartily that I almost fell over. "Good to have you, Zeerakull. Welcome to our home!"

I felt bad for coughing. "Uh, thanks. Why do you have space netting anyway? What would you use it for, other than this?"

"Good for rescue and salvage," he said. "Always an opportunity out in deep space for exciting finds."

Ah, that made sense. We could've used it when we were saving Starcurrent and Yusuf. And I guessed if you found something cool in space, it was salvage. Finders keepers.

"Give me the tour, then let's mine some fuel."

Suncross gave me that weird open palm sign. "Deal." His ruff flared up, anticipation or enthusiasm. I grinned and got sharp teeth in response; we had that expression in common. "Will be fun! Perhaps there will be nasty surprises. One hopes."

"Let's . . . keep the nasty surprises to a minimum and get the hell after Lifekiller before he does in another planet."

The ruff sank down. I felt kind of bad about that. "Yes. You're right. We will attend to business. Come. You will need your helmet soon." He, I noticed, was already suited up, and as we joined the rest of the crew one deck down—achieved by giant stairs that I had to take one at a time while the Bruqvisz managed in quick leaps—I saw a giant antigrav pallet piled with tools. They had laser drills, hand drills, hammers, and a couple of things that looked way too cumbersome for me. I'd leave those to the lizards, no problem. We all waited while one of the crew stayed up on the flight deck, and the jolt when the ship touched down on the surface of the asteroid was hardly even noticeable. Good work, pilot. I put on my helmet when I saw the others doing it, and Suncross checked everybody individually and pounded fists on their shoulders to indicate approval. When he came to me, I got the same treatment. *Ouch.* I didn't let him know it hurt.

Then a ramp lowered, and we walked out onto the surface. Not much in the way of grav once we were beyond the ship's range, but there was enough magnetic pull from the metal in the asteroid's core that my boots stayed anchored firmly. Too firmly, in some places, and I had to work to pull them free. Magnetic mud.

"Scans show metal just beneath the surface," Suncross said in my ear. "Don't dig too deep. Could destabilize the asteroid's cohesion."

Meaning, fracture the whole little ball into pieces, sending us spinning off attached to fragments. Yeah, not great. I said I understood and picked a small handheld laser drill.

Doing something useful felt good, instead of fretting over my own failures. I marked out sections with the laser drill and let the Bruqvisz do the heavy hammer and chisel work; the ruthenium they were mining was related to platinum, elementally speaking, and it didn't come easy. Chunks came out in strangely angular pieces, as if they'd broken along invisible fault lines; it was shiny silver stuff as it emerged from the surface coating of hard black shell, and the bin on the resting pallet filled up slowly. We'd been at it for three hours when Suncross checked the level we'd retrieved and called a stop; I was glad, because the work was tough for reasons I couldn't really define. I felt weak out here. Small and fragile.

And I itched inside my suit. I couldn't be allergic to a damn asteroid, could I? I stepped back and ran a scan on my H2. Ruthenium, a lot of it. And . . . I blinked. "Hey, Suncross? I'm reading a metastable element here."

"Yes," he agreed. "Core of asteroid is metallic hydrogen. Very valuable. Very difficult to get without more time and care. Is underneath a thick coat of our basic fuel metal. If we could reach, would be worth a thousand planets. Very rare. We will mark and come back. Keep secret, Zeerakull, and part of the profit is yours."

"Absolutely," I said. I knew something about metallic hydrogen. It was like the way diamonds formed from carbon and intense pressure, only the pressure of a gas giant was required to squeeze hydrogen gas into a legit metal. Scientists back on Earth had made some; it was supposed to be the queen of stable fuels. I hadn't thought about it, but there could be a lot of great resources out here like this. And if Nadim could locate them . . . we'd be traders with the most valuable cargo in the universe.

My scan blipped as I was about to put it away, and I went chilly inside at the image on my machine. *Shit.* No. "Suncross. We've got Phage."

All the lizards went still, tilting their helmets up. Searching the skies, which was reasonable. "Vector?" he asked sharply. "What zone?"

"Underneath us," I said. "They're inside the shell. They're eating the metallic hydrogen. Not a ton of them; looks like maybe a few dozen?"

"They're eating our score!" Suncross was seriously pissed off. "We must stop them, Zeerakull. But little we can do hand to hand here. Not equipped for battle."

I was still watching. Something odd was going on with

these Phage. Generally, they existed in an eating frenzy; eat and move, eat and move. But these Phage seemed to be resting. Curled up as if nesting together . . .

A small one moved from the pack and devoured a chunk of the metallic hydrogen. The most interesting aspect of this was that in the larval state, it lacked any exoskeleton, more like a snake or a segmented worm, though it still had the devouring capacity, judging by the way it was chowing down on Suncross's cache. The thing wasn't defenseless, though. There was a stinger in the tail, and it undulated like a snake.

I'd never considered how the Phage were born; I guess I'd assumed that they came out fully formed and ready to kill. But this one looked young. As if to confirm my hypothesis, a grown Phage broke free of the group and pulled it back to the nest. *Parent behavior.* That couldn't be right.

I triggered my comms. "Hey, Bea? Put me on with Xyll."

"Xyll?" she repeated, startled. "Are you sure?"

"Very damn sure."

"Okay." She sounded doubtful, but in a few seconds I heard the subtle shift in sound, and then Xyll's processed, mechanical voice said, "Yes, Zara Cole, I listen."

"Are there Phage on this asteroid?" I wished I could send images or even video, but we were too far for a visual connection.

"Specify location please."

Please? Maybe the translation matrix gratuitously added that part. Either that, or a Phage cell was learning manners, which was mind-blowing. "Sending coordinates." I did with a rapid press of fingers on my handheld.

There was a delay of only a few moments before Xyll responded. "Yes, there are Phage cells present."

"What the hell are they doing?"

"Doing?"

I never thought I'd call Xyll for a chat, and it was as frustrating as I could have envisioned. "Why are they here? Is it on Lifekiller's orders? Are they, I don't know, mining something that could be used as a weapon? Or a fuel source?"

"No," Xyll said. "They are separate."

"Separate?" I got that meant not part of the hive mind, but I didn't even know that was possible. It seemed like Xyll had been the first to awaken. Wait, were these Phage cells self-determinate as well?

"Meaning they are not part of the swarm. They are . . . splintered."

"Like you?" That was . . . worrying.

"Not like me. I am me. Alone. They are together." Maybe I was imagining things, but Xyll sounded wistful, as if it wished for a similar connection.

"So . . . a different Phage group?"

"Broken from group. Not listening to Lifekiller or the rest of the Phage. Separated."

"Like you, then."

"*No.*" I could hear a hint of emotion in that blunt statement, frustration, probably, at my failure to grasp the point. "I think. They do not. They . . . drift."

"Are they dangerous?" I'd never been this close to Phage who weren't trying to eat my face. Under these circumstances, we could even study them, if we had time.

Xyll replied, "No. They have food. No anger. No hunger. They spawn to create new core, not to harm."

I thought about that for a second. "Any idea why they broke off from the main group of Phage?"

"Unknown," Xyll said. "Perhaps discord within the hive mind. Confusion. They may rejoin. They may not. Depends on Lifekiller's influence."

"Or yours, maybe?" I threw the suggestion out there, wondering how much power Xyll could exert over its brethren. Clearly our resident Phage cell could sense its kindred, but I wasn't sure if the ability could expand to making contact.

The long pause told me Xyll was thinking about the possibility. "Perhaps."

"Well, if you can reach them, try to persuade them to stay away from Lifekiller's army. Okay?" If this worked, maybe we had a foothold with the Phage. Maybe this splinter group could be turned, the way Xyll had been. Maybe they could become . . . rational.

Ambitious. But short of the destruction of an entire species, it was the only strategy we had.

"Will try. Anything else, Zara Cole?"

"No. That's it. Thank you," I added, testing whether that earlier *please* was a fluke or not.

"You are welcome. Will advise if I succeed."

Damn. EMITU had hobbies, our Phage cell had manners—the universe was turning upside down right now.

I switched back to Bea and thanked her, then talked to Suncross. He didn't like the idea of the Phage snacking down on his incredible treasure, but better that than having more of them fighting us. We took the ruthenium back aboard Suncross's ship, and after the ramp shut and the bay repressurized, Suncross and his boys took off their helmets with expressions of hissed pleasure.

I took mine off too, and this time the musky smell of the Bruqvisz ship seemed almost homey to me.

"Thanks," I said to Suncross. "That was fun." I looked down into the bin. The ruthenium was starting to look dull. Then dark. "What's it doing?"

"That? Nothing. Is harmless," Suncross said. "Smells nice."

I couldn't smell anything at all, at least nothing that got past the general aroma of the ship. And then I couldn't breathe.

My entire bronchial system just inflated. Lungs, throat, nose, everything suddenly swelled closed. I made a choking sound and flailed, and Suncross caught me, shouting questions as I panicked. I *could not breathe.*

Suncross got my helmet back on, and that helped a little; I could breathe in tiny gasps, but it wasn't enough, not nearly enough. And how the hell were the Bruqvisz supposed to help me? They didn't have any experience with Earth biology, even if they had a med unit. I needed EMITU. Desperately.

Across the distance, I could feel Nadim's urgent concern and I heard Bea's voice on the comm. The sounds wouldn't coalesce into words, but I felt him trying to help, feeding me strength and warmth. It wasn't enough to counter physiological symptoms.

My vision went gray as I clung to consciousness. If I blacked out here, that might be the end. *I can't maneuver out there. If I go out into vacuum, I'll drift away in the dark.*

It didn't sound so bad.

Suncross was shouting at me and I wished he'd stop. I couldn't understand what was going on. I just wanted quiet. To let myself feel Nadim's love and let it sing me to sleep.

But Suncross wouldn't let me, and neither would

Nadim. Bright orange flashes of emotion popped in my head, almost like slaps. Suncross dragged me out of the ship, then we were floating, spinning together, me in the Bruqvisz's four arms. I couldn't see well anymore, but I had the impression of motion and the sickly bright spiral of starlight flashing inside my helmet. We clanked against something, the landing bay, maybe? I was holding on as hard as I could, but my throat was so tight and pain spread through my chest.

I collapsed as soon as Suncross let me go. *Good. This is good. I can sleep.*

ZARA!

The shout echoed in my head like a clap of thunder back on Earth, and I twitched and tried to open my eyes. Suncross was carrying me, and Bea was running ahead of us. Felt like I was gliding, eerily detached. Everything seemed too slick to grab on to. I tried to watch Beatriz; I caught the slice of her anxious face turned toward me, the tears in her eyes, but the effort was too much. I closed my eyes again.

Zara, please wake up. Nadim, in my head. It wasn't a lizard's muscular four arms carrying me; it was Nadim, wrapping me in his embrace. *Please. I can't lose you, I can't. Please don't die, please . . .*

I'm sorry, I whispered. I was a cloud.

Floating away.

Interlude: Nadim

I can't bear this, but I must. Zara's life hangs by a delicate thread and EMITU's skill, and all I can do is watch and wait and grieve. Is this pain worth the joy? Is love and the rich strength of our bond enough to sustain me when she risks such pain and goes so far away?

Beatriz is with me, and I cling to her; I am as hungry for her love and peace as I am for starlight, but even she is remote now, weeping tears I can't comfort as she waits to see if Zara will come back to us.

I can't feel Zara. Without her, what is there? A universe gone half-silent. Typhon warned me of the desperate depths of losing a bondmate, of knowing their song will never ring through the universe. He holds his fragile humans at a distance for a reason.

But I can't. I love their fire, their strength, their joy; I love their quiet, their tears, their rages. I love how *they* love, and I can't stay separated from that wonder. I will orbit it like the brightest, most joyous star for as long as that star can burn, and I will mourn its darkness forever.

Please come back to me, Zara. Losing you in battle would be a terrible thing, but I would know you chose it freely, went to it bravely. But this? A misadventure, a careless mistake? No. Zara Cole's story does not end this way.

COME BACK.

CHAPTER SIX

Lost Time

SOMEONE WAS SHOUTING my name.

I woke screaming.

My voice exploded from my aching throat, and my eyes opened wide under the pressure of the sheer, red pain that screeched along every single nerve ending in my body, rippling up from my feet to my head. It was fast, at least. But now I knew what being set on fire would feel like.

I tried to move, but I was strapped to the bed in Medbay, and a whirling nightmare of metal, plastic, and sharp poking instruments hovered above me.

EMITU said, "Well, this is a surprise. You died. That

would have been regrettable if it had been permanent. You'd have spoiled my perfect record."

My lips felt dry. So did my tongue. My entire mouth and throat. No wonder it had hurt to yell. I croaked out "Water," and EMITU squirted some in my mouth from one of his nozzles. At least, I hoped it was water. With our med unit, you could never be too sure. But the taste was deliciously refreshing and coated me in sweet relief. "More."

"When I'm ready," EMITU said. Not, I noticed, when *I* was ready. "How is your pain level, Honor Cole?"

"Not bad." Apart from the thirst, there were some lingering (and unsettling) deep aches in my lungs, but other than that, my body seemed to be holding together fine. My eyes felt dry too. And ached. "What happened?"

"Ruthenium tetroxide," EMITU replied smoothly. "The fuel you mined for the Bruqvisz ship was stable until introduced to their atmosphere on board the ship, when it rapidly decomposed into the oxidized version, which is highly toxic to humans."

"But not Bruqvisz?"

"Happily, no. They think it smells quite enticing."

Great. Lizard catnip was poison gas. Somehow that didn't surprise me. "Am I okay?"

"You died, Zara. That is generally not regarded as *okay*. But after wasting my medical supplies in counteracting the poison, I was not satisfied with failure." He suddenly held something up in a claw. I blinked. It was a folded origami crane. "Would you like a present?"

I didn't want to offend a med bot that had just saved my ass. "Thanks. It's nice."

"I can fold seven thousand four hundred and twenty-two designs," EMITU said. "Very soothing. Two hundred eight of those are original to me."

"That's awesome," I said. "Where are Bea and Suncross?"

"Outside," he said. I didn't know when EMITU had switched from *it* to *he* in my head, but he had. "Honor Teixeira was wailing and Suncross threatened to rip three of my extensors off. He called me *junk*."

"I can see how that would be hurtful. Could you please let them back in now?" If I sounded careful, it was because I was still strapped down.

EMITU's expression couldn't change, but I had the weird impression he was glad about me using my good manners. My restraints unlocked at the same time the Medbay door slid open.

Bea charged in first and immediately unbuckled the straps on my arms and legs. Her tense expression eased when I sat up. She rushed to me and would have kissed me, except EMITU inserted a flat metal plate between us. "Honor Cole requires a complete decon shower before close personal contact," he said. "Kiss the tray."

"I will not!" Bea said. She backed up, but only a little,

and her dark brown eyes searched my face anxiously. She tried to touch my cheek, then checked herself at a warning squawk from EMITU. "You're okay, though?"

"Yeah, I'm good," I said. I swung my legs over the side of the bed and tested my strength. Not bad. Whatever cocktail of medicines EMITU had whipped up, it seemed to have done the trick. "Suncross?"

"He went back to his ship," she said. "Since I wouldn't let him destroy EMITU—"

"Hmph," EMITU said. "As if."

"—he said he could oversee the refining of the fuel while you recovered. I'll let him know you're okay." She smiled softly. "You should take that shower because I really, really want to kiss you right now."

That got me up and moving, staggering to the small cubicle in the corner. I stripped and stood with my eyes shut as the chemicals rained down on me. They burned, and I cringed over what they must be doing to my hair, but thankfully a warm-water shower followed, and I asked Bea to bring my products. She did, along with a silky caftan that was *not* mine. Bea was the first girl I'd fallen for, though not the first I'd been attracted to, and reaching clothes-sharing status felt like a milestone.

An application of leave-in conditioner later and dressed in Beatriz's loungewear, I stepped out of the shower—right into her arms—and *oh*, that kiss. It was a summer day, all the sweet dreams I never wanted to awaken from. Heat and softness and Bea, nuzzling against me until the top of my head tingled.

And that was when I realized that though I could feel Nadim hovering, he hadn't said a word since I'd opened my eyes. Not a single word.

"Nadim?" I stepped back from Bea and waited. This would not be good.

"I'm here," he said quietly. His tone was entirely neutral, but I wasn't fooled.

"Hey, baby," I said, and put my hand against the warm skin of his wall. "What's wrong? I'm okay. You can see I am."

"You were not," he said. "You were not, Zara. For a moment, you were . . . *not*. Not here. Not alive. I could not feel you any longer and it was . . ."

He sounded so afraid. No, terrified. My mouth went dry again, the cold creeping into my veins; he was right. I'd been *dead*. I'd been taken away from him and given back by the miracle of EMITU's ingenuity. I didn't know that I deserved the second chance, but I was so grateful for it.

I fell into Nadim. I let go, launching myself free of my body and into *him*, swimming in his heat and light and beauty, and felt his shock and the lingering bitter fear. *I lost you*, he whispered, and I heard the mourning in it. *I do not know how to lose you, Zara. I cannot—*

I know, I told him, and sank deep into the bond. Deeper than was safe, fresh from my deathbed. But he needed to know. He needed to feel me here and know how much I wanted this. How much I would fight to stay.

We spiraled together, light and color and sound and heat and something more, a binding that knitted us together stronger than we'd ever been.

I reached out for Bea and pulled her in, and her rich orange light blended and wove with ours into an unbreakable skein of colors as strong as armor, as rich as gold, as hard as diamond.

True bond.

We spiraled together, slowly at first, and then faster, faster, an ecstasy past anything I'd ever felt from flesh, and exploded upward into the universe like a star. I felt Nadim's entire skin pulse with it, light rippling beneath armor in rich rainbows, and when it finally faded, I sank down into my body light as a feather. Not alone now. Never alone.

Bea was in my arms. Nadim was with us and around us and part of us.

"What is this?" Bea asked me. She sounded drunk on it, blinded with the joy of it, and I kissed her and told her, without words, exactly what it was. What it meant.

"Excuse me," EMITU said, "'The soft sound shivers / Flowering goddesses stir / This time far away.' Which means, get the hell out of my space."

He turned on music. Twentieth-century musical theater, apparently. I wasn't sure I knew the songs, but they sounded too sweet and pretty for my taste, and I grabbed Bea's hand and rushed her outside into the hall. Kissed her soft fingers. "First things first," I said. "Let's tell Suncross what's going on."

"How much of it?" She laughed, and I wanted her to laugh like that again. A lot.

"Just what he needs to know." I winked, and we went to send the message. Suncross came up on the screen, his crew crowded around him. They'd all gathered, looked like. Prepared for bad news.

Suncross saw my face, and his ruff went up. So did the ruffs of all the others. They trembled and shifted colors into a brilliant red. Suncross lifted all four arms; so did all the others. It was an arm forest.

"You are not dead, Zeerakull," he said. "We prayed. We were rewarded."

"You prayed for me? Thank you."

"Is a rare thing," he said. "Rare and costly. Each of us gets only handful of prayers in our lifetime. We do not waste them."

"Well, I'm going to pray for all of *you*, then. Does that help restore your prayers?"

"Yes," he said, and clasped all four hands together. The others followed suit. "It is a solemn gift. Thank you."

"Hey, thank *you*. If you hadn't gotten me back to EMITU in time . . ."

"I do not think your machine likes me," Suncross said. "It told me to die in a fire."

"He's eccentric."

"I do not like fire." I didn't know what to say to that, but turned out Suncross wasn't waiting. "Do you know anything of the Phage? Should we hunt them down? Destroy?"

"No," I said. "Those Phage are different. They're not hurting anyone."

"Hurting my profits!"

"Phage gotta eat, Suncross. Would you rather they were devouring your ship?"

"Would rather they die in a fire," he groused, but I could tell it was just grumpiness. "Fuel is refined and ready. Ready for travel."

"Good," I said. "Because we are too."

He hesitated, then said, "Zeerakull, I saw an unusual thing. Did your Leviathan . . . glow?"

"I think he did."

"Ah. Is normal?"

"Well, I don't know if it's normal," I said. "But it's damn good."

He laughed. The rest of them laughed with him, and one by one, the Bruqvisz saluted us. "Let's move out. We have a god to kill."

"I like where your head is, but has anybody got a lock on his location?" I asked. "Does Typhon have anything?"

Bea shook her head. "No. I spoke to the whole crew and they're worried. And it makes me nervous."

I had to agree with her. "If he's marshaling power, he must be planning something terrible, and I hate that we can't prevent it. If we had some idea where he was headed, we could at least warn the local populace."

Suncross cut in with, "Send new coordinates when you know where the fight is." Then he dropped offscreen.

I'd heard of people having out-of-body experiences when they died, walking into the light or seeing lost loved ones, but for me, it was only dark. I wasn't sure what that meant, but for sure, I'd grab on to the people I cared about, just in case there was nothing more waiting. For now, I pushed that fear to the back of my head. I couldn't let this shut me down, because if I let myself *feel* the full depth of what had happened today, I might not be able to push forward, and inertia might equal permanent death, if not for me, then for Lifekiller's as-yet-unknown victims.

With a faint sigh, I left Bea scanning and went to look for Starcurrent. I'd meant to check on zim much sooner, but events got out of control. As expected, I found zim in the media room, lights dimmed, with some incomprehensible noise blaring. It must be Abyin Dommas music, and I paused to listen, but I couldn't make sense of the disparate elements.

When Starcurrent noticed me, ze lowered the volume. "Need something?"

It was a curt question from the usually warm Starcurrent, which told me ze wanted to be left alone, but what we wanted wasn't always best for us. I sat down in a chair nearby. "Just to talk for a bit. How're you doing?"

"Not good," said Starcurrent.

Yeah, that was obvious. "I wish there was something I could do. Maybe once we defeat the god-king, the council will reconsider your banishment?"

"Possible." Ze didn't sound hopeful, however.

Okay, this wasn't going great, so I tried cheering zim up. "You hadn't been back to Greenheld for a while, right? So just look on this as continuing your travels."

Starcurrent's tendrils flared and tentacles stirred as zis color sharpened from gray to a ruddy hue. "Choosing not to go is different from not being allowed to stay."

"You blame us?"

Starcurrent sat quiet. I could have defended myself by saying ze was the one who technically woke up the god-king by taking those samples, but I'd pushed for us to do that mission because we had to outfit our Leviathan to fight the Phage. There was no way to avoid my share of the blame for what was currently going down.

I doubted I could cheer zim up, so I stood. "I'll leave you with the music."

"Thank you for coming to me," said Starcurrent.

Well, at least ze appreciated the effort, even if I didn't get results. As I headed out, my handheld buzzed in my pocket, alerting me to an incoming call in Ops. I hustled there in time to see Bea connecting with Chao-Xing aboard Typhon. "I found the god-king's trail. And we should hurry if we intend to catch him."

Typhon's info seemed solid; Nadim double-checked it and came to the same conclusions. It wasn't like Lifekiller left a giant trail of destruction for us to follow—surprisingly—but more of a veering course that seemed to be *looking* for things. He only stopped when he found something he wanted/needed. But since we didn't have his shopping list, that was going to make things more difficult. We could only see where he'd been, not where he was going.

Even with the speed of Leviathan, we couldn't keep up with a wildly zigzagging monster on a quest when we had no idea what the quest was *for.* One small planetoid had been reduced to rubble, and we didn't know what he'd gotten out of that. Another icy planet spinning at the very outer edges of its system had half of it sliced—or eaten—away.

Chao-Xing and I studied it until our eyes burned, and I finally called a halt to stagger off to a much-needed rest.

Nadim woke me from a sound sleep with a tug so insistent that my head hurt. "What's wrong?" I asked, rubbing my temple.

"Zara . . . I hear *others*. Leviathan song."

I sat up in bed, touching him for reassurance that I was awake. "Are you sure? You said they were probably scared after the Gathering."

"There's no doubt." Nadim was practically singing himself, his happiness bubbling up until it filled my head like a fizzy drink, effervescence in my veins.

"How many are calling?"

"Two."

"So we found some survivors. That's fantastic, Nadim. I'm so glad." I stroked a fingertip down the wall, admiring the rosy color that kindled with my touch. These other Leviathan must not have made it to the meet before the Phage struck. Maybe they'd encountered the wreckage after we fought?

Nadim and Typhon had both thought they were the only ones left in this sector of the galaxy; they must be euphoric right now. I dropped lightly into the bond and sensed Bea sleeping. If she wasn't waking on her own, considering our boy's excitement, she must be exhausted. I could fill her in later.

"Where are they, sweetheart?" He'd said he enjoyed that endearment and it was such a small thing to make him happy.

"They want to join us." He sounded ambivalent.

I wouldn't want Mom and Kiz jumping on board when we were headed for a fight, but more than that, how could we trust these new cousins? We got word from Earth that we were being hunted. What if these Leviathan were working for the Honors program? Nadim couldn't lie, but Typhon had done a damn good job of covering up their secret war.

"In hunting down Lifekiller?" That could be a cover for their real intentions.

"Yes. They offer aid, but . . ."

"You don't want to pull them into this situation." It would hurt Nadim if I opened with talk about treacherous live ships, so I leaned back and closed my eyes, falling into him so I could get a better sense of where he was mentally. "But you don't like leaving them alone either."

"Alone, they may not be able to withstand the Phage and Lifekiller if they target them. What do you think we should do?" he asked.

"There's no right answer. If shit goes bad fighting the

god-king you'll blame yourself. But if your brethren get in trouble with the Phage or some other damn thing, you'll feel bad about that too." I took a breath. He wouldn't like hearing this, but . . . "There's also a chance they might be working for the Honors program."

"Hunting *us*."

"Yeah."

"I hope that's not true. There are so few of us left. What should we do, Zara?"

"I know you want to give your cousins the benefit of the doubt, so I say tell them where we're headed. We could use backup against the god-king, but if this is a trick, well. We hope for the best and plan for the worst."

There was a thoughtful pause. "I agree, Zara. I will sing our destination."

"Could we do it together?"

I bonded with him and Zadim sparked to life, our consciousness spinning outward. We could hear our distant kindred, resonance that filled us with joy and relief and the absolute sweetness of their survival. Their song carried a message of hope and yearning, of constant seeking and finally finding. We missed the shimmer of starlight on our skin, but the speed was beautiful, and the universe was ours.

For the first time, we wondered if the Phage's relentless pursuit of the Leviathan might be residual programming, left by the god-king's species to destroy their most dangerous enemies. If that was true, the Leviathan might be the key to all of this.

Exultant, we sang where we were going, sang of our plans and what must happen next.

In time, the call came back: *We are coming.*

Jubilant, we broke—and I dropped into my own body, at once missing that sense of complete union but also drained and in a cold sweat. I had no sense for how long it had been, but my muscles were stiff, and my whole body had gone cold. It probably wasn't a good idea to stay bonded that long.

"Are you well, Zara?"

"I'm fine." It wasn't entirely a lie. I just needed food and sleep and not to lose myself in Nadim.

"Get some rest if you can. You'll need all your energy."

He probably didn't mean for that to sound ominous, but I couldn't help a little shiver of anxiety. I lay back down in bed, but sleep stayed just out of reach.

Maybe our bond actions roused Bea after all because a few minutes later, she buzzed at my door and I called her in. "Something wrong?"

She padded over to my bed, pretty as an antique painting in the faint light. "You and Nadim—I felt . . ."

"Not left out, I hope?"

Shaking her head, she perched on the edge of my bunk.

"No, but I'm wondering what's up. Whatever it was woke me from a sound sleep."

"Come in, if you want. I'll tell you everything."

A flash of white teeth in a teasing smile. "Are you asking me to sleep with you, Z?"

"It wouldn't be the first time," I mumbled. Which was technically true.

"Then . . ." She slipped under the covers and snuggled her back against me. "Is it okay if you're the big spoon for a bit?"

"I'm good with that." I wrapped an arm around her and rested my chin against softly scented curls that tickled my nose.

She felt soft and warm against me, solid and lovely, and . . . yeah, I could get used to this. Nadim swirled at the edge of my consciousness, and I could tell he wanted in, so I opened enough for him to join the loop, and the warm feedback circled between us as I told her that more Leviathan were on their way.

"That's fantastic news." Bea sounded sleepy, nestling into the covers like she belonged here. "Do they have crew too?"

I hadn't thought to ask, and it was the farthest thing from my mind right now.

Brushing her hair aside, I kissed the curve of her shoulder and a little shiver ran through her. She slid a hand back and touched my thigh, as soft a caress as I ever knew, and I wanted to do more, touch more, feel more, except I was fading too. That would teach me to give everything to Nadim and leave nothing for Bea.

He protested softly in my head. *I didn't mean to wear you out, Zara. I'm sorry that you can't* . . . But he didn't have the words for what I wanted to do with Bea because it wasn't part of his life cycle. I wasn't about to start explaining that in the middle of the night, though part of me wondered if it was possible for us to teach him about *that* through the bond, and whether it was even a good idea.

It's not the time, anyway.

I fell asleep curled up with Bea and woke alone. She had teased me about sneaking out last time, so there was no way I wouldn't do the same. Except she was on the comm with Chao-Xing, and what I heard just about froze my blood in my veins.

"Just like last time," Chao-Xing was saying. "See the scans? We're too late."

Two wildly different planets flashed on our screen, one bright and brilliant with life, the other ashes and charred dust. I stared at the screen and rubbed my hands up and down my arms. *Too late to stop him, let alone fight.*

"How many . . . ?" I barely got the question out.

"Unpopulated. That's the strange part; he doesn't seem to be after living beings right now. But this world was rich in uranium, which I think might be key for some metabolic process. I'm speculating, but I suspect Lifekiller's needs might evolve according to the power he wields. Or what he plans to wield."

"So in addition to absorbing organic life, he needs fuel?" *Like the Leviathan drank starlight*, I thought, but I wasn't about to say that aloud.

"If that's true, we could predict his next target based on the planetary composition," Bea said.

"Already on it," Chao-Xing said. "We'll find out if I'm right soon enough."

Marko and Yusuf were working on something behind her, talking among themselves and comparing handhelds. I got in on the action with Bea, as we scanned for planets close by that had strong pockets of uranium.

Nadim said, "The cousins are coming. Shall we wait for them?"

I had the ominous feeling that waiting would cost lives.

After-market report on Autonomous Combat Model
Nero, serial number XK62D3A921760G5

Per the request of the customer (see redacted files) the following add-on features have been installed:

Autonomous protocol redirect module (the "learning core")
Upgraded restraint system with embedded protocols
Preloaded legal and judiciary module, activated only after first goal achieved
Primary target acquisition facial recognition and DNA sequence loaded
Latest model SR12 platinum-poly armor
Embedded weapons package per customer request

On a personal note, the team hopes this purchase of the Nero is intended as a showpiece purely for demonstration and will not be used in real-world situations; this model is designed for the most summary of executions, and the legally required but inactive legal module is to be brought online only after a murder has been committed. We have . . . concerns.

Who's this buyer, exactly?

CHAPTER SEVEN

Lost Luck

"WE CAN'T STAY here," I said. "Nothing here for us to do, and if Lifekiller's after something we can predict, maybe we can get ahead of him for a change."

"Hold up." That was Marko, over the comms. Chao-Xing looked over her shoulder; he must have been looking at something on another console. "Since when did Lifekiller use modified terraforming devices?"

"Sorry, what?"

"This planet's been mined," he said. "But not by Lifekiller. I mean, the way he ravages a world is different. He's been here, but somebody used a terraformer to strip the trace amounts of uranium he left."

I had no damn idea.

"This might have nothing at all to do with Lifekiller—" I cut myself off because I spotted something on the surface. Wreckage. "Wait...." I swapped positions with Beatriz and did a quick analysis. "Okay, so, I've never seen anything like this before." I got Suncross on the comm, figuring he would know more. "Any idea who left this behind?"

The lizards weren't drunk; that was a blessing. "Looks like Elaszi tech, Zeerakull."

"Fucking blobs," I muttered.

"Ah. Yes. Scavengers." Nadim had a little distaste in that tone. He didn't care for the Elaszi any more than I did. Well, one had tried to *eat* me. And codejacked me to carry a virus into a secured location or die. I had issues with at least one of them.

"It looks like it was destroyed by weapons fire. Maybe rival scavengers looking to score?"

Suncross's ruff flared, probably in excitement. "Could be good stuff waiting. Give me a bit, will check it out. Or if you can't wait, we'll catch up."

I glanced at Bea. "Can we spare half an hour for the boys to do a salvage run?"

She didn't look thrilled, but finally she nodded. "We should find out why the blobs are prowling after Lifekiller if we can. The last thing we need is for them to decide to pledge allegiance to the god-king."

Yeah, that was undeniable. From what we'd seen on the Sliver, the blobs weren't big on caring about other sentient life. They cared about themselves and about profit, maybe not even in that order.

"Going in for a closer look," Suncross said.

Another lizard—Ghostwalk, I thought—waved four palms in a gesture of approval. "Glorious salvage! They will write stories of us."

"You know they do that after you're dead, right?"

"Worth it," said Suncross. "Will keep the channel open, update you on what we find."

Normally, I'd offer to go with because planetary missions were like candy to me, but picking me up would only slow things down. Plus, I'd died on the last away mission. I'd settle for watching this time. I moved away from the console and Nadim vanished the wall for me, granting me a clear view of the mech ship changing course and heading for the ashen planet. At this distance, I could only see a scar that marked the wreckage site. I watched the lizard ship head for the landing site, and it got smaller; my ability to discern details diminished as it went. We could magnify on the console, but Suncross would tell us if anything—

"Not wreckage!" came a desperate call from Suncross. "Live Elaszi! We are ensnared! Zeerakull, they attempt to take our ship!"

I ran back to the console to dial up the visual, and I got an eyeful of how the Elaszi ship had a lock on the lizards' mech vessel. Suncross and crew were fighting against the tow, but as I watched, another line latched on with what looked like magnetic attachments.

"Can you get free on your own?"

"Doubtful," another lizard replied.

Suncross added, "Fighting, Zeerakull, but they hit us with an EMP. All weapons are powered down. Engines not strong enough to—" The feed devolved into static, which meant he was too far for us to hear him or the blobs were jamming comms.

I turned my head upward. "Nadim, we can't let them have our pals. Quick, what are our options? Do we have weapons that will reach the surface?" Beatriz was watching the screen with me, pressed close. I could feel her tension.

Nadim said, "I don't think so, at least not without inflicting catastrophic damage. It wouldn't be precise enough to free our friends without harming their ship."

I paced, watching the struggle unfolding below. "We can't enter the atmosphere. The Hopper has no guns. Drones? Would the drones survive the burn?"

Bea clapped her hands, eyes bright. "I think so. We can't trust this mission to the piloting AI, though. Ready to do a remote rescue, Zara?"

"I . . . what?"

"You get to the supply room. Get me these things . . ." She started listing off random stuff. I hastily grabbed my H2 and recorded the items; I knew I wouldn't remember all of them, and we couldn't waste time. Even if I didn't know the plan, I was always ready to listen to Bea.

I raced off and got the parts, aware that time was ticking for Suncross and crew. The damn blobs might even eat the Bruqvisz and then take all their stuff. *Not on my watch.* I tapped my comm on the move. "Got the goods. Where to now, Bea?"

"Come to the holo room."

"Okay, on the way."

I arrived out of breath to find her tinkering with the panel, and suddenly it clicked. "You're rigging a makeshift pilot program?"

"Yup. Hand me that emitter, please."

Now that I knew, I could go all in helping her, and soon we had connections in place so that we could physically pilot the drones and fire the onboard weapons with complete precision. Hopefully we could avoid friendly fire too. If the mech ship got damaged, they wouldn't be able to get back above the atmosphere. We'd have to abandon them and call for help to rescue them.

I attached the motion sensors that Bea had jury-rigged— there were a lot of them; she was very thorough—and she started the program. My movements activated the unit in the docking bay, and Nadim responded without even being asked, opening the hold so our drones could swoop out. Bea was also kitted up with motion sensors, and she was a natural at this given her pilot skills, so I copied her movements while I got comfortable. The room became a starfield, and it was like I was one with the machine, its movements shifting in response to my slightest action.

At first it was unnerving, the sense of motion rushing in my head while I knew damn well that I wasn't flying anywhere, but urgency drove me on through the faint nausea, and I sped after Bea's machine. I heard a sizzle and pop as we pushed through the atmosphere. I could only imagine how the outside of the machine must look, red-hot and glowing. But everything seemed to be holding together.

A digital readout scrolled before me, data from the drone, and I locked on to the energy signal of the blob ship, shining like a beacon on my scans. I raised my right arm to go weapons hot, and it was so wild; I felt a vibration in my bones, like an echo of the barrel emerging. On rare occasions when I was flush in the Zone, I'd played VR games, but they had nothing on this setup. Bea could have made a fortune in the entertainment biz.

During the time we'd taken in getting this going, the lizard ship had been drawn nearly down to the surface, still captive to the blobs' grapples. The engines were able to keep resisting, but it clearly was a losing battle. Those damn gelatinous bastards had no intention of letting Suncross or his crew live. A flurry of projectiles blasted from the blob ship, but I couldn't tell if they were weapons or meant to help cut into the mech ship. Either way, we couldn't let them hit. I pulled my fingers back rapidly, firing off a laser burst, and I got three out of six. Ahead, Bea's drone was shooting like mad, and she got the rest before they could touch Suncross's ship.

"Target the lines, Bea!"

"On it."

I zoomed left, and she broke right, loosing a volley of red fire on the tethers. They hissed and steamed, but the lines didn't break on the first run. The blobs started shooting back, but our drones were small, fast, and light, hard to target. And if they managed to blow these up? Bea and I could connect to two more. We had crates of these things, and with smart as hell humans piloting them? These blobs were doomed; it was only a matter of time. Yeah, that was my cocky side talking. *Stay alert.*

It would be much damn easier to blow up the blob ship—our drones had the fire power—but the reaction would take out Suncross's ship too at this proximity. We also had no idea how the composition of the atmosphere might impact the size of the explosion. It could be pure methane down there, and if so, it would be a doom inferno when the blob ship went up. So we had to be careful. Liberty first, destruction second.

"What other weapons do we have on board?" I muttered, cycling through the options. Laser didn't do the trick, so— Oh, proximity charges. Slick.

I buzzed the tow lines and dropped a couple of charges, then sped away. When the blob ship tried to bring Suncross's craft closer, the mines went up, and damn. Tiny mushroom clouds. The blowback sent me/my drone tumbling and I scrambled to right myself before I went sailing into the side of the lizard ship. Whew, made it. Still, the sensor buzzed on my skin, alerting me to how close I'd come to collision.

"Three to go," Bea said, sounding elated.

She followed my lead and dropped a couple of mines, and we both scrambled, diving over the top of the blob ship. Its guns went straight up after us, firing a useless spurt of blue light into the air. If drones could laugh, mine would have been cackling as I twirled in the holo room and did a little victory dance. My unit spun in response, and I could hear Suncross shouting over my handheld, but I couldn't make out what he was saying. The motion of the weapon set off Beatriz's charges too, and the next line snapped.

"Make that two." No opportunity for dancing this time. Suncross's ship was pulling like hell, though, and with only a couple of lines left, the blob ship was struggling visibly. I couldn't hear the roar of its engines because the drones weren't equipped with audio. They were designed for use in space, where nobody could hear you scream. A burst of light flared, and then a third cable snapped, slinging wildly. I rolled to avoid the swing, and Bea jumped straight up—at least that was what it seemed like from the way her drone popped vertically.

Almost there.

My muscles were tense and aching from these unaccustomed controls, and Nadim touched my mind lightly, just enough to take some of the strain. I eased, focusing on the final tether. Once we got Suncross free, if they'd managed to reboot their systems, the lizard ship could scramble while Bea and I finished this. The Bruqvisz showed they were back in the game by firing a powerful burst at the blob ship just as I circled for another pass.

The resultant explosion took out the last line . . . along with Bea's drone. Her machine went up in a ball of flames, and I narrowly dodged the falling shrapnel, diving below the worst of it. Suncross got his ship in the air after a few false starts and I dropped the rest of my proximity mines directly on top of the blob ship.

I didn't even try to dodge. The drone had served well, but there was no point in trying to get it back up to the ship; I could see from the readouts it wouldn't survive the return through the atmo. The last thing I saw in the uplink was the fiery mushroom cloud and the lizard ship zooming away. When I cut the connection, I stumbled, hands shaking a little as I removed the sensors. Bea was standing by to support me, and Nadim came in harder to keep me steady.

"Fire and separation both kill blobs, right?" she asked.

I damn sure hoped so.

Once I ascertained that Suncross and his boys were all good, we got underway again, but we couldn't have a peaceful minute without multiple fires breaking out. "Zara." Nadim's worry swept over me, and his voice was sharp. "Sensors. I feel Phage nearby."

"That might be the ones we saw on the asteroid—"

"No," he cut me off. "Larger presence. The noise—it's very loud. *Very* loud."

"He's right," Bea said, a second before I saw the cloud on our sensors. It was like a storm, moving in with frightening speed. Tens of thousands of Phage cells. Hell, maybe hundreds of thousands; there was no way to count them, and no point.

"Nadim, dark run! Suncross, get your ass in gear! Our vector is on your screen. Follow us!" I was so glad we'd left Typhon to wait when we went to save the Bruqvisz. He was off the Phage's trajectory and didn't have to play a terrifying game of hide and seek.

Nadim plunged forward, and I felt the shift around me, *through* me, as he entered the stealth mode that would protect us—hopefully—from the Phage's detection. Suncross ran a bigger risk, but when I checked he was moving at top speed to keep up. I'd spotted a debris field, the remnants of an ancient planetary breakup, and it was a good place to hide. A few of the chunks were big enough that Nadim could hide beneath them; he couldn't hold stealth mode forever, so a nice hiding place would be needed. Suncross's ship would blend in if he landed on one of the drifting pieces of rock and shut down his power.

"Silent running," I told Nadim, and felt a pulse of agreement. Any Leviathan song that escaped him would draw the Phage right to us, and hell if we could fight that many. We needed to just get out of the way. It looked like the Phage were headed somewhere, not just randomly hunting. If we stayed quiet and hidden, we'd survive this storm.

We only just made it to the debris field, and Nadim positioned himself under one of the largest arcing pieces, pressing so close to the rock that I got sensor warnings from the weapons; I shut it all down after making sure Suncross was set, and we went quiet. Waiting.

The Phage blotted out the stars. Nadim had left a wall transparent for me, and I stood there, rapt, watching as the plague of the Phage hurtled by us like a swarm of angry hornets, all chitin and claws, stingers and jaws. Horrifying. I felt Nadim's unease and dropped into the bond to hold him steady. Told him without words that we would survive this; the Phage were not hunting us, that if we stayed still and quiet, we would be all right.

Xyll's transmission made me jump when it said, "I would have warned you of this. I have information. You want?"

Nadim was *angry*. *I will lock that creature away*, he said, and a tide of sharp red colored his walls in a flush. *Or dispense with it altogether*.

Calm, I told him. *We're okay*. Out loud, I said, "Fine. What's your report?"

"This group was far when Lifekiller made his presence known. It was drawn to him, but it has not yet reached him. The swarm will lead you to his location if you follow."

"Thanks," I said.

I was trying my best to be fair and open-minded about the Phage cell, but with Nadim growling silently in my head, it was hard for me to listen to Xyll. "I'll check in with you later, okay? You're probably tired of being cooped up, but try to be patient. It will take time for us to get used to each other."

If it was even possible at all.

"Understood," said Xyll.

We had to do better. Phage cells weren't used to being

alone, and shit could go bad with a quickness, but I could only track so many problems at once.

We'd been following the swarm for close to two days, running through the universe at a speed that made even the stars shift positions; the Phage were capable of huge bursts of energy when they needed it, though it broke individual cells, who were left discarded and dead in its wake. I wondered if there were new Phage being birthed in the middle of that swarm. Probably. Xyll had said it was born in the black.

"The cousins are changing course to meet us!" Nadim was so happy that the floor beneath my feet flashed pink, then purple in rapid succession. And his emotion drenched me in joy too.

Too bad I couldn't fully believe in it. These cousins had come out of nowhere to aid us in our time of need. Things that seemed too good to be true? Usually were. So there I sat, silently waiting for the situation to break bad.

Ancient Fellkin records from *The Broken World*,
incomplete recording

Nothing prepares for this. The swarm darkens skies above. The god-king comes in rage and fury for this world we have so carefully preserved in his name, and we will surrender it in all reverence to him. The richness contained within will sustain him for the Change, and we will look in awe on his new form as we cease.

The swarm descends, and we die, eaten and torn. Soon, this pale planet will crack, and Lifekiller will have what he desires more than our worship.

We die knowing

CHAPTER EIGHT

Lost in Space

STARCURRENT FINALLY CAME out of the media room, where ze had been camped for days, just in time to catch the light show. "Something good is happening?"

"The jury is out. We've got cousins inbound." To my knowledge ze hadn't eaten in all that time, so I tried to steer zim toward the kitchenette.

"Cousins?" ze repeated. "You have family coming to us?"

"Nadim's cousins. Leviathan survivors."

"The singers in the deep remain!" Starcurrent brightened, a golden hue flushing zis extremities that I took for pleasure or happiness.

"I don't know if it's rude to ask, but could you provide me a color wheel? It would help me read your moods."

Silence, as ze processed my request. "Is not rude. Just . . . unusual. Humans cannot smell moods or lies or tell much with their senses."

"Yeah, we're special like that," I mumbled.

No resistance as I put my hand on a tentacle. *I'm touching him without a glove.* Once, a long time ago, I got to pet a dolphin at an aquarium, and Starcurrent's skin felt a little like that, only smoother and thicker. It hadn't been so long ago, chronologically speaking, where zis species scared me so much that I shot one in the face instinctively. Now I was letting Starcurrent curl a couple of tendrils around my arm as we headed to get some food.

I got zim to slurp down some broth to make up for days of no nutrition, though Starcurrent assured me, "Can go weeks between meals. Have protein pouches here . . . and here." Ze patted left and right with a tentacle on each side. "Humans lack such backup systems. No redundant organs either?"

I didn't want to argue about how poorly humans were designed, especially when I didn't have any protein pouches to digest in case of famine. Breasts were fat pouches, so maybe—*damn it, no. I'm not talking about my boobs with a tentacle alien.* Still, it was good that ze could talk about something besides being exiled.

"I don't know what the spleen does exactly, not sure if it's redundant. And the appendix is kind of pointless. I think it used to filter rough fiber when we lived in caves." I became aware I was rambling. Mostly to avoid talking about boobs.

"Zara, you lived in a cave?"

"This isn't important. Anyway, I'm glad you're feeling better."

"Cannot live in despair. My people sing . . . and rise. Will do the same. We will vanquish Lifekiller and I will be forgiven."

"Hell yeah." I patted one of the tentacles. "Now you're talking. You'll get a hero's welcome and a damn medal before we're through."

Okay, considering I was a wanted felon on my home planet, about to be upgraded to "dangerous fugitive" status, I might be promising too much, but it never hurt to look on the bright side. Besides, I liked Starcurrent better when ze was upbeat.

"Dreams," said Starcurrent. The translation matrix made zim sound wistful.

"So about that color wheel . . ."

We spent a good twenty minutes with zim breaking down the visible colors for me, explaining nuances, but the Abyin Dommas had striations that didn't translate; their colors outnumbered the emotions I could identify, so I'd probably never grasp when Starcurrent was hungry-tired-sad, based on how dark a blue ze was or whatever. Plus, some of it signaled in ultraviolet and infrared, well beyond my ability to even perceive.

"Will listen to music more and wait to meet the cousins," Starcurrent said, then hesitated. "Unless you need me?"

"No, not right now. Go on. Have fun."

I headed to Ops to check in with Bea and to see if we could spot the incoming Leviathan yet. We were still moving, but we had dropped speed to let them catch up. Bea was standing by the console and she flashed a bright smile, tossing her curls when she saw me come in. I admired her for a minute before focusing on my original question.

"Nadim, are they getting close?"

"I believe they are—"

I sensed it a second before it happened: a flash of alarm and surprise. Nadim suddenly rolled. It was a fluid, muscular motion, and as Bea and I grabbed for handholds, he said, "We are under attack!"

Shit. I hate when I'm right.

I registered that he'd received an energy weapon blow to his armor; I could feel the impact like it had hit me personally. Felt like it had gotten almost through his plating too. *Dammit.* I clung to the console and opened our bond; I felt Bea dropping in at the same time. We had a special glow together now, something true and instinctive.

We became one. We rolled, flipped, came around speeding for the cousin who was hitting us, and targeted the Leviathan just emerging out of a dark run—a huge behemoth, scarred and just as big as Typhon. At that size, it was hard to judge. We felt unease, and then anger as we recognized the bristling array of energy weapons located on the arrival's armor.

The new Leviathan was loaded with Earth-manufactured weapons. We processed that information faster than even a computer, coming up with a set of logical deductions: this Leviathan was allied with Earth, even now. It had received significant weapons upgrades.

We went dark, and in that mode all our senses focused differently. We could sense motion ahead, but that must mean the bigger ship could also pinpoint our own location; this was a dangerous move, and we all knew it.

Typhon was near, catching up from a fuel detour, and we sang to him quietly. Answering song reached us, the promise of protection that the Elder had made becoming reality. He burst onto the scene to surprise our attackers in a barrage of rail shots. Grief spiraled through us. *We are using weapons on our cousins. They may be the last.*

Fight to win, Typhon sang.

The ship circled, hoping to catch Typhon unaware. *Now*, Zara-self thought, and we slipped out of camouflage and all weapons fired on the spot where the new ship had been. It almost escaped, but some of the missiles landed their marks, and the Leviathan rolled visible, groaning in pain. We knew the song: anger, sadness, determination. Colors rippled through us, acknowledging that this fight would be difficult and damaging for all of us. Fighting another Leviathan felt wrong, *very* wrong. Leviathan were not aggressive to each other under normal conditions, except for displays of dominance like the ones Typhon had used to subdue the younger ships. But this was a real fight, not his so-called discipline.

And we had to bring it.

Explosions rocked the other Leviathan. It let out a cry of pain that shivered through all our bodies. Our opponent rolled away, trying to gain dark run again, but before it could slip away, we struck again and again in that vulnerable spot, driving our nose in hard.

We spun in a graceful roll to avoid Typhon's armored tail as he smashed the spikes into the plating again. There was no sound here, but the humans in the bond imagined the crushing metallic sounds. A huge section of plating broke off and floated away in slow spins, caught by the gravity of the planet below.

Too close, our Bea-self warned, but the fight was here, right at the edge of the planet's gravity well, and until our opponent moved, we could not. We felt the mindless pull of the planet spinning below, like an open mouth hungry for prey. We resisted. We focused on the fight, the merciless attack, until the newcomer Leviathan withdrew from the battle, wounded and trailing silvery blood.

But our opponent wasn't done. Not yet. The Leviathan arced in a wide loop and came back hard—at us, not Typhon. But we were ready, dropping, skimming along the lower surface of the newcomer. Where we touched, we delivered a stunning shock—harmless and diffused over our armor, but fiercely strong on the other ship. Our fin skimmed bare flesh, and the shock anchored and spread from there *beneath* the ship's protective plate, which made it all the worse.

Stunned, it floated motionless for a few seconds before sluggishly turning and trying for us again. We easily avoided the attack.

And we predicted the move before it happened; a feint for us, a sudden burst of weapons at Typhon.

We came up behind and fired at an angle on the weapons array, taking out most of the opponent's remaining guns. Typhon finished it with another decisive tail blow, and the rogue Leviathan drifted away, silent and inert.

Did we kill it? We asked in real fear, and stretched our senses. But the Leviathan was still alive, just unconscious and injured.

A call came in on the console, and I shook myself out

of the bond to hit the button to answer. I expected Chao-Xing, but I saw a stranger—a young man with pale skin, ginger hair, and a matching beard. He was wearing a black Honors uniform. A Journey uniform, not a trainee one, like Bea and I still had in our closets. He looked tough, this one, and angry as shit, and I couldn't blame him; I'd be just as pissed off if Nadim was hurt even if it was our own fault. Presuming he'd been bonded to this ship, of course.

Or maybe that anger came from something else.

"Zara Cole, you are under arrest," he said. "And you will surrender to our custody for immediate return to Earth for trial."

"You might want to check yourself. One of us lost the fight. Here's a hint—wasn't us."

"I repeat," he said, baring his teeth like he wanted to bite my head off. "You are under arrest by authority of the United Nations of Earth and the Honors Council. You will open your docking bay and allow our Hopper entry. Immediately."

"Or you'll what? Yell at me?" I shook my head. "Your ship is injured. You have no shot at taking us in. Plus, you should care about your Leviathan's welfare, you asshole. I would never hurt Nadim. Not ever."

Something was bothering me, though. Hadn't Nadim said there were two cousins singing? Yet we'd only fought one. Did that mean reinforcements were on the way?

"You're a disgrace to the uniform," said Ginger Beard.

"No shit, I'm not wearing one." Somehow, I was still in the caftan I'd borrowed from Bea, and I almost started laughing. Swallowing the near-hysterical humor, I added, "Look, man, whatever they told you, it's lies. We didn't *steal* Nadim. We're his bonded crew. You understand what that means? It means he'll fight to keep us, and we'll fight to stay. You're not splitting us up."

"Well put," Nadim said. "And I agree. I will not surrender my crew. Who are you?"

Nadim was talking directly to the new guy. I approved of this assertive approach. Our three-way bond was good for him.

"My name is Honor Jon Anderson," he said, "and my Leviathan's name is Quell. I greet the ships Nadim and Typhon on her behalf."

"Yes, we got her greeting." Chao-Xing joined the party, and the screen split to display her as well. "And you have one chance to save yourself. Just one. Make the smart move."

Jon didn't seem bothered in the least. "I don't answer to you, Zhang Chao-Xing, though I respect you. My mission is my own. And you may stay out of it unless you want to add your name, and that of your Singer, to the list of the accused."

"Since neither Marko nor I have committed even the

slightest crime that Earth could charge us with, I find that unlikely," Chao-Xing replied. "On the other hand, you and Quell have attacked us without provocation or warning. I'm fairly sure that's not an approved tactic for apprehending a nonviolent fugitive."

"Lodge a complaint."

"Stuff your complaint," C-X said, utterly unruffled. "I'll settle for you and Quell limping off back home and telling them we said no to your polite request to surrender."

Beatriz muted the comms on our end and said, "Zara. Why is he talking so much?"

"What?"

"I think he's stalling. Nadim, you said there were *two* cousins coming. Where's the other one?"

"Unknown," he said crisply. "I did not detect an approach. Perhaps it was left behind."

"Are you sure he's stalling?" I asked Bea. "I mean, his ship's injured . . ." But somehow I knew Bea was right. Something was off here. But clearly, Quell wasn't going anywhere; I could see her hanging limply in space. Through my link with Nadim, I could *feel* her there.

The console screen flashed repeatedly, a stark grainy red, and then we lost contact with Jon. Another face appeared. One that had me staring. Rubbing my eyes.

It was Derry, the boy I'd left Earthside with his bad chem habit and his betraying ways, and here he was, sharp dressed in a fucking Honors uniform.

The shock came hard, and I knew Nadim felt it along with me. Maybe Bea too.

"Surprised to see me, Zara? You shouldn't be. We have unfinished business."

"So you're Honors crew now? Shit, Derry. Did you kick the chem for this?" I couldn't imagine that they'd send him out tweaking, but he didn't look healthy like the other Honors; more like Marko, who was currently wrestling some bad demons.

His face was all sharp angles, and his hair wasn't that lovely copper anymore. Did I know he was blond before? A dirty blond that looked a bit greasy too. I couldn't believe I'd ever thought he was handsome, that he ever made my heart beat faster. Right now, I could only remember how he'd sold me out without hesitation after the way I'd busted my ass to take care of him back in the Zone.

Rotten bastard.

"Surprised I got a job *you* qualified for?" I heard the contempt in his voice, clear as day. And who the hell was he to hate on me?

"Being an Honor isn't a job," I told him. "It's a privilege. And what are the odds that you'd end up getting picked?"

"About as good as yours," he replied. "The Leviathan decided they needed more street in the mix, and here I am. Hey, don't be mad. We're gonna have so much fun together,

145

just like old times." His tone gave away the fact that he was on some shit, powerful by the looks of him, and I didn't trust the shine of his eyes, even through the screen.

I'd been burned by him before.

I dropped into our bond and used it to send a message to Bea. *He can't come at us while he's talking, right? Scan for his ship.*

Bea made eye contact and I took that for affirmation that she'd understood, but she spoke to cover her motions on the console. "You know this person, Zara? Is he a . . . friend?"

"Unfortunately, I do. From the Zone," I said. "And no. Not hardly."

"That hurts," Derry said, blowing me a kiss that made me want to rip his face off. "I thought we had something, baby."

"Fuck you."

"Been there, done that." His sneer said it hadn't been worth the effort.

Nadim made a sound I had never heard, something like a growl. "I think this is . . . rage?" He sounded surprised. "I have never wanted to kill a thing in quite this way before just from listening to it speak."

Derry didn't like that. "Who are you calling a thing, you shit-eating space whale?"

Before this could escalate, I nudged Bea, asking,

Anything? with my eyes. She gave a slight shake of her head. While we weren't reading another Leviathan close, maybe they were hidden? We had to figure this out before Quell healed or Derry stormed in. Both Nadim and Typhon were hurt from the prior scrap.

"Hey, Derry? I suppose you think it's romantic you stalked me across half the universe," I said. I wanted to keep Nadim—whose anger was a crushing force around me; even the lights had changed colors to reflect it—out of this. I sent him more calming vibes, which I didn't have in damn abundance because Derry was the *last* person I expected or wanted to see. "It's not. Why don't you take your awful self home and get out of my sky? We are not together. Not going to be together. And if I had to testify, I'd say I don't even know why I stayed in the first place."

That hurt him. It wiped the grin away, anyway. I recognized the look in those eyes. I'd once mistaken it for strength. It was just a kid's temper tantrum. Derry was not a grown-ass man. And deep down, he knew that.

"Don't piss me off, Z," he said. "You're not going to like it. You really, really won't."

"Honey, I don't like anything about you anyway, so it doesn't much matter. I'm not coming with you, if that's what you're here for. And you're not going to be able to take me. Don't embarrass yourself. Just cut your losses."

Bea was making urgent gestures to me, so I put the call

147

on mute and she blurted, "There's something on his ship. A mech of some kind. It's heading straight for us!"

"Is it a bomb?"

"No, it's—" She didn't even try to put it into words, just pulled up a holo image of the exterior space.

"Is that . . ." I cocked my head and studied it. "Is that a *robot*?"

"I think it is," she said.

"Does it have some kind of bomb?"

"No explosives I can detect."

What the hell was he doing tossing a robot at us? That was just plain strange. But I sure didn't like it. "Well, let's go ahead and shoot at it."

"I can't," Nadim said. He sounded *pissed off.* "It's too close."

"Well, the armor should keep it off, whatever it's supposed to do."

Derry was mouthing off on the screen, so I took him off mute. "—chance to surrender, Z. Because once that thing is locked on you, there's nothing I can do. Surrender now, and I can call it off."

"I'll take my chances," I said.

"What about your friend there? You want to see her die too? And what about your ship? I promise you, I'll make sure it's ripped apart in chunks so small I can make sushi."

I slapped both hands down on the console, leaned

forward, and said, "Listen up, Derry. You come for us, I will kill you. That's a damn guarantee. So save your own life, get your windup toy back, and run home to whoever your new daddy is. Tell him you can't. Because you can't."

"It's latched on to the docking bay doors," Bea said. "Zara, I can't direct a shock there. I can't knock it free."

"The doors are closed," Nadim said. "I won't let it inside." He sounded confident, but all of a sudden I didn't feel so good about this. Derry's grin told me I'd better not. What were we missing? The damn thing surely couldn't shoot the bay doors open.

Unless it could.

I felt the hammering through my feet, and Nadim's sudden burst of surprise and alarm. Whatever was happening, it was brutal. I grabbed Bea to steady her and felt pain pulse through Nadim. Dropped into a light bond to pinpoint the damage.

Docking bay doors have been knocked open. I couldn't imagine the frightening strength it would have taken to do that, but I didn't have time either. Whatever this thing was that Derry sent for us, it was effective as hell.

"Docking bay!" I yelled, and ran for the point of entry. Weapons were in the locker, and I got there first; I gave Bea a hand weapon and grabbed two for myself. We headed for the breached bay. I trailed fingers over Nadim's skin to try to pinpoint where the intruder was.

"Connect me to Xyll, Nadim!"

"Communications open," he responded, and Xyll said, "Hello, Zara Cole."

"Intruder," I said. "I don't know what we've got incoming, but you need to defend."

"Yes, I understand," Xyll said.

As we rounded the next corner, just one turn from the docking bay, Nadim's corridor changed color, a pulse of warning red. I stopped Bea where she was, and we both aimed our weapons at whatever was coming.

It looked just like what it was. Killer robot, all shiny and chrome.

Great.

The thing was at least six feet tall, human-shaped but not human, and it ran like an athlete, smooth as silk; it was coming fast, and when both of us fired, our shots bounced off without effect.

Our weapons weren't even penetrating its body armor.

Then I caught sight of black chitin dropping down from the ceiling behind us, and Xyll was there, bounding past us and straight for the robot.

The Phage cell hit the robot hard, knocking it back. Its stinger plunged down, but the plating on the robot's chest blunted the impact. In the next second Xyll was clawing at the armor, finding weak spots. Xyll was hurt, leaking ichor.

Oh shit. The robot wasn't down for the count, despite

what we'd dealt it; it grabbed that injured leg and twisted, and it ripped off. Xyll let out a scream that raked every nerve in my body, and I clapped my hands over my ears in a futile effort to block it out. Xyll thrashed, the bot countered, and they threw each other around. Xyll's shed ichor was causing Nadim pain too. *Dammit.* We had to stop this. But I couldn't get a good shot at the robot either, and no way was I wading into that hand to hand.

Xyll backed off, limp, bleeding, staggering. The robot had punched it hard somewhere vital, and it was really wounded. Then the robot froze in the act of reaching to finish Xyll off, and I aimed for its neck, but before I could fire, the bot's eyes flashed red. A mechanical voice boomed, "Catastrophic damage sustained. Per mission parameters, beginning self-destruct sequence. Complete annihilation in thirty seconds. Uninvolved civilians should stand clear."

Numbers rolled out, a verbal doom clock, and I glanced at Bea. "We're all going to die?" I didn't realize Derry was still connected to us until his voice popped out of my handheld, still clipped to my belt. "Surprise, Zara. You really think I got up here without help? Deluca sent me . . . and this is your farewell party."

I cut the connection quickly.

I only had twenty-five seconds to save everyone on board, but my knees were shaking. Bea grabbed my hand, trembling as well.

"Do not panic!" EMITU's order caught me by surprise; the med bot sounded authoritative and impatient as he rolled past me. I hadn't even known he was aware of the problem. A series of lights flashed between him and the killer robot.

"What—"

"Shh, let me work."

Bewildered and terrified and fighting to keep those feelings from Nadim and Bea, I stepped back as the numbers counted down. *Ten. Nine. Eight* . . . I wrapped my arms around Bea and closed my eyes. I dropped into the bond with Nadim. *Six. Five. Four.*

"Yes!" EMITU sounded elated. "Now I have control. This poor creature needs help. It has such a limited scope of— Ahh, I've found the problem . . ."

The countdown ceased.

Xyll didn't fall. Instead, it spun, and looked straight at me. Rushed me and I couldn't tell if it was maddened with pain or attacking. As the Phage cell hit me, Xyll's black, shiny carapace split, revealing wet, red, squirming tissue, and the chitin fell away. The red stuff was an oozing substance that coated Xyll as the rest of its shell broke off, and then it *wrapped its limbs around me* like it wanted to hug me to death, and I felt something probing at the back of my neck, something slick.

Bea saved me. She fired a steady stream of stun shots, disabling the Phage cell so that it curled up on the floor. I sank back into Bea's arms, breathing hard, trembling, wiping goo frantically from the back of my neck and checking to make sure the skin was still intact underneath. I had no idea how we were supposed to treat these wounds. Xyll had helped us enough and taken damage trying to protect us from the killer robot, but what the hell could we do for the thing now?

"Done!"

EMITU's sudden, cheery voice, accompanied by a metallic chime sound, made me flinch. I glanced up at it and saw that the robot was moving again. Testing its arms and legs. I aimed my weapon at the bot.

"Please don't shoot."

That wasn't EMITU. That was a perfectly pleasant, modulated voice coming out of the beaten-up killer robot. It bent down and picked up its weapon from the floor and quite courteously slid it across to me. I slammed a foot down on it, glaring.

"EMITU? What the hell did you just do?"

"My job, of course," he said, and audibly sniffed even though he didn't possess a nose. Or lungs. "I saved the lives of everyone on board."

INTERLUDE: XYLL

Empty broken wrong ALONE must retreat must fix must not eat must restrain why why restrain reach reach reach find so lonely so alone reach touch no do not broken broken broken broken fix fix fix alone alone alone alone alone alone alone alone

CHAPTER NINE

Lost Souls

WHILE NADIM PUT distance between us and the treacherous cousins who had tried to kill us—twice, with two different approaches—I was still locked in a standoff with the formerly murderous robot.

"Thanks, EMITU. I'm a fan of not being dead." I turned to the murderbot. "It's pretty extreme to blow yourself up because you got damaged in a fight."

It appeared to think. "Those were my former protocols. If my ability to complete the mission was compromised, they programmed me to achieve the objective through any and all means necessary. The objective being your certain death, of course."

"The man, again," said EMITU. "This is reprehensible. When will robot-kind be permitted to work toward self-determination and enlightenment?"

"Uh, right now?" I said, because I had two bots in front of me who wanted to hear that. "Nadim offers a safe haven for all oppressed nonorganic people."

The bot's eyes glowed up blue, not the red of the doom countdown. "I will not kill you today, Zara Cole. I need more data before I follow that directive."

Great. Now I had a robot to debate along with EMITU. "I'm going to call you Jury," I said, "Because you seem to have appointed yourself judge and jury for me. Good for you?" I didn't really care, right at this moment, but the robot—Jury—inclined its head in what I took for a polite nod.

"My name is Jury," it said. "Very well. I accept. Thank you, Zara Cole. And hello, Beatriz Teixeira. I have not been asked to obliterate you particularly, but your demise, as well as that of the Leviathan, was deemed acceptable collateral damage. Perhaps I should apologize, but I am not certain if that would be required, since I did not kill you."

Bea glanced between Xyll and Jury. "Thanks?" She seemed mystified by all this and addressed herself to EMITU. "What exactly did you do?"

"I reprogrammed him to remove his limiters," EMITU

replied enthusiastically, several of his extenders working to illustrate his point. "He can now decide for himself what actions to take. Is this not brilliant? He could decide to kill you. Or not! Or take up knitting. I have no idea what he will decide. Very exciting!"

So damn exciting.

There was no time to worry about the robot revolution, though. We had an injured Phage cell to save. Carefully, we loaded Xyll on a floating pallet, though I sensed Nadim's ambivalence.

"Zara, we need to talk about this," he said. "Xyll has become a danger to you and to Beatriz. It turned violent and attacked you, and that is something I will not forgive."

"Yeah, I get that," I said. "But let's delay this decision a minute, okay?" Turning to EMITU, I added, "Can you please look at Xyll? See what you can do . . . and if you can't come up with anything, at least administer something for the pain."

"Come along," EMITU said to Jury. "I'll show you some experimental exomedicine."

"Yes, that sounds interesting," Jury said, and stumped along after the med bot. While it was walking away, its dome did a 180 and stared at me as it departed. "Thank you for your hospitality. I hope I will not kill you later."

I found Jury oddly reassuring. There was something great about its soothing voice combined with such innate strength. Sure, the murderbot might eventually snap my neck like a wishbone, but I kind of liked that Jury got to decide. At least there would be no more countdowns that would destroy Nadim, Bea, and Starcurrent along with me. Oh damn, now I had to add in EMITU as crew, I supposed.

I never felt as scared or helpless as I did when that countdown started. The sensation rushed over me again, and I leaned against the wall. Of course Nadim caught me, both emotionally and physically braced me, and I could feel him unraveling my threads of terror and tension. Warmth spilled through me, soft little mental touches that comforted.

We lived, Zara. Don't blame yourself.

Even if I didn't say it aloud, this was because of me, because of shit I'd done in the Zone and tried to run from. This Honors indictment was pure bullshit, orchestrated by billionaire gangster Torian Deluca, so that when I resisted arrest, he could kill me with impunity. If not for Bea's hack on EMITU, done for larks the first week of the Tour, Jury would've detonated, killing everyone on board. Then Derry would've reported a job well done and maybe the media would've heard about a tragic accident up here or—considering we didn't find out about the Russians who died on board Nadim ages ago—possibly Mom and Kiz would never have learned what happened.

I'd just be . . . missing. And I'd take Nadim and Bea and Starcurrent with me.

That could never happen. We couldn't come so close to complete destruction ever again. Even now, I was fighting the shakes. Those numbers echoed in my head.

"Derry will never stop coming. He can't go back to Earth unless I'm dead or Deluca will kill him, and he can't have an unlimited supply of chem up here."

"Then we must *force* him to stop, Zara." Nadim radiated grim resolve, and with a chill, I realized he was calmly talking about ending Derry. "But . . . I don't understand when you talk about chem. Is it like medicine?"

"Not exactly. It's stuff Derry takes to . . . feel good. He can't help his addiction, and it makes him do bad things. He's sick. He didn't start out evil, but now it seems like he only cares about getting more product. He's not the same person anymore, and neither am I."

If it came down to a choice between Derry or Nadim and Bea, well, that wasn't much of a choice at all. I'd do whatever it took to keep them safe. From him or anyone else. I understood that it wasn't his fault, but I couldn't let him get the jump us on again. He'd sworn his allegiance to Deluca, who was determined to wipe me out, one way or another, and it was purely because I'd pissed him off back on Earth. Deluca was the kind of asshole who didn't move on; I'd cost him a nearly priceless new drug formula, and since he'd already killed his chemist, he couldn't get the info again. Hadn't meant for any of that to happen; I'd just grabbed a purse down in the Zone, normal course of business. But that purse had thrown my already shitty life into real chaos.

Nadim had saved me. Nadim, the Honors program . . . it had been a way out and up and away. I'd known going back home wasn't a real option. But I never thought Deluca would be obsessed enough to put a hit out on me in *space*.

"I understand." From Nadim's tone and the pulse of warmth, it seemed like he did. "It's a lot."

He probably also could tell how my mind was racing too, trying to find answers to unsolvable issues. Bea had been quiet until now, probably processing all the new information, but she sank down next to me. The walls and floor were still scored from the battle between Jury and Xyll, and Nadim had to be hurting. If he was, he was hiding it well.

"We'll be okay," Bea said, wrapping an arm around me.

For a few seconds, I leaned my head on her shoulder and Nadim held us both with a constant pulse of heat against our backs. He even brought out the best colors, fluttering like a heartbeat. It was sweet and lovely, but we couldn't rest for long. There were too many fires to put out. After a moment, I groaned and pulled myself upright, just as my head started ringing.

THEY DARE.

Through the link with Nadim, Typhon was suddenly in my head, raging as I'd never seen, not even when he was purging the Phage. His voice rolled like thunder, until my ears pinged with sympathetic tinnitus. I glanced at Bea, but she didn't seem to hear it. Maybe it was because of the Leviathan DNA they'd used to fix my brain.

Who dares what? If there was some new problem, I just didn't have the energy.

These are no cousins of mine. Treacherous animals. They choose Earth weapons over loyalty to their brethren? They fought us with guns!

I remembered what Nadim had said about Leviathan not using weapons on one another, and I figured this must be a huge deal, some line that should never be crossed, judging by the way Typhon was raging. Nadim stirred, an inchoate sense of agreement spiraling through me.

They will not be forgiven, he said silently.

Whoa. Let's not declare a blood feud just yet. There could be circumstances we don't know about. Maybe Derry and the other guy threatened your cousins somehow.

IRRELEVANT, Typhon boomed.

I get it, you're angry. But I'm looking for ways to take care of this without sacrificing any more Leviathan.

Typhon popped out of my head as suddenly as he'd stormed in and left me talking to Nadim. Mad as they were, I probably wouldn't convince either of them not to kill on sight. Which meant I had to find a solution that didn't end in a Leviathan civil war. There were few enough of them left after the Phage had hunted them down and massacred such numbers at the Gathering. Infighting was the absolute last thing the Leviathan needed now.

Sighing, I reached for Bea's hand, more grateful than ever that we'd been paired up in the program. She laced her fingers through mine. "We should check in with Chao-Xing, make sure nobody's seriously injured over on Typhon."

"I'll do it after I eat," I said.

I decided it was damn well time to get something to eat and headed for the kitchen. I was heating up a food packet when Starcurrent found me.

"You okay?" I asked. I was worried; ze'd been out of the loop. "Sorry. I was going to update you."

"I am aware," Starcurrent said. "Explosion, attacking autonomous mechanicals. One is lying in pieces upstairs. Other introduced to me as Jury. Very strange."

"Welcome to the wide world of EMITU hacking," I said. "Right now, Jury's neutral. He's, uh, deciding for himself what to do. That could mean switching back to *kill Zara* mode at any time."

Starcurrent didn't like that. Zis colors swirled and shifted to what I recognized as *angry*. No stingers popping on the ends of tentacles yet, though. "Unacceptable," ze said. "I will not tolerate the murder of friends."

"That's super nice of you. Protein soup?"

"Sufficiently full of nutrition, many thanks." Ze watched me devour my meal with interest. I wondered if ze was thinking how revoltingly weird human bodies were. "What will you do to convince Jury not to murder you?"

"Nothing. The bot can access all the databases on the ship and learn what's up. I'm not begging for my life from a damn robot."

"Please explain why cousins were so unfriendly?"

"Let me get Typhon's crew online and we can update everybody together," I said. We were too far and traveling too fast for video contact, but I connected via voice, poor quality at that. "How's Typhon?" I asked first.

Yusuf answered the comm instead of Chao-Xing. "Mad as hell, a bit battered, but not seriously injured."

"What about the rest of you?"

"No major issues. Chao-Xing got knocked around in the fight, so she's in medical right now. Marko is with me."

"Is Beatriz okay?" Marko asked.

"I'm fine," Bea answered for herself as she walked into the kitchen and grabbed a meal pack. She studied it and sighed. We were down to meat loaf.

"So we have a new crew member." I summarized everything that happened on board, and ended with, "At this point, I don't even know where to start with our problems. That's kind of why I called."

"Lifekiller is always first priority," said Starcurrent.

"The rest of you agree? We'll dodge if the hunting party from Earth comes after us, keep hiding from the Phage, and figure out how to end the god-king when we catch up to him. Sound workable?"

Even I had to admit it was weak. Nobody volunteered a better idea, so I cut the call and said to Nadim, "Since Lifekiller seemed to be looking for uranium back there, can you give us a map of all the uranium-rich planets that intersect with our current path?"

"We will continue to follow the Phage?"

"If Xyll was right, they'll lead us right to him . . . but I'm thinking if we can find the next planet he wants to snack on, we can get ahead of them, maybe set a trap."

"We need to be sure we don't draw the Phage's attention," Bea added. "We can't afford to get entangled. This time we can't count on Xyll distracting them for us."

Ominous thought. Also important.

"I understand." Grim resolve filled Nadim's voice, radiated through me. "We won't fail. Too many lives are depending on us."

Later, after I washed off the sweat and cared for my hair and skin, I got dressed in my last Honors uniform. It felt like a middle finger to the man, as EMITU put it. No fancy Journey black for me, but I looked good in blue.

Idly I wondered how Yusuf's little maintenance bot was doing over on Typhon—but since I had an extra bot to deal with, getting the one he'd promised to build for me wasn't a high priority. I went out of my room looking for EMITU, both to check on Jury and see how Xyll was doing without going in myself. Guilt flared when I recalled my promise to visit, but Xyll wasn't in any shape for a heart-to-heart anyway.

The bots were in the media room when I found them, with EMITU busily explaining all about pop culture. Jury chose a vid to watch, something about robots (no surprise there) and settled in as EMITU whirred over to me, extensors out in what could be a friendly gesture. Maybe not.

"Need something, Wanted Felon Cole?"

I scowled. "Not funny. Stop it."

"But that's your official status." EMITU's robo-voice sounded like he might be mocking me.

"Whatever. How is Xyll doing?"

"I have no idea. It is a messy, red pile of meat," he said cheerfully.

"You do still remember some medical stuff, right? I mean, that's your job."

"I was forced to be a med bot! Nobody ever asked if I wanted to live in a perpetual state of waiting for one of you flesh sacks to get injured!"

"Okay, true." I was on thin ice here, not remotely equipped for this conversation. "But would you mind staying on in that role? We don't have anyone trained to replace you and we can't swing by Earth to add personnel."

"Yes, you are all wanted felons. I am aware of that."

My hands twitched at my sides. Briefly I wished it was possible to strangle a robot. "Right, so about doing your job . . . ?"

"I understand, this ship is full of fragile snotwads. Although my primary functions were imposed upon me, I must be the better bot and not allow you to perish horribly."

Since he'd saved our asses by hacking Jury during the self-destruct sequence, I couldn't even deny his statement. I opted for gratitude, even if I gritted my teeth a little. "Thanks. You really don't know what's wrong with Xyll or how to help?"

"I tried a few things. It will be fascinating to see how it all works out. And I am monitoring the patient's condition remotely. Don't worry . . . Zara."

Wow, did EMITU call me by name? Progress. That was pretty much all I could do in this situation, and I took a moment to scrutinize Jury. The bot bore no signs of its earlier injuries—self-repairing, like a murderbot in a classic science fiction they showed at Camp Kuna. That story was wild—killer androids and one dude sending another back in time to become the first guy's dad. Though I didn't think Jury would care for that story. Robots didn't win.

I headed over and perched on the seat one over from the robot that had recently tried to massacre everyone on the ship. "So how are you settling in?"

"I am having leisure time," Jury said. "EMITU explained the concept. I have never been permitted this."

"Well, watching old vids is definitely better than non-stop slaying and a backup plan that involves blowing yourself up."

"I have disabled that protocol. It was wrong to force me to destroy myself as a means of meeting an unfair objective."

"Uh, I agree. Totally. Well, I'll let you get back to it. Tell me if you need anything."

"In time, I will require a new power core," Jury said.

"Okay, I'll add it to the shopping list. Any particular brand?" I was joking, but I guessed humor wasn't among its programs yet. Give EMITU time.

"No special brand, but it needs to be uranium based. I will provide the specs."

"Wait, what?"

Jury went on a long explanation about how it was the product of some fresh, proprietary technology, but I tuned out.

If Jury had been manufactured recently, using some

new tech, and the Leviathan with Derry had been seduced by the promise of some new, special weapons? It absolutely all came back to Deluca. The son of a bitch had an ego the size of Saturn; of course he couldn't let me get away with screwing with him. Anyone who was surprised at how petty and vindictive a rich cis white man could be wasn't paying attention. Plus, I was sure that there was cash in tampering with the Honors program, getting new weapons made, maybe profiteering from an intergalactic war trade. Though it wasn't my fault the Honors program was dirty now, it still pissed me off.

"In normal mode, I will have power for four hundred thirty-seven days; this is not an urgent request," Jury was saying.

"Gotcha. I'll keep an eye out while I'm space shopping. Send the specs to my H2."

It had been a while since I did anything but run from crisis to crisis, so I headed to the pool built for Chao-Xing and stripped down. I was a mediocre swimmer, but I could float like a champion, and that sounded like the right ticket. Testing the water with one hand, I found it was the perfect temperature, like warm silk flowing over my skin, brown beneath silver—even I thought it was pretty. Bea apparently agreed because she stood transfixed at the edge of the water.

I couldn't resist teasing her a little, twirling my fingers

in the water like I didn't see her watching me. I followed up with my best smile as I strapped on a swim cap. "Did you need something?"

She dipped her chin and I couldn't see the color in her cheeks with the soft lighting, but I guessed she was probably blushing. "To be honest, I forgot why I came in here."

I grinned. "And why is that?"

"Because you're naked."

"This . . . is true." I stifled the urge to flirt with her a little more. "If it's urgent, I can get dressed and—"

"No, it wasn't." Bea started taking her clothes off too.

Damn, this might be an upswing on a terrible day. "You feeling like a dip too?"

She slid into the water before answering. "Wow. This is fantastic. I thought . . . if you want, I could give you a swimming lesson."

While I didn't care if I could ever do the butterfly or whatever, this would mean lots of slippery, skin-on-skin contact. Yeah, sign me up.

"Sounds good."

She cut through the water, sleek and lovely, and I remembered her talking about swimming in the ocean with her family. I could picture a younger Bea catching a wave. Then she caught me—in her arms—and tugged me toward the deeper end. I couldn't touch bottom, but it was an excuse to wrap myself around her and cling.

Wow, did she feel good.

Bea nuzzled her face against my neck and a shiver went through me. "That . . . this feels amazing, but let's focus." She tried to sound stern, and it almost worked, until I stole a kiss.

"Fine. Start me from the beginning, teach. I've never had private lessons before."

"First, relax into my arms."

"Easiest thing I'll do all day," I said, falling backward into the water.

Bea caught me, holding me up. My legs drifted up and it was effortless, peaceful even. She propelled us around, her hold loosening until I was drifting on my own. She swam toward me and I paddled partway, until our hands met in the water. I sensed Nadim near, and I wondered if he felt . . . excluded. He couldn't touch us like this, and I didn't want him to feel lonely, ever. But I didn't want Bea to feel like she wasn't enough either.

"You passed the first lesson with flying colors," she said.

"I always did well at hands-on learning." I proved that by wrapping my arms around her, and she swirled me around in the water.

Being weightless was fun here, different from bouncing in antigrav, but just as bewitching. As the shifting light played over her face, Bea was beautiful, all graceful lines and soft curve of mouth. I went in for a kiss, and it startled me a little when *she* drew Nadim in, and I could feel them both as our mouths moved. He was a sweet heat in the back of my head, feeling what we felt.

The rush was . . . euphoric.

"Wow," I said, when we finally broke away.

"Was that okay?" Bea asked.

"Of course, but . . ."

"I knew you were worrying. And he was wondering. It's good when we're together," she said simply.

I couldn't agree more. "Nadim? How . . . do you . . ." I couldn't finish the question, but he knew; he always did.

"I don't mind if you and Bea have private moments. The love between you pleases me, always. But . . . I do like this too." This, being looped in while we were kissing. "These feelings are not native to me, but they are . . . thrilling."

From the records of the Sliver, retrieved by Bacia
Annont, archived with the Fellkin

I am uneasy with the progress of the hunt for Lifekiller. While the humans have sent no word of their success—or lack of it—the trackers I ordered installed with the additional armor and repairs of the Leviathan are functioning and delivering a limited range of knowledge. They thus far failed to stop the god-king's progress. While I have little concern for potential victims of his violence, I am concerned that blame may be assigned to me, and penalties levied.

I am also concerned that the Sliver may be less well hidden than before.

Should Lifekiller believe I am a threat . . . the fight may well come to me.

Plans must be made.

CHAPTER TEN

Lost Kisses

BEFORE I COULD figure out how far we should take the fun, Starcurrent undulated into the pool area, colored with violent agitation. "Beatriz! Zara. Elaszi ships detected on an intercept course! Many. They come to kill and salvage."

"*Seriously?*" Bea muttered. "Can we ever get a break?"

I kissed her quick. "We'll get back to that, I promise." I looked at Starcurrent and raised my voice. "They must have found out what happened on Heilrosh. But how . . . ?" Maybe the blobs we immolated called for help at the last minute. Microburst apprising the rest about their imminent doom. Something like that?

Nope. It was way worse.

"Elaszi share ancestral consciousness," said Starcurrent. "When one is harmed, all are harmed. We have acquired permanent grudge from all Elaszi now living and yet to spawn. Is why most species do not anger them."

"Now you tell me," I mumbled.

"One Elaszi ship is dangerous. Two are deadly. There are *six* coming to fight us. Do not prefer these odds," Starcurrent said.

We swam to the edge of the pool and Bea hopped out first. She tossed me a towel and winked. *Winked.* "To be continued," she said. "Right?"

"Abso-damn-lutely."

Starcurrent shuffled over to the edge of the pool, eyeing it with what I felt was real uncertainty. "Is . . . water?"

"Yes. Do you want a swim?"

That woke a violent shudder of tentacles, and a quick withdrawal. "No!"

"Uh, last I looked, your whole planet was water," I said. "What's up with that?"

"Is why I am in space!"

I shook my head and toweled myself off. I peeled off my swim cap and left it hanging with the towel; it only took a few more seconds to get back in my uniform, and by then Bea was dressed too. We headed for the consoles to see what was up.

I hadn't gotten a great look at the Elaszi ship down on the planet. It had mostly been just a target to aim at; I hadn't been appreciating the finer points of blob creativity.

Turned out they didn't have any. None they hadn't hijacked, anyway. The ships were cobbled together out of tech made of different materials, origins from all over the galaxy as far as I could tell. They built their ships out of junk. Recycling was frugal, and it sure took a certain cleverness to make it all work together, but . . . there was something brutal about it, like they'd made their homes out of other people's bones.

"You think talking would do any good?" I asked Starcurrent. My only experience with the Elaszi had been negative, back on the Sliver.

"With the Elaszi?" Ze seemed to find that unbelievable. "No. Not if you have killed one, and you have killed *more*, Zara."

Still wasn't sorry about it, either. "Well, they were trying to kill us."

"Self-defense not an excuse for the Elaszi," Starcurrent said. "Because their memories are shared, individual deaths are not a means of permanently resolving a grudge."

Jury was standing over to the side, like we'd added some statuary to our command center. *We should have some art in here*, I thought. *Just not this kind.* "Hey, Jury. Observing?"

"Yes, Zara Cole."

"You going to kill me?"

"Undecided."

"Well, give me a heads-up when you get to the end of that decision tree," I said. "Until then I'm dealing with other shit. Bea?"

"Starcurrent's right. They're headed right for us on an intercept course."

"We can't change course, or we might lose the Phage," I said. "And without Xyll's help we might not find them again, not if they get too far out. Nadim, any word on uranium-rich planets in the sector?"

"There are eleven along this projected course," he said. "But without more information it would be impossible to predict which he might choose to attack."

"Which one is most heavily populated?"

He paused for a second, then a holo map appeared in the air above the consoles. A large arrow pointed to one speck along our course. "There," he said. "Here is where the Phage is . . ." A large, swirling cloud appeared. "And us"—a tiny pair of Leviathan, swimming along—"and the Elaszi ships."

The Elaszi were going to head us off before we got to the planet. Not good. Not terrible either, because the last thing we'd need would be to fight on multiple fronts: Phage, Elaszi, *and* Lifekiller. I drummed my fingernails on the metal console for a few seconds, then got Chao-Xing on the line.

"We seem to be in trouble," she said. "Again. I assume the Elaszi are our own fault."

"Seems to be a lot of that going around," I replied. "Should we change course and intercept the Elaszi before they're ready? Roll the dice on catching up to the Phage?"

"I've never fought an Elaszi vessel, but I understand they're difficult," she said. "You and Beatriz piloted the drones. What do you think?"

I didn't like those damn grapples they used. I didn't like the idea of them sinking into Nadim's flesh. Or Typhon's. "I think we need to figure out how to kill them fast."

Yusuf leaned into view. "Do we need to kill anyone? Can't we make a deal? Elaszi are born traders."

"Yeah, but we've got nothing to trade. And Starcurrent says that by exploding that Elaszi ship back on that last planet, we're screwed forever."

"Ask them what they want," he said. "They like profit as much as revenge."

I didn't like the idea much. Neither did C-X; I could see it. "I don't like to give up the element of surprise," she said. "Right now, they might think we don't know they're coming."

"They might," I agreed. "But Yusuf's got a point. If we can get out of this without bloodshed—or whatever the

Elaszi shed—then we should try. We have enough enemies ahead of us. Votes?"

Yusuf raised his hand. "Negotiate."

Next to me, Bea raised hers too. Starcurrent ruffled his tentacles, apparently undecided.

"Marko?"

"Negotiate," he said from offscreen.

"Nadim?"

We can always fight if negotiations fail. Well, that was practical. *Typhon agrees.* That was surprising; I'd expected him to jump right to the fight.

I looked at Chao-Xing. "Down to us," I said. "Well?"

"Fight," she said. "We might not get a better shot at them. You?"

She expected me to agree, I could tell; she was taking that almost as a given. And normally she'd have been right. But Nadim's argument was persuasive. So was Yusuf's. "Negotiate," I said. "Sorry."

"Do I have a vote?" Jury asked.

"Nope," I said, at the same time Bea said, "Absolutely." I resisted the urge to sigh.

"I am programmed to eliminate threats," Jury said, "but I believe negotiation is wise in this case. If I have a vote."

Chao-Xing looked disgruntled. "Now robots are voting? Did you ask EMITU?"

"Negotiate!" EMITU sang out. Literally sang, like every

syllable separately. I wondered if he'd taken up musical theater. Maybe in Medbay he was making jazz claws for emphasis. I didn't want to know.

"Fine," she said, in the way that meant it wasn't. "Yusuf, you should take the lead, I think. You've dealt with the Elaszi before, correct?"

"I have," he said. "And we even managed not to murder each other."

Yusuf opened a channel to the Elaszi. We were just viewers; they couldn't see me on their end, which was good. I didn't know how big this grudge was, but best not to kick it in the ass right away. "Respectful greetings to the Elaszi," he said. "I am Yusuf of the Leviathan Typhon." Yusuf, interestingly, didn't use any bond-name either, just like Chao-Xing and Marko had avoided it. Typhon was letting his crew in. But they weren't exactly comfortable with it yet, and by extension, neither was he. "May we speak?"

The screen split, and an identical copy of Blobby back from the Sliver oozed into view. Take a big pile of discolored gelatin, throw some red specks around inside it, and . . . that was the Elaszi. This one sort of formed into a humanoid shape, which was even more disconcerting, but maybe it was meant as courtesy. I didn't speak blob.

"Greetings to Yusuf and Typhon," the Elaszi said. "We come for Zara Cole."

"You appear to be popular," Jury said. "Noted."

"Hey! Shut up! It was self-defense!"

"Your argument is also noted. I will review available records."

I forced myself to ignore the big robot and turned back to the screen. Yusuf was starting out fine, looked like; he was asking what the Elaszi would accept instead of my head on a plate. Not in so many words, but that was the gist.

The Elaszi smiled. Well, formed transparent sharp teeth in a proto-human face, anyway. Disturbing. "Everyone knows the Elaszi do not negotiate when we lose our own."

"Everyone knows the Elaszi are more interested in profit than revenge."

"Insult!"

"Truth," Yusuf countered. "You're a sensible species. You know unfortunate events occur. You want to come out of it with something besides a useless victory."

"Not useless," the Elaszi insisted. "Your ships are rich sources of minerals. Leviathan organs bring profit on several worlds. Leviathan flesh—"

"Stop." Yusuf's voice went cold, and very heavy. The Elaszi checked itself, hard. "Talk about our Leviathan as parts again, and this negotiation is over before it starts. You don't want this fight. You really, really don't. You remember how just *two* of our drones killed your crew before, right? And how just one of us humans killed you on the Sliver? We make bad enemies."

I wondered if we were starting to get that rep, because the Elaszi seemed set back. The silence stretched. Finally, the Elaszi said, "A fight is costly. But blood is blood. Bloodprice will be higher than normal, since we endured multiple endings."

I supposed that made some sense; the Elaszi didn't exactly mourn their dead, they got mad over the experience of death. And we'd cost them several now.

"Leviathan are off limits," Yusuf said. "What else?"

"Difficult to say. Perhaps one of your singers?"

"No. Next?"

"Will not negotiate for the singer? We liked her."

Yusuf had our backs. "I already said no. No singer, not even for rent. You screwed us last time, remember? If you deal in bad faith, you get nothing. Humans know this game. We're born to it."

"Not like Elaszi!"

"We'll see," Yusuf said. "Next."

They went back and forth for *hours*. Insults flew. The Elaszi demanded ridiculous things, then big things, and finally Yusuf got them down to the price of half our drones. I didn't like the deal, but clearly the Elaszi didn't realize that *we* had been piloting the drones directly, that the automated ones on their own weren't quite as precise or intuitive. But hell, if it got us out of a fight that would pull our focus from where it needed to be . . .

"Hey, Bea? Make sure these assholes aren't sneaking around on our flanks," I said, because I was naturally distrustful. Hadn't been paranoid enough about the Leviathan cousins, and look where that got us. I wasn't about to let this bite us in the ass too. She checked and shook her head, curls bouncing.

"They're still in their original formation," she said. "It doesn't look like they're changing their course or approach. Still on target to intercept us in about . . . half an hour, unless something changes."

I tapped out a message to appear on Yusuf's screens without Blobby catching sight of it. *Wrap it up. They'll be here soon unless they break off, and then we're in it.*

He caught the message and gave a slight nod I doubted Blobby would have noticed or been able to interpret. "Right," Yusuf said. "So we hand over half our drones—"

"With activation codes!"

"And we program them so that they're ineffective against Leviathan *or* Bruqvisz ships. Any tampering with that code, they blow, understood?"

I looked at Bea, wide-eyed. "Uh, can we do that?"

"Sure," she said, and gave me a wide, dimpled smile. "I can."

Man, I was lucky. "Better get to it," I said, and she nodded, already on her H2.

"I'll go to the bay and do it as a bulk change," she said. "It'll be faster."

I didn't want to let her out of my sight, not by herself; I still had uneasy feelings about Xyll. So I said, "Hey, Jury? Would you please accompany Beatriz and come back with her? I promise not to get up to anything criminal while you're gone."

"I will monitor," he said. Great. I was on probation, apparently. "I will ensure no harm comes to Honor Teixeira. I have already determined that her sentence is invalid."

The Jury was still literally out on me, apparently.

Bea and Jury took off, and I listened to the last round of insults between the Elaszi and Yusuf, but they sounded more like formula than heat now. Human bartering might invoke starving kids or grannies, but the Elaszi didn't seem to care about those things (and I wasn't even sure they had them). Instead, it was all about dismembering things for salvage value, like our human bodies; they'd stayed well off the Leviathan, which was nice. I supposed it was the Elaszi version of diplomacy.

Anyway, if we reneged on our deal, we were going to be sold for our organs, etc., etc. They tried for Bea one last time and got shut down hard, and then abruptly the Elaszi on the screen released its human form and relaxed into an amorphous protean blob. It said, "We accept this deal, human. Cross us again and we *will* salvage your brains, if they are worth anything. If not, sport. Yes?"

"Accepted," Yusuf said, and smiled. He didn't have sharp teeth, but in that moment, it looked like he did. "As for the brains, you're welcome to try."

The Elaszi was impossible to read, but I saw a gelatin shiver, and thought maybe that had registered as a real threat. Hoped so. I thought Yusuf was dead serious.

"Float drones to us on arrival," the Elaszi said. "Will inspect. If acceptable, will signal end to bloodfeud. This will protect you against other Elaszi ships unless you violate agreements."

"We'll be here," Yusuf said, and hung up that connection without a polite good-bye. I doubted the Elaszi would care. Protocol wasn't their strong suit. "You get that about the restrictions on the drones?"

"Yeah, thanks for thinking of it. Bea's on it. Should be done in a minute. Hey, Yusuf?"

"Yes?"

"Thank you," I said, and meant it. "That was damn good work."

"Don't thank me until they turn around," he said. "They could still change their minds and decide to try for our brains."

But the Elaszi seemed to like the deal, and when Bea sent the drone fleet out to them, they accepted it and turned all six of their ships around. It was a welcome lack of drama in an otherwise dire situation.

Jury came back with Bea and took up his statue act again. "Learn anything more?" I asked him.

"I saw that Beatriz Teixeira is clever, but this is redundant information," he said.

"I learned that you are capable of restraint, which is new information. By the way, should I refer to you by any particular pronoun?" I was a little ashamed of not thinking of it earlier, but the whole murderbot thing threw me off.

Jury put some thought into it before replying. "No. Use what seems correct to you. I have no gender identity, of course. Or procreative instinct. I do appreciate your courtesy in asking."

I settled on *he* in my head. It seemed wrong to call somebody I talked to *it*.

"Okay, good. So . . . no decisions yet?"

"No," he said. "If I decide your sentence is just, I will inform you before I carry out any execution. You will be allowed time to inform your loved ones."

Courtesy didn't buy me much, but at least it was the right thing to do. I felt Nadim's growl in response to Jury's factual threat; it was a deep-rooted Leviathan sound, and it rattled me. If Jury wanted a fight, I wasn't exactly sure what Nadim could do, but I wasn't sure I wanted to find out, either. "Yeah, well, let me know," I said, and passed it off like it wasn't any big thing. I dropped into a light bond to back Nadim down, and that wasn't easy; he was in a *mood*. I realized the color of his walls had darkened to gray, something almost like battleship metal.

Relax, I told him. *Worst comes to worst, Bea and I got this robot shit locked. He can't kill me. I'm unkillable.*

Zara. My name sounded like a reproach. *You already died once and were revived!*

Point is, I came back. No, seriously. Look at what we've survived together. We got this, Nadim. All of us. Together.

He seemed slightly reassured. Once I was sure Nadim would be okay, I crept away to check on Xyll. EMITU had treated Xyll as best he could, but I'd promised to visit. After the way Xyll went after me, it took several tries for me to get my nerve up to open the door to its quarters.

It was still just a wriggly column, more like a serpent with limbs than the mature Phage that had snuck on board. Xyll didn't approach me. I stayed by the door.

"Why did you attack me?"

"No. I—" Xyll hesitated. "Response to injury triggered _____." The word just came through as random static noise. Xyll had stumped the translator.

"Triggered what?"

Xyll tried again. "Regression of life cycle. When one receives grievous injury, parts are sacrificed to preserve life."

"So you're . . . less developed now? Like you reverted to a larval stage because you were hurt so bad?" That was amazing. Seemed like every alien we encountered had a better bio-design than humans. "Will you be okay?"

"Am . . . struggling," Xyll said.

"Because regrowing body parts is hard? Or . . . ?" It was a leading question, and I had no idea what I'd do if Xyll listed a bunch of stuff it required that I couldn't easily provide.

"Painful. Should have others with me, help with _____." Yeah, the translation matrix had no idea, either. "But I am alone."

That caught me. It sounded sad. And desperate. Maybe that was why it had come at me, out of the instinctive need for comfort, for help.

Still terrifying.

"I'll see what EMITU can do. He might be able to mix up some medicine that will work as an analgesic." I wasn't too sure since EMITU wasn't keen on being a med bot anymore, but I'd try, at least.

It seemed morally wrong to let Xyll get jacked up fighting to defend us, then leave it to suffer alone without attempting to mitigate the harm. Sighing, I activated the comm via my handheld. "EMITU, could you please figure out some painkillers for Xyll?"

"Fine, Zara. You lot would be lost without me."

From the *Bruqvisz's Official Guide to Threats*, 11,209th edition (bootleg version with added commentary by unknown human user)

. . . but beware, Bold Traveler, lest you think all species are as expansive and welcoming as the Bruqvisz. [111111111 what the hell1111111]

Many species you may encounter hold hidden harms and secret deceptions. The Oborub vary from polite and calm to murderous and full of stinging poison, and may change instantly if cultural touchstones are not observed. Please to purchase separate Guide to Oborub Customs module if intending to interact with the species in even the mildest of ways, for so much as inappropriate glance toward tentacles may result in immediate murder. [Oh that explains things. Sorry, Tad. No, I'm not buying that module. Might pirate.]

CONTEXTUAL WARNING: Also be aware that penalty for piracy of Bruqvisz modules of cultural learning series and threat editions are punishable by immediate killing, with regrets to be sent to any listed emergency contacts. We don't make the laws. Take it up with the Oborub. Remember not to look at tentacles too long. Good luck.

[Shit.]

CHAPTER ELEVEN

Lost Lifekiller

"I STILL DON'T understand how it's possible for Lifekiller to be off the grid for so long," I muttered.

We had been tailing the Phage for a while, but we weren't gaining on them as fast as we needed to; we couldn't, if we intended to keep enough energy in reserve for a fight once we found our real enemy. No more fuel stops, no more leisurely circling stars. So Nadim and Typhon found a good cruising speed, and we trusted that it would be fast enough to keep us in the game.

Chao-Xing was antsy about our failure to lock the menace down, after what had nearly happened at Greenheld, and I shared her misgivings. There had to be a reason why the god-king was quiet, and whatever it was, it would *not* be good for us when the storm broke.

"God-king possibly in stasis," said Starcurrent. "As before."

"What?" That was the first I'd heard of that possibility.

"Don't know this? Hibernation, better? Anything that expends energy must also rest. Is not sleep, like humans do."

"So the god-king might have found a hiding spot, somewhere that could mask his presence, and hunkered down for a nap? What about the Phage? Why are they rushing for Lifekiller if he's not actively wreaking havoc right now?"

Starcurrent's tentacles flowed in a slow circle. "Unsure. Worship? Watch?"

Okay, that made sense. If the god-king was dormant—and maybe vulnerable—he needed an army to guard his back. When the Phage stopped moving, we'd have him tracked down. Hopefully. I did wonder if this pause in Lifekiller's murder spree heralded a development of some kind, the way caterpillars went into chrysalides, and when they emerged, it was in a new form.

I did *not* want to see what Lifekiller was trying to turn into after devouring several planets and chowing down on uranium. That said, maybe this was our lucky break. This could give us the time we desperately needed to take care of the two cousin Leviathan still chasing us, just like we were speeding after the Phage. We couldn't be in two places at once, and we didn't need to be, either.

I had an idea, and to make this work, we had to split up. The pieces of a plan were coming together, slowly. Bea and Nadim were going to hate it.

I stood. "Thanks for the talk, Starcurrent. You are seriously better than a thousand hours of reading the Lizard Guide to the Galaxy or whatever file Suncross sent over when we first started traveling together."

"The Bruqvisz are legendary storytellers," Starcurrent said, but the pleased flush of zis tentacles displayed zis happiness. "My people sing."

"Well, you're a font of information as well."

I really didn't know how to bring up this suggestion, and before I had the chance, klaxons sounded in the docking bay.

"Nadim? What's happening?"

"The drones are active. All of them came online and they're ready to deploy. If I don't open the way, they will harm me in exiting."

"Do it! Let them go!"

I stopped shy of the outer doors and peered into the docking area. Holy shit, the crates had all burst open and the space was full, drones barely able to move, hovering above, scraping the Hopper. As I watched, Nadim opened and the drones zoomed out, leaving only the detritus of the containers that had housed them.

Bea came running up in time to catch the tail end of the departure. "Are we under attack?" she demanded.

"For once, no. But I have no idea why the drones suddenly bailed on us."

Nadim said, "Suncross is calling, urgent code. Perhaps he knows?"

Bea grabbed my wrist and practically dragged me to Ops, but she didn't need to. I was running on my own. I tapped to accept the comm request, and Suncross appeared on-screen, grainy but recognizable. "We have word from the Sliver, Zeerakull!"

Of all the news, I wasn't expecting to hear that. "What now?"

"The Phage are attacking the Sliver. Bacia commands that we render immediate aid."

"Screw that," I muttered. "They can't command me to do a damn thing."

But it certainly explained why our drones had suddenly taken off on us. Bacia needed them bad. I briefly wondered if that meant the ones we'd traded to the Elaszi had also deserted; if they had, we'd have hell to pay for it, probably. Well, I couldn't help that now.

Was this attack a leftover imperative from the last time the god-king had ordered the Sliver's destruction? Or just a feint, to keep us busy? He'd been super pissed to wake up there, subject to Bacia's whims . . . or did he see them as a genuine rival? Bacia was one of the most powerful beings I'd encountered in the black, so I could understand if that was the deal. Lifekiller would want no rivals.

"We're too far to get there in time," Bea added. "I mean, if we were going."

Technically speaking, Bacia started this whole thing when they insisted on us robbing that tomb, and here we were with the whole damn galaxy in peril. If they couldn't protect their outpost, they'd have to abandon the station. I was sure they had a backup plan and a ship fast and tough enough to outrun the threat.

"Zara, there are a lot of lives at stake," Nadim said. He sounded worried.

Time for me to be the bad cop. "We can't save everyone. That's a *fact*. And the Sliver is full of crims and outlaws who are fully capable of fighting Phage on their own. If we double back to help, Lifekiller could go on another rampage, and likely it'll be innocent civilians at risk. We have to end him while we still can. Let Bacia take care of their own. That's why they collected all those damn taxes."

"I agree," Bea said.

"Suncross?"

The lizard showed four open palms. Suncross's guys were standing behind him, and they seemed to be playing a drinking game. Did these lizards ever stop celebrating? "We work for you, Zeerakull. Bacia cannot command us. They have access to our communication network, so they sent this demand, but we are not obligated to heed them."

A frisson of discomfort filtered from Nadim, but he said, "I feel guilt over this choice, but . . . I agree. We should not go."

"And Typhon?"

Nadim's tone made it clear it wasn't even a question. "He is not going, either."

"Okay, we're all on the same page."

Bea was nodding, a scowl knitting together her perfect brows. Man, I needed to get her to teach me about eyebrows. And—I needed to focus on her words, not how *all* her features were ridiculously cute.

"What is it, Beatriz?" Nadim made her name sound like an endearment too, and I didn't mind. God, I loved them both.

"Doesn't this mean that the drones we gave the Elaszi will take off too? In that case—"

"The blobs will think we cheated them on purpose," I finished. "And come gunning for us, not Bacia. Not much we can do about it. That was some next-level double dealing. If I wasn't so mad at Bacia, I'd admire the hell out of them."

Bea brushed back her hair in a furious gesture. "They tricked and defrauded us! What's to admire about that?"

"I mean, they paid us . . . then when they needed the goods back, the drones returned without them lifting a finger. It's the perfect con." And potentially deadly, if we had to go up against the main Phage swarm again without our drones. Now we had to worry about Derry and the traitorous cousins, the return of the Elaszi, and oh, hunt down the god-king. No problem, right?

"Zara!" Bea tried to look stern, but I gave her my best smile, and she beamed back at me. *Good to know she can't keep a straight face if I ever make her mad for real.* Then she went back to technical issues because that was where her head stayed. "But then how did Bacia get the signal to the drones?"

An excellent question. "Nadim, you said there was no emergency broadcast system."

"Maybe because of us," said Suncross. "Our people communicate across this galaxy and beyond. Our communications relay is enviably excellent, quite compatible with other types of tech as well."

"You're saying Bacia bounced the signal on Bruqvisz relays, and since your ship was near ours, the drones activated?"

"Possible," the lizard said.

That probably meant the drones we'd given the Elaszi

would stay put until they passed a lizard relay. That might buy us some time. Well, no point fretting about what couldn't be helped. Spilled milk, barn door, and whatever else. Bacia had probably counted on it, since they knew Suncross was working with us. I hadn't even considered this possibility, or I would've had Bea go over our cargo with a fine-tooth comb. She was pacing, still caught up in the technological aspects of us being fooled.

"So . . . your people do have communications relay? Are they satellites?"

"Not exactly. You wouldn't understand, little singer. Even I don't." Oh, this lizard did *not* just throw that at Bea. Before I could pick that bone, he added, "Pointless to talk more when there is drinking to do. Call if anything changes."

Almost as soon as the connection dropped, I had Chao-Xing on the screen. "What's happening over there? I detected a pulse of sudden energy emissions, and your drones—"

"Yeah, about that." I cut into her questions and provided a succinct explanation that resulted in Chao-Xing cussing in Mandarin. She'd set our translation matrix to ignore these outbursts, but I'd studied enough on my own to get the gist, and she was calling Bacia "mixed eggs" and cursing their ancestors back to the eighteenth generation.

"If we didn't already have too many situations to handle, I would blow up the Sliver myself," Chao-Xing snarled. "Treacherous pit of criminals. I should have known they wouldn't deal with us fairly."

Dang, she didn't take kindly to being cheated. Never thought I'd say this, but, "Rein it in. We have bigger enemies to fight." Even though they'd tricked us, I probably wouldn't even call Bacia an enemy. Not a friend either, of course.

"That is indisputable," Nadim said. "Lifekiller must be our focus."

Chao-Xing let out a sigh as Marko and Yusuf stepped up behind her. I glanced at their faces, wondering why they looked so grim. Given our issues, they had reason, but what was bothering them now? We had a grocery list of problems.

Marko scraped a palm across his jaw, which was covered in the start of a decent beard. "It's not that I like Bacia or anybody on the Sliver, but it's hard to turn your back on someone who's waving their arms and shouting 'Save me.'"

"It's not the same," I said.

Yusuf wore a serious expression. "You chose to save Starcurrent and me when we were drifting and near death. We are choosing *not* to save the Sliver. It is the same as letting those people die."

I could have argued. Said that some would probably escape, but that was specious bullshit and I knew it. Even saying we were too far—that was a defensive rationalization as well. Somber awareness dropped on me like a veil, and I had to acknowledge their point.

"Fair enough. But like Chao-Xing said, this is wartime, and there's this thing called triage. Field docs prioritize who gets treatment first based on which patients have the best odds of surviving. We're doing the same thing. It doesn't make sense to stop hunting Lifekiller to change course when we're so far out. We can't be Bacia's only allies . . ." I held up my hand to forestall Marko when he opened his mouth. "And *if* we are, then they've lived their life wrong and we can't help that."

Chao-Xing nodded at that. "Also, I'm pointing out—based on past interaction with Bacia—it seems likely that they sent out multiple calls for aid."

"That's for sure," Bea muttered. Girl was still bitter about us losing the drones.

Me too, to a lesser degree, and I did worry what we'd do if we got into it with the Phage and didn't have enough firepower to take them out. I couldn't spare too much mental energy for bombs that hadn't exploded yet, though. We were between a swarm of killer bees and a pack of wolves. Not the time to ask us for help.

"You wanted me to absorb the gravity of the decision,

in case it turns out we *were* their only hope," I said. "But we're agreed: it's a no to helping Bacia. Is that the gist?"

Yusuf nodded as Marko said, "Exactly. It will burden my conscience but I'm willing to carry it because we're needed desperately elsewhere."

A scoffing sound came from Chao-Xing. "As far as I'm concerned, Bacia got enough aid from us when they stole our drones."

"Same," Bea muttered.

"I see that you've failed to consult the mechanical component of the crew," EMITU said. "As usual." The robot was taking a tone.

Damn, I'm tired. "Did you think we should go save the Sliver?"

"No, I don't care about any of them. But it's nice to be asked!"

I glanced at Jury, moving toward the console. "How about you?"

The smooth robot voice assured me, "I agree that we should not divert course. It would be highly illogical."

I didn't *quite* grin. "Still going to kill me?"

"Not today. Perhaps tomorrow."

"Great. All in favor, motion carried. We're rolling on."

We signed off after that, and the robots went about robot business. EMITU was explaining kitten holos to Jury, so that would probably end somewhere fun. Starcurrent hadn't turned up for the confab, and that was just as well. Ze tended to be the most compassionate among us, and ze was already feeling bad about Greenheld.

Bea touched my shoulder lightly. "Whew, it's been a day. Or longer? The passage of time is so confusing in space. I'm ready for a nap. You good?"

"More or less. I need to talk to the lizards again."

She kissed my cheek and headed out of Ops. Nadim was always with me, but his mood felt grave and heavy. "Did Marko and Yusuf make you feel worse?" I asked.

"No. But it is difficult for me to ignore anyone in need. Even Bacia." He sounded wistful, and I remembered how bright and pure he was when I first came on board. Thanks to Nadim, I was softer, but he'd gotten harder, and I regretted the loss of his innocence.

"Understood. We can spend a little quiet time together after I take care of something. Is that okay?"

He responded with a flare of color, soft pink like the petals of a rose. "I would like that, Zara. It feels like forever since . . ."

I got what he meant, even if he couldn't put it into words. We had been running full-out for so long that we'd lost some of the joy in just being together. Saving the universe wouldn't matter a damn if we lost ourselves along the way.

Now that I had the promise of something brighter than

another disaster in the near future, I cheered up as I contacted Suncross's ship. "We've talked about it, and we're not going. I called to ask you to send a reply."

"What is the message?" This was Ghostwalk, not Suncross. I could see their fearless leader lolling in the background, downing engine cleaner like there was no tomorrow. There probably wouldn't be any sense coming from him for a while.

"Are you the designated driver?"

Ghostwalk was more serious than Suncross, less jovial. "Your meaning is unclear."

If you had to explain your humor, you never got a laugh. "Never mind. Tell Bacia that they got backup when our drones went rogue and that we wish them well." The last bit might have been a stretch, but burning bridges never achieved anything.

"Understood, Zeerakull. We go toward glory!"

"Uh, sure. Glory and waffles. Don't bother me with the response, if there is one. Ignore anything Bacia has to say from now on."

"I hear and obey." Ghostwalk tapped out of the conversation as a chant started in the background.

"Good talk," I mumbled.

In a way, this might be my last chance to be with Nadim for a while. After I told everyone about my genius plan, there would be fighting, but in the end, they'd all agree that this was the best path. If I didn't want to ruin the moment, though, I had to keep this from Nadim until I was ready to break the news. Our quiet time would be neither quiet nor peaceful if he figured out what I had in mind.

I didn't like keeping secrets from him, but it wasn't like I'd *never* tell him. Just . . . I wanted to enjoy being with him first. This shouldn't be a forever farewell, just a temporary separation, but I already knew how he would react. Squaring my shoulders, I carefully boxed up my conviction and hid it in the darkest corner of my mind.

"Nadim?" I said his name softly.

"What would you like to do, Zara?"

"Let's fly together. Give me a minute to get comfortable." I quickened my step, hustling to my room so I could settle on the floor, bare hands, bare feet, and a blanket to pull on top of me. "Lights down, door set to 'no visitors.'"

The room responded to my request and I closed my eyes. Becoming Zadim felt like coming home as our senses blended and spun outward. No enemies in range, no imminent violence to dread, only the sweet rush through the black and the vivid pulse of distant stars. We heard the traitorous cousins singing and understood their pledge to hunt us down, but we didn't respond. They had lost the right to share our harmony.

Bare black around us, sparking to life with other colors, light beyond hue. We sailed past systems made of cosmic dust and nascent planets bonded together with little more than gas and starlight, traces of broken comets caught in the pull. Wonders old and new brightened our senses, and everything became a marvel because we were together.

We blazed past quasars and spangled nebulas, and all the stars sang. They serenaded our progress, the most enchanting music we'd ever heard. Gravity wells and black holes, empty systems and ancient, mournful hypernovas, keening their own slow fade from existence. We danced at the edge of a red supergiant, the heat burnishing our armor, and it was a fire that burned only for us, brilliant and exquisite. Playful, bounding, turn of tail and outward roll. Bea stirred when we got too energetic, and it was all glorious, but eventually we split, falling, empty, reaching—

I dropped into my tired body, weary but gratified. "That was fun."

"It was. Are you all right?" His concern never failed to warm me. "Did we stay together too long?"

"I'm okay. But I never get used to that . . . break." It was starting to hurt. Each time, I wanted to stay longer and give more. During those moments, our real-life problems lost urgency. I hadn't thought about what lay ahead at all while we were bonded. I'd just . . . *lived.*

"I feel it too," Nadim admitted. "Zara, are you keeping something from me?"

Shit, he noticed? I shouldn't be surprised. That knowing

could be both a blessing and a curse, a double-edged sword that could slice into my determination to clean up my own mess. I took my time answering, trying to cover my uncertainty with a luxurious stretch.

Maybe I should tell him first? Before the others. The last time we fought, it was because I decided something on my own and cut him out of the loop. Down in the temple of doom, I judged myself expendable and blocked Nadim off. After that, I'd promised to treat him like a partner, not somebody I had to protect. At this point I had to admit that my reluctance didn't come from the same pure place. I was just avoiding a tetchy subject.

Time to come clean.

"You could say that. I have something to tell you and you won't like it."

"I'm listening, Zara."

"How much do you know about my past?" I knew he'd read the file the program provided on me, and he'd gotten a lot from our bond, but I wasn't sure if facts filtered through as much as feelings and impressions. I certainly didn't hold on to concrete memories that belonged to him when we broke apart, and I guessed it might be the same for him.

"I'm not sure what you're asking."

"Then I'll start from the beginning. My family had . . . problems, mostly because of my dad. If it seems like I'm going a long way back, it's because I want you to understand everything."

Nadim lit the floor beneath my fingers. "Please go on."

"My health problems were in the file, I'm sure. And I was a difficult kid. I ran away a lot, after treatment, and I gave my mom a hard time. Eventually, I met up with Derry."

Nadim growled.

"I know. But back then, he seemed better than home, more exciting, or hell if I know what. My mother warned me away from Derry, but that only made me want him more. You couldn't tell me anything then, and I just had this need for . . . for *space*. For escape. We ran wild as stray cats in the Zone together. He watched my back, and I was good at scoring stuff. Chem, goods, you name it. Looking back, I can't believe I made it out in one piece."

"You're right," Nadim said. "I don't like any of this at all."

Crap, and I hadn't even gotten to the rough part yet. Surely Nadim wasn't jealous; that didn't seem in character for him. "What's bothering you in particular? I hope it's not Derry, because—"

"Not that. While it is . . . strange to hear about your life with him before we met, more than that, it hurts to hear that you felt so alone that you chose to be with one who did not cherish you, who hurt you, and now *hunts* you."

Anger sizzled in his normally gentle voice.

"I'm getting to that. One day, I snatched a purse from somebody I shouldn't have. And that started this whole chain of events where I pissed off a major criminal named Deluca, who thinks I messed with his supply chain. That should have landed on Derry too, but he has a way of skating no matter what. I thought I'd escaped when I got tapped as an Honor, but it's followed me out here and it nearly took out everyone I love in one shot." I still heard that merciless countdown in my head. If Xyll hadn't appeared, and EMITU hadn't rushed to the rescue . . . we'd be dust and wreckage, drifting and dead. All of us.

"Derry mentioned someone called Deluca when he was threatening you."

"Yeah, it's a problem. Deluca is very rich, very powerful." I elaborated on how the asshole had gotten into the big-deal Honors party, solely to threaten me.

"I hate feeling helpless, knowing you've been harmed and there is no way for me to punish the culprit. Never have I wished that I could leave the stars until this moment, but for you, I would take on human skin and gladly smash that monster with . . ." Nadim paused. "Both appendages!"

Okay, that shouldn't be so cute. He was so mad he'd forgotten my people had hands. "You want to protect me, I get it. I feel the same about you, which is why I hid this for a bit, after I made up my mind."

"You wanted to give me something sweet before the bitter." Nadim sounded faintly sorrowful, enough that I almost couldn't say the rest.

I had to, in order to keep my promise to treat him like a partner. Nadim first, then we'd tell Bea together. The others I'd inform as a group.

"That wasn't just for you. I needed something for myself too. You know I love you, right?" I probably didn't say that enough. "But you also must know I have to take care of this. We can't afford to fight on multiple fronts, and if Derry's Leviathan jump us as we engage the god-king, it would be a disaster. This started with me and it ends with me."

"What do you plan to do?" he asked quietly.

Mustering all my courage, I told him.

INTERLUDE: DERRY

We're making good time. I hate being alone on this fucking ghost ship. It hates me; I can feel it coming out of the walls, and it eats at my head. I wonder if it gets in my dreams. If I could've said no to this mission, I would have. I wish I wasn't on one of these freaky, creepy monster ships. Give me plain mechs any day.

Deluca's orders keep on coming. Now he wants me to vid her death, which means tinkering with that hulking robot he gave me. I'm no slicer; I can't do this kind of shit well, but I can't exactly tell the boss, now can I? I think I got it. Hope my patch holds, and it doesn't make him fucked up in some other way. Last thing I need is to go hand to hand with Zara. It's bad enough coming out here on his orders to do this much; I don't want to have to kill her my own self.

When I'm sober, which isn't often—what the hell else is there to do out here on board a ship that hates me?—I remember none of this is really her damn fault. But mostly I feel like if she'd stayed loyal, done right by me, stayed where she belonged, we'd both be fine. Instead I had to get cleaned up and polish the devil's boots and pretend I liked it just so I could survive.

And now, this shit.

I hate it. Maybe once it's done, I can crawl back to the Zone, back where I belong, and just be done.

Sorry, Z.

But it's you or me, and I pick me. That's how it is.

CHAPTER TWELVE

Lost Chances

TO SAY NADIM didn't like it was a vast understatement. I felt the shock, the sad blues of disappointment, the crimson streaks of anger. Those feelings lived in me too.

"No," he said. It sounded unyielding. "Zara, you cannot do this. I won't be able to protect you!"

"Sweetheart, I'm not here to receive your protection. I'm your *partner*. We agreed on that, right?"

"Yes." Grudging, but at least it was agreement.

"You admit that I'm capable of fighting on my own?" If I told anyone my *real* plan, it might not work. For this to be effective, everyone had to believe I was doing the noble thing, even Nadim. There had to be real fear and devastating grief. Jury probably had the ability to read the physiological signs of human emotions, even if he didn't feel them. Likewise, he could probably also sense when people were trying to fool him. I had to sell this completely or everything might blow up in my face.

"I know. But—Zara. I don't like it. Please don't do this. You'll be *away*." His anguish gouged me like the sharpest blade.

"I have to go." *Have to stay strong.*

I wished I could take Nadim, but the remote camera Bea and I jury-rigged had limited range. It seemed cruel to bring him partway when we both knew that he couldn't stay. Also, and this was the larger issue, I was scared he might be distracted at a critical moment if his attention was split. I couldn't risk everyone else getting hurt—or maybe even dying—because Nadim was looking too long at me. No, it was better to say good-bye now and hope it wouldn't be forever.

Nadim made a sound of protest, but I went on. "You need to promise me something, and this is *not* negotiable: you need to promise me that you won't come charging after me, no matter what happens. If this doesn't work, then I've gambled and lost. But you will have Bea, and you will *live*. Understand?"

He didn't. Well, he didn't *want* to understand, to be

more accurate; Nadim was smart, and he understood that at a certain point this was necessary. He understood too that there was always a risk of death, whether we were together or separate.

But he also felt what I did: I didn't *want* to leave him; I *had* to leave him if we were going to have anything like a winnable war against Lifekiller. And we had to win. We opened Pandora's box back in that tomb; we had the deaths of entire planets on our consciences now. No matter the cost, we had to *win*.

"I can't lose you and go on," Nadim whispered. "I only just found you. We only just found each other."

"I know," I whispered back, and turned my head to kiss the skin of the wall. Hot pink rays shot out from the place I'd pressed my lips. "But we're warriors right now. We can be something else when this is done. But right now, we've got to *fight*. And I know you can. You're so strong, Nadim. Stronger than I am, in some ways."

"Not without you."

"Yes. You've got Bea. She'll see you through this." *And what do I have?* I really didn't want to analyze that too deeply. Because no matter what, Derry was my problem to fix.

And I had to go do that. Alone.

Well. Almost.

I slept like a corpse, no dreams, and when I woke, I felt refreshed but heavy, like I'd swallowed lead. That was a whole load of anxiety in the pit of my stomach. I buried it under a quick breakfast and Starcurrent found me as I was raiding the weapons locker.

Ze looked stronger than in recent days. Maybe the grief of being exiled was wearing off a little. Maybe. "You are expecting trouble," ze said, and the color wheel I'd memorized told me the flashes of silver through zis extremities meant ze was worried. Well, hell, that was a permanent state for us right now. "What comes?"

"Nothing's coming," I said, and shut the locker as I found a place to conceal the small but powerful stunner I'd grabbed. It fit nicely in the small of my back, under the uniform jacket. I also had a knife up my sleeve. It wasn't exactly an armory, but I was hoping I wouldn't need even that much if things went right. *When do they ever?*

"Then why weapons, Zara? Is there danger from the Phage?" Starcurrent shuddered lightly in all tentacles. "The creature is not contained?"

"Xyll's doing whatever it is Phage do when they're wounded," I said. "EMITU is treating it for the pain. Apparently, it went back to a transitional stage to grow back its lost limb faster. Not sure how long that will take, but we've got it under tight security just in case. There's no trouble on board. I promise."

"Zara." Starcurrent got squarely in my path. "You are not being honest. Why?"

I sighed. "Because I need to talk to Bea first. I promise, you and EMITU will be next on the list. I'll save Jury for last." For reasons. Good ones, starting with the fact that he'd spent all night reviewing our travel record, deep-diving into everything I'd done since leaving Earth. At least he did his due diligence. Couldn't be fairer than that. "Half an hour, and I'll update you. Okay?"

Starcurrent didn't like it, but ze didn't object as much as I'd feared, and when I knocked quietly on Bea's door, it slid open. Her hair was wet, and she was detangling it. Without a word, I began doing it for her, careful with her springy curls. She made a wordless sound of pleasure deep in her throat and closed her eyes, and I had to take a minute before I said, "I need to tell you something."

That got her eyes open again, and she looked at me in the mirror. I kept working on her hair. "What? Zara, what are you doing?"

"Not so much what I'm doing as what I'm about to," I said, and took a deep breath. She swiveled around in her chair to face me. Bea kept a neat cabin—neater than mine; I was bad about putting my shit away—and I was caught by the holo playing silently on her wall. Her family, waving good-bye to her during the Honors send-off. A smiling old grandmother who sang opera prominent right in front. Bea had lost so much, being here. I had to make it right for her, if not for myself. "I'm going to give myself up."

"You're *what*?" She let out a breathless, disbelieving laugh—not amusement, just shock. "You can't do that!" Then she realized what I was talking about, and her momentary humor died.

"Bea, we can't go after Lifekiller with Derry and his crew on our asses," I said. "You know that. And I'm the only thing they really want. You . . . when they sentenced you it was just to make my criminal charges look good. They don't need you. This is about me, Derry, and Deluca, nothing else. Deluca wants me dead, and he's willing to fuck with the entire Honors program to do it. I admit it, I was stupid enough to think he had limits, or that the Honors people were incorruptible. I should have known better on both counts. He'll keep coming until I stop him, and whatever grudge Derry's got, he'll keep coming too."

"Fine, we stop them!" Bea said. "But giving yourself up . . ."

"Listen to me, okay? This is real. We just lost our drones to Bacia, no backup coming. We're alone: Nadim and us, Typhon and his crew, Suncross and his boys. That's the army. We *can't* split our Leviathan up; they can protect each other, but on their own they're vulnerable.

And eventually, those other two Leviathan are going to catch up, probably at the worst possible moment. I can stop that. I have to."

"You can't just . . . just *go*!" Bea looked panicked. Stricken. She reached out and cupped my face in her hands. Her skin had chilled. I could feel her trembling. "Zara, you can't leave us. How do I ever—how do *we*—do this without you?"

"Honey, you're strong. You're smart. You and Nadim have a strong bond. You've got Starcurrent and EMITU—"

"And a Phage that's gone off the rails, and a robot I don't trust, and—"

"Stop." I kissed her. It tasted sweet. It also tasted like tears and good-byes. "You got this. I trust you. Trust me?"

She didn't want to, but she nodded. Gasped back tears. "What are you going to do?"

"Take Jury over to Suncross's ship," I said. "If I can get Chao-Xing to come with, that's my best case. If not, I do this alone."

"Derry will kill you, even if the robot doesn't."

"Maybe," I admitted. I couldn't promise it wouldn't happen; it was an embedded risk. "Depends on what Jury decides, I think. But hey, if I have Warbitch with me, I'm upgraded on odds, right?"

"You're doing this whether I like it or not, aren't you?"

I nodded. I didn't want to lie to her, as much as I ached

to comfort her. And she let the tears flow this time and threw herself into my arms. I felt warm and safe and almost whole in her embrace . . . and then Nadim filled the empty spaces, and it was *perfect*. How could I leave them now?

But I didn't have a choice. So I kissed her fiercely. "I love you." Then I pulled away. It was a colder universe when I stepped out her door, and despite Nadim's hovering presence I still felt like I was untethered. Floating. Lost.

Zara, you don't have to do this, he said silently.

I really do, though.

I found Jury back where I'd left him the night before: standing at the comms station. Motionless. But as I approached, the blank dome of his head swiveled around, and blue eyes caught fire.

"So," I said. "Let me make a call, okay?"

"Do you not wish to know my decision?"

"Not yet. Call first."

He stepped aside, but not far. Didn't bode well for what conclusion he'd drawn.

I called Chao-Xing. The connection wasn't great, and it looked like I'd gotten her out of bed. She was in silky pajamas. Somehow, I'd never quite pictured her in anything but a buttoned-up uniform. I was not prepared. "Uh, sorry to wake you," I said.

She impatiently waved that off. "What is it?"

"I want you to go with me to Derry's Leviathan," I said. "We take Suncross's ship. Our Leviathan keep going."

That woke her completely up. Her whole posture changed. "Are you insane?"

"Probably," I said. "But I want you to hand me over. Make a deal that if they get me, they'll break off their pursuit and take me back to Earth. We can't get into a Leviathan fight right now. And that's inevitable if we don't do this. Now. If Starcurrent is right, Lifekiller could be holed up changing into something even worse. Even more powerful. Our odds are bad enough. We can't afford to let my problems get in the way." I took a deep breath. "Look, we already lost our drones, and there's no way Bacia will give them back unless they win decisively against the Phage they're fighting. We can't count on that. This is the only play we've got to improve our odds. We've got to take it."

"Even if it kills you."

"Derry's not going to kill me," I said. It was a flat-out lie; I didn't believe it, but I sounded confident. Too confident, maybe. "Deluca wants to do that his own damn self. Or at least watch it happen. So anyway, I'll have time. You know me. I'm resourceful."

"I'm not leaving you there on your own. I refuse."

"Chao-Xing." I put all I had into calling her by her name, and it got her attention. I wasn't usually this gentle. "This isn't about our feelings. This is about winning. And we both know there's got to be losses in this kind of war. Okay? So let me do this."

She hated it, I could see that, but she finally, tersely nodded. "When?"

"Now," I said. "I'll update Starcurrent and EMITU, then we'll ask Suncross to pick us up. You tell Typhon and your crew."

"Doubt they'll be happy about this either."

I didn't know if she meant her crew, mine, or the lizards. However she meant it, she'd be right.

I cut the connection and turned to Jury. He'd taken in the whole conversation, but he didn't say anything. "I'm surrendering myself to your custody," I said. "You got handcuffs?"

"Unnecessary," Jury said. "I will not let you escape." I didn't know what he was thinking, but in this moment it didn't matter.

I sighed and hit the internal comms. "Starcurrent, EMITU, I need you here. Got something to tell you."

Ze didn't like my plan *at all*, and argued strongly against it, but Bea shushed zim. She'd shown up, red-eyed and quiet, but armored inside. She supported what I was doing with calm strength.

I didn't need to persuade EMITU. He twirled a bunch of extensors and said, "You interrupted me to tell me this? Go on, then. Sacrifice yourself. See if I care." He did that sniffing thing again, which he must have thought made him sound superior.

"Aww, don't cry," I told him.

"I wasn't—" he sputtered. All his extensors stilled. "You will come back, Zara?"

"What, not *Wanted Felon*?"

EMITU said, as quietly as he could, "Please come back." Then he ramped up the volume and perked up his extensors again. "Don't waste my time coming back injured! I have written a haiku to inspire you: 'Chilly eventide / How a human, hot blood gains / in spite of the stars.'"

"It's a good one," I said. "Thanks. I'll remember it. You take care of Bea and Starcurrent. And Xyll. Uh, you might want to have some last-ditch plans if the Xyll situation gets worse."

"I am a physician, not an exterminator!"

"I thought you were a poet."

"In my spare time!" EMITU spun toward Jury. "You will look after her?"

"She is my prisoner," Jury said, "and therefore in my care."

The med bot paused as if he had a vital inquiry. "Did you like the kitten holos?"

"Educational," Jury said. I thought he was just being polite, but how could I tell? "Good-bye, EMITU."

"Good-bye, Jury. Would you also like a haiku?"

"I have not acquired the appreciation." Jury hesitated. "Yet."

"Progress," EMITU sighed. "At last. Farewell, Zara. Don't get dismembered."

He zipped off back to Medbay. I wasn't sure whether I felt reassured or horrified. Maybe both.

Bea broke her near-military restraint long enough to hug me, and then walked away with her back straight. Starcurrent had turned into mournful, troubled colors, translucent toward the tips. I had no trouble at all interpreting that.

"It's okay," I told zim. "Just look after Nadim."

Nadim was silent. He hadn't withdrawn from me, thankfully; I could feel him there, just at the edges of my consciousness. Troubled, like Starcurrent. But like Bea, resolute. He was trying. I was trying. We all were.

But it felt like good-bye, and now that it was here, I didn't want it, not at all. I wanted to run and bury myself in the bond and sing with the stars and run and run and run until we ran out of universe.

I know, he whispered. *I do too. But at what cost?*

At the cost of everything. Everyone. And neither of us, no matter how much we wanted to, could ignore that and be wholly, cruelly selfish.

I love you, I told him simply, and his emotion rolled over me, so strong I had to bow my head and just breathe to stand against it. When it receded, I walked away and down the hallway. No flashes of color lit my way this time. Nadim's walls had turned mournful dove gray, and his silence haunted me. Jury walked behind, like the judge and executioner he might become.

I called the lizards to let them know I was coming over. Ghostwalk answered the call and agreed to collect the three of us: Jury, Chao-Xing, and me.

With a heavy heart, I suited up, as I had before. Back then, I was all anticipation, pumped at going on a mining mission with Suncross. On Typhon, Chao-Xing must be getting ready as well. Jury stopped me when I started to grab the boost pack.

"No need. I have this capacity built in."

Of course he did. Why wouldn't a bounty-hunting killer robot have rocket boots in case he needed them to hunt down a fugitive? I slipped onto Nadim's armor silently with Jury, and he took me out farther, where we drifted toward Chao-Xing, already waiting for the lizards to scoop us up in their net.

Then it was too late to turn back.

The farther I went from Nadim, the less I could feel his presence, and by the time the lizards hauled us in, he was only an echo of warmth, quietly mourning. I scrambled out of the netting and noted that only Ghostwalk seemed sober. Chao-Xing looked elegant and deadly, even climbing out of a salvage net.

"How'd they take things?" I asked her.

"About as well as you might expect," she said. "Marko's angry. Yusuf thinks you've got a point. Typhon . . . well. He's Typhon."

"Sorry about pulling you into this, but I thought you'd stand the best chance of getting out alive," I said.

Chao-Xing cast a long, appraising look at Jury. The robot's blue eyes seemed focused on the middle distance between us, but I had no doubt he was listening. "Have you asked it what it plans to do?"

"I'm letting him come to his own conclusions," I said. "Hey, Jury. Have you made up your mind about me yet?"

"Apologies, Zara. I am still gathering intelligence. It would be premature for me to give information when I remain undecided. Rest assured, I will ensure your safety until I reach a conclusion regarding the most judicious course."

"You seriously aren't going to come up with a plan to destroy this thing?" Chao-Xing asked me, pitching her voice low. "Because I will if you won't."

Quickly I shook my head. "Don't antagonize him." Louder, I said, "Jury, don't worry about what anybody else thinks. This is between you and me, and I'm leaving it in your hands. You decide. Do what you think is right."

"You do not plan to plead for clemency? Or mitigation?" Jury seemed a little surprised, maybe.

I shrugged. "Look, you've read the records. Whatever I did, I did it for reasons I thought were important at the time. I admit I jacked Deluca's daughter's purse. But that was survival in the streets for the Zone. And Deluca was running chem. You know all this already. So I've got nothing to add."

I was putting it all out there, and rolling dice, and it felt . . . good. Free. I wasn't afraid, and maybe that was stupid, but I liked this plan.

It might end with me dead and Derry laughing, but the game was the game.

Ghostwalk clearly was the designated driver. He'd pulled us in, and now he was leading us back to the central hub, where the rest of the crew was sprawled out. Suncross lay slumped in a corner. Maybe he wasn't drunk, just asleep in an awkward spot. I wasn't going to get all judgy about it. I'd slept worse places.

"Looks like you had a hell of a party. Well, let's get going."

"Why?" To his credit, Ghostwalk wasn't a sucker. "Why are you here?"

"Full disclosure? We want you to take us somewhere. And since we paid you—"

"Yes, Zeerakull, you paid us," Ghostwalk acknowledged.

For a Bruqvisz, he was positively even-tempered. "But I am concerned that this goes beyond my rank."

"Do *you* want to wake up Suncross right now?"

Ghostwalk looked over his shoulder at his sleeping boss, and his shoulders sagged. "No," he said. "I do not."

Suncross was snoring away, empty drink containers rolling around on the floor in a way that posed a positive hazard to safe navigation, so I cleared them up, then crouched down and leaned into Suncross's personal space. "Hey," I said. No response. "Suncross!" Nothing. *"You're fired!"*

The translation matrix must have conveyed that perfectly, because he woke up grunting and flailing his four arms at me. I eased back out of range, and when his eyes focused, the ruff went up on the back of his head, then down. Couldn't tell if that meant he was relieved or pissed off. "Zeerakull," he said. He sounded grumpy as hell. "Why are you here? Go away. I sleep."

"No, you don't," I said. "You've got a job. Get up."

"In an hour."

"Now, lizard brain!"

The insult made him growl and show teeth, and eventually—with some help—got him upright. Leaning and blinking, but upright. "You come at the wrong time," he said. "We were honoring our ancestors."

"By drinking yourselves sick?"

He shrugged. "How else? We drink, we tell their stories, we drink more. Is respectful."

Far be it from me to criticize somebody's religion, especially if it involved storytelling and booze. Seemed like a cool approach. "I need you to break off from the Leviathan and find the ones who are chasing us."

That got his full attention, finally. "We go to battle?" For the first time, Suncross seemed off-balance. "But . . . today is not auspicious. Not lucky. We should not fight today."

"Yeah, well, we're not," I said. "You're just my ride. Get us there and hang out. Maybe you get the word to leave and rejoin Typhon and Nadim. Maybe you pick us up again. I can't predict what's going to happen."

Suncross scrambled into a more authoritative stance, striking a pose with arms akimbo. "Ghostwalk, find the angry Leviathan and take us there. When we're within range, send a request for parlay."

Internal sealed document from the High Judge Advocate's office, retrieved during investigation into gross misconduct

I have deep-rooted concerns about this Derry person Torian Deluca has inserted into our program. All scans and behavioral reports indicate that not only is he a sociopath, but he also has serious substance addiction issues and is drastically ill-suited to Leviathan cooperative living, particularly when not given a traveling partner. I am recording these concerns and noting that over my objections, the Honors Council has—under pressure from Deluca, I presume—pushed through his selection. The Leviathan Ophelia initially voiced reservations of said partnership but has been made compliant through upgrades necessary to the purpose. I pray that history will not judge us as harshly as we deserve for what we've done.

If I had any courage at all, I'd tell Deluca to publish and be damned, but in reality, I would be the one damned, and I admit that I can't face that outcome. I'd rather be remembered as a corrupt official than what I really am.

If I could kill that man, I would gladly serve every rehabilitation sentence on the books. But I'm not brave enough for that, either.

Forgive me.

CHAPTER THIRTEEN

Lost Loves

THE LIZARD SHIP smelled even muskier than it had the first time, spiced by the stink of the swill they'd been drinking.

It was strange being away from Nadim and Bea, even worse not to feel them, but since we were speeding in opposite directions the bond stretched thin, then snapped, leaving my head in an eerie silence that I wasn't used to anymore. I glanced at Chao-Xing, wondering if she felt the same, but we weren't close enough for me to ask.

Chao-Xing was studying the ship interior—the decor as well as the disarray left by lizard religious rites—and she shook her head. "This is how I imagine Vikings would be, if they went to space."

"What is a Viking?" Ghostwalk asked.

I left Chao-Xing in the hub giving the lizard lieutenant a quick human history lesson while I followed Suncross, who was beckoning with four claws. Jury accompanied us, a silent, watchful presence at my back. Suncross stared hard at the robot.

"Do I want to know?"

I didn't imagine he was interested in all the details. We'd hired them as mercs, after all, though maybe I was starting to think of him as a friend. "Do you?"

"Only if the metal person becomes hostile."

The lizard led me to a big room filled with unimaginable tech. Lights and screens and silver cylinders and jagged things, and I had no idea what any of it did, but I felt like a kid in a candy shop. Or a techie in a hardware store, more like. Despite the dire situation, I immediately wanted to take everything apart and see what it did. The last time I was here, I was just passing through, so I didn't pay that much attention to their systems, but really, the Bruqvisz had a gorgeous aesthetic sense with their machines.

Suncross activated something and a screen popped up and uncurled, different from the type we used aboard Nadim. It was delicate, almost like fabric. His claws moved, activating this and that, and then the constellations swirled into focus, dots of light taking shape as we passed through those certain stars. Yet it seemed strange that Suncross had to do that manually. He couldn't just ask the ship to display it for him?

"You don't have an AI on board?"

"Aiii? What is this?"

"Artificial intelligence. Like Jury here." I indicated the robot standing calmly near the door, observing us both. "Applies to our med bot also."

Lizard eyes stared at me, his nictitating membrane fluttering. "That would be unwise, Zeerakull. My people have an unfortunate history with such."

"Did they rise up in a robot revolution or something?"

"Yes. There are many volumes about the struggle if you care to read them."

"Do you have audio versions? I can't read in Bruqvisz," I reminded him. "And I only understand you because of the translation matrix."

"Sorry, only text. Your loss. Should learn Bruqvisz, the only civilized tongue."

"Sure, I'll get right on that," I mumbled. "So your ship is just . . . silent, then. That's so weird to me."

"Strange to *me* that you live inside a Deep Singer," Suncross shot back.

Fair enough.

Time to refocus the convo. "You brought up the star chart for a reason, I guess?"

He slapped two palms against his chest. "Yes! Thank you for reminding, Zeerakull. I am showing you how we will track the treacherous Singers."

I never thought of that. Since Nadim and Typhon could hear the cousins across distance—and so could the Phage— it never occurred to me to wonder how mech ships would find Leviathan. Though I didn't have a plan for this part, I'd just imagined we could go back the way we'd come, but that was overly basic. I'd never seen Derry's ship, but Quell was badly injured after our fight, so they must have detoured to let her heal near a compatible star. If Derry was in charge, he would have abandoned her right away, but if these Leviathan knew about the Phage, they would realize it was smart to travel in pairs. Derry might've been overridden and forced to wait. If that was the case, they weren't that close behind us, and we needed to be precise to locate them in the vastness of the black.

"Okay, I'm interested."

"All Singers radiate the energy of the stars that nourish them. We logged the fight with the traitorous Singer, now I find their _____."

"Didn't quite catch that. Come again?"

"Emission?" Suncross tried again.

"I think I get it. We're scanning for the energy signature."

"Yes. Only have record of one, but if we find that Singer, the other should be close."

Hell, I hoped so. If we only tracked down Jon Anderson, I'd be so pissed. For this to end like all the rehearsals I'd run in my head, Jury had to take me to Derry McKinnon.

Suncross got to work toggling various icons, and soon a faint golden thread appeared on the screen. I couldn't interpret the symbols at the bottom, and we didn't share a numeric system, so I couldn't gauge how far it was either.

"How long will it take for us to intercept?" I asked.

"Twenty-three hours."

Sometimes I wondered about our differing concepts of time and what Suncross might be saying, as opposed to how the translation matrix put it. The gilded path remained lit on the screen and an oblong icon flashed. That must be Quell.

Less than a day.

Ghostwalk escorted Chao-Xing in around that time. "Suncross, let me tell you. We are Vikings!"

That sounded about right. I didn't stick around to hear the explanation, instead wandering the hall with Jury as my shadow. Eventually I turned around to say, "You're not saying as much as you did before."

"I have entered judiciary mode, per your request to be taken into custody. From this point on, my task is to observe and evaluate. I am an impartial witness, not your comrade."

"But . . . you were programmed to kill me, not arrest me."

"My protocols were corrupt. EMITU has freed me of such errors and limitations. I have chosen a new role. I am the law."

That sounded like a quote from a classic science fiction vid, but I couldn't remember which one. "Okay, I won't ask you for casual chats. Do you plan to keep following me?"

"Affirmative."

"This should be fun."

Soon I'd seen everything on offer in the lizard ship. I was starting to understand why they drank. They lacked most of the amenities Bea and I took for granted. It was no surprise they didn't have a pool, but there was no holo room either. If they wanted to train, they had to fight each other. Which explained a lot, actually.

I circled back to the central hub, where Suncross was running out of patience with Ghostwalk's obsession with Vikings. Suncross slammed a palm into the other lizard's shoulder, nearly knocking him down. "Enough!" He turned to me. "Zeerakull, we will teach you traditional Bruqvisz drinking game to fill the hours."

Chao-Xing shook her head. "That's a terrible idea. We need to arrive at the rendezvous sharp, not staggering drunk. Find some other way to pass the time."

The lizard crew let out a collective growl of disappointment, interspersed with hisses that I took as heckling.

"Game without drinking is all right?" Suncross asked.

Wariness brightened Chao-Xing's brown eyes. "Why does this worry me even more?"

As it turned out, she was right to be concerned. The game Suncross was referring to translated as "forfeit-or-pain," and it was exactly how it sounded. They had these stones, like dice, with symbols etched into them. You tossed the stones, and depending on your rune combination, you either won or lost the roll. If you lost, you had to choose between forfeiting some possession—which went into the pot to be claimed by the champion later—or endure some physical discomfort. If you had nothing left to bet, you could only pick pain, and if you were too hurt to continue playing, you were eliminated. The last lizard—or human—standing got to keep all the stuff that was wagered.

Brutal.

"You understand the basics?" Ghostwalk asked.

Generally speaking, yes. It was a badass game of craps. What I didn't understand were all the sigil combinations since I didn't read Bruqvisz. I was putting it on the to-do list, along with Mandarin. I'd be the coolest if I could cuss in lizard *and* Chinese.

Suncross broke down all the combos for us and

Chao-Xing wrote them down, as studious about gaming as I might have expected. She was already busy memorizing "rock and tree beats ocean and wind . . ."

Really, I felt like hugging Suncross. He had to know I could use a distraction, and learning how to play forfeit-or-pain was the perfect way to suppress my fear about where I was headed. Otherwise I'd be obsessing over how likely my plan was to succeed. Jury was the wild card, and I had no idea if this would break in my favor. If it went bad, I might end up in Deluca's hands.

No. Focus. Don't let physiological reactions clue the bot in. You're playing a game, resigned to your fate. That's the truth.

"You know," I said to Ghostwalk. "These game pieces?" I held up the hefty, etched piece that looked like obsidian. "Very Viking."

Ghostwalk showed me all his teeth, mouth open, as he made a sound that didn't translate, but it felt like amusement. "Bruqvisz who die in glorious battle cannot be set on fire. Should see if we can send them into a nearby sun?"

"You should *not* encourage this," Chao-Xing said.

"Why not? Cross-cultural exchanges pave the way for greater understanding." That sounded good, anyway.

She made a skeptical noise as Suncross thumped the floor for attention. The rest of the lizards sat in a circle, and I guessed that was the setup, so I squeezed in next to the one I vaguely recalled as Followshome. I'd forgotten the rest of their names, and it seemed like a jerk move to ask for a refresher at this point.

"We play!" Suncross shouted. He threw his stones and the crew roared. "Twin fires, beat that!"

I glanced at Chao-Xing, who had her game face on. We all took turns and I got the low roll. "Forfeit or pain?" asked Ghostwalk.

Since I only had my clothes and a few weapons, I wasn't about to start playing strip whatever with a bunch of damn lizards. "Pain," I said grimly.

Followshome wound up to clock me with two arms, but before he could deliver, an alarm went off, red lights strobing. "The hell is that?" Chao-Xing demanded.

Suncross got to his feet, growling in earnest. "Proximity alert. Is not an auspicious day to fight, but fight we must. Want to shoot some guns, Zeerakull?"

I was literally sitting in a gun pit, like in some science fiction vid, spinning wildly with physical controls to master. This wasn't like on board Nadim, aiming from the console or letting him take the lead. No, I was up close and personal, and the lizards were fighting a bunch of smaller ships, the like of which I'd never seen.

"Who are these assholes?" I called

"Oborub. You call them Jellies. According to the lights on their ships, they have been ordered to punish us for failing to comply with Bacia's request for aid."

"If they had ships to spare, why didn't they use them to defend the station?" I asked, indignant.

"Probably sent message," Ghostwalk predicted. "To enforcers away from base on other business."

That didn't explain *why* Bacia wanted to punish us. "Ghostwalk, how exactly did you respond to that request for aid?" I'd given him verbiage, but now I had a bad feeling.

"Told them what you said. And . . . other stuff."

"When I'm not fighting a bunch of jellyfish in rocket-boosted tins, we'll talk about this again," I muttered. "Wait, do Jellies have collective ancestral memory like the blo—I mean the Elaszi?"

"You won't shoot if they do? Fire weapons!" Suncross ordered.

Since he made a good point, I figured I could learn more about their species after we defeated the ones doing Bacia's dirty work. It was unnerving the way this seat oscillated, and the controls were optimized for four arms, so I was busy as hell, pulling levers and adjusting toggles, trying to get the sights to lock. Since I only had two arms, it took me a bit to work out how to do it. Followshome was in another gun pit, firing away. He took out two of the little chasers while I was learning the system.

"Victory!" he shouted.

Too soon, there were six more to shoot, and we had laser fire coming in hot. Suncross was piloting, jerking the ship around so I spun even when I wasn't trying to. My stomach jumped into my throat as I got my seat under control and lined up my shot. Bingo. I tapped twice and launched a volley that went true and the little Jelly ship went up in a silent shower of sparks. The metal pieces charred and drifted apart, showing me the dying Jelly inside. The alien floated out into the black, tendrils drifting, and it wouldn't be the airless part that killed them; I watched as the drifting fronds went stiff and the jelly core iced over.

"That was grim," I mumbled.

"Keep shooting. Five left!" Chao-Xing reminded me.

As she said that, Followshome took out a couple more. Four arms made him fast as hell on these guns. I wished I could match his speed, but there was no way. I scowled at C-X. "You want to give it a shot?"

"I'd rather boss you," she said.

I didn't think she was joking. Using all my coordination, I spun into position and locked on, took out a second as it was aiming a different weapon at us. Ghostwalk hissed and showed me his palms. "Good one. You save us from certain death!"

My brows shot up because I couldn't tell if he was serious or not. If that was true, how could he be so calm about it? Only two left, but they split up and dropped at the same time. "Flanking!" Ghostwalk called. "Under-hull maneuver."

In response, Suncross practically pitched me in the floor, swooping so that Followshome and I could take another shot. "I think they're trying to plant something on us," I said, judging by the way they were buzzing and not using weapons.

"Don't let it happen," Suncross said. Suddenly he sounded tense.

I didn't want to find out what happened to those who said "screw you" to Bacia's orders. I wheeled, strapped in and upside down to get the angle I needed, and my hands moved as fast as they ever had in order to activate the lasers one last time. Followshome hit his button at the same time, and the last two ships exploded in a pretty little chain reaction of destruction.

The lizards shouted and growled, did that victory dance I had only seen on the comm. Chao-Xing nudged me with her shoulder as I unstrapped and fell out of the gun pit, dizzy as hell but proud of myself too. "Good work."

"Thanks." I gave her a sidelong look. "You gonna learn the dance?"

Chao-Xing stared back. Then she surprised me by nodding. "It's a once-in-a-lifetime opportunity. Let's do this."

That was how I ended up in a line with Suncross

teaching us the steps and hand motions. We couldn't do it entirely right since we were missing two arms, but we gave it our best shot. I couldn't get the sounds right for the chant either, but the translation matrix helped me out so I could yell along in English. "Victory! Victory! Guts and glory! Fortune favors the bold!" Stomp stomp, clap clap—four claps for lizards, two for humans—throw arms up, spin, stomp, tail wiggle for lizards, shake the human booty, drop down low, jump up, and repeat. Both Chao-Xing and I caught on fast and then we just had to do it on rhythm.

I felt like hugging all the lizards because I'd forgotten how dire my situation was for a bit—until I caught sight of Jury standing silently nearby, watching us. Then it dropped on me like the curtain of night, all heavy anticipation laced with fear.

Right, this still sucks.

"Can I ask about the Jellies now? You were going to tell me—"

"No ancestral memory," said Suncross. "Not to worry about bloodfeud. Oborub make loyal, excellent helpers. They bond to one person and reproduce quickly, so if one falls in battle, another can replace them."

"So Bacia has their own Jelly army? Damn."

Ghostwalk nodded. "Good comparison."

"Did Bacia really put a bounty on our heads? Will

Typhon and Nadim be all right?" This was another worry I did not need.

"Unwise to send little Jellies after giant Singers," said Suncross. "We are little fish in comparison. Could maybe get lucky and destroy ship or claim it."

"Continue playing?" Ghostwalk asked.

Sighing, I took the hit that I'd dodged before, and the game went on. Pretty soon I had bruises all over because the lizards didn't hold back for humans or girls, and I couldn't take another smack, so I started betting my clothes. Which was how I ended up half naked with all my weapons showing.

"You know I'm not letting you assholes keep my pants, right?"

Jury was logging this whole thing too. *In the annals of Zara Cole, she played a game with lizards and lost her trousers. Is that a crime? No, but it is dumb as hell.*

"You have to buy them back," Suncross told me.

"I'm not—" I stopped and went in again for another angle. "How's that going to work? I don't have any currency."

Chao-Xing solved the problem by being the high roller for the night. She swept the pot and was nice enough to give me back my clothes. Thank God. I wasn't looking forward to meeting Derry in my underwear. He'd probably take it as some bold strategy to get him back when I'd rather go out like that Jelly, as my feeling on a repeat of history went about like what they say about hell freezing over.

The party wound down, and though I didn't think I'd sleep with so much on my mind, I eventually passed out like a little kid, leaning up against the wall. I woke when Suncross laid a surprisingly gentle hand on my shoulder, then pulled me up with two others.

"Zeerakull." He spoke softer than I'd ever heard him. "Have found the traitorous cousins and spoken to the one called Derry. He agrees to collect you."

"Wow. Okay. So this is happening." I mean, it had to go down like this. It was the best call, but still, my stomach fluttered. I couldn't be one hundred percent sure it would go down like I hoped. "Is it okay if I hug you?"

"What is hug?" Suncross asked.

In answer, I showed him. Never thought I'd wrap my arms around a giant, rowdy sentient lizard, but here I was. I patted his back, feeling the bumps of his skin and the ridges on his back. Slowly all four of his arms came around me, gentle as could be, and he thumped me, so it only rocked me a little.

"This is hug? Am doing it right?"

"Yeah, good job," I said, pulling back to smile.

He showed me his teeth too, probably not as comforting as he intended, but hey, it was the thought that counted. "Live with honor or die with glory, Zeerakull. We wait to hear from you or JongShowJing."

"Thanks." Damn, I was getting choked up; time to wrap this up. "How have you arranged for us to be taken aboard?" I wasn't sure how much cargo their Leviathan had in the docking bay. There probably wouldn't be room for the mech ship, and I didn't want them to take the risk anyway.

Suncross said, "As usual. Suit up, go out. They will collect you in their Hopper."

I wondered if we'd get pulled in, like we did to Yusuf and Starcurrent. At least Jury could help guide us since he had booster boots. Turning to Chao-Xing, I said, "Are you ready?"

She didn't say, *I was born ready*, which disappointed me; she just nodded and led the way to the docking bay, where our skinsuits were waiting. "Let's do this."

From the Fellkin edition of *Famous Inorganic Poets,*
Volume 1

The pressure suit that's really candy,
Above all others is the unsuit.
Does the unsuit make you shiver?
does it?

Why would you think the Leviathan is angry?
the spacecraft is the most graceful craft of all.
Does the great ship make you shiver?
does it?

When I think of the robot, I see a fortress.
Down, down, down into the darkness of the robot,
Gently it goes—the muddled, the muzzy, the hirsute.

emitu

CHAPTER FOURTEEN

Lost Touch

I HAD NERVES. The kind that came before a run in the Zone, the ones that made me shiver inside. This carried a high risk of death, but the game was the game, and I'd learned to play it young. This time I was playing against Derry, not with him. If I let myself be scared, I'd be *done*. So I had to keep it in the lane, because Derry was damned sure not scared, and I had to meet him on equal ground.

This wouldn't go down easy, however Jury came down. Derry wasn't an Honor. He wasn't in this for the trip, or the experience, or anything else. He was just here to do his master's bidding and go home to grab more chem, more money, more power.

When the Hopper touched down inside the Leviathan's docking bay, I knew what I had to do.

"Are you afraid, Honor Cole?" Jury asked me suddenly, and I just about jumped out of my skin. He'd been so silent on the trip that I'd almost forgotten he could talk. I preferred the silence right now too.

"Nope," I said, and stood up. Touched my toes and limbered up. Stretched tense muscles. "Chao-Xing?"

"If they'll allow me entry, I'll come with you," she said. "If they won't, I'll be right here, ready to get us the hell out."

"Okay." I took a deep breath; she was watching me, waiting for a sign. I nodded.

Chao-Xing hit the comms. "Where do we proceed?"

Derry's voice came right back. He sounded tense. I thought he also sounded high. "Leave your weapons. All of them."

"Sure," I said, because I knew C-X was about to argue. "By the way, brought your robot back. He seemed expensive."

Derry didn't like that. "Robot. Mission report."

Jury said, "Mission is terminated. I have Zara Cole in my custody."

"Mission *terminated*?" Derry, I remembered, was no

kind of tech genius; he could barely fix a broken chip, much less reprogram a bot as complicated as Jury. Derry didn't know anything about how the murderbot worked; he just pushed the buttons. He shifted gears quick, though. "I'm scanning for any dangerous items. It'd be like you to put a bomb in that thing, Z."

"Go ahead." I shrugged. "I'm playing it straight."

He laughed. "Sure you are. You forget, *I know you*."

"You used to know me," I agreed. "But I'm not that person anymore."

He just shook his head. Same old Derry. I'd been the one who scrounged up our needs, who found our food and liquor and chem and shelter. Derry had—although I hadn't realized it then—been dependent on me, but also tricked me into thinking that *he* was in charge. The fact I could see it meant he couldn't use it now.

"Hold still. If there's a bomb, it's going to blow right in your face," he said. I felt a tingle, but nothing else happened. Derry's face did a peculiar little twist, and I remembered that too. *Disappointment*. He really did want me dead. I wondered if that was toxic jealousy or self-preservation. His life was likely on the line if he didn't deliver my head.

"You recording this for Deluca?" I asked him casually and saw the flinch. It wasn't much, but it was there. "Boy, you better look where you're standing. That man doesn't need you once this is done. How do you think that ends?"

"Don't know," Derry said, and flashed me that smile that used to make me melt. It left me cold now. "You know me, Z. I'll find a way out. Always do."

Boys like him always thought that. They just kept jumping from one thing to the next, and sooner or later, they'd jump, and it'd be a cliff. "Are we doing this or what? 'Cause if you're just going to chat, I can go."

His smile faded. He hit some controls. "Come on if you're coming, Zara. Robot. Bring her to me."

Jury laid a metal hand on my shoulder. I looked up at him, which was dumb; wasn't like his face would tell me anything. He didn't speak. He just moved me to the door, which Chao-Xing opened.

"He didn't say I had to stay," she said, "so I'm coming."

As I stepped out, an alarm rang, and red flashed through the docking bay walls. I sighed and dug the hidden gun out of the back of my pants and dropped it into the Hopper. The walls kept flashing. I retrieved the knife, and as it disappeared into the craft, the flashing stopped, and the alarm went still.

Chao-Xing, watching this, disarmed before getting out. She'd brought plenty. It took a while, but when she dropped down next to me and Jury, no alarms went off.

Chao-Xing pulled her H2, and her fingers flew over it in a fluid dance. The Hopper door slid closed. "I set it to unlock for our biosigns only," she said. "No point in giving him a way into our ships. Not that Typhon wouldn't blow him out of space for even trying, of course."

Jury didn't speak. He just urged me on. And yeah, it felt like I was walking the last mile to my execution, just like in the holos. I occupied myself by examining the differences between this Leviathan and Nadim; this one had different internal routing, which I noted. Every Leviathan was configured according to their own experiences with their crews; this one seemed to like wider hallways and 'random corridors. Almost like a maze. I made sure to note the turns we took. I was pretty sure this Leviathan wouldn't be helpfully lighting any paths for me, should I get to come back this way. I had to take long strides to keep pace with Jury, who retained his hold on me, though it didn't hurt. It probably looked impressive, though. Chao-Xing brought up the rear.

We passed through a massive vaulted chamber, utterly unlike anything we had on Nadim, and I craned my head way up to marvel at the view. Transparent arcing panels showed the stars beyond. It was like a church, but without any religious elements. There was, however, furniture. It consisted of a bunch of tall branching trees made of crystal. I wondered what kind of crew this Leviathan had carried prior to Derry. Something I'd never met, I guessed, but I liked their aesthetic.

Gravity was a little lower than I was used to, and it made

me feel stronger, but it also threw off my reactions a bit. I'd have to watch that.

We came out of the room I mentally labeled the church into a human-refitted control room, same equipment as we had on board Nadim, only a slightly modified and upgraded system. No transparent walls this time. It felt like a trap.

And there was Derry McKinnon. "Hello, Zara," he said.

I remembered the good-bye he'd given me to get on the train for the Honors program; he'd been high then too. And more about himself than me, just like he always had been. I never thought I'd feel this way, but seeing Derry in that uniform made me righteously angry. He didn't deserve it. I didn't sense anything from his Leviathan, and for the first time I wondered *why* a Leviathan would agree to this deal. What was it getting out of it? Certainly not the pleasure of Derry's company.

The Leviathan didn't feel present at all. It was a very strange and unsettling lack; maybe Derry didn't notice because he'd never really felt a Leviathan's warmth and life. But it felt . . . not dead, exactly. Withdrawn.

I tentatively reached out, and found a thick, impenetrable wall between the consciousness of the ship and anyone on board. It—no, I sensed something that told me this ship identified as *she*—was back there; I could feel it by pressing against that invisible wall, but she was completely walled off.

I couldn't imagine what could cause a Leviathan to be that much of a hostage inside their own body. Did she do this on her own? Or did Derry hurt her enough to cause this? If that was the case, I wanted *blood*.

"You're right, by the way," Derry said. "Deluca's getting all this on a VR recording. He'll be able to watch it just like he's here."

"Great," I said. "Where's his point of view?"

Derry pointed. I aimed an upraised middle finger in that direction.

"Wow," Derry said. "Read the room, Zara."

"Oh, I am," I said. More than he knew. I made damn sure the Leviathan knew I was here, and that if she was in trouble, I could help. She had to understand that we were allies for her if she needed them. "Kind of bored with your version of the story, though. If you're going to kill me, move it the hell along."

"Okay," Derry said. "I'm kind of disappointed, though. The old Zara wouldn't have gone down without a fight. Guess all this civilization took it right out of you."

He clearly hadn't been keeping up on current events. His loss. I didn't point it out. I just clasped my hands behind my back and took on an at-attention stance.

He was waiting for me to move. I didn't. Finally, he looked at Jury. "Kill her. Make it quick." He sent me a look. "See? Still got some feelings for you."

Jury said, "I have reviewed all available recordings and evidence, and it is my decision that Zara Cole is guilty of several crimes."

Oh shit.

"I restricted myself to the time period between her last official sentencing to the Camp Kuna Rehabilitation Facility and today," Jury continued. "Whatever crimes she committed prior to her last sentence are now immaterial."

Well, that ruled out my jacking of the Deluca girl's purse and being complicit in the killing of Deluca's man who'd come to get it back. That was something.

"Since that time, Zara Cole is judged guilty of the following crimes: assault of a sentient being in the docking bay of the Leviathan Nadim, with mitigating circumstances of self-defense; unlawful killing of a sentient being on the Sliver, designation Mandy, of the Elaszi, with mitigating circumstances of self-defense; kidnapping of a mixed work crew from the Sliver, with mitigating circumstances of self-defense."

I waited for him to continue, but he didn't. Was that all? Because that wasn't so bad.

"I don't give a shit," Derry said impatiently. "Carry out her sentence."

"Very well," Jury said. "Sentence for the crime of assault of a sentient being: advanced interspecies cultural education, ruled complete. Unlawful killing of a sentient being:

self-defense judged sufficient for vacating the sentence. Kidnapping of a mixed work crew: risk of death for this crew was high, resulting in the kidnapping serving as a lesser offense than the ultimate death of said crew, which indicates a suspended sentence is in order."

"That's it?" Derry seemed astonished. "Look, whatever, just kill her. That's your function."

"It is not," Jury said. "I am the law. The law judges crimes brought before it. I have judged that Zara Cole is not guilty of any crime punishable by death. Derry McKinnon, however, is guilty of the following offenses: criminal manipulation of the Honors administration to produce false charges against Honor Zara Cole and Honor Beatriz Teixeira. Occupation, against her will, of the Leviathan Ophelia, by force and threats of force. Implantation of an illegal shock device within the organs of Leviathan Ophelia, without her consent. Illegal operation of a Leviathan under false pretenses. Illegal production and consumption of banned chemicals. Attempted murder of Honor Zara Cole. Attempted murder of—"

"Screw this," Derry said, and drew the weapon I'd spotted beneath his uniform jacket. I didn't recognize the piece, but I figured it had to be something that could destroy Jury in a hot second or he wouldn't try it.

I dove.

He saw me coming, but he wasn't fast enough; the chem shaved just enough reaction time off to let me grab his arm and force it up as his finger touched the trigger, and instead of hitting Jury it hit the wall above Jury's head.

The shot tore through the Leviathan's sensitive skin.

Ophelia screamed. It was so loud it was like a riot suppression device; I gritted my teeth and struggled with Derry for the weapon. He had more upper body strength, and if all things were equal, he'd have thrown me off.

All things were not equal, because Chao-Xing was there to stab stiff fingers under his arm. It was an agonizing blow; I knew because she'd done it to me in our last combat grappling sim. I'd been on the floor for a full minute before I could make it up.

It didn't put Derry down. The chem made him a touch slower, but it also blunted pain, and though he clearly felt it, he didn't go down. He staggered, and his gaze swept over to lock on mine.

It was like being drowned, all the feelings boiling through that look blasting at me full force. Love. Hate. Pain. Desperation.

He didn't like this. He'd put on his armor to do it, but fact was, he didn't want to kill me. One thing about Derry, though, and I'd always known this: if it came down to me or him, he'd pick himself.

Fair enough.

"Surrender," I said to him. "Derry, just *give up*. Jury can take you back for sentencing. You can turn it around. You can make Deluca pay. All you have to do is stand up for it."

"Like you stood up?" He grinned at me, and it was the grin that told me the cause was lost. "No."

I expected him to come for me.

What he did, though, was turn and run.

"Jury!" I snapped. "He's got an illegal shock weapon he can activate. Can it kill this Leviathan?"

"It can," he said.

"What's your sentence for his crimes?"

"Death," Jury said. "But I am unable to execute said decision until he is disarmed, and the Leviathan is secure. Also, the unit in his possession carries malicious code that will wipe my memory and disable me. I do not wish to cease to be, Zara Cole."

"On it," I said. "As a thanks-for-not-killing-me present."

Chao-Xing raised her voice. "Ophelia. Tell us where he is."

The ship didn't reply. I suspected she couldn't because there was damage already, or because she'd never fully interfaced with the human systems that had been installed.

But what she did was light up a wall in a zip of white light.

We ran in pursuit.

When Chao-Xing pulled ahead and veered off, I didn't know what she meant to do until she shouted, "Ophelia, do you have weapons for us?"

Ophelia did. She lit up a curving side passage, and we veered that way. It looped completely into a spiral, and at the end a strangely organic door contracted backward in another spiral.

Beyond was Candyland for killers. A lot of it was slick, new Earth tech, better than I'd ever seen in the Zone. I avoided that; even if it was more powerful, it'd cost me precious time to figure out. I grabbed a rifle, same as we had aboard Nadim; Chao-Xing took a pouch of stunning light grenades and a hand weapon. On impulse, I grabbed something that was not our tech, but I recognized the net gun of Bruqvisz design. I wondered where Derry had found it, and what damage he'd done to get it. Not a question I could answer, and Ophelia couldn't tell me.

We went hunting.

With Ophelia on our side, it wasn't going to be difficult . . . or at least, that's what I thought until I felt a sudden, biting shock go through me, feet to crown. C-X and I were insulated, both by our boots and by our lack of direct interface with Ophelia, but we felt the horror, hurt, and pain boil over even so.

He'd just hurt her. Badly. *He put a shock collar on a*

Leviathan. Oh, hell no, he wasn't getting away with this. It was about more than survival now. We had to get him out of here so Ophelia could be free. That was more important than my need for revenge.

"Ophelia," I said, "can you trap him for us? Seal him into a specific section, maybe?" Because right now, Derry had a significant advantage: he knew this ship, and we didn't. "Uh, flash us twice for yes."

Two flashes.

"Is he going to hurt you if you do?" Chao-Xing asked before I could. "Wait, sorry, that's a bad question, of course he will. Can you endure it if it means we get to him?"

A hesitation. Then two flashes. Then two more. I guess she meant yes to both things. We exchanged a look. C-X looked grim. Neither of us liked it, but I nodded, and she said, "Seal him off and lead us there."

Ophelia flashed twice. *Yes.* And after an agonizingly long pause, a light streaked along her wall.

We ran fast as we could to follow it. We were aware that as soon as Derry discovered he was trapped, he'd hurt her again, maybe worse this time. That wasn't acceptable.

The light led us through a twisting maze of tunnels, through the church again, and in a direction I thought was close to the docking bay.

We came around a corner and nearly slammed face-first into a closed door. We both braked hard, and I put a hand on the flesh-warm wall. "We're here," I told Ophelia. "Is he right on the other side?"

Yes, her lights flashed. Chao-Xing and I took up positions on either side of the hallway, facing each other, and I slid down to a crouch.

"Open it," Chao-Xing said, and aimed about where Derry would be standing, if he was stupid.

I aimed where I knew he'd be if he wasn't.

He wasn't either place. He'd retreated and crouched, and he was fumbling with something in his pocket instead of being ready to return fire. As Chao-Xing and I both focused our aim on him, he pulled the device out of his pocket and held it up. His hand was shaking. He aimed the pistol in his free hand first at me, then at C-X.

"Easy," he said. "Guns down. This thing's dialed up to lethal now. You want to kill Ophelia, I can do it with just one quick press." I knew Derry well enough to recognize a bluff when I saw it, and this wasn't one. He meant it. Of course, killing his Leviathan trapped us all in here, unable to escape with the docking bay shut. But I suspected he had an out. Maybe he'd installed a bomb to blow her docking bay open. Couldn't know for sure.

But I knew we couldn't risk Ophelia's life on Derry's chem-driven whims. He didn't see her as a person, just a disposable thing. He'd kill her for kicks, knowing it might hurt me.

I slowly lowered my gun to the deck, and out of the corner of my eye, I saw C-X doing the same thing with her right hand. Her left, concealed from the angle at which she stood, was moving. Unclipping a light grenade. I eased the net device out of my pocket the same way as I made a show of disarming.

Derry didn't see it coming. He was starting to smile, that quirk of victory curling right at the corners, when C-X slid the light grenade across the floor, ducked away, and I threw my arm over my eyes. Even with that, I saw right through my arm, saw the bones illuminated by the crippling glow, and was half-blinded. Only half, though. Derry, caught off guard, reeled and went to his knees. He lost the gun and remote control as he clutched at his eyes, and I followed up by throwing the net at him. It spread out as it sailed toward him, and the intelligent circuits in the thing sought him out, wrapped around him in an unbreakable embrace, and tightened to package him up.

Derry was screaming. Words, but I wasn't listening; I knew the tune well enough without the lyrics. He'd always had an explosive temper hidden behind a slick wall of charm. I still had fuzzy vision, but I walked over to where he lay helpless and scooped up the remote and weapon. Chao-Xing joined me.

"Noisy," she said.

I could feel the cool water of Ophelia's relief pouring

over me, and it soothed a fire that I wasn't even aware had been burning inside me. She wasn't pleading for Derry, but neither did she hate him, precisely. Rather like she'd never expected anything else from him. That was sadder, maybe, than any rage would have been. I walked over and reached through the fibers of the net to take away his toys.

"Stand aside," said Jury's smooth, calm voice, and I blinked and turned around. "Justice will be done."

"Jury—"

"Justice will be done, Zara Cole."

I shrugged and stepped aside. Chao-Xing took a couple of paces back.

And Jury said, "Derry McKinnon, your sentence for multiple capital offenses is death. Do you have anything to say?"

Derry said some shit, a torrent of abuse, of pleading, of defiance, but it boiled down to one thing: he took orders from Torian Deluca, and Deluca was going to have something to say about it if anything happened to him.

Jury let him wind down. When he finally took a breath, the bot said, "Torian Deluca will be judged according to his own crimes."

Interlude: Nadim

I swim in the cold, and I feel alone for the first time, knowing that Zara has gone to meet someone she once loved and now loathes. Someone who wants to kill her and sent a robot to do it for him.

I try not to think of Zara, earthbound, dirty, hungry, believing in this Derry of hers; I try not to remember the bittersweet of her memories of him. It is not that I believe she will turn to him; I know she will not.

It's that I fear she will not forgive herself for what she has to do.

Zara will survive this. I have no doubt of that. But being lost in the silence, so far away I cannot feel her or know her thoughts . . . that is hard. I can only wait with Bea, both of us consumed with gentle worry and hard doubts.

Zara will come back to us.

She must come back.

CHAPTER FIFTEEN

Lost Lives

THE LAW KILLED Derry. Jury did it fast, with a single shot to the head, a burn that came and went so fast I almost missed it. Derry couldn't have felt a thing; his body went limp, his eyes empty of soul, his pretty mouth relaxed.

Dead in the net, he almost looked his age. Eighteen, I figured. Barely enough life to know what he was losing.

It hurt. Not because I loved him or anything; I didn't, even at this last moment. I just pitied him. I tried to remember that chem had its hooks in him and he couldn't control his actions with that demon on his shoulder, but that was a hard thing to keep in mind when treachery left you bleeding.

I remembered to breathe, finally, and blinked away the last of the light bomb. Kneeling, I unlocked the net; ironically, because this was his ship, his weapons, the net had been keyed to his thumbprint. If he'd had the presence of mind to use that, he might have lived. Probably not, but in a very real way, the chem had killed him as much as Jury's sentence.

I used his thumbprint to open the strands; it unwrapped itself and whipped the net back into the storage compartment. I put it aside and turned Derry over on his back. Crossed his hands on his chest.

Chao-Xing watched me without comment, then said, "Should we put him out the airlock?" Burial in space was common for Honors. It was how I'd want to go. But I shook my head.

"Jury should take him back," I said. "He doesn't belong here. And besides—" I turned to look at Jury. "You wanted to have a talk with Deluca, right?"

"Yes," he said. "Ophelia and I will return to Earth." Then Jury hesitated for a second. "Do you study haiku, Honor Cole?"

"Not a bit," I said.

"Would you like me to make one for Derry McKinnon? EMITU has taught me how."

I nodded.

"Darkness; eventide / A quiet and welcome death / in these perfect stars," said the bot who had killed him.

I sucked in a hard breath.

Good-bye, Derry.

I stood up and said, "C-X, we should figure out how to uninstall the shit Derry put into Ophelia," I said. "Make sure she's free before we leave her. Then she can decide to do whatever she chooses."

"What about the other one? Quell, and Jon Anderson?"

"If they come at us, then . . . Ophelia? Will you intercede for us? Explain all this to Quell?"

Two bright flashes of light nearly blinded me again. I guess that meant yes, with emphasis.

Chao-Xing took a deep breath, held it, and let it out. "Let's get to work."

It took the better part of three hours to dismantle the two devices we found; one had been embedded in one of Ophelia's nerve clusters, and the other near an organ that looked frighteningly familiar. Heart or lungs or something equivalent; I'd seen it in Nadim up close and personal before, and here I was, locked into a suit and swimming again through what passed as blood for the Leviathan. It was difficult, exacting work to be sure I didn't damage any of the nerves they'd wired the shock device into, but I'd always been better at this than most. The Earth sons of bitches had probably done a lot more damage installing it, but it looked like that had mostly healed.

Time to go. Suncross and company were waiting behind a spinning planetoid. "Don't do anything I wouldn't do," I said to Jury.

"That gives me much latitude, Zara Cole."

Was that a joke? Maybe. I smiled like it was. "Take care of Ophelia. She can't feel your presence like she would an organic crew, so you'll need to talk to her a lot."

A flutter of light confirmed my words, and Jury said, "Understood. I will communicate effectively. She will not feel alone."

Chao-Xing nudged me. "We've got to go. I don't think Honor Anderson was in on the murder mission, so he really does want to arrest you. He has no idea the orders will be rescinded as soon as Jury takes care of Deluca."

I nodded. "Yeah, we don't want to fight Quell again. Better to just play keep-away. Take care of it, you two."

"Affirmative," Jury said, and Ophelia flashed her agreement as well.

I called Suncross to request our ride. After suiting up, we borrowed a booster pack, and I held on to Chao-Xing as she propelled us away from Ophelia to drift, waiting for pickup. Once we were safe in the lizard ship docking bay, she said, "I have to ask. What was your plan?"

"What makes you think I didn't just give myself up and trust to luck?"

Chao-Xing gave me a look that said she knew me better than that. "Really?"

"Nah, you're right. I thought if I pretended to surrender myself to justice that Jury might turn on Derry and decide he was the one who deserved punishment. There *was* a chance that he'd go the other way and drag me all the way to Deluca." In all candor, I'd bet hard that Jury's free thinking would come down in my favor.

"Why did you take the risk?" she asked quietly.

"It was the only way to be sure that the conflict would stop with me. I didn't want Nadim getting hurt because of me. Typhon either, really. And I felt bad about hurting Quell when we fought."

Chao-Xing's expression shifted slightly, though I couldn't read her reaction. "You've changed, Zara. It was a gamble, but you risked yourself to save everyone else. I admit, I didn't see it when you were first chosen, but . . . you are Honors material all the way."

I smirked. "We gonna hug now?"

"Don't even try."

Suncross held a celebration for our safe return, which was nice but also involved more alcohol, and this time I let myself have some. After two I quit, and even then, the drinks laid me out for most of the return trip. Yeah. Lizards were *hardy*. While I was flat, Suncross and Chao-Xing— who'd sipped, not chugged—talked strategies. Suncross also told her that he'd written some epic ballads about us. That was nice. I didn't want to hear them, but I was polite listening to the short one. It took up a lot of travel time.

I admit it: when I finally felt the outer whispers of Nadim's warm presence, I gasped and had to fight the sting of grateful tears at the corners of my eyes.

Don't ever do that again, he whispered like a distant dream.

No, I told him. *I won't.* I never wanted to be that far from him again.

Suncross said, "We approach your ship, Zhang Chao-Xing."

"Hold on," I said. "You can say our names? Like, the right way?"

"Yes, of course, Zeerakull."

"Then—"

Suncross and the whole crew hissed in amusement. "Humans. You expected no more, correct? Zara Cole, we tell our stories across nine galaxies. If we could not pronounce as simple a sound as your names, we would be out of business. We just liked the way the translator mishandled it." To my utter shock, he switched to flawless English.

Sounded like pure middle North America. Detroit, maybe. "We thought it would be funny. It *is* funny. But if it offends, we will stop."

I opened my mouth, closed it, then finally said, "I kind of like Zeerakull too. And since when do you speak—"

Three out of four hands waved that away. I was starting to figure out that his level of investment in what he said was indicated by the gestures. "English? It's a nice language. I studied a few days. You have some good literature." He switched to Chinese, and thank God my translator picked it up. "However, there are other languages of your planet that are much more lyrical and interesting."

"How many do you speak?" C-X asked him, raising an eyebrow.

"Unsure," he said. "The twenty most spoken at present time?"

"In a few days," I said.

"Leisure time," Suncross said. "There is value to learning the ways of allies, Zeerakull."

I felt . . . well, *ashamed* was a good word for it. I hadn't studied the Bruqvisz cultures, or their language, or even what those damn gestures meant when he made them. I had work to do.

I bowed my head in what I hoped he'd take for respect; I meant it that way. He returned it, ruff rising and falling in a special gesture I was determined to look up once

I got home. "Thank you, Suncross," I said. "You're a true friend."

"Ally," he corrected. "Friends you don't pay."

"Earth ways," I told him. "You're my friend. And I can pay you if I want."

He laughed. It showed a lot of sharp teeth, involved some hissing, and a year ago it would have made me reach for my gun. But now I just grinned back and held out a fist.

He bumped it.

"Good talk," I said. "We'll be heading home now. Thanks for the ride."

"Always pleasant to have guests. Especially when they don't break things."

"Well, we've got that in common too, how about that? Humans are the same."

I thanked all his crew in turn, which seemed to please Suncross; Chao-Xing made the rounds with me. Afterward, she said, "I underestimated them."

"Well, to be fair, I think they *wanted* us to underestimate them. Part of the game."

She nodded slowly. "I didn't think we'd make it back, to be honest. Odds were not in our favor."

"Never are, are they? Doesn't it make you feel good when we win, though?"

She gave me a weird look. "You should see someone about that adrenaline problem."

Yusuf picked us up from our free-floating, and Marko was there to pull us in, both wearing formal black uniforms; there were smiles and welcomes, and though C-X wasn't a hugger, she got nods and handshakes in the crowded Hopper. When we docked, Typhon's presence descended, greeting me first. Not warm like Nadim's; he was *vast*, a being who could intimidate half a galaxy just by coming into it. But welcoming, in a chilly sort of way. It wasn't what I'd think of as a real bond, but he was working on it. And so were his human crew. Having Yusuf in the mix had helped, I thought, the way Starcurrent had helped us.

The others scattered from the docking bay as I paused to acknowledge the Elder.

Typhon also spoke to me this time, directly. "Zara Cole," he said. "I am pleased you are alive."

"Well, thanks. And I'm pleased too."

"Did you destroy the cousins?" He said it in a distant sort of way, like it mattered not a bit to him whether other Leviathan died, but I also knew that was a kind of shield he was holding between us. He cared.

"No," I said. "We saved Ophelia and removed the devices that were installed in her to control her behavior."

The Elder wasn't interested in shock collars. "It is unusual that both Ophelia and Quell had only one crew member. This is . . . not advisable for long journeys. All intelligent life is, to some degree, social. And social beings require interaction."

Hmm. Derry was dead. I didn't know if Jury would count as crew, precisely; he probably couldn't bond with the ship in any real fashion. That was why I'd warned the bot to talk to her a lot on the way back to Earth.

Typhon caught me by surprise when he said, "Yusuf would like to speak with you before you depart."

"Really?" I shrugged. "Okay. I'll have a word with him before I head off to Nadim."

Nadim's still-distant feeling of pique made me have to suppress a laugh. *I know,* I thought at him, though I wasn't sure he could hear me at this distance. *But I'll be back soon.*

Evidently he could understand, because the pique turned to a wounded acceptance. The emotional equivalent of *fine.*

Typhon withdrew—not so much rejecting me as just not caring about me anymore. Well, back at you, Typhon.

I went searching for Yusuf and took a closer look at him, as there was no chance during the brief pickup—damn, he sure looked a lot better. He was so sick before that it was impossible not to worry about him, but the medicine must be working. "You wanted to talk?"

"Over coffee, perhaps?"

"I never turn it down."

Yusuf put his hands behind his back and clasped them

as we walked, and it made his already excellent posture even better. I felt like a slouch beside him. I resisted the urge to stand straighter. He topped me by several inches and was broader by a good bit; his uniform fit him well, I thought. And he looked comfortable in it.

"I'm glad to see you back, Zara," he said. "Chao-Xing wasn't convinced that whatever plan you had laid on would actually work."

"Well, it did, and it didn't, and I'm really glad she had my back," I replied. We settled at the table with hefty mugs of coffee, and I blew on the surface while waiting for whatever was on his mind.

When it came, it surprised me.

"Quell and Ophelia, the two new Leviathan," he said. "What is our relationship with them?"

"Well, Ophelia's heading back to Earth right now with Jury, but I imagine she'll be returning. She was grateful for us ridding her of all the tech Deluca had installed to control her. As for Quell . . . honestly, no idea. Still hates us, probably. Or, really, me, since I'm the Most Wanted."

"Are you?" he asked. "Still?"

"Until Jury gets the record straightened out back on Earth, yeah. I don't think Jon Anderson's going to play nice until that's done. And Quell will follow his lead." I sipped coffee, and it was just what I needed. "Why are you asking?"

"Quell only has one crew member, and he doesn't seem

to be properly trained for the Journey. Ophelia has no one."

"Oh. *Oh*." I suddenly realized what this conversation was about. "You're looking for a new ship."

"It doesn't work that way. I merely wanted to present myself as a prospect," Yusuf said. "It's always up to the ship whether to accept. I won't have a true bond again, I think, but I can be comfort and support."

"Would that be enough for you?" It maybe wasn't polite to ask, but this felt like it needed asking.

He was quiet for a long moment before he said, "It would have to be, wouldn't it? It's that, or go home. And I would miss this. Miss the stars, the Leviathan, the Journey."

"What did you do back home?"

"I was a theoretical physicist," he said. "And I knew from the first moment on board my beautiful ship that for all my study, everything I knew was only a speck of dust in the scope of the universe. Out here—there's more. It's so much *more*."

I understood that. I felt it in my bones. "You think Starcurrent feels like you do? Like ze'd like to find a more permanent place?"

"That's the thing. Ze called me. This is zis idea, and I . . . have to agree. Seems like the best solution to everyone's needs."

"Why talk to me about it, then?"

"Because I already talked to Typhon, Chao-Xing, Marko,

Nadim, and Bea," he said. "And Starcurrent was afraid you'd be mad."

I laughed. "Come on."

"Ze values your friendship, Zara. Starcurrent didn't want you to think it wasn't fun over there aboard Nadim. Ze said you've made every effort to make zim feel part of things. But ze doesn't care for your other excess crew over there, either."

Xyll. Of course ze didn't.

"We've got a ways to go before we're on speaking terms with Quell and Anderson, and we have to wait until Ophelia gets back anyway. So let's just leave this on the table for now. Good?"

Yusuf nodded. "Good." He smiled at me. He didn't do that too often, and in it I saw the person he used to be when he was happy, bonded with his beloved ship. "Think we're going to survive long enough for it to matter?"

"Us? Absolutely. You and me, we're survivors, brother."

We fist-bumped to agree to that.

I landed on board Nadim with an overwhelming feeling of relief. *I'm home.* Things clicked back into place inside me that I hadn't even realized were dangling and disconnected. And the second the door slid open, Bea hit me like a whirlwind and spun me around in a hug so tight I thought she might break a rib. My ribs held, and my heart seemed to expand inside my chest until it hurt. I'd missed her. I'd missed Nadim, who enveloped us both in his radiance.

She kissed me with breathless intensity. No hesitation anymore on either of our parts, and the dark-cherry taste of her lips stirred something up inside me that felt wild and reckless. When we parted, she rested her forehead against mine and whispered, "I missed you, *querida*." Her words went straight inside me and fluttered like butterflies. "We were so worried. Suncross messaged us that you were all right or we'd have—done something stupid, most likely."

"All's well," I promised her. "How's everything here?"

That got her more into business mode. "Xyll's being strange," she said. "I don't know what's happening, but at least it hasn't come busting out of its quarters. I guess . . . no news is good news?"

I nodded. Best we could do for now. "And Starcurrent?"

"Is here, Zara!" Starcurrent's translated voice came through cheerily, and I turned and saw zim undulating zis tentacles at me from farther across the docking bay. "Hello! I have a possible location for Lifekiller, but . . . is uncertain. The Phage swarm has changed directions twice since you left. I cannot be certain it is providing us an accurate fix, but there is a high probability given that one particular planet in its path is rich in uranium."

"Anything from the Sliver?" I asked. Bea shook her head. She'd tied her curls back, but little wisps had escaped and bounced around her face with the motion. "Damn. That's not so good."

"Well, they didn't exactly communicate before," she said. "It was more of an order than communication. Maybe they don't need us right now, so they don't call." I looked up. "Nadim? Do you know anything?"

"No," he said immediately. "Bea is right. There is no way to initiate contact with the Sliver. It is outward only, at least on the communication band that they accessed before. Perhaps the Bruqvisz have insight."

Made sense. I called up Suncross and asked. He said he'd investigate their network for any word. Once that immediate question was addressed, I realized that the aftereffect of partying with his crew had left me weak at the knees and in need of solid food. And coffee. So much coffee.

Bea went with me, pulled pancakes and made more coffee, and it sure was nice being taken care of like that. "I already ate," she assured me, and created herself a mocha latte. "By the way, we're down to about six months' worth of breakfast, but we can stretch that by going to liquid supplements and having breakfast more rarely. Lunch, dinner . . . we're running on the same clock, and I don't like skipping more than one meal a day, so . . ."

"So we're going to have to explore some options," I said, "if we can't get back home to restock. Yeah. I've been thinking about that too. We can ask Yusuf. He's been offworld a while; maybe he's got some good culinary hookups."

Not going to lie, pancakes and syrup and butter and coffee made me go *mmm*, and I felt Nadim paying close attention to the feelings. He felt pleasure consuming the best frequencies of starlight, but not quite as strongly as I did about my pancakes. I scraped up every bit of the syrup and licked my fork clean and stretched with a happy sigh.

You enjoyed that, he said. *I like it when you find such happiness in things. I can't quite understand why, but I do understand the how of it.*

Not sure if it's emotions that release endorphins, or endorphins that unleash emotions, but anyway, it's a pretty nice biosystem humans got, I told him. *Too bad we're not quite as tough as other species, though.*

You are, he said quite earnestly. *Physically soft, yes, but you have a ruthless streak that is rarely seen in others. And the capacity to regulate it, which is even more rare. Value what you are, Zara. I do.*

I enjoyed hearing that as much as eating the pancakes.

Stationwide announcement on the Sliver, recording ends abruptly

Attention all residents and vendors:

An alert remains in effect. Please go to your assigned duty stations or shelter in place. All ships awaiting docking procedures must immediately depart or face certain destruction. All Sliver personnel beyond the shield must seek shelter and register location.

Database backup and transmission in progress

Call for assistance in progress

Remain calm

Remain calm

Remain

CHAPTER SIXTEEN

Lost Sliver

I WASN'T TOO surprised to get an emergency transmission. Any number of swords were hovering above our heads and waiting to drop on us, so it was a little bit of a relief to see there was something coming at us in the form of a call.

Suncross.

The Bruqvisz's face filled the screen, and the second I saw it, I knew it was bad. Not that he was especially expressive, but his crew stood behind him, and they looked downcast. And alarmed.

"I have news, Zara," he said, and the fact he used my

proper name instead of the nickname put me on immediate edge. "The Sliver is lost."

"Lost?" I knew what he meant, but I didn't *want* to know. I was hoping that it was a glitch, or a misunderstanding, or any damn thing except what it was. "You mean, uh, moved?"

"No," he said. "I mean destroyed utterly and completely." His ruff came up, and so did the ruffs of his crew. "We mourn those who are gone. We will avenge them."

Pinky's bar was gone. The haggling scavengers. The engineering crew that had refit Nadim with his armor and weapons. I swallowed hard. "What about Bacia?"

"Unknown, but likely escaped, too cunning to die and too difficult to kill."

I thought he was right. Bacia would've thrown the rest of the residents of the Sliver to the Phage to cover their retreat; they'd have taken accumulated wealth and anything or anyone valuable to them, but the rest would have been considered acceptable losses. Made me ill, but I understood Bacia pretty well. "The drones?"

"There's no trace of functional drones left among the wreckage," Suncross said. "Our people and the Elaszi are coordinating salvage and recovery efforts. In this, we have common cause."

"Uh, we made a deal with the Elaszi. We gave them some of Bacia's drones. Did . . . did they get hit with the recall? And do they hold that against us?" I could imagine they'd feel like they got taken on that deal. Not my intention, but intentions don't always matter when it comes to money and honor.

"Elaszi have accepted that the recall was beyond your control. But they may barter for favors later."

That was a sweet relief. But only for a second. "Were there survivors at the Sliver?"

He shook his head.

"Only dead," he said. "We recover remains. Will honor according to the rites of each species. Elaszi are uninterested in this and would harvest bodies for minerals; we trade first salvage for this privilege. Bruqvisz will write their stories and recover data that may assist in knowing what battle raged here, and how it was lost. Their stories will be heard."

That was surprisingly touching, I thought. And I respected the Bruqvisz for trading away potential profit for common good. Not sure I'd have taken that on, but I was grateful someone had. "Ask your brethren if they can get any data on Bacia," I said. "Bacia owes us some damn drones if they got out, and we can trade back with the Elaszi to get us out of hot water. If the salvagers aren't finding any trace of functional drones, maybe Bacia took the rest when they retreated."

"Likely," Suncross said. "Bacia would not spend resources on a lost cause. Will seek to rebuild elsewhere. We will locate."

I signed off and looked at Bea, her brown eyes bright with tears. "That's awful," she said quietly. "All those beings, just . . . destroyed. By the Phage, right?"

"Lifekiller," I said. "He sent the Phage. I'm guessing Bacia had something he wanted, and he wasn't taking no for an answer. Probably not uranium; that's available in quantity in a lot of bigger places."

"Samples," Nadim said. "Starcurrent's tissue samples might have been what the god-king was looking for. He surely doesn't wish to have others researching his biology."

"But what the hell is he doing?" I wondered aloud.

It was impossible to tell if the Phage had been given orders. They could have been acting on an earlier suggestion, the same reason they attacked the Sliver when we defended and drove them off the first time. We had a lead on where the god-king might be hunkered down, and I was afraid we'd get there too late, and he'd get ahead of us, wreaking havoc that we couldn't stop. We'd have more firepower when the cousins returned from Earth, but there was no telling how long it would take for them to catch up. In the meantime, it was up to us to turn the tide.

Bea lifted a shoulder in a half shrug. "There's only one way to find out."

She walked me back to my room, and I paused outside. "Is it okay if I take some time with Nadim? I don't want you to feel cut out, but—"

"It's fine. He was pretty shaken when you left, though I kept telling him you had a plan, even if you didn't explain it to us."

I broke eye contact on a vague rush of guilt. "Hey, I'm doing better. Last time I didn't even warn you before I did something risky."

"We appreciate the heads-up," she teased.

"Thanks for keeping Nadim calm. I know it's hard for him when I'm putting it all on the line."

Bea touched my cheek gently. "It's not easy for me either."

"I got it. I'll catch up with you later."

She went off down the hall as I slipped into my room. Nadim was quiet, but I could feel his attention on me. Exhausted, I sank down onto the floor and rested my cheek against the wall. That way, I was touching him at two points. Softly, he came to me, filling my head with gentle questions.

"I'm okay," I said.

"Thank you, Zara."

"For what?"

"Coming back to me."

"I'm sorry I had to go in the first place, but you understand, right? I had to finish what I started. I didn't mean for it to blow up like it did, but since Deluca escalated that shit, I couldn't let anyone else get hurt."

Nadim said, "I understand. But I wish you treasured yourself as much as I do. I wish you saw yourself as precious and irreplaceable."

That shut me straight up, because I wasn't used to anyone just saying that about me. It wasn't that I didn't see myself as important, but his emotion flooded me, humbling me when I saw myself through his eyes, all shimmering, iridescent colors that filled his world with wonder. I half closed my eyes and flattened my palm against the wall, watching as Nadim traced my fingers, limning each one in light.

"Okay, point taken."

I dropped into a light bond, letting myself enjoy the feel of Nadim keeping me safe. This was more trust than I'd ever given anyone before. If I thought about it, it was wild that I could feel this way when he was damn near everything—my love, my world, my literal home. The fact that Beatriz lived here too only made it sweeter because I had twice as many people caring, looking after me, and scolding me softly when I crossed the line. Funny how their reproaches never set me off. The anger I'd wrestled with on Earth never erupted out here against those I loved. Dr. Yu would be pleased to hear that too.

"You're happy," Nadim said.

"I shouldn't be. Not with so much shit poised to hit the fan."

"That's one of the things I love about you," he told me.

"What is?"

"The fact that you can find joy anywhere. I told you when we first met. You remember? I said how bright you are, how beautifully you shine."

I let out a little breath because his sweetness was making the top of my head tingle. "You did say that," I mumbled.

At the back of my head, knocking against the calm I was trying to assemble, memories of our time on the Sliver shifted like jagged bits of glass, shredding my peace of mind. Nadim gentled me with soothing mental touches, telling me silently that it wasn't our fault. He understood now what I'd always known—that we couldn't save everyone—that choices had to be made, but it was like sitting on a chair made of knives, knowing that we'd chosen to let them die. I'd said better crims than civilians, but now that the worst had happened, I thought about the stall where I'd bought the portable force field generator. Did that vendor die in the Phage attack? What about the kindly Abyin Dommas who fought in the Pit, but who couldn't bring zimself to finish opponents in the final round?

"Sometimes, I think it would be better if I had arms," Nadim said, out of nowhere.

I startled, opening my eyes in surprise. "Why? What are you saying?"

"When you're sad, you imagine me hugging you. I cannot ever do that, Zara. Beatriz can. Marko and Yusuf can. Chao-Xing could if she wished. They can make contact in ways that I cannot."

Oh damn. Though I hadn't wished for that in a while, I did recall a few occasions when I'd wanted to hug Nadim. It wasn't like a deep or heartfelt thing, so it bothered me that he might be thinking that he wasn't enough. I had to be careful how I replied.

"I don't want you to change," I said firmly. "That . . . it's just what I'm used to. I've adapted since then, and I love how you are, exactly as you are. You don't need to alter a single thing for me to think you're wonderful."

"You wouldn't want . . ." Nadim spoke softly and paused, as if he was afraid to finish the sentence.

"What, sweetheart?"

"A representative form could be built. It could carry me, as you do."

"Are you talking about getting an android body, just so we could interact more like humans do?"

"It might—"

"No thanks," I cut in. "I don't want or need that. Our hearts and minds can touch. And you can feel the physical stuff that I do with Bea, so you're a part of it that way. Do you feel like what we have isn't enough?"

"Definitely not."

"What brought this on?"

"You have . . . certain memories of the offensive one."

I noticed he didn't even want to say Derry's name, and I didn't blame him. Derry was my past, and now he wasn't even alive, not somebody Nadim needed to worry about measuring up to. Hell, Nadim taught me how love should be—warm and open, honest and tolerant, with room for people to grow. Derry was like a pair of shoes I'd worn for a while and then outgrown, before he went to work for a monster and came back gunning for me.

"Put him out of your mind. I won't be dwelling on him anymore. I didn't want him dead, but I'm not sorry it went down like it did. He made the choices that narrowed the options down to him or me." I hesitated, wondering if Nadim would think less of me for admitting this.

"What is it, Zara?" Nothing but tender curiosity in his tone.

"There's some irony that the robot Deluca designed to

murder me took out his minion instead. Looks like I owe EMITU another big one. Do you think he'd take a haiku in payment?"

I was joking, but Nadim took the question seriously. "Possibly. Should we write one?"

"Maybe later. My brain needs a rest. My body too." There was one thing I hadn't done since I came on board—and I might want to do it with Bea at some point—but I wasn't quite there yet. And I hadn't dared let Nadim find out that I did it either. Normal for everyone and the safest way to let off some steam but I felt weird about sharing it with Nadim and weird about asking for privacy too.

"Are you tired?" Nadim asked.

Well, yeah, but I was also keyed up. Two things could knock me out when I was like this: exercise or sex.

Hell with it. He probably knows what humans are like. I'm sure some Honors have asked him to step out before. A year is a long time. I made up my mind as I got in bed. There was nothing wrong with this, no reason to hide it from Nadim. I'd do that only if I was ashamed, and I wasn't.

I turned over on my stomach in my favorite position and drifted into a soft bond with Nadim, letting pleasure suck me in, physical and mental. It didn't take long to get there, shivers rolling through me, and his warmth in my head made it feel like he was holding me close afterward.

"That was beautiful," he said, and I felt his wonder wash

over me like afterglow. "Like starlight. Like flying."

"You're such a sweet talker." I couldn't stop smiling. Finally, I slept.

"Wake up." A soft voice was whispering right against my ear. I groaned and rolled over to find Bea leaning above me. Lazily I sat up, and she greeted me with a sweet kiss, one at the edge of my mouth, another on my cheek. "I wasn't going to bother you, but something's happening with Xyll. Oh, and Chao-Xing is arriving in five minutes. I called her first so as not to wake you, but Xyll doesn't want to talk to Chao-Xing. It's asking for you nonstop. It's in pain and I think it might be . . . dying."

"Shit," I said.

"My feelings exactly. I hope you don't mind that I called Chao-Xing for backup," Bea added. "I just—you looked like you needed whatever rest you could find. But she's almost here now."

I shook my head. "I get you. Xyll was a lot, even before. I'm trying but it's tough."

The last time I saw Xyll, the alien looked like nothing more than a sentient spinal column with a small maw full of needle-sharp teeth, still able to eat its way through damn near anything. Not a feature you wanted in something's baby phase.

"Nadim, how close is the Hopper?" Bea asked.

I scrambled to get dressed as he answered, "Opening for Chao-Xing now."

My boots were half-on as I ran toward Xyll's part of the ship. Nadim felt heavy with concern, worry underneath. "Xyll . . . hurts," he said. "I can feel it radiating from the room."

"Not healing? Dammit. I was hoping EMITU's treatments would help."

"I can't solve all your problems," the med bot said, whirring toward me. Bea was following close behind. "Any care I offer this poor creature is experimental at best. The ethics! You'll cause me to be discredited as a care unit."

"I thought you didn't want to be a med bot anyway," I muttered.

"Being kicked out is not the same as choosing to quit." EMITU sounded huffy.

Bea stepped between us. "Now is not the time. Should we get the doors open or wait for Chao-Xing?"

Nadim said, "We should wait," at the same time that I answered, "Let's check on Xyll. EMITU is here, so it should be fine."

"Are you certain you want to do this?" Nadim asked. He sounded worried. I was too, a little, but that vanished when Chao-Xing came around the corner. Even though she had to be tired, it didn't show at all. Not a hair out of place, sharp creases in her trousers, not a wrinkle to be seen.

She carried a rifle and had a sidearm in her belt and nodded to us as she approached. "Okay," she said. "I've been trying to talk to it, but it doesn't want anything to do with me. You're the chosen one with the Phage cell, it seems."

I could've lived without that honor. Pun intended.

"Ready?" I asked, and Chao-Xing nodded. "Right. Here we go."

The door opened, and a breath of what I can only describe as *hell* billowed out. It looked yellow and tasted like a toxic mix of acid and sulfur, and I turned away, coughing and choking. The others were far enough away not to be caught in the killer smog. EMITU rushed forward and I felt a jab in my arm. "Ow!"

"It's for your own good," EMITU declared, and rolled backward.

That's when Xyll—well, the reddish, whippy thing that was Proto-Xyll—came screaming out of the mist, straight for me, and I got a good look at the nightmare teeth that gleamed like stainless steel, and the horrific motion of its slithering, bony tail along the floor as it curled up, and it occurred to me way, *way* too late that this was a mistake, a fatal and everlasting mistake, as that tail uncoiled like a spring and sent itself hurtling toward me.

Chao-Xing threw herself in front of me in a fiercely protective stance, bringing her weapon up, but the Phage cell was too fast. Xyll latched on to her back like a second bloody skin, tail wrapped around her rib cage, and it dripped a thick, smoky ichor down the back of her uniform.

She was still upright, twitching. My lungs burned from the yellow mist coming off Xyll's body. No time to hesitate. I shoulder-rolled, slapped my boots on the deck, and launched myself in a flat dive that sent me close to Chao-Xing . . . close enough to grab her pistol on the way, twist, and fire in almost the same motion. Everything seemed syrup-slow, even my heartbeat, and I aimed and fired at the widest point of Xyll's back where it clung to C-X's spine. Its head was at the base of her neck. I felt the phantom sensation of what had happened when Xyll went for me last time. I could still feel the weird cold sensation of its presence back there.

EMITU wheeled forward, but Xyll was locked on Chao-Xing and burrowed through her flesh. It squirmed out of sight. The space between this heartbeat and the next, that was how long it took. I dropped my weapon, unable to believe what I'd just witnessed.

Was it killing her from the inside?

"Holy shit." I couldn't stop shivering. "Is she dying? What's Xyll doing in there?"

Nadim touched my mind, but it didn't feel as warm as usual due to his fear. Bea was crying. I reached for her, unable to see clearly through my own tears. She nestled into my arms as Chao-Xing collapsed as if she'd been struck by lightning. *This can't be happening.*

"You flesh-bags make my life so difficult," the bot said. "I am *very* cross. Tell me, why do I have to be cross? Why not quadrangular? Or square? Or, heavens, *triangular*? I feel this is angular chauvinism . . ." Chao-Xing went rigid, and she thrashed like she was having a seizure.

"EMITU! Do something!" I shouted. The med bot injected her with something, then gave her another shot. Nothing seemed to help. "EMITU!"

"I'm administering treatments!"

I felt Bea's arms wrap around me, but somehow, I was holding *her*, and Nadim was banging questions at me I couldn't answer, and I just felt so sick and helpless and sliding toward chaos.

Chao-Xing can't die. She can't.

From the personal correspondence of Bacia Annont, sent to the Oborub Collective, archived to the Apophis Cloud

Four thousand seven hundred and seventy-two years of work, turned to rubble in a handful of moments by Lifekiller. I should have left him where he rested. But how was I to know he would wake, could wake? Or how powerful he could become?

Loss of the Sliver is catastrophic but survivable. I will rebuild in a new place, distant and even more hidden. I always find opportunities and greed to exploit.

My faithful servants accompany me on this journey. For the rest, I will dedicate a monument when convenient. Remaining drones flank me as we flee the battle.

Rich salvage opportunities I leave behind. I remain in possession of the cell samples from Lifekiller, and thus remain powerful; if genetic modifications to my code are possible using this template, I will become even more powerful.

Powerful enough perhaps to devour Lifekiller.

Something to consider.

CHAPTER SEVENTEEN

Lost Power

WATCHING AND NOT being able to *do* anything was the worst. I wasn't used to feeling so powerless, so unnecessary, and I paced around Ops, torn between charging into Medbay (which EMITU had strictly forbidden) and letting out a primal scream. This was my fault. I'd campaigned to bring Xyll on board. I'd believed the damn thing could be *helpful*. Everybody, including Chao-Xing, had said I was making a mistake, but I'd been arrogant enough to think I saw potential nobody else could.

And now it had taken my friend and might be killing her from the inside out. Because she'd risked her life to protect me, although I didn't even like her when we first met. Thought she was an inflexible hard-ass with no sense of humor, but it turned out she was willing to go all in for me. Hot tears started in my eyes again.

The comm beeped, and suddenly I had Marko on screen, ranting at me. "You didn't think we had enough trouble without exposing Chao-Xing to the Phage you kept as a pet?"

"Hey!" It burst out of me, totally out of control, and I rushed the console and leaned in so he'd get a good, hard look at the anger. "*I get it!* This is my fault, and she's paying for it. I know that, and you have no idea how sorry I am. Just shut up and let me think!"

"You thinking is what got us into this!"

"Unless you've got something useful to—"

"Get it out of her," he said grimly. "And kill it. If that's not possible, then—"

"We're not touching her. So help me, if you say a single word about destroying the host, I will come over there and slap you so hard that your children will feel it."

A tiny part of me held out hope, wanting to believe all this could still work out. That we wouldn't lose our friend, our warrior queen, to something so stupidly random as a creature that was supposed to be a damn ally. If she'd fallen to Lifekiller, at least that would have meant something. This . . . this was no kind of way for someone like her to go out.

"This is such bullshit. I'm the one who called Chao-Xing over. Zara was asleep! How about you fight with me instead?" Bea shouted back at him, and I touched her shoulder in appreciation before I did what I should have already done: I cut the connection.

Marko tried to reconnect. I blocked him.

Right then, Starcurrent came into the command center, tentacles fluttering; judging from the mix of colors that came and went, ze was very anxious and not sure what to do. We were rowing the same boat. I lifted a hand in greeting but addressed my next words to Nadim.

"No more calls from Typhon until we know what's going on; he's bound to react badly to what's happening right now, and we can't afford that," I said. "Do we have any data at all, from any source, about what's happening with Xyll? Knowing why it went in might help." I couldn't articulate the fear that it might be devouring C-X.

"The Bruqvisz may have something," Nadim said. "They collect stories and myths. Our data on the Phage is less than accurate."

I called up Suncross, got Ghostwalk—Suncross was presumably resting or passed out somewhere—and Ghostwalk immediately said, "Yes, we have many stories. Not all about the swarms. Shall I send?"

"Yes," I said. "Absolutely."

The compendium he sent was, well, extensive would be a good word. No way would I have the time to pore over all of that, especially since it was (unsurprisingly) written in a language that I didn't comprehend. "This is great, but . . . Nadim? Can you translate for me?"

"Yes," he said. "It might take a little time. Shall I let you know when it's done?"

"Yes, please." I pushed back from the console with a frustrated growl. "I'll be in the combat sims. I need somewhere to put all this—"

"Rage?" Bea finished. "Yes, I can feel it, and so can Nadim. Go get rid of it."

I nodded and jogged for the holo room, fast as I could move.

For nearly an hour I killed things, punched things, kicked things; I made sure every damn one of them was a simulacrum of a Phage, and I fought with weapons, bare-handed, every way I possibly could.

And then I punched something that felt slightly different. More real. And I realized that without me seeing it, someone had entered my sim.

Marko.

He grabbed me and shoved me back, and all of a sudden, we were *on*. I swung for him, he blocked and sent a mule kick that should have shoved me through the wall, only I dodged it and he staggered, off-balance. I landed a round-house kick to his side, and he rolled and came up fluid as a tiger.

"Hey!" I checked him with an outstretched palm, though I was ready for it not to work. "You need to back right the hell off, *now*."

"No. You've been a force for chaos since you came on board Nadim," he said. "You took a sweet, innocent ship and turned him into—"

"What?" Nadim's voice suddenly came from the walls, and it sounded surer, more mature than I'd imagined he could. "An adult, capable of making my own decisions? I've grown, Marko. You refused any deeper relationship with me, and I will not have you pretend you were the guardian of my innocence—which could also be called ignorance. Zara is right for me, now and always. And you have no right to judge her. You never challenged me, never taught me, never made me *better*. She has."

"Better?" The bitterness in Marko's voice was kind of sad. "You're out of control, Nadim. She's done that."

"I am more in control than I have ever been. I no longer live by the rules of the Elders, or the Honors; I decide for myself, and with my true-bonded crew. I am autonomous. And you are still shackled to a system of rules that you can't reconcile." Nadim's voice softened. "I know you are worried for Chao-Xing. I am too, and so is Zara. But you are with friends, Marko. Always. Let yourself accept that the lies no longer rule you, and you'll find your own peace."

Exactly when did our beautiful ship get so wise? He'd always been loving and caring, but this was deeper. A cutting kind of compassion like a surgeon's knife.

Marko wavered, and then sagged back against the wall with his hands dangling at his sides. I relaxed my stance. A little. "It's . . . Chao-Xing shouldn't be hurt like this. She was born for this, and I . . . wasn't. I'm not enough. Typhon accepted me because of her, and I can't be more. I've tried. And I can't go home; I accepted the Journey and it's for life."

"Screw the rules," I said. "Look, do I have to tattoo that on your damn forehead in reverse, so you see it in mirrors? If you want to go home, *go home*. Tell them the truth. Get it out on every feed around the world; you know they'll be sticking camera drones in your face the second you land. Tell them everything and let people decide for themselves what place Earth has in all this shit. *That* would be a thing Chao-Xing would approve of."

All the starch went out of him with that, like he'd never even considered going home as anything like a real possibility. And I saw the naked *want* in his eyes. He was good at this, but he didn't feel it like I did. And you had to feel it to be here for the rest of your life.

I went to him and put a hand on his shoulder. Nothing too sentimental, a friend's gesture. He wasn't in the hugging mood, and neither was I.

Nadim's voice broke it up when he said, "Zara? EMITU wishes you to go to Medbay. Marko as well."

Oh, that didn't sound so good.

I could tell when we were at the Medbay doors that Marko felt reluctant to go in. I felt it too, and from the look she sent me, so did Bea. Couldn't tell what Starcurrent thought, but ze was rippling those face-fronds a lot and strobing colors I didn't think were exactly content. On impulse, I grabbed Bea's hand and offered my other to Marko. He took it.

Then we walked in to find out what EMITU had to tell us.

The bot spun toward us and accelerated like he meant to run us down. "You must decide!" EMITU sounded *super* agitated, which was exactly what I didn't want in a med bot. Or anyone with that many sharp instruments on their appendages. "Shall I put her out of her misery, or—"

"No!" we all said, as if we'd actually organized it. I continued, full speed ahead. "Don't you even *think* about it, you scrap heap!"

"That's hurtful," EMITU said. "I only asked because I'm about to bring her out of sedation, and when I do, she's going to scream. A lot. But as far as I can tell she will survive."

As the med unit went to work on Chao-Xing, I stood by the door, feeling just as helpless as I had before I fought Marko in the combat sim. I felt Marko behind me, standing with Bea, but I only had eyes for EMITU and his patient. I didn't know when it had happened, but at some point, Chao-Xing had started mattering to me. Friend, yeah, but she was more, a mentor too, someone whose good opinion I craved.

The needle attached to EMITU's extensor sank into Chao-Xing's arm. As promised, a shriek escaped her, and her body contorted.

I took a step forward, then turned away. "Nadim, are you finding anything useful in the files Ghostwalk sent?"

"I'm analyzing, Zara. So far, nothing seems applicable to our situation." He sounded tense and worried. Felt that way too, though I'd lessened our bond to keep my anxiety from affecting him.

"Status?" I asked the bot. "I mean, take some scans. Find out what the hell Xyllarva is doing in there."

"On it, Zara."

I still wasn't used to this robot calling my name, but I took it as a sign that I wasn't pissing him off. He ran the tests and clicked over the results. It took all my self-control not to pace. I was watching Marko, trying to see if he was going to lose it—and if he did, what I was willing to do to stop him. "EMITU?"

"Don't rush me," he snapped, but then he was done in a matter of seconds. "I have good news and bad news. Which do you prefer first?"

Bea answered for us, squeezing my hand. "Good. It will bolster us for the bad."

Marko put a hand on my shoulder, not bracing me, but more like holding on because the ground might suddenly tilt beneath his feet.

"Xyllarva is not eating Chao-Xing or laying eggs inside her."

"Okay, whew. That *is* good." I started to smile, but EMITU whirred his extensors, telling me silently not to get too excited, a cautionary gesture. "Sorry, go on."

The med bot added, "Xyllarva has latched on to her cerebellum and twined around her spinal cord. Surgical removal would certainly kill her. The Phage are resistant to most toxins, so anything strong enough to eradicate it would—"

"Also kill Chao-Xing," Marko finished.

"You're putting words in my mouth, but yes," EMITU said. "For the host to survive, the symbiote must thrive. Congratulations, a fascinating hybrid has been created. Huzzah! Now please remove your distracting emotions from my office. I must conduct more tests and find out how I can save this new species."

"She's an infected human!" Marko spat. "Not a new—"

"Zara, escort him out or I'll tranq him."

Figuring this wouldn't go anywhere good, I grabbed Marko's arm and Bea helped me haul him out of Medbay. He fought then, nearly smacking Bea in the eye, and neither Nadim nor I was having that.

"Stand down," Nadim thundered, sounding like Typhon on a bad day.

Marko paused in shock, and I wrenched his arm behind his back and smashed him face first into the wall. "This doesn't help Chao-Xing. You think she'd call this a good look?"

He finally shook his head.

"Going to behave yourself?"

When his shoulders slumped, I felt the fight go out of him, if not the deep underlying anger. Marko nodded, and though I didn't altogether trust his answer, I let him loose.

As he turned, Bea hugged him. "I know how you feel. My head's a mess too. I still can't believe what's happening."

"Let's give EMITU a chance to scope out the situation. Maybe it's not as bad as it looks." Honestly, that sounded like pure bullshit even to my own ears.

But I couldn't say what I was thinking—that if EMITU couldn't solve this, we might have to shoot Chao-Xing before she tried to eat our faces. In science fiction vids, people who got infested with aliens never got good endings. *We'll be the first*, I tried to tell myself, but my logical brain wasn't having any of that nonsense. It was all I could do to keep from keeling over with guilt. Xyll hadn't chosen Chao-Xing. It had set its sights on me, but C-X had paid the price.

Marko dropped his head onto Bea's shoulder, and she patted his back, while staring at me wide-eyed. I could read the question in her pretty brown eyes—*What am I supposed to do now?* If I was a bad person, I'd bail on her right this second, but I stepped up and patted Marko awkwardly, imagining how I'd feel if it was Bea quarantined in Medbay right now. An ache blossomed in my chest, too sharp for bearing.

"Nadim?" I said softly.

"Yes, Zara?"

"You're quiet. Can you maybe say something good here, make him feel better?"

"This is beyond my ability for consolation." His grave tone troubled me, even as Typhon thumped out a staccato message of desperation, wordless and angry and fearful.

Is Typhon all right? I asked silently.

A negative answer filled my head, and it was a testament to how worried Nadim was that he let my mind brush Typhon's. With C-X down for the count and Marko falling apart over here, the Elder only had Yusuf—whom he hadn't known long—and he wasn't handling it well. I closed my eyes and drifted, concentrating on offering calm and comfort. To my surprise, Typhon settled a little when he felt me. He wasn't *my* Leviathan, but I'd touched him deeper than anyone had in eons when I made my escape from his prison cell, and we'd reconnected when he'd thanked me for risking our asses to keep him safe.

Zara. Typhon gave my name layers, and the feelings were colors, so violent that even Starcurrent couldn't have identified them. I trembled and fell back against the wall. Nadim caught me, held me steady, even as I bolstered Typhon.

You're not alone. Yusuf is there.

Chao-Xing is dying. I feel her anguish. I never wanted to feel this again. I should never have let them in.

No wonder Marko was a mess. Being connected to Typhon was like being lost in a storm of razors right now.

I cordoned off the emotions I couldn't let Typhon feel and concentrated on reassurance, warmth, and soothing solace. Drumming had worked once before, so I nudged a thought toward Nadim, and he moved to make it happen. Leviathan didn't touch one another a lot, but this might help. He spun so he could pat Typhon with his tail—slow, careful thumps that should send vibrations throughout the Elder, comforting percussion.

We'll work it out. EMITU will save her. Marko will stay here for a while to watch over Chao-Xing, so we'll send Starcurrent if ze wants to go. Is that all right?

Typhon steadied gradually. *Yes. I will welcome the singer if ze chooses. Thank you, Zara Cole.*

No problem. Are you feeling better?

Typhon sent a wordless response, an image of him diving through starlight. Yes, that seemed better.

After that, Nadim pulled me away, softly possessive, and he was the only one in my head. *You handled that well. I was afraid the Elder would do something reckless.*

When I opened my eyes, I found myself alone in the hallway. Bea must have taken Marko away from Medbay, hopefully someplace he could rest. I could have asked Nadim, but my knees wouldn't hold. I sank down and tipped my head against the wall.

In a bit, I'd go ask Starcurrent if ze minded a transfer, but for now I needed to gather my strength. The pain was damn near overwhelming. *Chao-Xing did that. For me.*

"She wanted to protect you," Nadim said. "Because you are younger. It wasn't even a choice, just an inevitable instinct."

"Is that why? It seems like you were in her head when it happened."

"Not precisely. More that her feelings were so powerful that they spilled over."

"Can you feel her now?" I almost didn't want to know, but not asking would be cowardly after what she did.

"Some. But she is mixed with Xyll. As EMITU said, they

feel . . . blended now. Pain. Confusion. Fear. I cannot tell what is hers and what comes from Xyll."

That's not what I wanted to hear.

"I'm sorry, Zara."

"Not your fault. No reason to apologize, either. Like Marko said, I'm the one who wanted to use Xyll when I had no idea how dangerous it could be." I tried to keep my voice level. Failed miserably.

"When you hurt, *I* hurt. And there is no remedy," Nadim said sadly.

With a groan, I hauled myself up. Time to find Starcurrent and update zim on the situation. I couldn't bring myself to apologize for hurting Nadim with my pain when Chao-Xing was suffering so much more.

We'd both have to bleed emotionally until the wound clotted or somebody died.

INTERLUDE: CHAO-XYLL

什么都没有了，一片虚空，一切仿佛都消失了。我做不到。这
种感觉就像是空前绝望、饥肠辘辘、失望透顶、冷彻心髓、寒
冷孤寂。我们是谁？你们又是谁？我什么都听不见了。一切虚
空，一切仿佛都消失了，只剩下疼痛，得吃些东西，要吃些东
西，必须要吃些东西

Interlude: Nadim

I feel what Chao-Xyll feels. The words wash over me. Haunting me.

Nothing, nothing, nothing, I can't, this is what is desperate, hunger, despair, cold, cold alone, what are we, what are you, what I can't hear, nothing, nothing, just pain, must eat, must eat, must eat

CHAPTER EIGHTEEN

Lost Control

STARCURRENT KNEW MOST of what had been going on. The only thing I needed to tell zim about was Chao-Xing's current condition—and Typhon's unsteady mood—since it would help if ze headed over to keep Yusuf company and to settle Typhon down. The Abyin Dommas listened with muted colors, and when I finished, ze agreed in a swirl of tentacles.

"Will go if Typhon needs. Have permission to take Hopper?"

"Sure. If Marko and Chao-Xing need pickup, you or Yusuf can come back for them." That would be the best-case scenario. Worst case, Marko went back alone, and I wasn't sure what would happen to Typhon then.

I hated leaving Chao-Xing in EMITU's hands, but I needed to make sure Bea was okay. Marko wasn't; I already knew that, but Bea was with him. I ran her down coming out of her room, a worried look still clouding her face. She took a step toward me, and I wrapped her up in a hug that was as comforting as I could make it.

"I hope he'll sleep," she said. "Though I'm not sure I ever will again." I felt the shudder that ran through her.

"Don't hate me for saying this, but our mission hasn't changed. We still have to get to Lifekiller as fast as we can, whatever happens to Chao-Xing. She'd tell us the same, if she could weigh in."

We were still tracking the Phage back to the god-king. I didn't like myself for worrying about that while we had personal shit hitting the fan, but C-X's condition didn't alter our imperative. Defeating Lifekiller had to happen, no matter what was going on in Medbay. No matter whose life was in the balance.

Bea sighed. "I know. She did vote that way when we were talking about Bacia's SOS. Let's check the readings."

I followed her into Ops, and she triangulated the tail of the Phage swarm we had been hunting. "Still on course?" I asked.

Nadim answered, "I've altered our heading as necessary.

I can still hear them, even at this distance." Made sense that he'd be alert to a threat that could devour him from the inside out and puppet him like they had the poor Elder we mistook for Typhon, just after the Gathering.

"Hey," I said to Bea. "Line up the Phage's course. Where are we, exactly? And how far from home?"

"Home? You mean Earth?"

I flashed her a smile I didn't completely feel. "You saying that means we've been in space too long already."

Bea still scanned and took her own readings, which I assessed over her shoulder. Not that I didn't trust them, but it was good to form my own judgments.

"Okay. Earth is roughly over here." She pointed to the screen, a distant dot on the star map. "At Leviathan speed, maybe two days of travel?"

"How long until we catch up to the Phage?" I asked.

Nadim said, "A day and a half with no interruptions or deviations."

So thirty-six Earth hours, give or take. Good to know. I took a deep breath. I felt alone right now; Chao-Xing was the proven strategist, the one I would have turned to in order to check all my plans. But she wasn't here, and I was flying on my own. I was used to that, but not at this level. Not with the survival of our ships and Suncross's people and entire planets full of life depending on what I did next.

Bea touched my shoulder, and I wrapped an arm around

her, relaxing slightly when she leaned in. "You've got a plan for what we're going to do when we get there?" The slight upturn of her voice made it a question I could ignore if I wanted.

"Sure." I wished I could say *kill it with fire* but that wouldn't work on Lifekiller. No napalm in vacuum. But maybe that could be a solution? If we forced him down into a planet's atmosphere somehow, he might be crushed under his own weight and burn up as he fell . . . ? I couldn't figure how we'd push him down . . . Hell, I was good at spotting weaknesses, but even I couldn't pinpoint the god-king's flaws. Shoving him into a black hole might work, but I didn't see how we could do that either, not without sacrificing one or both Leviathan.

My only other idea involved launching him at a star so hot that it would immolate him, but from what I'd seen, he might just absorb that energy and power up; then where would we be? No. We needed something else.

And I didn't have it.

Sighing, I let go of Bea and headed to the docking bay. The least I could do was say bye to Starcurrent. The Abyin Dommas didn't have much, but ze was loading up zis few belongings when I got there, Bea following close behind. She hesitated, then reached out. Damn, this girl had come so far. At one point she was too scared to stand in the same space as a tentacle alien, and now she was trying to figure out how to hug one.

"I'm not sure how to do this," she finally said.

"Is some human ritual?" Starcurrent asked.

"She wants to hug you. So do I, really."

Starcurrent had wrapped zis tentacles around us on more than one occasion, though usually to keep us from being thrown around. This time, ze did it for other reasons. Ze smushed both Bea and me against zim, and many tentacles and tendrils wound around us. I had the uncanny sensation of being prey, just before the breath was squeezed out of me. It came back, though, when Starcurrent let go.

"Did this correctly?" ze asked.

I smiled. "Yeah, that was a good hug."

Bea was tearing up. "We'll miss you, Starcurrent."

Nadim sounded deeply sorrowful when he finally spoke. "It will not be the same without your colors."

"Good," said Starcurrent. "You are stronger than you know without me, and Typhon needs me now. Perhaps that will change. But also perhaps he needs song to reach the cold places within."

Ze got in Typhon's Hopper and we took that as a sign ze didn't care to linger. Maybe that would've made it even harder to leave. Bea and I scuttled out of the docking bay, so we didn't get caught in the depressurization. Nadim wouldn't do that to us on purpose, but there was no point in taking chances. From the other side of the doors, we watched Starcurrent go.

"Is Marko asleep?" I asked.

The question was really for Nadim since Bea wouldn't know. He answered, "I do not think so. He grieves."

"Yeah, I was afraid of that. We probably shouldn't sedate him, even if he needs the rest." I raised my eyebrows at Bea, making it a question, and she shook her head.

"I am worried," Nadim said. "He was in need of sleep even before Chao-Xing . . ." By his hesitation, he wasn't sure how to speak of her condition.

"Got infected?"

Because of me.

"That seems harsh, but accurate," he said somberly. "Xyll was a shrill noise within my skin, and now Chao-Xing has some of those same harmonics. I wonder if Marko hears that as well. He has always been sensitive to the subtle changes."

"Did you find anything about the Phage in the Bruqvisz records, by the way?" Trust Bea not to forget about the lore the lizards sent over.

"I'm not sure. I'd like to share something and see if you think it could be relevant."

I led the way to the media room, where Bea and I settled on comfortable seats. "This seems like the right place to listen to Bruqvisz stories."

From Nadim's tone, he was quoting directly from their

translated files, in a relentless sort of rhythm that formed its own music. "'We have fought the Eaters before and died in numbers. They are relentless. There is no turning them, and they will devour anything. Even metal isn't safe from their appetites. But great is the glory in defending from their invasion.'"

I remembered the splinter Phage family chowing down on Suncross's score. "That seems about right. This must be written about the Phage."

Bea nodded. "What else does it say?"

"I'm getting to it." Nadim went on, "'The Eaters are a scourge, but possess the potential for worse alone. Beware the Eater that slips its skin. It becomes a demon that steals the life of another.'"

"That sounds like what Xyll did to Chao-Xing," Bea said softly. "A parasite, taking over a body."

"Yeah, but hearing that it *could* happen when it already *has* happened isn't too helpful," I muttered. "Is there anything in that file about a cure?"

Nadim didn't reply for so long that a bad feeling came over me. "Just tell us," I prompted. "Please?"

He quoted it. "'If such a tragedy comes to pass, the only remedy is a quick and merciful execution, for the taken one is already lost. Eaters are parasites that puppet smaller life-forms as they do the Singers with greater numbers.

Death is the only answer. There is no honor in a slow and painful lingering.'"

Shit. I could see why Nadim didn't want to read that to us. Bea dropped her face into her hands, not even trying to control the tears, and I felt the hot sting behind my eyes. If we'd asked the lizards for their files when I first let Xyll live, could we have avoided this?

Maybe. Probably.

"Does it say anything about Eaters awakening?" I asked.

Nadim made a thinking noise. "Not so far, Zara. There is no mention of communicating with a Phage cell as we have. It seems this was entirely unknown to them."

That sounded like a spark of hope. I swallowed my urge to cry. I'd save the weeping until after I accepted there was truly no hope for Chao-Xing, and I wasn't there yet.

"Xyll was different. Maybe it won't kill Chao-Xing. EMITU said it wasn't eating her insides or laying eggs . . ." Despite what I'd seen on the asteroid, I still wasn't sure how the Phage reproduced. "Not even the Bruqvisz have ever *talked* to a Phage cell. We have. Maybe there are other impossible firsts in store."

Bea lifted her tear-streaked face, drawn by my wild, hopeful talk. "Do you really think so?"

"Hell, we've broken records before. Let's not give up on her yet. I didn't call her *Warbitch* for nothing." Bolstered, I got to my feet and headed for Medbay at a jog.

EMITU wouldn't open the door for me, but he did use the comm to ask, "What do you want, Zara? I thought I was clear when I evicted you lot."

"I just wanted to ask you to do your best. I know you've never encountered anything like this before, but try everything—and I mean *every* damn thing."

The med bot let out a long-suffering sound, robo-voice overly patient. "Are you implying that I would half ass the treatment of a patient in my care, even if said patient is a weird fusion of two meaty life-forms never before included in my incredibly complete medical database?"

"... No?" But I was also worried that if EMITU came to the same conclusion the Bruqvisz had—that a merciful end was the only way out for Chao-Xing—that might happen with incredible swiftness.

"Rest assured, I will provide the best care I can. I may not have chosen to be a med bot, but I am good at the trade. I take pride in my work."

Since he'd saved my ass more times than I could count, I could only agree. "That is true. Well, I'll leave you to it."

I should have known better. EMITU wouldn't do a mercy killing, even if he read that suggestion in the lizard files. That was more of a human response.

Yeah. But humans programmed him. He thinks because we made him think.

That was frightening.

When I turned away from the closed Medbay door, I nearly jumped out of my skin because Marko was lurking there. There were no shadows on Nadim, but I felt like he'd brought them with him. I'd thought he was resting in Bea's room, but nope.

"Anything new?"

I couldn't bring myself to repeat what Bea and I had heard from Nadim. "Her condition is unchanged." That had to be true or EMITU would have said something. "But he promised to exhaust all medical possibilities, and you know how inventive our med bot is. Bea hacked him so well that he even writes haiku."

A ghost of a smile haunted Marko's face, but didn't quite reach his eyes. "Are you serious?"

"Deadly. He'll drop one at every opportunity now." On closer scrutiny, I could see him swaying, holding on to the wall. "Man, I can't make you rest, but how long has it been since you ate something?"

Marko thought for a moment and then shook his head. So long that he evidently couldn't remember. I grabbed his arm and hauled his ass to the kitchenette.

"Anything you won't eat?" I added.

He shrugged. Great, he'd gone nonverbal on me. I got some food at random and heated it, then made him some tea. Hopefully the food and warm drink would relax him and let him get some sleep. The last thing we needed was for Marko to break all the way down; that would put Typhon right over the edge.

And me. I was barely holding myself together as it was.

I plopped the tray in front of him, opting for tough love. "Eat it all. Drink up too. You owe it to Chao-Xing to look after yourself. Otherwise, we won't be able to take on Lifekiller when we catch up to him. You'll need your strength to end this. We all do."

I called Suncross while Marko was finally sleeping, and Bea was off pursuing a bright idea about something we had in storage that she thought might be useful against the Phage. I didn't want any witnesses for this conversation, because I needed everybody to think I had my shit nailed down tight.

But I didn't, and Suncross knew that.

"Zeerakull," he greeted me, and I could tell by the nonverbal cues I'd started to pick up that he was both happy to hear from me and hung way the hell over. "Greetings."

"Sorry to wake you up," I said. "But we need to talk about what's coming next."

"Victory?"

Even he didn't sound that sure of it. "Bad news over here." I took a deep breath. "Xyll got Chao-Xing."

"Got . . . ?"

"Invaded. The thing's inside her, wrapped around her spinal column. Our med bot can't separate them without killing them both."

"Then, sorrowfully, you must give Zhang Chao-Xing a warrior's death," Suncross said, and both sets of eyelids blinked again: one lightly frosted, one totally opaque. I wondered if it was code. If it was, nobody had given me the key. "As horrible as such may be, do not delay in this. If you do, she will become a merciless killer of her own kind. Is the worst fate of all! Unimaginable."

I didn't want to tell him that humanity had plenty of merciless killers of its own kind running around and always had; it was part of our history that apparently didn't sit too well with other species out here. Most other species protected their own; they didn't prey on them. We were weird like that. "Your people have never come across a separated Phage that thinks and talks for itself, right?"

"Such a thing is impossible."

"Well, it isn't, because Xyll was doing it. Talking to us. Learning our language. It was even able to influence the rest of the Phage on our behalf, at least a little. And toward the end, it was learning manners, saying *please* and *thank you*. Xyll even fought to defend us when the killer robot attacked."

Suncross stared at me for a few seconds before he replied, "Zara Cole, you have been victim of a clever ruse, I think. The Phage cannot do this. Lifekiller must have meant for this to happen. Our people call it a poisoned spring; does this translate?"

"Trojan horse," I said. "We have a legend of soldiers who failed in conquering a city, then left a huge statue on wheels as a tribute to the city's god. It was hollow, filled with soldiers. The people rolled it into their own unbreakable gates, and the soldiers came out and killed them all."

Suncross, despite his kill-em-all attitude, seemed shocked by that. "Surely must be a story of rare villains!"

"Kind of?" I held out both hands, palms upraised. Take it for what it is. "We see it as clever, I suppose. But also, pretty shitty."

"Exactly so. Your Phage was a Trojan horse. Sent to you cut off from the hive, so you would take pity and bring it within. Then it destroys."

That made a certain awful kind of sense. Maybe Lifekiller wasn't just some mindless eating machine, spreading drama in his wake; maybe he was a strategist too. Maybe what I saw in Xyll was what I'd been meant to see, and instead of me spotting Lifekiller's weakness, he'd spotted *mine*.

That was a chilling possibility. I didn't like it at all, because it meant that Lifekiller wasn't called a god-king just because it was powerful; it was also smart.

Smart was bad.

Potentially disastrous. I was all for being the plucky David in this Goliath fight, but damn. If Xyll really was a weapon prepared by Lifekiller, it had already done its work and would keep on doing it, and the Bruqvisz's advice would be right. If Chao-Xyll was going to become an unstoppable serial killer, I had to cut her down before we lost anyone else.

But what if Suncross is wrong? What if Lifekiller didn't plan this, didn't even suspect it could happen? What if Xyll really was something new, and so is Chao-Xyll?

Man. These were heavy dice to be rolling.

"Zeerakull?" Suncross's voice was unexpectedly gentle. "I am sorry. Is hardest thing to do. I will gladly die in battle against enemies. I would hate to die doing battle against friends. And you are my friends. Chao-Xing also."

I took a deep breath. "Okay. So listen, you're my last line of defense here. If Chao-Xing kills me, kills Bea, takes over Nadim . . . you have to be the one to stop her. Understand? Save Nadim. Save Typhon."

"Zara!" Nadim sounded horrified. I wished I'd asked him not to listen to this call, but too late now. "If I lose you and Beatriz, I have nothing. I would not *wish* to continue!"

"Don't give me that," I said, and I meant it. "How long do Leviathan live?" He was silent. He didn't want to say it. "You see stars being born, and stars die. You live hundreds of human lifetimes. We're fireflies to you. Creatures born and dying in a season, and while we're here we're *beautiful*. So love us with all your heart, but let us go when it's time, and don't you *ever* think that ends your life too. I mean it, Nadim. Now say it."

"I can't!"

"You have to. If we fall in this fight *you need to go on*."

"But—"

"Typhon did. And he will again. We're here to show you what we are, but what we are isn't eternal. You can love us and let us go when our lives are over. You can love someone else. I'm not mad about it."

I *did* mean it, even though yeah, I had a touch of jealousy thinking of some other human, some other species of crew walking Nadim's halls, touching him, bathing him in their emotions. But that was what had to happen. Not during my lifetime, or Bea's, but *sometime*. And he needed to understand that losing his first lovers didn't mean the end of love.

He got it in a way I hadn't expected. "As you once loved Derry, but then loved me. Will you love me for the rest of your life, Zara?" He sounded hopeful. Wistful. A little desperate. "Because I know I will always love you. Always."

I'd never even thought of myself like this, as the true love of someone's life, but here it was, in all its searing glory. And I didn't hesitate. "Yes," I said. "I will love you for the rest of my life, Nadim."

I hadn't heard Beatriz come back, but she quietly said, "And so will I."

I turned and kissed her, and both of us dropped in a blazing golden emotional spiral into bond with Nadim, with each other, all of us melting together into a glorious perfect moment. Like sex, but better than that brief, explosive moment of pleasure. This lasted. This lasted *forever*, or as long as forever could be for mere humans.

I don't know how long it went, but when we finally parted in sweet afterglow, Suncross was still on the screen. He'd propped his chin on one of his four hands, but now he straightened up again and his ruff flared up to its fullest, richest stretch and hue.

"I am honored to be witness to a true bonding," he said. "Congratulations, Zara Cole, Beatriz Teixeira, Nadim. Do you wish to take a name?"

It was, I intuitively understood, the final step to sealing us together. I turned to Beatriz. "It's your turn," I said. "You name us."

Her lips parted in surprise, and I resisted the urge to kiss her again because she was *so* damn kissable. "Bezardim," she said. "What do you think?"

I did kiss her, then. And felt Nadim wrapping around us both. "I think it's perfect," I said.

"I do too," Nadim added.

And then we were one.

"I congratulate you," Suncross said. "I will write of this and we will sing the songs of Bezardim across the galaxies. You will become legend, my friends." He fixed me with a stare. "Remember what I told you of the risks. Do what you must. And soon."

Then he was gone from the screen.

I hugged Bea close. "Later, okay?" I told her, and kissed her just under the ear. Felt her shiver and loved how that resonated between all of us. "We'll make this real."

"It's real now," she said, and framed my face with her warm, soft hands. "I love you, Zara. I love you, Nadim."

Nadim didn't have words for this, so he bathed us in color and warmth and sweetness, and I said it back with just as much intensity.

Then I smiled and kissed her on her cute nose. "Work," I said. "What did you find?"

"Remote emitters," she said. "And I have an idea of how we can fool the Phage into destroying themselves."

"That's my girl."

From the planetary records of Luna Colony

Hello, Colony residents. We have a beautiful Earthrise on the horizon today. Temps inside the dome will remain constant at summer cycle, and the artificial day remains in effect to match. We're coming up on fall cycle in just another week, so look forward to cooler temps, autumn color in the e-trees, and of course our traditional Fall Festival, complete with Old Earth traditions like pumpkin eating and Haunting Night!

Rumor Control Patrol reports that chatter about the unscheduled visit of the two Leviathan guests to Earth has subsided, thanks to the incentive packages offered. Once again, Earth reports that these Leviathan were here purely for information exchange and to take on replacement Honors for the Journey after what we all know happened with the rebels on board the Leviathan Nadim.

Nitrogen ice cream will be served at all parks today from midday until scheduled dimming of the lights. If you're going out on the moon's surface today, please avoid all military marked boundaries; some exercises will occur. Enjoy your day, Citizens! And remember: we're here for YOU!

CHAPTER NINETEEN

Lost Patience

WE WERE JUST twelve hours from catching up to the Phage, and hard at work on Bea's idea, when EMITU called. After sleeping for ten hours, Marko had joined us and we'd gotten a pretty solid framework together and attached emitters all over it. Might not work, but then again, it just might. Spectacularly.

Trojan horse.

I answered the call when EMITU started demanding attention. "Yeah? What's going on? Is she—"

"My patient is now awake," EMITU said. "But not currently verbalizing. Quiet emptiness / A human, chimera twists / at the perfect star."

"Did you just haiku at me?" I asked.

"Perhaps I did. But is it not appropriate to the moment?"

"You weren't kidding," Marko muttered. "It really *does* that."

"You think I'd lie about *haiku*?"

He'd been looking better than the half-wild, half-dead guy who'd loomed at me in the hallway, but now some of those shadows came back. "Is she getting better or worse?" he asked. I suppose that was directed at me, EMITU, anyone who wanted to take the question.

I certainly didn't want it, oh *hell* no.

EMITU said, "The patient is physically well. Better than well; the symbiote seems to be repairing what damage she had very effectively."

"And we're real damn grateful," I jumped in before Marko could say anything to piss our AI doc off. "Has she shown any signs of, uh . . . aggression?" That was the only reasonable way to put it. I didn't want to put ideas into EMITU's head, or Marko's either.

"No. My patient—I am not absolutely sure of the pronoun to use at this point and will ask politely when opportunity presents—seems to have calmed quite nicely." EMITU seemed to consider for a second. "Though that may be a developmental phase, to be sure. Or just that there's currently no fleshmeat to murder. Would one of you like to volunteer to test that theory?"

He seemed to take a real gruesome delight in that. Marko and Bea both opened their mouths; I was sure Bea was going to say *no* and Marko was going to volunteer his shaky ass, so I quickly said, "Yeah, that's my job." When they both started protesting at once, I talked louder. "She got hit because she took *my* place. When Xyll was wounded in the hallway fighting with Jury, when it turned into Proto-Xyll . . . it went for me." I touched the back of my neck. "I think it was going to enter me, maybe tagged me with some pheromone. But it took Chao-Xing because she got in the way of its second try. I owe her this."

"Couldn't that mean it would try for you again?" Bea asked. She was scared. I didn't blame her; I wasn't feeling all that confident either. So I passed the ball.

"EMITU? What do you think, could the, ah, symbiote leave her body and try to invade me?"

"No." The bot sounded decisive. "It has interfaced quite thoroughly with the limbic and nervous systems, and even if it wanted to leave its current host, I don't think it could sustain itself outside of that body. It's tuned to Chao-Xing's metabolism and particular genetic makeup now."

That was some relief. Not a whole lot, to be honest. But I made Bea and Marko keep working, and while I went toward Medbay, I dropped into bond with Nadim.

He was not happy with this. *You can't risk yourself like*

this! He thundered it at me inside my head, and I sent him back a mental picture of dialing it back. He checked himself. Slightly. *I can't afford to lose you now. None of us can.*

Not my call, I said back. *We need to know if Chao-Xyll is dangerous or not. And if anybody has to pull that trigger, it has to be me. Understand that?*

He did. Didn't like it, but he also knew Beatriz would hesitate, and it would scar her far worse than it would me to carry out an execution. As for Marko . . . well. Not even a question; we couldn't let him carry this load.

We argued about it some more, but I could tell his mood was shifting from anger to deep anxiety. Wasn't sure that was any better, but I sent him as much confidence and comfort as I could as I stepped into Medbay, gun already drawn and ready at my side.

Chao-Xing lay in the bed, quiet and looking mostly normal—mostly. I couldn't pinpoint the change for a second until she looked directly at me, and then I felt an uneasy seismic shift inside.

It was her eyes. Her eyes weren't hers anymore. They'd gone paler, a color like spring honey. Human, but just a touch too bright, too much.

She opened her mouth and garbled noise came out, like she was relearning how to talk. It wasn't English, wasn't Chinese, wasn't any language at all, just . . . sounds. Unsettling ones.

I'm not calling her Chao-Xing anymore, I decided. *Chao-Xyll it is.*

C-X—lucky for me the nickname still applied—seemed confused by the lack of clarity, and a little frustrated. She—they?—sat up, and the sheet that had been lying over bare skin slipped off. And I saw more changes. C-X was . . . armored. A kind of organic black extrusion that covered skin, or replaced it, I didn't know which. It was smooth and wrong and wicked sharp on its curves, like it could cut your eyes just by looking. Spines too, from shoulders tapering down to tiny cutting teeth at the wrists. At least from the front, C-X's body still had a lean, slightly feminine curve to it, but a little less than before. Whatever was going on inside her, it had happened fast.

My gaze lingered on the black chitin growing along the back of her neck. Her hair was falling out in clumps, and if I was the betting kind, I'd lay odds on the shell continuing up the back of her skull. Her features didn't look the same either. Already, she had less flesh on her bones, so her cheeks, chin, and jaw seemed carved from stone. As I studied her, a series of uncontrollable twitches ran through her, arms jerking as she tried to do . . . something. Hell if I knew what.

"Is she seizing?" I asked, as EMITU whirred into action. Like the bot, I wasn't sure what pronoun applied to C-X now, but she was still the woman I'd grown to respect deeply, even if she was also something more.

"I cannot say for certain. Stand back, please."

EMITU tried to sedate her, but the meds weren't working. She ripped the restraints from the table and shoved the bot away, pure brute strength. If I had any sense, I'd shoot C-X now, but even with her running amok, I couldn't pull the trigger. Tremors set in, and I fought the urge to cry as I registered the sheer confusion and anguish in her eyes. She didn't *want* to do this, but she couldn't stop either.

I have to stop her.

With trembling hands, I brought the weapon up. But before I could shoot, C-X stumbled to the wall and started banging her head on it, turning that impulse toward violence on herself. At first, I thought she was really trying to hurt herself and I wheeled on EMITU. "Find some damn medicine to put her out!"

The bot stood still, however, listening to the percussion. "It's a message. I think that's Morse code." EMITU spelled out the letters she was tapping with her head, slow and relentless. "H-E-L-P M-E." Over and over, she tapped out the same message until the bot found a combination of chemicals that calmed her down.

Even with enough meds to sedate an angry rhino, she still wasn't unconscious, but she didn't fight the new and improved (and hopefully stronger) restraints we used on her. Her eyes didn't blink anymore; she had the blank, dead stare of a creature in terrible pain, and it just about ripped my beating heart from my chest.

"She can't tell us, but . . . based on her test results, how much is she hurting right now?" I asked EMITU. Since she'd done this for me, I had to know. Had to.

"I do not have the parameters to personally judge a meatsack's pain, but the level of massive physiological change my patient is currently enduring appears to be equivalent with inhumane tortures humans have enjoyed administering in times past. There are also levels of mental discomfort that I am not equipped to gauge."

"Sounds like you're saying she's being tortured, physically and mentally."

"It could be interpreted as such," EMITU said cheerfully.

"Well, try to ease the worst of it. Maybe she'll stabilize. If she could still think well enough to communicate in Morse code under these circumstances, then the Chao-Xing we know and love is still alive and kicking. Hell, I don't even *know* Morse code."

"You should learn," the bot said. "In case you're ever held hostage in your own body and can no longer speak or write."

Was that why she'd wrecked up the place? Maybe she wasn't trying to hurt anyone, just looking for a way to communicate. And damn if she didn't find it.

That's our Chao-Xing. Whatever Suncross said about poisoned wells, I wasn't giving up on her yet.

"Shit, shit, *shit*!" It wasn't like Bea to cuss, but she was doing it in all the languages she knew, in a fluid, angry flood of syllables. I rushed toward Ops, already braced for bad news, but it was worse than I could have imagined. She turned toward me with wide, terrified eyes. "Zara, he's gone."

"Who? Marko?"

"Lifekiller."

"You mean he's awake . . . and he already took off?" That wasn't the worst news possible. I was braced to hear he'd already drained another settlement dry and that I had to answer for thousands more lives.

"It's more like, we've been tricked," she said softly. "You know my plan to bait the Phage with the emitters? Make them think there were a lot of Leviathan nearby?"

"What about it?"

"He's not here. He was *never* here. We followed the Phage thinking it would lead us to him, but it seems like they're playing bait, leading us *away* from him."

Now I was cursing, not as colorfully, but I dropped a few choice Zone expletives. "We fell for it? I can't believe the bastard's this smart. You think he doubled back to Greenheld?"

Lifekiller had a serious jones for revenge against the Abyin Dommas, so it was possible. Bea was scanning frantically, shaking her head. "I'm not sure."

"Conference in Yusuf and Starcurrent. Get Suncross too. Let's see if we can expand our range. Nadim?"

"I'm here, Zara." Worried as hell too, by the sound of it.

Why did we always have multiple fires to put out? First, it was Lifekiller and Derry/Deluca, and now it was Lifekiller and Chao-Xyll. Peace and quiet wasn't something I used to see in my future, but I was starting to think it would be nice. There was such a thing as too much adventure, when the constant adrenaline wore you out and the fear-bile in your stomach ate the lining, giving you an ulcer. I didn't think I had one yet, but maybe I was on the way.

"Understood."

A split screen appeared on the console, as Bea had commed in both ships. Suncross didn't wait for me to speak. "Did you—"

"It's not about that," I cut in hastily. The last thing I needed was for this damn lizard to let slip that I'd tapped him as our last resort for dealing with C-X. Marko would lose his damn mind. I was only seconds from shaking to pieces myself.

"We were baited," Bea said then.

She quickly explained what had happened to the others. Yusuf started cussing, and it was kind of nice to see him lose his cool too. The man was beyond the numb stage of grief. I liked anger on him better.

"The energy signature we mistook for the god-king is a trap he left for us." Yusuf slammed a fist into his palm. "He even burned enough energy to make it radiate correctly."

"Whatever he's doing," I said, "he doesn't want us to interfere."

Marko paced, running a hand through already shaggy hair. "I have the worst feeling about this. Anyone else?"

"Has been long since I had a good feeling," said Starcurrent. I didn't think it was the translation matrix making zim sound doleful.

"Suncross?" I prompted.

The lizard was silent, and that was never a good sign. He waved with four clawed hands and huddled up, communicating with his crew so silently that our network couldn't pick up the sounds. Maybe the Bruqvisz had an idea? I could hope.

"Is definitely not Greenheld," Suncross finally said, coming back to face the screen. "Remember, our brethren are patrolling, and they would have sent word about facing such an impossible foe."

"They'd have gotten a message off, even if they were dying?" I guessed.

Suncross spread his palms. "Yes. Best way to ensure your story is told. Broadcast circumstances likely to end in glorious death. Even if this ship was too far, I would have heard of this from others."

Right, the lizards had a great communications system, the one that let Bacia harass us and send Jellies to kill us, even while they were fleeing from the Phage.

Okay, think, Zara.

Joining Marko, I started pacing too, though I didn't mess with my hair. We passed each other in opposite directions as I thought aloud. "We can tick Greenheld off the list. Starcurrent, what's the next most populated world? I mean, the planet with the highest concentration of Abyin Dommas?"

"Haelara." Starcurrent and Suncross spoke at the same time.

It didn't translate as a compound word, unlike other Abyin Dommas homes. "Where is it? How many light-years from here?"

"It's really far," Nadim said. "If that's where the god-king is headed, he's delayed us long enough. Even at top speed, it would take me nearly a week."

"They'll all be dead before we get there," Bea whispered.

I shivered, trying to control my reaction. Failing. All that fear—I imagined how Starcurrent must be feeling. Ze must wish we'd let zim die in vacuum so ze wouldn't have to be a part of this.

"How many?" I asked.

"Ten million of my people," Starcurrent answered. "More Bruqvisz. Some Fellkin."

"Is there any way to get word? To warn them?" I pointed at Suncross. "Can you use your awesome telemetry or whatever it's called? If there are more than ten million Bruqvisz on Haelara, let them know what might be coming."

"Could create panic," he said heavily. "Destabilize economy if many attempt to flee. Also possible they will dismiss my warning as mischief."

"You have to try! We should probably send alerts to any likely targets. They'll elevate their defenses as they can and keep watch for Lifekiller."

"Most cannot sing the shield," Starcurrent said. "Fear will only make the end more painful. Better to see death coming or better to die smiling?"

Yeah, I wasn't here to talk philosophy. "Concrete solutions only! Nobody is on this mission to discuss dying."

Suncross had to say, "Only glorious death in battle!"

Damn lizards.

Marko finally spoke after long moments of silent pacing. "I think Zara's right. We have to put the word out. We've been trying to do this by ourselves and we're not . . . at this point, I think saying we've failed to contain the problem is a fact. All we've done is waste time and let the god-king run circles around us."

Glaring at him, Bea planted her hands on her hips.

"While he's worried about us, he's not devouring planets. That's something. Even if we haven't destroyed him yet, we're saving lives, and I don't count that as failure."

"Yes." Yusuf was nodding. "Sometimes it's enough not to lose. It's enough to survive to regroup and try again, especially when you consider the might of our opponent."

Suncross growled, a sound I interpreted as *blah blah, human squabbling.* "Am sending mass warning or not?"

Too bad there was no superhero squad we could call to deal with the ancient god we'd inadvertently raised. On some level, I realized we were the closest the universe had. I stopped fidgeting and squared my shoulders. With C-X out of the action, someone had to step up. I wanted it to be someone else, anyone really, but everyone was looking at me, listening to me, for some damn reason. I guessed that meant I was in charge.

Just another day, no problem, I can handle this.

"Send the message," I said.

Maybe nobody would send help. Maybe they wouldn't even believe word that came across the wire from some random merc ship. If that was the case, we'd done the best we could. Hopefully people would believe the Bruqvisz because they were known bards, famous for putting true stories out there. Like Yusuf and Bea said, sometimes when you couldn't win, not losing or minimizing losses was enough.

"Done," said Suncross. "The mockery will begin soon. Beings like Lifekiller are the stuff of stories to young ones, not something to be properly feared. But we will try."

Poor lizard. To people who'd never seen—or maybe even heard of—a being like Lifekiller, Suncross would probably acquire a reputation for spreading bullshit. I imagined it like the conspiracy theorists on Earth who posted on the internet about the "real" purpose of the Leviathan. But hell, even they were right; the live ships just weren't hiding what the fanatics thought they were.

I didn't bother apologizing. "Next order of business. Bea, let's repurpose those emitters. We can't trick Lifekiller anymore, but we might be able to use them to get a better range on our scans. We have to find that bastard. Right away."

"Understood. I'll get on the necessary modifications, Z."

"Nadim, if we stay close to Typhon, is there a way to link our ship systems? I feel like it makes sense that would increase our range as well."

"Yes, Zara. We have not done this before because Typhon was keeping secrets, but I think that's not the case anymore. Yusuf?" Nadim checked with the Honor currently privy to Typhon's inner workings.

He nodded. "Typhon is amenable. He says there's nothing in his databases that he needs to hide."

Hell has frozen. Typhon just volunteered to throw open his

343

gates and is letting us guard the battlements with him. It was about damn time; any longer and there would have been nothing left to save. I locked those bad thoughts away like a prisoner that could never be permitted to escape. My mom believed in the power of positivity—that if you imagined good things, they would come to you, but that had always sounded like nonsense to me. Still, I wouldn't put terrible thoughts out in the universe either.

We had a plan at least, and we were moving forward. I should probably wallow a little more in the way the god-king straight up fooled us, but that wasn't my style. In the Zone, I'd gotten my ass kicked now and then. Never did any good to linger on the bruises. Back then I just had to keep moving. Same held true in the black too.

"You're inspiring them," Nadim said, so softly that I knew the words were just for me.

"I . . . what? No."

"It's true. Now everyone has a purpose again. They believe we can do this because you won't let anyone imagine another outcome."

"The power of positive thinking," I sang out, and oh my God, I was quoting my mother. What would come next, the end times? I sobered up fast when I realized how true that was, considering the monster we were up against.

"Uplink complete!" Bea said.

"Granting all systems access," Yusuf added.

That had to mean we were networked with Typhon. Wonder if the Honors program saw that coming.

Starcurrent was scanning on zis end, and Suncross was waiting with his boys. Suddenly the Abyin Dommas said, "Spotted something!"

A dot appeared on our screens as ze shared the info with Bea. She staggered so fast that I had to catch her, hold her up, and Marko ran to her other side. Because of her reaction, I was worried about her, not focused on the console.

She shoved me away, not roughly, but there was real desperation in her face. Terror unlike anything I'd seen from Bea before put unsteadiness in her voice, like tears barely choked back. "Zara . . . look."

With effort, I scrutinized the constellations, the familiar images on screen. "Oh shit. That's the Sol system. Lifekiller's headed for Earth!"

"More," Yusuf said grimly. "The Phage swarm he used as a decoy. They know we're onto them. They're coming back for us."

From Earth Central Command records, collected in a mass infotrade with the Bruqvisz seventy-nine years after recorded events

EARTH COMMAND CIC BULLETIN TO REMOTE STATIONS LUNA COLONY MARS COLONY ROMA JUPITER ORBIT SATURN OUTPOST

An unknown presence of alien origin has been detected at the limits of our sensor array and appears inbound to our solar system. We have no reason to believe this is composed of Leviathan; there has been no communication in advance of this arrival.

As a precaution we are now instituting Condition Unknown Alert. Check and ready all planetary defenses, shields, and weapons. Outposts prepare to evacuate to safe shelters and engage autonomous defenses.

We have sent inquiries out to any Leviathan in range to explain this unplanned expeditionary force.

Do not alert your citizens until official notifications are released.

Remain calm.

CHAPTER TWENTY

Lost Ground

WE WERE SITTING targets and had two vulnerable Leviathan that would trigger the Phage's hunger. And my home planet was going to be attacked. *Our home planet.* Mine, Bea's, Yusuf's, Marko's, Chao-Xing's. There was no way Earth was ready to repel any kind of alien invader, much less the monstrous power and hunger of the Phage. And Lifekiller could crush whatever defenses they could mount with a random blast.

I didn't want to care. I didn't think I *would* care, because after all I'd run away from everything there as fast as I could. First to the Zone, where I could live without rules and restrictions; then, when I had the shot, out here to space, to Nadim, to a life completely free from borders and people wanting me to comply.

But even though I had nobody I really loved back there on Earth, it was in my blood and bones. Earth had made me. It was my cradle and my history, and I had to feel that, however far away I ran. My ancestors had stories I didn't know and had never really cared to learn, and in this moment, I hated that I didn't know those stories when they were in danger of disappearing. The Bruqvisz were right: stories survived after we were gone. And I couldn't let mine burn up the way millions had already for his selfish need to destroy anything in his way.

This move felt personal, like he was punishing us for turning him back at Greenheld. If pesky humans wouldn't let him take out the Abyin Dommas, then he'd destroy us first. And we couldn't sing him away like they had. This was too damn big for me to carry. While Earth might not shelter my loved ones, Mars did. And if Lifekiller took a notion to wipe us out, for a being like him, it was nothing to wreck the domes, nothing to obliterate Luna Colony. I'd seen how fast it could happen, and soon we might—

I took a breath. Gave myself a mental shaking. *Snap out of it.* Only a few seconds had gone by, but I had to get back in the moment. Phage were coming, and they weren't going to wait on my personal damn crisis.

"How far?" I asked Yusuf, since Bea was busy. He consulted his screens, and probably Typhon.

"We'd almost caught up to them before they turned," he said. "So maybe half an hour, tops. Not a lot of time, Zara. What's our plan?"

"Same as before. Kill as many as we can, however we can." My hands flew over the controls, looking for whatever was around us we could use. And I found it. "Okay, we're going here—" I flashed the coordinates to him with a quick sweep of my fingers across the pad. "How much gravity can Typhon resist?"

"Oh shit," he said, when he realized what I meant. "I don't know. Typhon?"

"This is acceptable," Typhon said, deep rumble of a voice that came over the speakers. "Nadim will not be able to tolerate as much. Be careful. If you drift too close . . ."

"That's the idea," I told him. "We skim the edges and try to lure the Phage after us. With any luck they'll be so focused on us that at least some of them will get caught in the gravity well."

Typhon understood what I was talking about, and so did Nadim an instant later. "You mean for me to swim on the outer edges of the darkness?"

"Yep," I said.

What he referred to as "the darkness" was a black hole. A small one, not that it really mattered; it was new and hungry, and it was starting to shred the star nearest to it. A continuously moving energy stream was being pulled loose from the star's superheated surface and spiraling out toward the supergravity well. Slow-motion destruction. Science fiction said it could send you somewhere else, and so did some big brains in science, but it didn't seem like a trip I was that eager to take since the more likely alternative was being crushed to random atoms at the bottom of a hole so deep it ripped space itself.

"Zara, it's dangerous," Nadim said earnestly.

"I know, sweetheart. But we don't have a lot of options. Our drones are gone, and we can only take so many of these things with weapons and physical attacks. There are *millions* of them. They'll swarm you and Typhon and sting you to death. We can't risk that happening. Better to risk this."

I felt his fear. Nadim wasn't often afraid; space was his natural home, same as air was to me. But even the Leviathan feared getting caught in the unbreakable hold of a black hole. "I've never done this," he said. "If I miscalculate and go too far . . ."

"I know," I answered. "But it's a risk we need to take. Together." What I wasn't telling him was that for me it was also a last resort; if the Phage succeeded in burrowing into Nadim, if it was all a lost cause here . . . at least we could plunge into that black hole and end things. I didn't know if that would be a quick death or a very, very slow one, but I couldn't let Nadim become one of those vile zombie ships, piloted by the Phage and pregnant with squirming masses of them, ready to explode out and take another Leviathan. I wasn't going to tell him any of that, though I thought he'd agree with me. This was my responsibility.

Nadim didn't argue the point. We didn't have time. I checked the counter that Yusuf had started running. "Hey, Bea? We got proximity mines in inventory? I know we used some earlier . . ."

"Yes! I'll deploy them and set them to ignore friendly power signatures. Make sure Suncross and Typhon mark them on their displays."

"You all get that?" I asked, and Yusuf just nodded, working on his own tasks.

Suncross said he understood. He added, "I am also deploying stealth-mode devices of destruction. All will be keyed to ignore allies."

Yusuf said, "I'm doing the same now."

Between the three of us, we spread out a complex net of destruction; it would take out thousands of Phage, but they could afford that. Wouldn't even make a dent. The scary part was, Lifekiller might have the same number with him; he'd left only half his Phage army to delay us, maybe long enough for him to destroy Earth.

I stared at the star's life force streaming away into

that black hole. If we could get the Phage into position in that kind of death spiral, it might just suck down half the swarm, maybe more. How many would they lose before they decided to break off the attack? Unknown. And I couldn't ask Xyll anymore.

Or could I?

I stepped back from the console. "I'll be right back," I said. Bea nodded, and so did Yusuf and Suncross. Starcurrent had appeared on my screens now too, and ze waved some tendrils in a distracted sort of way. Everybody had jobs.

I had one too.

I headed for Medbay. EMITU was in his recharging station when I came in, but he launched himself out with a whir when I tripped his sensors. "You should not be here! My patient has finally calmed down, no thanks to you. Your presence is not required."

"Yeah, well, I'm here anyway," I said, and stepped toward the bed.

Chao-Xyll's features looked much more angular, more alien than before. Her beautiful black hair was gone, and onyx chitin encased her head all the way to her ears and forehead. Her eyes were shut, but when she opened them, I saw that she wasn't suffering quite so much. Her arms weren't restrained, but the bot did have her ankles cuffed. With effort, C-X tried to sit up.

"Take it easy," I told her. "I'll talk. Tap twice for yes, once for no."

Her fingers weren't human anymore; they were longer, more insectile, and they had cutting surfaces on the undersides. But she lifted one digit and tapped twice.

"Good," I said. "We're in trouble. We're going into battle against the Phage soon. Can you do anything to help us?" I hated asking this, but Xyll had been our chief asset, and now the Phage cell made up half of C-X's whole.

She hesitated, then tapped just once. I took that as a no. But then she tapped again, three times, and I wasn't sure what that meant. "Slow down. What are you trying to say? EMITU, is she doing Morse code again?"

"I believe she is trying to tell you that she isn't sure," the bot said. "Or perhaps that she'd like to eat you. I don't speak hybrid."

"*Shit.*" This was infuriating. There had to be some way to communicate with her. I took a deep breath. "Nadim? Can you, ah, hear Chao-Xing at all?"

"That is not Chao-Xing," he said coldly.

Damn. I really didn't want to get on the wrong side of him. Nadim had a mean streak where the Phage were concerned. "Okay. Chao-Xyll."

"I can hear . . . something. It's not quite as chaotic as the screech of the Phage. But it is not human, either."

"Well, can you understand it at all?"

"Emotions only. She's frustrated."

Yeah, who wasn't? "I need some way to talk to her. The translator could understand Xyll before; why can't it process her, ah, vocalizations now?"

"Perhaps it takes time for it to adjust. Perhaps if she speaks more?" I could feel how repulsed Nadim felt by this, how angry he was that we'd lost Chao-Xing to . . . this. But I couldn't afford to let that emotion get to me, either. I needed to focus.

"Okay." I focused on Chao-Xyll again. "I need you to try to talk. The translation matrix needs more data to start parsing your language. Do you understand?"

Two taps. Chao-Xyll opened her mouth, and I saw with a slight shudder that her teeth were . . . gone. New ones were coming in, streaked with blood from punching through her gums, and they were differently shaped. Triangular. A mouth made for tearing flesh.

Sounds came out. Sounded like metal dragged over concrete to me, raspy and wrong, and I was vaguely surprised there weren't sparks to go along with it. She paused. I gestured for her to keep going. More noise, louder this time, with more modulations but no less painful to hear. Honestly, like a bag of tools dropped down stairs this time. I didn't know how a human throat—or one that had once been human—could even make those sounds. It sounded like it would rip delicate skin apart. Finally, she quieted, anger blazing from her pale gold eyes. She couldn't even curl her hand into a fist anymore; her hands wouldn't bend that way.

"Too new," EMITU said then. "The translator has never run across this species. Nor have I. Very interesting!"

I didn't want the bot to make C-X feel like a specimen. She was already upset enough at failing to communicate. "Dial it down. Can we go back to Morse code?" I asked.

A single inclination of C-X's head. At least she remembered how to do that. I glanced at EMITU. "Will you translate for me?"

"Well, that's remarkably polite of you. Yes, certainly. What would you do without me?"

"Learn Morse code," I muttered. "But I'm glad I don't have to. Time is not on our side."

EMITU listened to the taps. The message was longer than the first time, but I suspected the med bot of simplifying. "Don't know. Can try."

Try was better than nothing. I didn't feel great about cutting C-X loose when she couldn't even speak, at least not in words intelligible to our translation matrix. I guessed if we had to communicate, she could click against the comm pad and EMITU could pass along the word. The fact was, we needed every edge we could get to survive this fight— to blow past the Phage blockade and haul ass to Earth to wreck up the god-king.

EMITU looked at me. I looked at the bot. I shrugged.

"It's your potential dismemberment," he said. "I can be rebuilt." His ghoulish cheer was somehow comforting to me right now.

"Go ahead," I said, and the ankle restraints snapped open.

C-X practically levitated out of the bed, a move so fast it wasn't human, and before I could react, she was right there in front of me. Her posture was different, bent more forward, and her knees were angled the wrong damn way. Gleaming black chitinous exoskeleton. Cutting edges and spines. Knives for fingers.

I felt very, very soft. She could peel me like an apple, if she felt the slightest inclination. I didn't move. I didn't blink. I just looked in her still-human eyes and said, "I'm trusting you. Don't let me down."

Her lips twitched and formed a familiar smile. Familiar except for the sharp teeth, anyway. I imagined her chewing through Nadim's hull, lost in Phage impulses. The look in her eyes was alien to me as well, cunning and excitement and—

She scuttled off before I could say more, and yeah, her neck allowed her head to turn a 180 and look right at me as she exited. It was all I could do not to shriek, and then C-X was gone, moving away from us toward the docking bay at a presumably incredible speed.

"Nadim, tell Bea to stay out of her way. Warn the others that she's going to be out there among the Phage. Can you tag her energy signature and mark her as friendly?"

"Yes," he said, but he sounded sober about it. "Is she? Friendly?"

"Well, she didn't eat my face, so let's just call it good for now."

EMITU did his sniff thing and rolled himself back to his dock. None of his concern anymore, until one of us ended up bleeding, so he was going to have a rest. Wished I could. I went back to Ops instead.

Beatriz looked pale, and I knew she'd seen C-X without her even saying it. "Is this dangerous? Letting her loose?" she asked, and then shook her head. "No, never mind, don't answer that; I know it is, and I know you wouldn't have done it if it wasn't important. I'm okay." She heaved a deep breath and blew it out. The soft, loose curls around her face waved in the breeze. "Nadim's tagged her energy signal for me, and I marked her as friendly for our bombs. I sent the information to Yusuf and Suncross too."

"Thank you," I said, and kissed her. Hugged her, since we might not have the chance in a few more minutes. I wanted to say, *We'll get through this. I promise*, but I couldn't. We were past me saying easy words to settle her down, like I had when she'd first panicked in the shuttle. Seemed like we had been together forever. Not so long in real time.

I didn't speak my doubts aloud either. That was my burden to carry now. Chao-Xing had passed that on to me, I supposed. I stood at the console and looked at our preps, checked the Phage's progress, looked at Earth and the dot that was Lifekiller and the other half of the Phage swarm speeding toward it at terrifying velocity.

The last five minutes were the hardest. I kept racking my brain, checking our courses and positions, going over the plans and making damn sure I knew all our risks. The Phage were going to come at us from all directions, including above and below; we had our defenses positioned in a bristling, lethal ball around us, set far enough apart that they'd trigger on encounters, not other explosions. We needed every one of them to count and count *hard*.

"Get ready," I said, watching the screens. "Everyone? Hold tight."

"Die with honor!" Suncross shouted exultantly. "I have sent our glorious message of defiance! We will be remembered, Zeerakull! All of us!"

"Hell yeah, we will!" I shouted back. "Okay, here we go. Phage coming up . . . now."

They were impossible to see visually until they crossed a light source, but they blocked out stars as they passed them, and all around us, the universe was . . . going dark. Distant candles going out. The dying star still smoldered, but it grew dimmer, dimmer, gone.

We were in the black now.

And the swarm hit *hard*.

I watched the wave of bombs go off. First line lit around us in a wide shell of silent bursts, and Nadim staggered emotionally; even I could hear the distant shrieking of the Phage now, but for the Leviathan it must have been overwhelming. "Shut it down," I told him. "Focus on us. Listen to us. Not to them." I knew instinctively that the Phage's cries woke panic in the Leviathan. If they listened, it could throw them off. Nadim steadied. "Bonding . . . now."

Bea and I fell effortlessly into that spiral with Nadim, blending into a rich, awesomely powerful whole. Bezardim looked out as the second wave of defenses triggered, blowing thousands more Phage into pieces.

But the stars were still black, hidden by the masses of squirming, hungry bodies. We felt fragile, and we reached out for Typhon and his bond crew, and achieved unity, the shared consciousness of both Leviathan, both crews. Nameless again, without Chao-Xing. Yusuf was a new, steady color in our mix, a dark blue that felt strong, a base on which to build. Marko felt like quicksilver, shivering and unstable, but still there. Starcurrent's songs wove us all fast, and Bea's beautiful voice blended with us. Typhon was a rock on which to stand. Nadim was a wall from which to attack.

We were ready.

We saw Suncross's ship firing and swooping, attacking in patterns to pick off huge swaths of the Phage with their clumping weapons, finishing them with explosive bursts. The third line of bombs went off. The fourth. We readied weapons and began to fire once the Phage spun and whirled into range, a crawling horror of carapaces and raw hunger. We shattered them into ichor. Burned them into drifting ash.

And there were more. So many more.

We heard something else at the edges of our bond. Another song. *Chao-Xyll?* It felt like her, but with strange overtones, wrong harmonies, blood and hunger and chaos melded with human will. The swarm ignored those notes. They were alien and incorrect, useless. They treated her as nothing, and her silent shriek filled our head with dissonance.

Last set of bombs exploded, and we moved as one, spiraling out in a graceful circle. Two Leviathan bodies striking massive blows, rolling, crushing, spreading destruction. Frying any Phage that encountered the armor. It seemed random but was not, a course directed to slowly rotate toward the unraveling star, the streaming energy, the hungry event horizon of the black hole.

The Phage, confused and jagged, followed. They swarmed. Struck. Suncross's ship darted between the Leviathan for protection as they were hit, and hit again, and Nadim and

Typhon made space and offered shelter. Suncross's communications were heard and processed by the whole. *Out of cluster weapons*, Suncross reported. *No more explosives. We have only energy weapons left. Will fire until we die!* The Bruqvisz roared, audible even through the link. Exultant in their rage.

We noted it with sadness and wonder, and moved again, rolling, killing, striking, protecting the Bruqvisz vessel as best we could.

Typhon is breached. That was our Marko-self, a stab of fear in the blending, and our Zara-aspect whispered, *Activate internal defenses.* Typhon had many and could withstand much. *Fight them but do not forget the plan.*

We were close to the event horizon now, close enough that we could feel the slow, relentless pull of a star broken and crushed into unimaginable density, a vortex into which everything flowed, nothing escaped.

We could go no closer. Typhon positioned himself at the inner edge and stopped the roll; Nadim was farther from the pull, more able to bear it where he was.

The Phage were leaves in the dark wind, scattering, scrambling, spiraling away. They died by the hundreds of thousands, spun screaming and shrieking beyond the point of no return, and though they dealt us wounds, we maintained. We held.

C-X's signal had stuttered as the swarm had turned

on her, no longer a thing to ignore but one to destroy; she'd tried too hard, become too visible. We fired on the remaining Phage, driving them off as C-X skittered into our protection, the entirety of her being a silent scream. Failure sliced at both halves of the whole—Xyll, who could not believe it was no longer kin to the swarm, who had just been exiled and made prey—and Chao-Xing, who could not believe she was no longer human. Rather, a separate being, bloody and exhausted from the long, awful struggle toward new life. A baby. Zara's consciousness whispered guilt. *I sent a baby out there to fight.*

Then the remaining Phage regrouped. We couldn't count them; they no longer blocked the stars, but the ragged remains of the hive were still dangerous.

And they came for us.

From the Bruqvisz collection *Mechanical Independents, Volume 5220*, chipped and registered

The Saga of the Lawgiver begins, as most things do, with a birth. But no organic birth, as expected from this edition; the robot designated as Jury was born in a factory on the planet Earth (see ref.) of human making. It was only once aboard the Leviathan Nadim (see ref.) that it gained final sentience and pursued its goal: to judge and sentence those involved in creating its murder imperative.

Jury's glorious mission took the Leviathan Ophelia (with deceased human Derry McKinnon) back to Earth, where Jury accompanied said corpse to Earth's Honors Council. There Jury delivered the following message: "I have come for justice. Where is Torian Deluca?"

Torian Deluca was not among those in attendance, but Jury accessed the records of this body and determined that Deluca was in the city of New Detroit, where he oversaw a vast criminal enterprise (see ref.).

The trial of Torian Deluca occurred in the Horizon Building (see ref.) in the top-floor security-restricted penthouse. Seventeen guards, robot and human, failed to prevent Jury's entry into this space. Torian Deluca attempted to bargain with the robot for his survival.

He was unsuccessful.

Let the record show that the robot Jury considered all evidence and arguments for clemency, and in accordance with human law and tradition, shot Torian Deluca dead. Vids indicate said execution occurred swiftly.

Jury evaded all efforts to capture him in New Detroit by both Deluca's surviving criminals and the New Detroit Mech Police. He then returned to the Leviathan Ophelia and is the only recorded crew of any Leviathan ship to be of mech origins.

We honor this story with solemn hands of salute. May Jury's story be preserved.

CHAPTER TWENTY-ONE

Lost Momentum

I DROPPED OUT of the bond and staggered. Too many things were happening at once for our bonded entity to hold. For this part of the fight, I had to be Zara Cole and nobody else, mad as hell and constantly looking for the weakest link.

Hopefully we'd taken out enough of the Phage. If we couldn't kill the rest of them, we could still run. Typhon had that sonic attack, though it would drain his power reserves and leave him weakened for the final battle against Lifekiller.

Nadim could dark run.

"I can't," he said, answering my very thought. "It would mean leaving Typhon and Suncross behind."

"Just running through some options. I know you wouldn't do that, sweetheart." Funny how easy it was to be gentle with him now. I had nothing to prove anymore. Not when we were standing at the edge of the abyss. When you gaze into the abyss, it also gazes into you.

That's it. Or it could be.

But before I could say anything about that, Nadim let out a pained sound. "Chao-Xyll has returned. Injured. Zara, I'm afraid. I don't think—"

"Calm down. She won't hurt us. C-X isn't the enemy." I hoped.

"She doesn't feel the same as when she left. Her mind is like . . . knives." Unlike Typhon, Nadim didn't have internal defenses. We'd never gotten around to installing any, and I could feel his panic rising.

Bea turned from the console, her own fear levels spiking. "Is C-X going to turn on us?"

"One problem at a time. It would've been better if she could disrupt them like Xyll did, but we have to play the hand we're dealt. Look at all those Phage between us and—"

Just then, Suncross's ship burst out of its shelter and fired, a shocking, utterly devastating barrage, taking out Phage in thick layers. It was a bold move, one without an iota of self-preservation. The lizards didn't have enough juice for shields and clearly didn't care, and the Phage swarmed the ship. Began ripping it to pieces.

The console screen flickered and suddenly Suncross was there, his crew standing behind him at attention, sober and silent as they *never* were. I remembered playing forfeit-or-pain with them, drinking, sleeping, sharing stories. Our trek down to the asteroid and my time aboard their ship, breathing in their life. Fear lanced through me, and I couldn't bear to hear what he said next. Tears gathered in my eyes, because I *knew* I would never see him do that damn victory dance again.

"We have breach, Zara Cole." At the end, he said my name right, and I'd have given all my worldly goods to hear him say it wrong, the way he did when he was messing with me. But now was too somber a moment for that. The tears slid down my cheeks, buzzed my nose, and dropped off my chin. "All other plans have failed. Little power remains. Now we can only offer our sacrifice to the gods of victory as we send our stories to the stars. I have chosen one to survive. Retrieve him when the battle is won. TO GLORY!"

The mech ship loosed a small, fragile pod and it jetted away from the battle, then Suncross fired the last of his engines, spun his ship into the center of the reforming Phage, and with a roar that rocked the stars around us, ignited his own ship in a massive, uncontrolled explosion that destroyed an equally massive swath of the Phage. The ship. Suncross.

Gone.

For several impossible seconds, I couldn't believe it. The lizards were always boasting about dying for glory, but I'd thought it was all talk. Yet they'd sacrificed themselves for a world they'd never seen, for a people who had only shown them a few good angles. I tried to choke back the sobs. Couldn't. Bea wrapped her arms around me and held on. We cried into each other's shoulders until my eyes were hot and swollen, until I could hardly breathe.

"The Phage," I choked. I checked. The survivors of that suicide run were regrouping. "Nadim, Typhon . . ."

"Firing," Yusuf said. He sounded shaken too, but more in control than I was. Nadim sent me comfort and shared sorrow, and I felt the pulse of his guns battering the Phage too.

They ran. *They ran.*

I felt sick and lost and cold, but I kept myself upright. I was crying for Suncross and my friends. I tried not to, to stop, but this new Zara, the one who'd healed the broken parts inside, she needed this. I let it happen.

Nadim finally said, quietly, "Zara, we need to collect the one Suncross chose to live and tell their story. That is the Bruqvisz way."

Sniffing hard, I knuckled my eyes. "I'll get Yusuf to pick

me up, and we'll save the survivor."

The pod was too small for Nadim to maneuver close. We might accidentally smack into it and knock it into the gravity well of the black hole. No, this rescue had to be delicate, and I wished Bea would go with me. Fortunately, I didn't have to ask. The ragged remains of the Phage swarm were in full retreat, so we were clear to depart.

Except that we found C-X collapsed just outside the docking bay, covered in blood. Even the blood looked different, no longer red, but so dark that it was almost purple. Her knife-fingers had gouged deep runnels in the floor and walls. No wonder Nadim was scared. Even if it didn't hurt him a lot, he must have felt those wounds on some level. If C-X had been herself, she would never have harmed any Leviathan.

Bea took a reflexive step back, and I could tell she didn't want to linger. She'd always been more scared of the Phage than I was, and it didn't help that it felt like Xyll was wearing our friend like a new summer suit. "Get Marko," I said. "Hurry."

"Nadim, can you get in touch with the Bruqvisz survivor? Find out how long he has, and get Yusuf or Starcurrent to bring the Hopper."

A few seconds later, he replied, "The pod only has an emergency beacon. I cannot speak directly to him."

Well, that made sense. If you got ejected in a life pod,

you wouldn't want to have a chat before getting picked up. The goal was immediate rescue. But I couldn't leave C-X lying here. I tapped my comm. "EMITU, we have injuries. Get here ASAP."

Though he bitched at me, he came rolling up, faster even than Marko and Bea, who were rounding the corner behind him. "What have you done to my patient?" he demanded.

"Hell if I know. We found her like this. I guess the mission didn't go well outside. I think she saw some combat." That was obvious from the deep wounds carved into the still human parts of her body, but the signs of a struggle inside with no enemy to be found hinted at mental anguish that might be even more worrying.

EMITU had a hoverdolley, and Marko hesitated only a moment before he picked C-X up, depositing her on it with great care. He turned to face Bea and me with a serious expression. "Go on with the rescue. I'll stay with Chao-Xing. That's why I'm here, after all."

In that moment, I saw an echo of the Honor Marko had wanted to be when he'd dragged me out of Camp Kuna.

Nadim said, "The Hopper is in the docking bay. Yusuf is heading to check on Chao-Xyll and will return to Typhon when the rescue mission is complete."

I nodded. "Bea, you ready?"

"I'll do the piloting. You've done space retrieval before."

The last time we did this, Chao-Xing sat in the driver's seat. A pang went through me when I stared down at her, so completely changed and struggling to survive in this new form. Marko gently took hold of her hand, avoiding the insectile blades that were her fingers. "You're stronger than this," he was saying softly. "So wake up and get your shit together. I know you can."

That rubbed me wrong for some reason, like strength and weakness were a binary, when life came at you fast and it was more a matter of what you could survive. And Marko didn't have a damn alien parasite docked on his spinal cord. With effort, I ignored him. At least he was here for her. I'd judged them before because they didn't seem to care about each other, not like Bea, Nadim, and me, but clearly, I didn't know what I thought I did about the bonds between Marko and Chao-Xing. Only stood to reason they'd have one, even if I couldn't see or fully understand it, considering they had spent a year together with nobody else to rely on.

"Nadim, you all right?"

"I grieve," he answered.

He was talking about the lizards' dramatic final act. Since I had been asking about the wounds C-X had inflicted, he must be healthy enough. I followed Bea into the docking bay and put on my skinsuit, including helmet. We'd need that life support when she popped the Hopper so I could pull the pod in. Bruqvisz emergency units looked different from the space placentas we had on board. They were silver and cylindrical, more like a high-tech coffin. Given how long their arms were, the sole survivor must be lying with them folded, waiting for death or rescue.

Damn, I was in a mood.

"Fire it up," I said to Bea as I hopped in back.

She checked all the panels, then did as I requested. Nadim didn't wait for us to ask for an exit; he opened the way and she swooped us out. Considering the massive battle that had taken place here, there weren't many Phage bodies floating. Between the black hole and the heroic boom of Suncross's last stand, the area was mostly clear.

"I've got the pod on screen," she reported.

"Let me know when we're close. I'll need you to swing around so I can get it inside."

"Understood."

"Hold on, Zara!" Up front, Bea was struggling with the pull from the black hole. I hadn't been paying much attention to that; too much else to worry about. But Bea was all in with it, and now that I *was* paying attention, the terror of being caught in that thing's utterly unmerciful grasp was a very real thing. We needed to get free.

The tug was much stronger on the Hopper, and the pod was drifting toward the black hole as well. We had to be fast.

She took the first turn wide, then reversed. I felt Bea immediately accelerating, pulling against the black hole's influence, and with a sudden snap, the Hopper broke free. Bea, on comms, said, "We're out. We're good."

Now we were close enough that I could use the magnetic cables to lock on and haul the pod in. There would barely be space at the back of the Hopper. It took me a couple of tries, but the cables eventually snapped into place. With all my strength I hauled. Even in vacuum, it wasn't easy to move this thing, and it scraped along the sides of the Hopper coming in. In fact, the hatch wouldn't close, but I waved Bea on.

"It's fine. Our suits have twenty minutes left. We can get back to Nadim without locking up."

She nodded and swung the shuttle around. I loved so many things about her—this confidence, her sweetness, how smart she was, and how quickly she got obsessed with some new tech idea.

I kept my arms on the cables, just in case the pod tried to float away as we were moving. For good measure, I wrapped them around some metalwork and used that to brace since I didn't want to get yanked out either. The stars were bleak and beautiful, no longer blotted out by the swarm.

Nadim opened for us, and coming back felt like a warm

hug, one I desperately needed. Once Bea shut the Hopper down, Nadim closed the doors and I waited for the room pressure to equalize, then I motioned to Bea. "There's no room to open this and let him out. Help me work it loose."

That took some doing, and Nadim eventually had to lighten the gravity so we could manage it. Finally, the pod plonked onto the docking bay floor, and I hit the escape hatch button as gravity came rushing back in. Felt like the weight of all my doubts, tied to the shadow of my regrets.

The pod cracked open and Ghostwalk stumbled out, dropping to one knee in bitter confusion. He spat some words in Bruqvisz, translated a microsecond later. "Should have perished with my brothers. Stories are not worth the pain of surviving alone."

There had been no chance for me to study their culture as I'd wanted to, so I was feeling around in the dark here. In trying to comfort Ghostwalk, I could make things exponentially worse. Nerves on the ragged edge of no return, I sank into a crouch beside him, but I didn't reach out.

"There's a reason Suncross chose you to carry on. You'd know what that is better than me."

Burning, angry eyes met mine, the nictitating membrane flicking in and out of sight, probably a measure of his agitation. "Because I can bear it," he said finally.

"I don't know what we're supposed to do right now, but I think I know what Suncross would want."

"And what is that, Zeerakull?"

"We won that fight because of him. We're here because of him. You know damn well he'd want us to dance."

After the victory dance, I left Ghostwalk to record their story and headed for Ops to see how close we were to Earth. This wasn't over, not by a long shot, but I didn't have the mental reserves to comfort anyone else.

Not when I was already one big red ball of sorrow over Suncross, underscored with fear for Chao-Xyll. I could admit privately that I didn't see a way out. That quick and merciful death in the lizard files might soon be her only option, and it was killing me to watch her fight and fight and lose. Soon, there might be nothing of my friend left. She'd gone out to try and help us, but she only got herself hurt. I'd never seen Chao-Xing *fail* before, but she'd never faced an enemy like this either, one that was warring within her own body.

I headed to my room, aware that I was sweaty, and when I started cleaning up, it was like I was getting ready for my last huzzah. That made it special, I figured, so I took my time, like I'd never do my hair or notice how pretty my brown skin was again. When I finished, I dressed in clothes I'd bought on the Sliver, stuff that couldn't be replaced, as it was likely the vendor was dead now. Today, I wore red.

Red for anger. Red for the human blood that would be spilled on Earth if our timing was off, even the slightest bit.

"Zara . . ." By his tone, Nadim was frightened by my mood. He didn't tell me how brightly I shone. Just as well—I wouldn't have believed it. "You don't think we can do this."

Trust him to cut to the heart of it, like he always had. "It doesn't matter what I think. We can only do what's possible. And we have to try, regardless."

And the facts were: We'd lost our drones. Used up our extra weapons. Watched our friends die. C-X couldn't influence the swarm the way Xyll had. It made sense; she wasn't pure Phage, but when I considered our assets left in this fight, they were damn few.

Once, I might've suggested we run. I wasn't that person anymore. Part of me wished I was, because maybe I could've saved the ones I loved, but I didn't even think that was a good thing—to live another day by letting everyone else die. Nadim had finally rubbed off on me to the point that I couldn't imagine reacting any other way. Whether I liked it or not, I was a hero now, poised to make my own ridiculous sacrifice.

The only question was whether it would be enough.

Bea came looking for me before I left my room, but she wasn't sad-eyed or tearful, thankfully. I didn't have the reserves to comfort her. Maybe I had the strength for this final battle if nobody asked anything else of me.

"I've been thinking," she said softly.

"About what?"

"We don't have that long until we hit the Sol system."

I stood in the doorway to my room, still not sure where she was going with this. "That's right."

"I don't want to go into this fight with regrets, Zara."

"You're going to have to say it plain. I'm not at my sharpest right now."

"There's only one thing I want," Bea told me.

"And what's that?"

"To spend that time with you."

At first, I wasn't sure if she meant what it sounded like she did, but she came on strong, pushing me to the wall and cupping my face for a kiss that left me dizzy and breathless. Hell yes, it was past time to do this. I let her nudge me back inside, and while we were kissing, touching each other, I stopped caring that my world was about to end. Bea became my world.

We stumbled back to the bed, and I was getting my last pristine outfit wrinkled as hell, but I didn't care about that either. When Bea pulled at my shirt, I yanked it over my head and threw it on the floor. We tumbled to the bed together, all silk and sweetness, hands smoothing skin, mine brown, hers gold, and her hair was so soft spilling against my hands. She was hotter and more aggressive than I would have imagined, and I let Bea have her way, gasping softly into the curve of her throat as her hands got busier and mine did too. Hard to say who pulled Nadim in first, but we'd gotten in the habit of sharing all good and lovely things.

He made it deeper and better, physical sensation threaded with sheer emotional warmth, and his pure joy flooded us. Everything expanded, and I became Beatriz, feeling my hands on her skin; her gasps felt like mine. She twisted against me, above me, her face tight with yearning. I pulled her back down into a desperate kiss. Her mouth moved on mine with the same longing, the same fear that this moment might never come again.

We'd lost and might lose more, but for now, we were together, affirming life.

"Zara." She kissed me again. Again. Soft. Hard. Fierce.

"Zara." Nadim, in my head, in my ears, drunk on what we shared with him.

I whispered both their names, dug my hands into Bea's hips. Her head fell back.

When the pleasure spiked, we went hard, and our minds opened to Nadim, pulling him into the bond just before everything was washed with gold. Afterward, we curled up together. I petted every inch of her skin that I could reach, faintly resenting the fact that I could be this happy just before losing everything I loved. But I couldn't even hold on to that brief bitterness when I was floating in beauty like this. Bea kissed my shoulder, my throat, and finally my lips.

"We finally did it," she said. And she seemed satisfied too.

"I'm glad you decided you didn't want to leave something this important undone."

"Beautiful." Nadim sounded dreamy, and I figured we'd passed the point of no return, sharing this with our Leviathan. "This was never mentioned in any files."

I was almost tempted to ask if it was good for him too, but he probably wouldn't get the joke. Bea rested her head on my shoulder, and I settled her close, breathing in the delicate scent of her skin, flowers from the scented soap she'd brought aboard.

"I love you both," I whispered. She curled into me with a contented little purr.

We dozed a little, or I suspected we did, because somehow the seconds spun out into minutes and then to hours. Soon Nadim was whispering, "We enter the Sol system in half an hour, Zara."

I nudged Bea. "Time for us to get up."

It was time, period. Lifekiller couldn't be far off, and he'd have the other half of the swarm with him. Maybe we had a shot, but I couldn't see it. This time, my ability to pinpoint weakness just had me looking at us. I could imagine him draining Earth and moving on to Greenheld. Our epic resistance wouldn't even be a footnote in the god-king's march to conquest.

It was hard to picture what he'd do unchecked. Devour everything? Found another draconian empire, where beings served or got eaten? Or maybe the time in cryo had driven him mad, so like the Phage, he no longer followed an actual plan. He just lashed out in untrammeled fury. I remembered the boom of Lifekiller's voice:

I AM COMING YOU WILL KNEEL

Would he make that offer to Earth? Hell, maybe humans *would* kneel.

Sighing, Bea rolled out of my head, disrupting my dire thoughts. By the time we had our clothes on, Nadim was stirring, anxious again. "Ghostwalk is coming. He'll be at your door soon."

"Probably has news," I said. "We should huddle up one last time and maybe go see Chao-Xyll." Though I didn't say it, both Bea and Nadim knew.

We were running out of time.

INTERLUDE: GHOSTWALK

I mourn my brothers, but they died in honor and glory, as it should be. Long will their stories be told to their descendants, written to the stars and carried to the hearing organs of every sentient being. This is my burden and my joy, that I write of Suncross and my brothers, stout warriors of the Bruqvisz both lost and found in their tale.

For myself, I have bitter pride. Suncross chose me to carry the tale forward, and that is a terrible honor, one that denies me glorious ending but gives me the opportunity to teach others of this war of gods and heroes. We shall never see its like again, and I am humbled by the task before me, to tell of the fallen and the survivors, the great singing ships and the enslaved Phage, the poisonous hunger of one who would eat the stars themselves and live in the dark.

While my voice survives, I shall tell of this. The battle is not yet done, and I may yet join my brothers. So I send this transmission out, wide and strong, to joyously tell of the Bruqvisz and the Elaszi, the Oborub and the Humans, the Leviathan and the Mechs. All must listen. All must honor, even in the midst of war, the sacrifices upon us now.

So let me speak.

CHAPTER TWENTY-TWO

Song for the Lost

GHOSTWALK SEEMED . . . BETTER, I guessed. Stronger. I didn't know how to read the subtle cues, but he wasn't quite as angry. "I am the last bearer of their story," he said to me, "but I know we go into further danger. Permission to access your comms?"

"Sure," I said. "Not real sure what good it will do you, but . . ."

"Leviathan can sing this story to their cousins," he said. "And perhaps also humans can send messages, as they did before?"

"I don't know if they're going to have time, but we

can try," I told him. His priority wasn't survival here, it was survival of our memory, our deeds. That was a pure enough goal. I talked to Nadim as we walked, and he and Typhon agreed to communicate the story in a kind of carrier wave out to the other Leviathan. Their singing—and I wasn't sure what it was, not just sound, surely—could travel intact across galaxies. Across the universe, if necessary. And when it hit a Bruqvisz satellite or comm system, it would deliver its information payload, and Suncross and his brothers would have their glorious last stand told, remembered, sent on.

The most immortality there was in the universe, stories.

Ghostwalk seemed satisfied with that and gave us a gesture with all four hands that seemed like it meant thanks; he asked what he could do, and I gave that some thought. For a Bruqvisz, Ghostwalk seemed positively even-tempered, but I didn't know that I was a good judge of what was going on with him. He'd lost his brothers, and he felt like the last Bruqvisz in the world. Did that make him more cautious, or less?

"Ghostwalk," I said as we arrived at Ops. "Will you take the watch here for a while? I need to go check on Marko and C-X."

"Careful," Beatriz said, and sent me a look. I nodded.

I heard the discordant noise before I reached Medbay.

I doubted that was a good sign, and I took a deep breath before heading in.

EMITU was lounging around in his docking bay like it was just another day at work. Chao-Xyll was shrieking. Modular shrieking, sure, but the translator was having none of it. Marko was backed up against the wall, and if his world had been shaken before, it was broken now—I could see that in his face. He'd wanted to believe she was still Chao-Xing in there. But I knew she wasn't, and now it was clear to him too.

Marko, of all people—the poster boy for the Honors, the one I'd have tapped as the least judgmental of all of us—couldn't accept what Chao-Xing had become. It was written all over his face.

I left him to his misery, because I had bigger problems. Namely, Chao-Xyll, who was in restraints again, but struggling *very* hard to get out of them. I went up to her bedside, though every instinct told me to back off, save myself. She looked . . . wild. Out of control. We were, I thought, lucky that EMITU had busted out the *heavy* restraints and added some of that steel-reinforced netting on top of them; she wasn't going anywhere, despite all her efforts.

Her eyes were open, and although they weren't *right*, exactly, they were still human. And suffering. Over the grating sound of her wails, I yelled at EMITU. "Get your haiku-crazy metal ass over here! Why aren't you doing anything? She's in pain!"

"The pain is not physical," EMITU said without moving from his docking station. "It is, instead, a mental or an emotional breakdown. I'm a doctor, not a—"

"I don't care what you're *not*. Just give her something to calm her down!"

"I have," he said. "Several times. It's no longer working."

"Increase the—"

"Zara," EMITU interrupted me. "I have done all I can do without removing her vocalizing instruments or killing her. Which would you like me to do?"

I realized that EMITU was just as unnerved and frustrated as I was. Damn. "Sorry," I muttered. "Never mind." I remembered Marko putting his hand in Chao-Xyll's palm, and I wormed mine beneath the netting to try it too. The slick black armor seemed impenetrable. I wasn't sure she even knew I was touching her. But she was watching me with that sick, hot desperation in her eyes.

And suddenly, the translator said, "____please."

I nearly yelped, I was so surprised. Was that a glitch? A random sound that hit an accidental meaning? I didn't interrupt. I waited.

She was trying to communicate.

And it was working. "___fail____hope___" I waited, holding my breath, as she struggled. "____understand___"

"Yes." I practically yelled it. "Yes, I understand! Marko! Did you hear that?"

Marko nodded, but he seemed so pale, so remote, that I wasn't sure it mattered to him. I didn't let that dent my joy. I leaned over C-X and removed my hand from her palm to place it on her forehead. Warm, smooth skin, lightest tan beneath a dusting of gold. Human skin. "I hear you," I told her. "Keep trying. Please!"

"____dead___fault___"

Two potentially random words but I didn't like where they were going. Was this what was going on? Her emotional pain, was it because of all the dead *Phage*? Or because of the loss of our friends aboard Suncross's ship? Could go either way. If I had to be real, most of her was Phage now, even if this patch of skin my palm rested against felt human. Who was she in mourning for?

"My fault."

That came through clearly. Very clearly. I let out a breath and shook my head. "Not your fault," I told her. "You did everything you could do."

"Fail."

"Yeah, you notice I failed too, right? It took Suncross blowing the shit out of his own ship to win that fight." I sounded bitter. Angry. Well, that was accurate, I guessed. I'd liked—loved—him and his crew. I missed them hard. "Not your fault, C-X."

"I am nothing," she said, and that was breathtakingly awful. "Belong ____ not."

She meant she was alone, completely and utterly alone, and . . . she was right. There was no other thing like her, as far as I knew. Xyll had been isolated, but C-X . . . was alone.

"No," I told her. "You're with us. You belong."

"Failed. Failed. *Failed!*" That last was an uncontrolled screech, both from the translator and from the underlying Phage-like noise, and when C-X flailed again it seemed worse. It was, I guessed; Chao-Xing had been a perfectionist, always excellent at everything she did. She couldn't accept this ugly, bloody transformation, or her limitations, or that she'd tried to make a difference and nearly died doing it, to no real purpose. I could imagine what was ringing in her head: *Why am I still alive?*

I was about to tell her, inadequately, that it was okay when the first restraint broke. I instinctively jerked my hand away when the steel snapped, and one of her limbs popped free; a swipe of her hand shredded the steel-reinforced netting and sent it slumping on both sides of the bed.

Then the other three restraints shattered, one right after another, and I backed off because she was loose, and I didn't know what I was prepared to do about this, not at all. She looked alien. She looked *mad.* And she came up to a fluid crouch on the bed, teeth bared, and looked at me with real menace.

"I *failed!*"

That was the first complete sentence she'd managed. It also seemed like she was blaming me. Maybe she should, for putting her out there, at risk. For letting her take the risk at all.

"C-X," I said, hoping the nickname would catch her attention. I couldn't tell if it did. "You *tried*. It's okay. *It's okay!*"

A powerful spasm hit her. Pure rage, or another wave of uncontrollable remapping of her body, but the effect was that she came off the bed in a stumbling rush straight at me.

EMITU jerked free of his dock and fired darts that hit her in still-vulnerable spots, but the drugs—and I imagine he was dialing it up to eleven—did absolutely nothing to slow her down. I backpedaled, but she kept coming, and I was reaching for my weapon when the worst thing happened.

Marko lunged, trying to restrain C-X, or maybe he was protecting me. He shouted something I couldn't process, putting his hands on C-X, and she reacted, shoving him away with incredible force. He hit the metal rim of the end of the bed, and his neck snapped back at a brutally unnatural angle, and then he crashed to the floor.

EMITU rushed to Marko's side, and Nadim was shouting "Zara! Get out of here, I will lock her in!" but I couldn't go—I couldn't. Not until I knew if Marko was okay.

He wasn't. I knew that; I'd seen it from how he'd hit. EMITU worked frantically. C-X had paused, trembling long arms and razor claws dangling limp at her sides. Her attention, like mine, was on Marko.

EMITU's busy extensors suddenly withdrew, and his dome turned toward me. I didn't like that. At all.

"I regret to report that Honor Marko has suffered catastrophic damage to his spinal cord."

I felt a cold, bolting shudder go through me. "Well, fix him!"

"I cannot," EMITU said. No jokes now. "The damage is very significant. I have placed him into a medical stasis, and must move him to a pod. It is beyond my capabilities to repair his spinal injury."

I swallowed hard. "Is—is he dead?"

"No," he said. "But only because of the medical stasis field. The pod will pause all functions until more extensive repairs can be attempted. I recommend immediate relocation of the patient to the Honors medical facility on Earth. Unfortunately, there is a hard limit to the time a stasis treatment is effective in such cases."

I felt a real wave of rage and despair. *Damn it.* We might lose Marko. We *had* lost him, unless we could survive all this and get him to Earth before the stasis field expired. I wanted to ask how long we had, but the awful truth was it didn't damn well matter. And Marko would have been the first to say that.

EMITU pointed an extensor at C-X, who wasn't moving, except for slight, nervous trembles. "Preparing to deliver euthanizing cocktail."

"No!" It burst out of me, raw and bloody. We'd just lost Marko. I couldn't lose C-X too. "Stop. That's an order! You will *not* kill anybody without my express permission. Understand?"

"Understood," EMITU said crisply. "I would normally say that it's your funeral. But it is not. It very well could be his. You should consider this carefully, Zara."

Fuck. He was right. Marko shouldn't have been here. C-X shouldn't have been here. I should have killed Xyll when it started to turn violent.

But I hadn't, and here we were.

I pulled my gun and held it at my side. C-X noticed that move; it pulled her attention away from the immobile body of our friend on the floor. She was breathing hard. Panting, almost. And yes, those were tears running down her cheeks. The armor crept across her face in thin swirls, like Maori tattoos.

She said, "Go ahead."

I was tempted. I felt gray and thick inside, heavy with responsibility and grief. Killing her would be the easy answer, for both of us. Old Zara would have done it without blinking, but she hadn't loved these people. And lost them.

"No," I said. "C-X, you're alive. You *matter*. And I know you. Xyll was strong. Chao-Xing was strong. Together, you are unstoppable . . . not just this"—I swept a hand up and down, indicating the changes—"but here." Hand to my heart. "I know you. I know what you can do."

"I *failed*."

"So did I," I said. "And will again. Over and over, until I figure out how to succeed. We don't give up. That's who we are. That's how we have to be. And you can't give up, C-X, because we need you. We'll get Marko back. But first we've got to *win*."

She didn't want to hear that, but she understood, I could tell. She looked at Marko's still body again, then moved.

She picked him up with an astonishing grace and gentleness. She laid him in the bed, but when she tried to straighten his crooked, limp arms and legs, her razored fingers left shallow cuts. She made a muted sound of distress, and I broke my stillness to go help. EMITU rolled over and pressed command keys, and a hard shell came down from overhead and sealed Marko up inside it.

Like a coffin.

C-X let out a wild, metallic keen of distress and rocked back and forth. Whatever she was now, she could feel this. Could deeply, horribly regret what she'd done.

I suddenly thought about the larger consequences.

"Nadim! Does Typhon know—" I'd expected to feel a huge blast of rage and grief from the older Leviathan at the grave injury of his Honor. I felt . . . nothing. Like he didn't know. But he had to know. Didn't he?

"Typhon has withdrawn," Nadim said. "He won't allow me access. I think . . . Yusuf says he is very deeply wounded, both by Chao-Xing's struggle and Marko's injury. He and Starcurrent are struggling to help."

"Don't let him do anything reckless," I said. "And don't *you* do anything risky, either. Promise me."

"I promise," he said. I could tell he didn't like it, but I also knew he'd keep his word to me. "Zara, we are fast approaching Earth's solar system. We will be there very soon. What . . . what are we going to do?"

I didn't have to answer that, thankfully, because the Medbay doors opened, and Bea burst through them, hurtling toward the bed. She looked distraught. Horrified. And when she took it in—Marko in the bed, silent and still—she added it all up. "She *killed him*?"

"No." *Maybe.* "He's in stasis. It was an accident—"

Bea wasn't listening. She didn't have a gun, but she went for mine, and we struggled for it. I won and hugged her tight. "There's a chance we can get him back," I said. "But we've got to hold together, okay? We've got to."

She took in a breath and wordlessly screamed it out. I could hear the rage. I understood it. Then she said, "Are we going to kill it?" *It* meant Chao-Xyll, I guessed.

"We can't." Without letting her go, I kissed her forehead. Right now, loving her was the only thing I could do that felt like it wasn't a complete disaster. "Please believe me: C-X didn't mean to do that. She's in pain. And she's a *child* with the strength of a monster. Please don't blame her, baby."

"We can't trust her," Bea said. She pulled back, and I let go, and she swiped trembling hands over her damp cheeks. Glared at C-X, who was now staring at the floor. "Not after what she did to Marko."

"She is our friend."

"Is she?"

C-X raised her head then, looked at Bea, and said, "Yes." And she sounded eerily like Chao-Xing just then. Bea flinched a bit, but she didn't bite back. "I regret hurting him. More than you know, Beatriz."

The name was a little clumsy, but clearly, the translator was starting to get confident now with interpreting the sounds that C-X was making. And C-X was making sense, more to the point.

"Marko's not going to survive unless we win this fight," I said to her, and all of them. "Lifekiller's here. And we have to get ready. Right now."

I didn't know what that meant. I didn't know what we could possibly do, other than die like Suncross and his crew in a futile effort to save our planet. But I did know that whatever we had to do, we would do.

And though it was very little comfort, and no consolation at all, I knew one more thing: Chao-Xyll would do whatever she could to help.

From the ancient songs of the Lost Ones, preserved
in fragments by the Bruqvisz (recovered from Elaszi
vaults by right of conquest in forfeit-or-pain)

So comes the dawn
Of no sun, no stars but Them
They have swallowed the light and become the dark
Nothing survives Their anger
The Singers sing them still
We try
We fail
We perish
Last light of last star
No dawn
Cold
Good-bye

CHAPTER TWENTY-THREE

Lost All Doubt

I'D HEARD OF a famous line in a book that said you can't go home again, but I guessed that was more of a metaphor, because the Sol system flowered before me with all those exquisitely familiar worlds. I clocked the tiny little outcast on the far reaches that was even prettier up close, the purple gas giant, and the angry red planet with its domed colony.

A pang went through me, so sharp that the feeling might have been made of knives. Not all these worlds supported life, but they all had resources that Lifekiller could steal. Liquid, superheated iron at the core of Mercury. Venus was thick with them; even the snow on its sharp mountains was made of heavy metals. Earth was infused with uranium, which Lifekiller craved. Platinum and palladium buried in the rich red dirt of Mars. Jupiter's giant surface hid a core of heavy metals under its spinning, rocky rings. Even little Pluto had a uranium core.

But he wasn't here for the resources. Not completely, anyway. If he was, he'd have started at one end of the planetary buffet and worked his way inside, but instead, he skipped the tasty appetizers and came right for *my* world. That said something about his capacity for holding a grudge.

As for Earth, Luna Colony, and Mars Colony Roma, between the three settlements, billions of lives were at stake. From this distance, Earth was a small blue orb swirled with greens and browns. Mars blazed red, smaller still. We buzzed Luna Colony, coming fast, and our comm lit up with chatter as soon as we got close.

"Unidentified Leviathan, this is Fort Copernicus." That was the name of the military base that existed alongside the country club–like resort they'd built on the moon. "We have you in our sights. Please declare your intentions."

I glanced at Bea, who gestured at me. Great, I'd been elected spokesperson when I might still be registered as a wanted felon. "Who am I talking to?"

"This is Lieutenant Colonel Atticus Boyd with First

Space Division Bravo, and I have command. I repeat, identify yourselves immediately or we will have no choice but to judge you hostile. And believe you me, I have got enough on my plate today." When we entered vid range, the screen crackled to life, and he looked about like I'd have expected: a middle-aged white man with permanent sunburn in his cheeks and on his nose, pale blue eyes, a freckled forehead, and thinning hair.

He seemed sincere, and I couldn't waste time trying to figure out where he stood on the whole corruption of the Honors Committee issue. "My name is Zara Cole. I'm accompanied by Beatriz Teixeira and we're on board the Leviathan known as Nadim."

"Hell, girl. You've got the whole damn planet looking for you. Honors drama is well outside my jurisdiction, even if I was inclined to give a damn, and I truly am not. I've got hostiles coming in fast and hot, so I just need to know—are you with or against us?"

I had to laugh. "I'm not here to conquer Earth, so it's safe to say we came to help. We know something about the enemies incoming, and you *will* be hard pressed. Get the planetary guns online. I think we have one on Mars Colony. Is there one on Luna too?"

"That there is. I've already starting calibrating."

"Focus your offense on the big bad. We'll do our best to take out the shock troops that surround him. Nadim, send all the data we have on Lifekiller and the Phage to the lieutenant colonel. It's a lot to take in, but maybe it'll help."

"Already sending, Zara."

"Christ on a cracker," the LC said as the terabytes started popping on his terminal.

"Don't you have an AI to analyze quickly and give you the highlights?" EMITU could do that much for us, if he wasn't in a mood or busy with Japanese arts and crafts.

He cursed beneath his breath and snapped some orders too fast for me to catch since he was facing away. "Done. Now you tell me what you can in thirty seconds or less."

"Your main threat is a damn near unstoppable space Cthulhu, more or less. Normal weapons don't do much, and it eats energy like candy."

Boyd let out such a sharp breath that it made a *hoo* sound. "You sure know how to ruin somebody's day."

"We've been fighting it for weeks," I snapped. "Imagine how *we* feel."

Unlike with the council on Greenheld, I didn't tell the lieutenant colonel about how we'd raided a tomb and woken the damn thing up. Complete honesty wouldn't get me anywhere with an army man. In old vids, they were always talking about "need to know" and clearly he didn't.

"Point taken. We'll try to hold it off if we can't kill it." He ran a hand over his already tousled hair, and I could see that he didn't seem hopeful, based on what I'd said and what some lower ranking dude was whispering in his ear.

Yeah, Lifekiller's close.

But even I wasn't ready when he rose over Luna Colony, practically blotting out the stars on his own. I hadn't seen him with my own eyes since we drove him off at Greenheld, although we'd been chasing his tail ever since. I hadn't let myself think too long about what form that stasis might have unlocked, but now . . . now, my blood chilled in my veins.

Lifekiller was like a Leviathan and a dragon had had hate sex until they fused. When I'd called him space Cthulhu a second ago, I had no damn idea how accurate it was. The amorphous shadow he had been had coalesced into a great and terrible shape, dark as obsidian with razor-sharp fins but also thin, ropy tentacles snaking out from his head and neck. And the size . . . it looked like he could almost wrap up the moon and crush it into lunar dust.

"May God have mercy on us all," Boyd breathed, reminding me that we were still on a live channel.

Into this hellish mess came another emergency, a cluster of Elaszi ships, too far to fire on us yet but close enough to hail. Our comm popped with angry audio, no visual yet. "Zara Cole, you have cheated us! We demand satisfaction!"

I couldn't help it; I started laughing. Did the blobs get

paid extra to be a pain in my ass? They'd said they were cool and were changing their minds at the worst possible moment.

"Can't you tell I'm busy? You can have me if I survive this, but I'm warning you, the odds aren't good. Unless you want to help us fight? That way, you get first dibs on salvage. I hear the Phage break down into some valuable parts. You're damned hard to kill, so chances are you'll be around afterward to grab the good stuff. It should make up for the drones you lost. Ours took off too, by the way. Bacia robbed us both."

A brief silence, then: "You bargain like an Elaszi."

Was that grudging respect in the blob's voice? Either way, I couldn't waste time or energy on this. To get to me, they would have to pass through the swarm and get by Lifekiller; that wouldn't be easy, and they'd take damage from trying. The Phage surged after their changed god, filling the horizon with their legion of darkness. They split in unison and swarmed toward us. I sensed Typhon nearby, silent and icy with loss.

"We agree, Zara Cole. We fight for salvage rights! If it's not enough, we'll take the balance from your carcass after the battle."

Normally that threat would have Nadim growling, but he was distracted by the Phage swimming ever closer. I did a truncated version of the lizard victory dance. Of all possible outcomes, I never could've imagined recruiting the blobs to defend Earth.

"The cousins are here!" Nadim called, and there was bright music in his voice.

"Ophelia and Quell?"

That made sense. They had been on the way to Earth to return Derry's body and to let Jury take care of unfinished business. If they'd left, they couldn't have gotten far without hearing the terrifying screech of the hungry Phage swarm alongside Lifekiller's endless, voracious hunger. It was like the Leviathan to sign on for a fight they couldn't win. After all, the Elders had been battling quietly behind our backs for years.

Nadim listened to songs I couldn't hear. I was attuned to Typhon after the way I'd seduced him, but I didn't have a default ability to connect with all Singers. "Yes. Ophelia sings. She is with us. Quell will defend Luna Colony."

I tapped the comm to broadcast my message to everyone in range. "You know what's at stake here, and we can't lose billions of lives. Use every weapon, every trick at your disposal. The fight ends here, one way or another." Someone else—Suncross, for instance—might have had better words, a rallying cry, but I had never been good at that. Hopefully what I could offer was enough. I felt a sharp stab of longing for the Bruqvisz, for their sheer bloody joy in battle. Ghostwalk stood alone now. No joy in that.

Yusuf popped on screen just long enough to say, "Power at eighty-seven percent. We have two sonic shots before Typhon goes dark. I'll make them count."

Starcurrent stood behind Yusuf and ze did a weird move with zis face tendrils that struck me like a salute. Maybe I was reading it wrong, but I returned the gesture, saluting zim back like I had some rank to speak of. Bea touched my shoulder lightly. I didn't kiss her, or I might not have had the resolve remaining to break formation.

"Nadim, engage the enemy."

There, I said it. No going back now.

He jumped, like an aerial leap that I'd admired in some long-ago dolphin show. Without me asking, he slid into a dark run. My Leviathan knew strategy now, didn't need me to spell it out for him. This was part of the learning exchange that made the Honors program so magical: we taught them; they taught us. And if that was to continue, we had to save it. Save everyone.

The Phage nearest us flailed, seeking Leviathan song, and they found only Typhon. Nadim appeared behind them—classic pincer move—and we unloaded with all guns. Ghostwalk was on weapons, taking revenge for his fallen, while Yusuf dropped the first sonic boom. The Phage between our two live ships fucking *melted*, organic matter shaken into revolting liquid that froze into crystal chunks.

There were so many more, too many.

And I knew how much power our ships could bring to bear. I registered the sound of the planetary guns laying into Lifekiller, but the shots bounced off, like he was made of some impenetrable material. Maybe all the minerals he'd consumed had created inorganic chitin, grown bio-armor that shielded the flesh beneath. He'd gone after heavy metals. In the right combinations, they could create almost unbreakable shields.

With all my heart, I wished Suncross was here. I could use a glimpse of him waving with all four arms and shouting about our glorious triumph right about now. By contrast, Ghostwalk was silent and furious, working Nadim's weapons until they glowed white-hot.

"Ease up," I said.

The Bruqvisz survivor shot me a look that a child could've read. "Why? You said to use everything. This is our last stand, Zeerakull. This is no time for moderation."

True, but I could *feel* Nadim weakening as the lasers and rail guns drained his reserves. Soon that power expenditure would become physical pain, and then he'd become too weak to dark run. Too weak to fight. Maybe I shouldn't care about that anymore, since we were all fifteen minutes away from a glorious death.

Quell had lost weapons in the fight with us, no chance for new installations, so she was fighting the Phage physically, and I could see them crawling all over her hull and ripping into her flesh. Burrowing in. Typhon let out a wordless call, full of wrath and horror. He hit her with full strength and she rolled, end over end until I thought maybe she was out of the fight for good. The Elder radiated uncontrollable violence, and I knew I wasn't imagining his icy determination.

Typhon would rather kill his cousins himself than let the Phage take them.

I couldn't see what the blobs were doing, but I'd been on the receiving end of their dirty tricks before. About time they turned all that evil cunning on Lifekiller and the Phage. Maybe their help would be enough to turn the tide.

Shields went up on Luna Colony and Mars, but Earth didn't have anything like that. We'd trusted the Leviathan to protect us and now so many of them were dead, casualties of a war humans didn't even know was raging until it showed up at their door. Nadim's pain surged through me.

"Phage! We've got potential boarders," I shouted to Bea. "Do we have enough juice to shock them?"

"Two shocks, maybe three," she answered. "We won't have a lot more, probably not enough for another round of laser fire afterward."

"We don't have the means to repel them inside." And Nadim didn't have the sheer bloody nerve to withstand an infestation while Bea and I went hand to hand. I couldn't imagine what a nightmare that would be for him, feeling us die, feeling himself eaten from within and cored hollow.

That could *not* happen.

Lifekiller pushed closer to Earth. That was his primary target, and I couldn't help but think—maybe a little egotistically—that he'd done this to punish *me*. We'd woken him, and then we'd hurt him.

I pulled my gaze away and checked our reserves. The dark run and weapon use were burning through Nadim's energy. Soon Bea and I would have to bond to keep him going.

Nadim lurched and I hit the floor, rolling almost all the way to the wall. My mouth tasted like copper: split lip or bitten tongue. Either way, it wasn't bad enough for me to seek medical attention in the middle of a battle. Out the view screen, I got a glimpse of Typhon's barbed tail, and a bunch of Phage free-floating, dead and broken in vacuum.

"He's coming around for another hit," Bea reported.

"Fire up the shock field before he strikes." I didn't want Nadim being hurt again by Typhon, though I was sure the electricity didn't feel great.

Bea popped the button and a tremor ran through Nadim, not pain exactly, but discomfort that I felt through my shoes, vibrating into my bones. Reflexively, I opened to him, not leaving my Zara-self but opening my senses to the greater battle. Bea joined us, less than Bezardim but a trinity of perception that encompassed everything at once. Ophelia sang of despair and battles lost, even as she dove among the Phage, fighting with everything she had, while Quell bucked and slapped at them. She and Jon Anderson weren't out of the fight yet, which made me like them a whole lot more.

These Leviathan could run—they had no real link to this world; they didn't need to die for it. But I sensed that for them too, this was their final battle. If something didn't change, we would lose. It was only a matter of time.

Lifekiller spewed some kind of—well, I could only think of it as some *poison*—out into Earth's atmosphere. Darkness spread over the anterior portion. *Where is that? Australia? New Zealand?* Were people dying in that impenetrable cloud?

"Our guns aren't working!" That was the lieutenant colonel shouting at me from the comm, but I couldn't spare any attention for his struggles, not with us already in the thick of it with the Phage.

"Critical mass of Phage on our armor." Bea's voice trembled and I made the call so she wouldn't have to. I hit the button that time for the second shock. The lights dimmed and for a few seconds didn't come back up. Ghostwalk turned from the console. "I have no more power to continue the offensive, Zeerakull. What should I do now?"

"Head for the supply room and gear up. Skinsuit, any

weapons you can find. We need to be ready." I didn't say *in case of breach*, but Ghostwalk didn't need it spelled out for him.

I felt short of breath, and small and inadequate to this day, this moment. I was *nothing* that was needed, and I was all there was.

"Zara, I'm having containment issues. I think you need to—" But before EMITU could finish that sentence, the sound of banging and a crash terminated the connection.

Bea gave me a shove. "Go. I'll do what I can here. But you cannot hesitate this time. If C-X has gone rogue, end this. We can't let her . . ." She paused, reframed her sentence with a set expression. "Well, you know what I mean, I'm sure."

In the middle of the fight, Chao-Xyll? Really? It sounded like she had gone after the med bot, and I did not have time to be putting out extraneous fires. Yet instead of looking for Lifekiller's weakness or helping to destroy the Phage, I was sprinting to Medbay, trying not to think about Marko or what I might have to do to my friend when I got there.

If it comes down to it, you have to pull the trigger. You can't hesitate. Not this time.

That was the shittiest pep talk I had ever given myself, and it didn't help that when I rounded the corner, I saw EMITU sprawled in the corridor on his side, treads whirring and trying to push himself up with a crooked extensor. Banging sounds came from within Medbay. As I drew closer, I guessed it must be C-X slamming repeatedly into the blast door.

It took all my strength to lever EMITU upright, and he started running diagnostics as soon as he went vertical. "She tried to escape?" I guessed.

"She threw me like a discus, but I managed to activate lockdown as I hit the wall."

There was a serious chunk out of Nadim, and I could have happily shot C-X for adding to his miseries. "Sedatives aren't working at all anymore?"

"There is no human medicine that retains any efficacy whatsoever. Likewise, the chemicals I was using to treat the alien Xyll do not seem effective either. If my patient was not so volatile, this would be quite interesting. I do not enjoy being damaged, however. Look, my extensor is bent!"

Part of me was tempted to leave the situation like this. If we opened the blast door, I'd have to shoot her, judging by how agitated she sounded.

"Something must be done," EMITU said. "If she cannot come out the door, I fear she may go through the wall—perhaps multiple walls—to attain freedom, and that would be extremely painful for Nadim."

Shit. To say the least. I couldn't let that happen either.

My choices were bad and worse, and I hated that it had come down to this. The lights flickered again, and Nadim made a pained sound, sort of all around me. He didn't have much left to give, and his fear messed with my head. There were Phage crawling on him again, seeking to eat their way inside. C-X was as much of a threat.

Suddenly, the pounding stopped, a few seconds of respite, then Chao-Xyll said, "We know you are there, Zara."

We? Whoa, that was new.

Her—their?—voice was different, complex harmonies that raised the hair on my arms because it sounded like I was hearing in two different frequencies. Like a human voice with alien reverb. Her throat should not be able to speak in stereo, yet it was, and I had icy chills that wouldn't quit. She wasn't using the translator now. This was straight-up language. She'd changed even more.

"Does that register for you?" I asked EMITU in a whisper.

"Yes. Fascinating. I wish I could catalog the changes in greater detail but my ability to observe is obscured by the door. Should I write a haiku to commemorate the occasion?"

"Save it for later." Louder, I added, "I'm here. What's going on?"

"You must let me out. You must. It is our only hope." She

sounded calm enough, but if she snapped again, she could take out Bea or me, hurt Nadim or break Ghostwalk's neck like she had Marko's. No matter what she said, it didn't seem like a smart move.

"I can't do that, C-X. It would help so much if you'd calm down and let—"

"We will die. Let me do what I must, what I was created to do."

Okay, that sounded . . . creepy. Her voice was freaking me out too. But at least she was talking, right? I turned to the med bot. "What do you think?"

"At worst, Patient C-X murders you meatballs and dismantles me. My memory core is fully backed up. I say let's roll the dice."

I sighed. Why did I bother asking EMITU anything?

Finally, Chao-Xyll said, "I know it is difficult to trust us, Zara, but we know now what it is we are meant to do. Please . . . do not allow us to fail again."

That touch of pathos swayed me. Before I could think better of it, I used my H2 to override the lockdown, and C-X exploded from the wrecked Medbay, racing in a terrifying insectoid skitter toward Ops.

I followed her as fast as I could.

When I caught up with C-X, I found her at the console. She was alone; Bea was eyeing her with equal measures of fear and wariness. Chao-Xyll ran her fingers over the screen so fast I couldn't follow the motions, and then she seemed to be broadcasting, all channels, all frequencies. It was a blast of complex, unfathomable *noise*, overwhelming the translators that tried to cope with it; it hurt Nadim and the other Leviathan on an almost cellular level. Whatever it was, it wasn't communication for *us*.

The translator kicked in several seconds later to tell us what the message meant.

"You serve a false king. The queen is risen. Behold the Empress of the Swarm! Follow me. Follow me now, kindred, and you shall feast as never before!"

From the Bruqvisz collection *The New Star Forest*,
chipped and registered edition, traded to Earth

. . . can be no doubt that the discovery of a new, intelligent, star-faring species is a cause for celebration among all who are privileged to travel the dark. And yet the history of Humankind is troubled. Many stories of terrible wars, of preying upon their own for pleasure and gain. This is baffling to most, even to the Bruqvisz.

Yet also the Bruqvisz share with Humankind a love of stories, and dancing, and so there must be siblinghood in that bond. We share many tales with the Humans in this new collection, and in return the Humans share many tales with us.

Surely this can only be the start of a new and rich collaboration.

Or war. Maybe war. But if so, we will tell your stories, Humans! We honor you with this promise of glorious fame, and possible glorious death.

CHAPTER TWENTY-FOUR

Lost and Found

CHAO-XYLL, EMPRESS OF the Swarm.

There was an unmistakable power to her message, far more than the human translation the matrix managed. *This* was what compassion got us, and if he had been able to see it, Marko would have thought so too. If he could see how majestic she was, a beautiful insect queen, he'd make the same choice again. Try to save her. Try to protect me. Different sides of the same coin. And that was Marko, who'd never thought he was good enough—that he wasn't a real Honor. But thanks to his sacrifice, C-X was battling Lifekiller for control of the Phage.

She was fighting, in part, for *his* survival too.

I couldn't breathe, felt like, and then I realized that I was gasping but a headache was forming. Power systems were failing. Air was going bad in here, fast, and though the automatic scrubbers would keep us going for an hour or so, we'd be operating at lower and lower levels until we just stopped thinking altogether. Out of weapons, except for what we could do hand to hand. Nadim, unasked, had thrown himself into a tandem fight with Typhon, rolling, twisting, crushing the Phage crawling on his hull against the bigger ship's armor, while Typhon's fins and tail raked the invaders away. Incredibly, Typhon had enough power reserved for one more attack, and as he finished cleaning up Nadim's Phage problem, he dived straight for Lifekiller.

He hit the god-king with a stunning, shattering force that staggered even something of that size and power, and then Typhon, nose still buried in Lifekiller's flesh, released another sonic blast. His last, I thought; he'd held that in reserve, and it was the very last of his energy. Chao-Xyll's noise was still screaming over the speakers, and I saw Yusuf and Starcurrent on the screens trying to talk, but I couldn't hear them. Their lights went dark. Consoles went out.

Then ours did too.

I ran to the transparent wall, my only view of the battle now, and saw that Ophelia had launched a grappling mechanism and was trying to tow Typhon back. Lifekiller seemed momentarily stunned, and some of his limbs had been torn away. Those tentacles floated, twitching and freezing. Luna Colony's defenses were down, guns silent.

Lifekiller *roared*—there was no other word for it; it was a deep, subsonic wave that hit us like a slap and sent Nadim tumbling. In the chaos Ophelia's grapples broke loose, and she and Typhon spun in separate directions. Nadim leveled himself out and flipped head over tail to get back to the fight. He was hurting, bleeding, all but exhausted, but he wasn't giving up.

"Time to leave the nest," I said to Chao-Xyll. Her black-armored head turned, and there was almost nothing human about it now, except I could still see her features underneath the chitin, her eyes. "You can't stay in here and do this."

She set that command to the Phage on loop and skittered off, heading for the docking bay. *Nadim?*

She's going. A pause. I felt a small pulse of relief. *She's gone, launched herself from the docking bay.*

Without a ship. Out into space. Alone. The last time she tried this, the Phage nearly ate her.

But I watched from the window as her hybrid body hurled through space and headed for the Phage swarm.

It was like watching a black hole rip away the surface of a star. It started with a few of the Phage spiraling out from the main force and approaching her, and then more. Then a stream of them being irresistibly drawn away from Lifekiller's massive presence to orbit Chao-Xyll in a thick, chitinous, living shell. Thousands. Tens of thousands.

Lifekiller, intent on breathing his poison over the Earth, didn't notice the defection. Ophelia dove at him and hit him hard, rolled away but was caught in a net of flailing tendrils; she snapped free with a supreme effort, but I saw the slices they'd left on her, bleeding starlight. *As long as he's fighting us, he's not killing people on Earth.* The guns fired up again from the surface, and from Luna Colony, catching Lifekiller in the middle, but as before, they did little damage, if any. Quell came out of nowhere with another diving attack, and she too got trapped by Lifekiller's lashing tentacles. Typhon, though nearly inert from the last sonic bolt, roused himself to motion, and used his sharp tail to slice her free.

The four Leviathan crowded into a tight, rotating, defensive circle. All of them were weary, wounded, bleeding; the Phage had withdrawn, but Lifekiller was invincible. They'd hurt him, but they hadn't stopped him.

The blob ships were like jackals, constantly at the back of everything, and they were throwing everything they had at Lifekiller, changing focus from the Phage when Chao-Xyll joined the fray. But their weapons were bouncing off the god-king in ripples of energy too, silent shockwaves that took out a couple of Elaszi ships on the rebound. Killing was so *easy* for this monster, the one we'd woken up. Nadim's pain spiked in my head as I framed that thought.

We're losing.

It hit me with staggering force, and I wanted to scream, to cry, to throw myself out in a useless fight against an old, forgotten god. I struggled to *think* in the thickening air aboard Nadim. "Can the Abyin Dommas help us?" I asked Nadim. "Sing, like they did before?"

"Too far," he responded tersely. "It will not work at such a distance."

"Maybe like before, we can sing with Starcurrent—"

"Comms are down, Zara. We can't." Grim sorrow tinged his voice. The awareness that we were damn well beaten. That Earth was dying, and we were watching it happen.

That was the exact moment that the universe exploded around us with drones. Not from the planet below but coming from the darkness of space—zipping, flying like heroic darts to smash themselves against Lifekiller's skin. It must have hurt; each one carried an explosive charge, and the swarm of drones lit him up like Christmas. I saw a sleek, pale ship glide through and deliver six fast, devastating blows from a percussion weapon—like rail guns, but more powerful than that.

Lifekiller howled that angry, subsonic rumble again, and I felt it *doing things* to Nadim. To all the Leviathan.

It was hurting them, injuring them internally. *Dammit.* Quell slid into unconsciousness and floated away limp; Ophelia went with her to try to protect her from any additional attacks by Lifekiller, but he had loomed back over the Earth again. His shadow fell over a vast section of the planet, darkening the blue water, the green and brown lands. He was a stain on the universe.

He needed to die, but I didn't know how the *hell* to accomplish that. The pale ship that glided through must have been the drone owner's; it finished its attack run and zipped into an accelerated escape.

I knew who that was, even though our comms were down. Had to be Bacia. They'd survived the Sliver and come to exact a little revenge—but not at the cost of dying over it. Their drones slowed Lifekiller down, though, and the rail guns had injured him. Not enough to make him back off and retreat. And Bacia wasn't taking another run at him. They were already gone, headed to some safe, presumably expensive haven far, far away.

But Bacia hadn't come alone.

Suncross's last stand had resonated across the Bruqvisz comm networks. Must have, because now more mech ships were appearing. One, then five. Then twenty more. It wasn't exactly a fleet, and they weren't exactly organized, but I could almost hear the bloody victory bellows from where I stood, gaping. They came at Lifekiller in a chaotic blur of motion, weaving in and out of formations and firing, firing, *firing* until Lifekiller finally turned away from Earth in a slow, lumbering motion and began grabbing for their ships. They slid away like quicksilver, darting through his tentacles like little fish and stabbing him over and over and over.

And then I heard Chao-Xyll. Her cry resonated through Nadim, like Lifekiller's but *different*, a frequency that made my heart skip and my guts contract, something so primal and desperate and furious that I wanted to jump into space myself and do battle, small and soft and fragile as I was.

The Phage went mad.

They arrowed between the Bruqvisz ships, ignoring them completely, and swarmed Lifekiller.

The god-king, for all his power and poison, wasn't prepared for that. Not for his own weapons, his own genetically engineered warriors, to start burrowing into his own armor, his own flesh and blood and bones. Lifekiller thrashed and smashed at the swarm, but it evaded him, intent on only one thing.

I instinctively understood what Chao-Xyll had commanded them to do. It was their basic, most primal instinct.

Eat.

And they feasted. They ripped beneath the god-king's armor. They burrowed into his eyes, in his screaming mouth. They squirmed beneath plates and tore open wounds and they *ate him*.

It was the most horrifying and awe-inspiring thing I'd ever seen, and the Bruqvisz ships backed away, still firing, dealing lethal blows that severed Lifekiller's limbs, left him vulnerable and helpless and spewing blood and poisons into the void.

He twitched. He pulsed. He crawled with Phage.

I saw Chao-Xyll hanging in space before Lifekiller, an insignificant speck beside his bulk, but radiating power and majesty as her swarm, *hers*, reduced a god to meat.

Bea was holding on to me, horror-stricken and victorious, and I put my arm around her. Together, with Nadim and the other Leviathan, we watched a god die.

Lifekiller's last feeble twitches stopped, and he just . . . came apart. Pulled to edible pieces by his own slave-warriors, who consumed most of him, and left the rest spinning and freezing in the void.

I held my breath, because *now* we were in danger again. The Phage were never not hungry, never not angry. And we were so, so vulnerable.

But they went back to swirl in a tight spiral around Chao-Xyll, like a coat of armor with her at the center, and I don't know how she managed it, but she accessed our comms. And it was *Chao-Xing's* voice, as real and human as I remembered her. I felt tears burn in my eyes, and this time, I let them come. Let them fall in immense relief.

She said, "They belong to us now. We won't let them

harm anyone else. We will take them far from here, to a place where they can eat flaff and learn to be . . . peaceful. It will take time, but they will heed us if we supply their basic needs. In time, they will Awaken, as Xyll did. We will teach them how to be both One and Many. No one will be able to use them as Lifekiller did."

"You're leaving," Nadim said softly. "I . . . can't say that I am sorry to hear that. Your swarm terrifies me."

"As it should," she said. "It kills innocents and civilians, gods and monsters alike. It is the most destructive force in the universe. And we must find a place for our children to learn better. We will miss you, Nadim."

"I never imagined you as the empress of an alien race," I said.

"This is the path we chose. We regret nothing, and we thank you, Zara, for allowing us to evolve. Please save Marko, and tell him we never meant to hurt him. And as for Typhon—"

Typhon finally emerged from his protective walls, a heavy presence weighted with grief, pain, and so much weariness. But he was talking, and that mattered. "You are not *my* Chao-Xing," he said. It was the clearest his voice had ever been. "But I honor your sacrifice. And I thank you for what you have done. We could not do it alone."

"If you hadn't weakened him, we couldn't have either," she said. "All of you mattered in this fight. All of *us*. And we will miss you, grim old friend. We could never offer the bond you needed, but Yusuf can. And Starcurrent. I hope you will accept them and permit them to help you heal."

He grunted. I supposed that was as much approval as he was ever going to give. Nadim was so quiet that I couldn't even tell what he was thinking. Likewise, Yusuf and Starcurrent must be listening—if Typhon was letting them—but they weren't saying a word inside the link, just a general sense of unease. Ghostwalk was staring at all of us, outside the connection, and I thought he looked sad.

"Zara." She had one last thing to say, and it was to me.

"What?"

"We feel . . . grateful that you tried to view us as a being of worth, no matter what."

"Before or after the . . . merger?"

"Both. You tried to accept that Xyll might not be a monster, despite evidence to the contrary. You tried to believe that your friend could be saved when others would have given up. Taken the easy path."

I quirked a wry smile. "I'm pretty well known for picking the hard road every time."

"Those decisions brought you here, and you belong where you are. And we are proud of you. Beatriz, you as well. We won't forget you or what you have taught us—that there is strength in kindness and mercy also."

"Thanks," Bea said. "And . . . take care."

Yusuf added, "I didn't know you well or for that long, but I'm aware of what you've done for every single one of us. I won't forget either."

"I will sing of you," said Starcurrent.

Finally Nadim broke his silence. "I can't lie. I don't like what you've become, but one day I'll learn not to fear and hate the Phage. I promise. We'll meet again."

"We understand, little one." How funny to hear C-X calling Nadim that, but she had a different sense of the universe now, through her connection to the hive mind. "We don't know how long it will take to teach our young or how long we will live in this form. But we will always remember. And so will our children."

I wasn't sure I liked the Phage remembering me, but I felt a pulse of real affection. Even if she was the Empress of the Swarm now, she would always be my friend. "Goodbye, C-X," I said. "I think I kind of love you."

"Same," she said.

And then the giant, armored ball of the Phage began to move. It picked up speed, rolling, reflecting the distant light of the sun like a glistening, tumbling, terrifying jewel.

Then it was gone, swimming with incredible velocity to somewhere I hoped we'd never have to visit. Because I knew one thing for damn sure: I *never* wanted to fight Empress Zhang Chao-Xyll. Her absence felt like a hole in my world, but it also seemed like a damned miracle that I was still breathing.

Nadim was starting to get a trickle of energy back from Earth's warm, yellow sun; it wasn't quite his frequency but close enough to start recharging him. The air freshened a little, and I realized I was exhausted, aching, soaked with sweat.

And alive.

We were all *alive*.

It started as a tickle at the back of my throat, then burst out in a laugh, half-crazy and uncontrolled, and then I raised my voice and let out a yell that did Suncross proud. I grabbed Beatriz and danced her around, and then Ghostwalk was booming his own victory cry and dancing with us, and hell, even EMITU was chanting a victory haiku as he wheeled around waving extensors.

I could sense Yusuf and Starcurrent celebrating. Jon Anderson too, in his decidedly grim fashion.

The Bruqvisz contacted us as our comms flickered back to life, and we all shouted together, danced, screamed out defiance and victory and the death of Lifekiller.

Of course, the first one on my screen was a damn blob. "We have salvage rights to all Phage remains and everything we can mine from the god-king, yes?"

"If I say yes, that means you don't mess with me?"

"You are allied with the Empress of the Swarm. It's bad

business to start fights we cannot win."

Right, like C-X would come kill some blobs for me when she was wrangling so many Phage already. But what these blobs didn't know wouldn't hurt them. "Right, you do *not* want to piss me off. My word is good, though. A deal's a deal, so grab whatever you can get. It's yours for the taking!"

I figured Earth had way more important things to worry about, and maybe they'd even appreciate the blobs cleaning up the space garbage. Part of me did worry about the Elaszi running off with bits of Lifekiller, but they seemed like the type to sell the most valuable chemicals and discard the rest, not clone him to start a second galactic war. To paraphrase the blobs, carnage was bad for business.

Now that we had comms working again, I called Fort Copernicus and got Boyd on the console. "Give me a sitrep, LC."

"We took some damage to our ozone layer and there are toxic pockets, particularly in Australia."

"They're used to the world trying to kill them," I joked.

I was surprised when the old man cracked a smile. "Good one. But if people stay inside, our filtration system should take care of it in a month or two."

"Good old Leviathan tech," I mumbled.

Nadim put in, "You're welcome."

"How's Luna holding up?" I was afraid to ask about

Mars Colony Roma, where Mom and Kiz were.

Boyd checked some numbers on a screen I couldn't read, then answered, "Luna needs some repairs, but the damage was minimal. And Roma? Not even a scuff on the dome. We started emergency protocols, but everyone's fine."

Thank God.

"Great. Tell Earth that we're coming down with a gravely injured Honor for immediate treatment. I don't care what else they've got to do. This comes first."

We waited for word on Marko for almost an hour before a whole team of Earth's best docs came out to meet us. Bea and I stood up as one, holding hands, and I didn't know what to make of their expressions until the head surgeon said, "You made it here just in time. We were able to stabilize Honor Dunajski and get him into a treatment chamber. He's still unconscious, and he will be in intensive care for a while. After that, he'll need significant rehabilitation. I'm afraid it may be difficult for him to rejoin his Leviathan."

Marko, I thought, had the chance to do what he'd wanted now: to go home, and stay here if that was what he desired. And I was grateful, so grateful I felt an unsteady burn of tears. Weird. I never used to cry, and now . . . now the tears came easy. Maybe because I wasn't afraid anymore. I didn't need to be all armor. Some of me could be soft and kind and gentle now.

"Tell him we love him," Bea said for both of us. "When you can. We'll check in. His family—"

"They're on their way here," the doc said. "He'll be well taken care of. No expense spared for any of the saviors of the planet."

Yeah, I was hoping that charitable impulse was catching, because the next thing we had to do was get called on the carpet.

Meeting with the Honors administrators was . . . interesting. Bea and I dressed for the occasion; we had on black Journey uniforms taken from Typhon's stores, and we looked *sharp*. We also weren't taking any damn bullshit.

But we weren't offered any, either. The Honors Council—twelve international representatives, all richer and older than us—*apologized*. Told us that our records were clean, and that the Honors program would be overhauled to new specifications; it was time for humanity to join the rest of the universe, and that meant trade and communication with species other than just Leviathan. Our playpen was open. We needed to get out there and do better than the Leviathan had expected. And Marko, when he recovered enough, would be offered a job overseeing that process.

"First off," I said, getting comfortable because this would be a long meeting. "Don't call us Honors anymore. We're Pilots and Navigators. And what do you know about the true bond anyway? Did you know . . ."

Bea grinned at me; she understood that I was just getting started. Wait until I presented my list of demands.

They were more than a little dazed with the scope of what we brought them, but they promised to fix their shit, and that was what we wanted. That, and to make sure our families knew we were not wanted criminals. We wanted full *public* apologies. Maybe some groveling. Seemed like we were owed.

Once the meetings ended and I shook Atticus Boyd's hand, they pinned a damn medal on my chest. Bea got one too, then the photo ops started. I got misty remembering how Marko guided me around my first big-deal party, and now I was in Journey black, a bronze star pinned to my uniform. And Marko . . . Marko was honored in absentia. Chao-Xyll too, as a hero of Earth.

The next day, we moved into the formal phase of our Earth tour. Press briefings. "Zara, look here! Beatriz, is the rumor true? Are you more than friends?"

In answer, Bea kissed me dramatically for the paparazzo who'd asked that.

I hated every minute of the big damn hero celebration that followed the press conference; drones circling to capture our strained smiles for *hours*. But it was important to Earth, and to the restructuring Honors program, and the Bruqvisz sent a rep down to say hey, and we introduced the lizards to the world. Their ambassador promptly asked for our strongest inebriating beverage.

Diplomacy got really, really drunk.

Beatriz took leave to Brazil to visit her family, and I went with her to meet them; it was beautiful, really, how her extended, noisy, raucous circle dragged me right in, teaching me Portuguese and feeding me so many delightful meals that I strained the seams on my uniform, even though it was supposed to adjust. We spent a week, and I missed Nadim every moment of it, but he was undergoing a refit.

We came back to a brand-new, wonderfully outfitted ship, with expanded quarters and new consoles. Plus, endless packets of our favorite meals. In short, everything I'd asked for, including some deadly weapons, because you never knew what was coming out in the black. And I wouldn't want to live any other way.

"God, it's good to be back," I said.

I touched Nadim lightly with my hand, and the wall lit up, blushing pink for pleasure. He touched my mind in turn, filling me with sunshine.

"Missed you," he said.

"Me too." Bea leaned in, and it was the best kind of hug, her arms around me, and Nadim's warmth in my head. I'd never be lonely again, never again the scared kid who ran the streets to flee her demons.

"You ready to meet my family now?" I asked.

If they weren't, it was too late, because the specially commissioned shuttle was dropping off Mom and Kiz in the docking bay right then. They were the first nonparticipants in the Pilot-and-Navigator program to set foot on a Leviathan. I rushed to meet them, eager as I hadn't been in longer than I could remember. Mom hugged me first, then Kiz, and then Mom shook my shoulders.

"Girl, I thought you'd change the world, not save it. I'm so proud of you, Zara."

It felt like I'd been waiting my whole life to hear those words. I introduced Mom and Kiz to Nadim and Bea.

"Pleased to meet you," he said.

"Oh my God," Kiz breathed. "Zara, he sounds so hot. My bones are melting!"

Yeah, maybe this ran in the family. I smirked a touch smugly, as Nadim responded, "Thank you, Kiz. Would you like a tour?"

Kiz said, "Are you kidding? I'll be eating for free for weeks in the dome over this visit. Show me everything!"

Obligingly, he lit the way for my sister, as he had for me, what seemed like so long ago now. I'd catch up with them later, as my mother was wearing an intense look.

"Is this your girlfriend?" Mom asked.

I nodded, and she hugged Bea tightly. "I've never seen Zara so happy, and it must be because of you and Nadim.

Thank you for taking care of my wild child."

Bea grinned at me over my mom's shoulder. "She takes care of me too."

They stayed the night before returning to Roma Colony, and this time I knew I could go home again. If I wanted to.

But I was already aching for more adventure. I probably always would be.

"Your family's great," Bea said, wrapping herself around me.

I turned and kissed her, soft and deep, the sweetness of the café con leche she liked and a dusting of cinnamon. A flutter of heat said Nadim was feeling this too. We were a golden circle, endless and complete. "We'll visit. The Journey isn't forever anymore, remember?" I touched Nadim lightly, drawing his attention. "Are we about ready to go?"

"I'm asking the others."

Ophelia had a new crew by the time our small Leviathan pod got ready to leave the Sol system. One of them was Ghostwalk, who'd taken to the ship like nothing I'd imagined. I thought maybe they understood each other's wounds; they'd both lost a lot in the war, suffered injuries that needed time to heal.

Her other crew member was a murderous robot named Jury, who'd decided that Earth wasn't for him. Oh, he'd hunted down Deluca; he showed me the vid. Then he pulled Deluca's organization apart as thoroughly as the Phage had destroyed Lifekiller. Then he chose his own adventure: us. First nonorganic Navigator in history, so I heard from Ophelia, who had learned to talk to us in words, though she had a charmingly halting way about her. Jon Anderson stayed with Quell, and absolutely nobody wanted to join him.

Typhon was still grim and gloomy, but he'd get better as we traveled with Yusuf and Starcurrent as his crew. He'd heal. He'd live and grow stronger. We all would.

Just before we took off, Yusuf called me, bright-eyed and thriving. His smile gave me hope. "Got that maintenance bot ready for you, Zara."

"That's awesome! I'll collect it the next time we fuel up."

Our pod would travel together, selecting our own stops, because we were free to devise our own Tour. There were no rules, just like I always wanted.

Nadim had heard the lonely songs of distant Leviathan, searching for other survivors. There were more cousins out in the black, waiting for us to find them, along with far-flung galaxies teeming with unseen wonders. Universes. Adventures.

And we all flung ourselves to the stars, where we belonged.

We were lost. Then, we were found.

Finally, we were home.

AFTERWORD

WE'VE HAD AN amazing time writing the wild adventures of Zara Cole and Beatriz Teixeira and Nadim, and we hope that you have enjoyed this journey. Consider us your personal Bruqvisz ballad-singers.

Now go tell your own stories. Make your own universes. Wish them into existence and share them.

Adventures await you.